S0-ACS-097

Presents.

**Glamorous international settings...powerful men...
passionate romances.**

Harlequin Presents delivers stories
of passion and escape featuring
alpha males and luxurious, jet-setting
lifestyles. Step into this sensational,
sophisticated world where sinfully
tempting heroes ignite a fierce and
wickedly irresistible passion!

Eight new titles are available each month!

ISBN-13: 978-0-373-20876-0

From passionate, suspenseful
and dramatic love stories
to inspirational or historical,
Harlequin offers different lines
to satisfy every romance reader.

EAN

HPIFC2018

HARLEQUIN
Presents CLASSICS

·⊰ **LYNNE GRAHAM RECOMMENDS** ⊱·

USA TODAY BESTSELLING AUTHOR

Sharon Kendrick

··········

Carrying the Greek's Heir
& Claimed for Makarov's Baby

2 BOOKS

GREAT VALUE

Sharon Kendrick

———

Carrying the Greek's Heir
& Claimed for Makarov's Baby

HARLEQUIN® PRESENTS® CLASSICS

ISBN-13: 978-0-373-20876-0

Carrying the Greek's Heir &
Claimed for Makarov's Baby

Copyright © 2018 by Harlequin Books S.A.

The publisher acknowledges the copyright holder of the individual works as follows:

Carrying the Greek's Heir
Copyright © 2015 by Sharon Kendrick

Claimed for Makarov's Baby
Copyright © 2015 by Sharon Kendrick

Recycling programs for this product may not exist in your area.

Printed in U.S.A.

www.Harlequin.com

CONTENTS

USA TODAY bestselling author **Sharon Kendrick** once won a national writing competition by describing her ideal date: being flown to an exotic island by a gorgeous and powerful man. Little did she realize that she'd just wandered into her dream job! Today she writes for Harlequin, featuring often stubborn but always to-die-for heroes and the women who bring them to their knees. She believes that the best books are those you never want to end. Just like life...

Books by Sharon Kendrick

Harlequin Presents

A Royal Vow of Convenience
The Ruthless Greek's Return
Christmas in Da Conti's Bed

One Night With Consequences

The Italian's Christmas Secret
The Pregnant Kavakos Bride
Secrets of a Billionaire's Mistress
Crowned for the Prince's Heir
Carrying the Greek's Heir

Wedlocked!

The Sheikh's Bought Wife
The Billionaire's Defiant Acquisition

The Billionaire's Legacy

Di Sione's Virgin Mistress

Visit the Author Profile page
at Harlequin.com for more titles.

Carrying the Greek's Heir

With special thanks to Iona Grey (*Letters to the Lost*), who makes discussing characters such fun.

And to Peter Cottee for giving me a glimpse into a businessman's mind.

CHAPTER ONE

HE WANTED HER. He wanted her so badly he could almost taste it.

Alek Sarantos felt the heavy jerk of lust as he drummed his fingers against the linen tablecloth. Tall candles flickered in the breeze and the rich perfume of roses scented the air. He shifted his position slightly but still he couldn't get comfortable.

He was…restless. More than restless.

Maybe it was the thought of returning to the crazy pace of his London life which had heightened his sexual hunger, so that it pulsed through his veins like thick, sweet honey. His throat tightened. Or maybe it was just her.

He watched as the woman walked through the long grass towards him, brushing past meadow flowers which gleamed like pale discs in the dying light of the summer evening. The rising moon illuminated a body showcased by a plain white shirt, tucked into a dark skirt which looked at least a size too small. A tightly tied apron emphasised her hips. Everything about her was soft, he thought. Soft skin. Soft body. The thick hair which was plaited in a heavy rope and fell down to the middle of her back was silky soft.

His lust was insistent—his groin the opposite of soft—yet she wasn't his type. Definitely not. He didn't usually get turned on by curvy waitresses who greeted you with an uncomplicated, friendly smile. He liked his women lean and independent, not gently rounded and wholesome. Hard-eyed women who dropped their panties with ease and without question. Who took him on his terms—which had no room for manoeuvre. Terms which had helped carve out his position as a man of influence and given him a lifestyle free of domestic tie or encumbrance. Because he didn't want either. He avoided anyone he suspected might be soft, or needy or—heaven forbid—*sweet*. Sweet wasn't a quality he required in a bed partner.

So why was he lusting after someone who'd been drifting around the periphery of his vision all week, like a ripe plum waiting to fall from the tree? Something to do with her apron, perhaps—some late-onset uniform fetish, which was playing some very erotic fantasies in his head?

'Your coffee, sir.'

Even her voice was soft. He remembered hearing its low, musical cadence when she'd been comforting a child who had cut open his knee on one of the gravel paths. Alek had been returning from a game of tennis with the hotel pro when he'd seen her crouching down beside the boy, exuding a general air of unflappability. She'd stemmed the flow of blood with her handkerchief as an ashen-faced nanny had stood shaking nearby and, turning her head, had seen Alek. She'd told him to 'Go inside and get a first-aid kit' in the calmest voice he'd ever heard. And he had. A man more used to issuing orders than taking them, he'd returned with the kit and felt a savage twist of pain in his gut to see the boy looking up at her with such trust shining from his teary eyes.

She was leaning forward now as she placed the cup of coffee in front of him, drawing his attention to her breasts, which were straining tightly against her shirt. Oh, God. Her breasts. He found himself wondering what her nipples might look like if they were peaking towards his lips. As she straightened up he saw pewter-grey eyes framed by a pale and heavy fringe. She wore no adornment other than a thin gold chain around her neck and a name badge which said *Ellie*.

Ellie.

As well as being cool and unflappable towards small boys, she'd spent the week anticipating his every need—and while that was nothing new to someone like him, her presence had been surprisingly unobtrusive. She hadn't tried to engage him in conversation, or wow him with wisecracks. She'd been pleasant and friendly but hadn't hinted about her evenings off, or offered to show him around. In short, she hadn't come onto him like any other woman would have done. She had treated him with the same quiet civility she'd exhibited towards every other guest in the discreet New Forest hotel—and maybe that's what was bugging him. His mouth hardened—for it was almost unheard of for Alek Sarantos to be treated like other people.

But it wasn't just that which had captured his interest. She had an air about her which he couldn't quite put his finger on. Ambition maybe, or just some quiet professional pride. Was it that which made his gaze linger for a heartbeat too long—or the fact that she reminded him of himself, more years ago than he cared to remember? He'd once had that same raw ambition—back in the days when he'd started out with nothing and waited tables, just like her. When money had been tight and the future uncertain. He had worked hard to escape his past and to forge a new future and had learnt plenty of lessons along the way. He'd thought that success was the answer to every problem in life, but he had been wrong. Success made the pill sweeter, but you still had to swallow the pill all the same.

Wasn't he realising that now—when he'd achieved every single thing he'd set out to achieve? When every hurdle had been leapt over and unimaginable riches were stuffed into his various bank accounts. Didn't seem to matter how much he gave away to charity, he still kept making more. And sometimes that left him with a question which made him feel uncomfortable— a question he couldn't seem to answer, but which he'd been asking himself more and more lately.

Was this all there was?

'Will there be anything else, Mr Sarantos?' she was asking him.

The waitress's voice washed over him like balm. 'I'm not sure,' he drawled and lifted his eyes to the sky. Above him, stars were spattering the darkening sky— as if some celestial artist had sprayed the canvas silver. He thought of returning to London the following day and a sudden, inexplicable yearning made him lower his head and meet her gaze. 'The night is still young,' he observed.

She gave him a quick smile. 'When you've been waiting tables all evening, eleven-thirty doesn't really feel *young.*'

'I guess not.' He dropped a lump of sugar in his coffee. 'What time do you finish?'

Her smile wavered, as if the question wasn't one she'd been anticipating. 'In about ten minutes' time.'

Alek leant back in his chair and studied her some more. Her legs were faintly tanned and the smoothness of her skin made you almost forget how cheap her shoes were. 'Perfect,' he murmured. 'The gods must be smiling on us. So why don't you join me for a drink?'

'I can't.' She shrugged as if in answer to his raised eyebrows. 'I'm not really supposed to fraternise with customers.'

Alek gave a hard smile. Wasn't *fraternise* an old-fashioned word, which had its roots in *brotherly*? An irrelevant word as far as he was concerned, because he'd never had brothers. Never had anyone. Well, nobody that mattered, that was for sure. He'd always been alone in the world and that was the way he liked it. The way he intended to keep it. Except maybe for this star-lit night, which was crying out for a little female company. 'I'm just asking you to join me for a drink, *poulaki mou*,' he said softly. 'Not to drag you off to some dark corner and have my wicked way with you.'

'Better not,' she said. 'It's against hotel policy. Sorry.'

Alek felt the stir of something unknown whispering down his spine. Was it the sensation of being refused something—no matter how small—which had started his heart racing? *How long since he had been refused anything and felt this corresponding frisson of excitement? A heady feeling that you might actually have to make an effort—instead of the outcome being entirely predictable.*

'But I'm leaving tomorrow evening,' he said.

Ellie nodded. She knew that. Everyone in the hotel did. They knew plenty about the Greek billionaire who had been creating a stir since he'd arrived at The Hog last week. As the most luxurious hotel in the south of England, they were used to rich and demanding guests—but Alek Sarantos was richer and more demanding than most. His personal assistant had actually sent a list of his likes and dislikes before he'd arrived and all the staff had been advised to study it. And even though she'd considered it slightly over the top, Ellie had got stuck right in, because if a job was worth doing—it was worth doing well.

She knew he liked his eggs 'over easy' because he'd lived in America for a while. That he drank red wine, or sometimes whisky. His clothes had arrived before he did—delivered by special courier and carefully wrapped in layers of filmy tissue paper. There had even been a special staff pep talk just before he'd arrived.

'Mr Sarantos must be given space,' they'd been told. 'Under no circumstances must he be disturbed unless he shows signs of wanting to be disturbed. It's a coup for someone like him to stay in this hotel, so we must make him feel as if it's his own home.'

Ellie had taken the instructions literally because The Hog's training scheme had given her stability and hope for the future. For someone who'd never been any good at exams, it had offered a career ladder she was determined to climb, because she wanted to make something of herself. To be strong and independent.

Which meant that, unlike every other female in the place, she had tried to regard the Greek tycoon with a certain impartiality. She hadn't attempted to flirt with him, as everyone else had been doing. She was practical enough to know her limitations and Alek Sarantos would never be interested in someone like *her*. Too curvy and too ordinary—she was never going to be the preferred choice of an international playboy, so why pretend otherwise?

But of course she had looked at him. She suspected that even a nun might have given him a second glance because men like Alek Sarantos didn't stray onto the average person's radar more than a couple of times in a lifetime.

His rugged face was too hard to be described as handsome and his sensual lips were marred by a twist of ruthlessness. His hair was ebony, his skin like polished bronze, but it was his dark-fringed eyes which captured your attention and made it difficult to look away. Unexpectedly blue eyes, which made her think of those sunlit seas you always saw in travel brochures. Sardonic eyes which seemed to have the ability to make her feel…

What?

Ellie shook her head slightly. She wasn't sure. As if she sensed something lost in him? As if, on some incomprehensible level, they were kindred spirits? Stupid crazy stuff she shouldn't be feeling, that was for sure. Her fingers tightened around the tray. It was definitely time to excuse herself and go home.

But Alek Sarantos was still staring as if he was waiting for her to change her mind and as those blue eyes seared into her she felt a brief wobble of temptation. Because it wasn't every day a Greek billionaire asked you to have a drink with him.

'It's getting on for twelve,' she said doubtfully.

'I'm perfectly capable of telling the time,' he said with a touch of impatience. 'What happens if you stay out past midnight—does your car turn into a pumpkin?'

Ellie jerked back her head in surprise. She was

amazed he knew the story of Cinderella—did that mean
they had the same fairy tales in Greece?—though rather
less surprised that he'd associated her with the famous
skivvy.

'I don't have a car,' she said. 'Just a bicycle.'

'You live out in the middle of nowhere and you don't
have a car?'

'No.' She rested the tray against her hip and smiled,
as if she were explaining elementary subtraction to a
five-year-old. 'A bike is much more practical round
here.'

'So what happens when you go to London—or the
coast?'

'I don't go to London very often. And we do have
such things as trains and buses, you know. It's called
public transport.'

He dropped another cube of sugar in his coffee. 'I
didn't use any kind of public system until I was fifteen.'

'Seriously?'

'Absolutely.' He glanced up at her. 'Not a train or a
bus—not even a scheduled airline.'

She stared at him. What kind of life had he led? For a
moment she was tempted to offer him a glimpse of hers.
Maybe she should suggest meeting tomorrow morning and taking the bus to nearby Milmouth-on-Sea. Or
catching a train somewhere—anywhere. They could
drink scalding tea from paper cups as the countryside
sped by—she'd bet he'd never done *that*.

Until she realised that would be overstepping the
mark, big time. He was a hotshot billionaire and she
was a waitress and while guests sometimes pretended to
staff that they were equals, everyone knew they weren't.
Rich people liked to play at being ordinary, but for them

it was nothing but a game. He'd asked her to stay for a drink but, really, what possible interest could a tycoon like him have in someone like her? His unusually expansive mood might evaporate the moment she sat down. She knew he could be impatient and demanding. Didn't the staff on Reception say he'd given them hell whenever he'd lost his internet connection—even though he was supposed to be on holiday and, in her opinion, people on holiday shouldn't be working.

But then Ellie remembered something the general manager had told her when she'd first joined the hotel's training scheme. That powerful guests sometimes wanted to talk—and if they did, you should let them.

So she looked into his blue eyes and tried to ignore the little shiver of awareness which had started whispering over her skin. 'How come,' she questioned, trying to make her voice sound cool and casual, 'it took until the age of fifteen before you went on public transport?'

Alek leant back in his chair and considered her question and wondered whether now might be the right time to change the subject, no matter how easy he found it to talk to her. Because the reality of his past was something he usually kept off-limits. He had grown up in a pampered palace of a home—with every luxury known to man.

And he had hated every minute of it.

The place had been a fortress, surrounded by high walls and snarling dogs. A place which had kept people out as well as in. The most lowly of staff were vetted before being offered employment, and paid obscenely well to turn a blind eye to his father's behaviour. Even family holidays were tainted by the old man's paranoia about security. He was haunted by the threat of stories about his lifestyle getting into the papers—terrified that anything would be allowed to tarnish his outward veneer of respectability.

Crack teams of guards were employed to keep rubber-neckers, journalists and ex-lovers at bay. Frogmen would swim silently in reconnaissance missions around foreign jetties, before their luxury yacht was given the all-clear to sail into harbour. When he was growing up, Alek didn't know what it was like not to be tailed by the shadowy presence of some burly bodyguard. And then one day he had escaped. At fifteen, he had walked away, leaving his home and his past behind and cutting his ties with them completely. He had gone from fabulous wealth to near penury but had embraced his new lifestyle with eager-ness and hunger. No longer would he be tainted by his father's fortune. Everything he owned, he would earn for himself and that was exactly what he'd done. It was the one thing in life he could be proud of. His mouth hard-ened. Maybe the only thing.

He realised that the waitress was still waiting for an answer to his question and that she no longer seemed to be in any hurry to get off duty. He smiled, expec-tation making his heart beat a little faster. 'Because I grew up on a Greek island where there were no trains and few buses.'

'Sounds idyllic,' she said.

Alek's smile faded. It was such a cliché. The moment you said *Greek island*, everyone thought you were talk-ing about paradise, because that was the image they'd been fed. But serpents lurked in paradise, didn't they? There were any number of tortured souls living in those blindingly white houses which overlooked the deep blue sea. There were all kinds of dark secrets which lay hidden at the heart of seemingly normal lives. *Hadn't he found that out, the hard way?* 'It looked very idyllic from the outside,' he said. 'But things are rarely what they seem when you dig a little deeper.'

'I suppose not,' she said. She transferred the tray to her other hand. 'And does your family still live there?'

His smile was slow—like a knife sinking into wet concrete. His *family*? That wouldn't be his word of choice to describe the people who had raised him. His father's whores had done their best, with limited success—but surely even they were better than no mother at all. Than one who'd run out on you and never cared enough to lift the phone to find out how you were.

'No,' he said. 'The island was sold after my father died.'

'A whole island?' Her lips parted. 'You mean your father actually *owned an island*?'

Another stab of lust went kicking to his groin as her lips parted. If he'd announced that he had a home on Mars, she couldn't have looked more shocked. But then, it was easy to forget how isolating wealth could be—especially to someone like her. If she didn't even own a car, then she might have trouble getting her head around someone having their own island. He glanced at her hands and, for some reason, the sight of her unmanicured nails only intensified his desire and he realised that he hadn't been entirely honest when he'd told her he wasn't planning to drag her away to a dark corner. He thought he'd like that very much.

'You've been standing there so long that you've probably come to the end of your shift,' he said drily. 'You could have had that drink with me after all.'

'I suppose I could.' Ellie hesitated. He was so persistent. Flatteringly so. She wondered why. Because he'd been almost *friendly* since he'd helped with the little boy who'd cut his knee? Or because she'd displayed a degree of reluctance to spend time with him and he wasn't used to that? Probably. She wondered what it must be like, to be Alek Sarantos—so sure of yourself that nobody ever turned you down.

'What are you so scared of?' he taunted. 'Don't you think I'm capable of behaving like a gentleman?'

It was one of those life-defining moments. Sensible Ellie would have shaken her head and said no thanks. She would have carried the tray back to the kitchen, unlocked her bike and cycled home to her room in the nearby village. But the moonlight and the powerful scent of the roses were making her feel the opposite of sensible. The last time a man had asked her on a date— and you couldn't really call this a date—was over a year ago. She'd been working such unsociable hours that there hadn't been a lot of opportunity for down time.

She looked into his eyes. 'I hadn't really thought about it.'

'Well, think about it now. You've been waiting on me all week, so why not let me wait on you for a change? I have a fridge stocked with liquor I haven't touched. If you're hungry, I can feed you chocolate or apricots.' He rose to his feet and raised his eyebrows. 'So why don't I pour you a glass of champagne?'

'Why? Are you celebrating something?'

He gave a low laugh. 'Celebration isn't mandatory. I thought all women liked champagne.'

'Not me.' She shook her head. 'The bubbles make me sneeze. And I'm cycling home—I don't want to run over some poor, unsuspecting pony who's wandered out into the middle of the road. I think I'd prefer something soft.'

'Of course you would.' He slanted her an odd kind of smile. 'Sit down and let me see what I can find.'

He went inside the self-contained villa which stood within the extensive hotel grounds and Ellie perched awkwardly on one of the cane chairs, praying nobody would see her, because she shouldn't be sitting on a guest's veranda as if she had every right to do so.

She glanced across the silent lawn, where a huge oak tree was casting an enormous shadow. The wild flowers which edged the grass swayed gently in the breeze and, in the background, lights blazed brightly from the hotel. The dining room was still lit with candles and she could see people lingering over coffee. In the kitchen, staff would be frantically washing up and longing to get home. Upstairs, couples would be removing complimentary chocolates from on top of the Egyptian linen pillows, before getting into bed. Or maybe they would be sampling the deep, twin baths for which The Hog was so famous.

She thought she saw something glinting from behind the oak tree and instinctively she shrank back into the shadows, but before she could work out exactly what it was—Alek had returned with a frosted glass of cola for her, and what looked like whisky, for him.

'I guess I should have put them on a tray,' he said.

She took a sip. 'And worn an apron.'

He raised his eyebrows. 'Perhaps I could borrow yours?'

The implication being that she remove her apron... Ellie put her glass down, glad that the darkness disguised her suddenly hot cheeks because the thought of removing anything was making her heart race. Suddenly, the moonlight and the roses and the glint in his eyes was making her feel way too vulnerable.

'I can't stay long,' she said quickly.

'Somehow I wasn't expecting you to. How's your cola?'

'Delicious.'

He leant back in his chair. 'So tell me why a young woman of twenty…?' He raised his eyebrows.

'I'm twenty-five,' she supplied.

'Twenty-five.' He took a sip of whisky. 'Ends up working in a place like this.'

'It's a great hotel.'

'Quiet location.'

'I like that. And it has a training scheme which is world famous.'

'But what about…' he paused '…nightlife? Clubs and boyfriends and parties? The kind of thing most twenty-five-year-olds enjoy.'

Ellie watched the bubbles fizzing around the ice cubes he'd put in her cola. Should she explain that she'd deliberately opted for a quiet life which contrasted with the chaos which had defined her childhood? Somewhere where she could concentrate on her work, because she didn't want to end up like her mother, who thought a woman's ambition should be to acquire a man who was a meal ticket. Ellie had quickly learnt how she *didn't* want to live. She was never going to trawl the internet, or hang around nightclubs. She had never owned a thigh-skimming skirt or push-up bra. She was never going to date someone just because of what they had in their wallet.

'Because I'm concentrating on my career,' she said.

'My ambition is to travel and I'm going to make that happen. One day I'm hoping to be a general manager—if not here, then in one of the group's other hotels. Competition is pretty fierce, but there's no harm in aiming high.' She sipped her cola and looked at him. 'So that's me. What about you?'

Alek swirled the whisky around in his glass. Usually he would have changed the subject, because he didn't like talking about himself. But she had a way of asking questions which made him want to answer and he still couldn't work out why.

He shrugged. 'I'm a self-made man.'

'But you said—'

'That my father owned an island? He did. But he didn't leave his money to me.' And if he had, Alek would have thrown it back in his face. He would sooner have embraced a deadly viper than taken a single drachma of the old man's fortune. He felt his gut tighten. 'Everything I own, I earned for myself.'

'And was that…difficult?'

The softness of her voice was hypnotic. It felt like balm being smoothed over a wound which had never really healed. And wasn't this what men had done since the beginning of time? Drunk a little too much whisky and then offloaded on some random woman they would never see again?

'It was a liberation,' he said truthfully. 'To cut my ties with the past.'

She nodded, as if she understood. 'And start over?'

'Exactly that. To know that every decision I make is one I can live with.'

His cell phone chose precisely that moment to start

ringing and automatically he reached into his pocket, glancing at the small screen.

Work, he mouthed as he took the call.

He launched into a long torrent of Greek, before breaking into English—so that Ellie couldn't help but sit there and listen. Though if she was being honest, it was very interesting listening to a conversation, which seemed to involve some high-powered forthcoming deal with the Chinese. And then he said other stuff, too—which was even more interesting.

'I *am* taking a holiday. You know I am. I just thought it wise to check with the New York office first.' He tapped his finger impatiently against the arm of the chair. 'Okay. I take your point. *Okay.*'

He cut the connection and saw her staring at him. 'What is it?' he demanded.

She shrugged. 'It's none of my business.'

'No, I'm interested.'

She put her drink down. 'Don't you ever stop working?'

His irritated look gave way to a faint smile which seemed to tug reluctantly at the corners of his lips. 'Ironically, that's just what my assistant was saying. He said I couldn't really nag other people to take holidays if I wasn't prepared to do so myself. They've been pushing me towards this one for ages.'

'So how come you're taking business calls at this time of night?'

'It was an important call.'

'So important that it couldn't have waited until the morning?'

'Actually, yes,' he said coolly, but Alek's heart had begun beating very fast. He told himself he should be irritated with her for butting in where she wasn't wanted, yet right then he saw it as nothing but a rather disarming honesty. Was this why people went on vacation—because it took you right out of your normal environment and shook you up? In his daily life, nobody like Ellie would have got near him for long enough to deliver a damning judgement on his inability to relax. He was always surrounded by *people*—people who kept the rest of the world at arm's length.

But the protective nucleus of his business life suddenly seemed unimportant and it was as if everything was centred on the soft face in front of him. He wondered what her hair would look like if he shook it free from its ponytail and laid it over his pillow. How that soft flesh would feel beneath him as he parted her legs. He drained the last of his whisky and put the glass down, intending to walk across the veranda and take her into his arms.

But she chose that moment to push the heavy fringe away from her eyes and the jerky gesture suddenly brought him to his senses. He frowned, like someone wakening from a sleep. Had he really been planning to seduce her? He looked at the cheap shoes and unvarnished nails. At the heavy fringe, which looked as if she might trim it herself. *Was he insane?* She was much too sweet for someone like him.

'It's getting late,' he said roughly, rising to his feet. 'Where's your bike?'

She blinked at him in surprise, as if the question wasn't one she had been expecting. 'In the bike shed.'

'Come on,' he said. 'I'll walk you there.'

He could see the faint tremble of her lips as she shook her head.

'Honestly, there's no need. I see myself home every night,' she said. 'And it's probably best if I'm not seen with you.'

'I am walking you back,' he said stubbornly. 'And I won't take no for an answer.'

He could sense her disappointment as they walked over the moonlit grass and he told himself that he was doing the right thing. There were a million women who could be his for the taking—better steer clear of the sweet and sensible waitress.

They reached the hotel and she gave him an awkward smile. 'I have to go and change and fetch my bag,' she said. 'So I'd better say goodnight. Thanks for the drink.'

Alek nodded. 'Goodnight, Ellie,' he said and leant towards her, intending to give her a quick kiss on either cheek, but somehow that didn't happen.

Did she turn her head, or did he? Was that why their mouths met and melded, in a proper kiss? He saw her eyes widen. He felt the warmth of her breath. He could taste the sweetness of cola and it reminded him of a youth and an innocence which had never been his. It was purely reflex which made him pull her into his arms and deepen the kiss and her tiny gasp of pleasure was one he'd heard countless times before.

And that was all he needed. All his frustration and hunger broke free; his hands skimmed hungrily over her body as he moved her further into the shadows and pressed her up against a wall. He groaned as he felt the softness of her belly and it made him want to imprint his hardness against her. To show her just what he had and demonstrate how good it would feel if he were deep inside her. Circling his palm over one peaking nipple, he closed his eyes. Should he slip his hand beneath her uniform skirt and discover whether she was as wet as he suspected? Slide her panties down her legs and take her right here, where they stood?

The tiny moan she made in response to the increased pressure of his lips was almost enough for him to act out his erotic thoughts.

Almost, but not quite.

Reason seeped into his brain like the cold drip of a tap and he drew back, even though his body was screaming out its protest. Somehow he ignored the siren call of his senses, just as he ignored the silent plea in her eyes. Because didn't he value his reputation too much to make out with some anonymous waitress?

It was several moments before he could trust himself to speak and he shook his head in faint disbelief. 'That should never have happened.'

Ellie felt as if he'd thrown ice-cold water over her and she wondered why he had stopped. Surely he had felt it, too? That amazing chemistry. That sheer *magic*. Nobody had ever kissed her quite like that before and she wanted him to carry on doing it. And somehow her bold words tumbled out before she could stop them.

'Why not?'

There was a pause. 'Because you deserve more than I can ever offer. Because I'm the last kind of man you need. You're much too sweet and I'm nothing but a big bad wolf.'

'Surely I should be the judge of that?'

He gave a bitter smile. 'Go home, Ellie. Get out of here before I change my mind.'

Something dark came over his face—something which shut her out completely. He said something abrupt, which sounded like *'Goodbye,'* before turning his back on her and walking back over the starlit grass.

CHAPTER TWO

'WAS THAT YOUR boyfriend I saw you with last night?' The question came out of nowhere and Ellie had to force herself to concentrate on what the guest was saying, instead of the frustrated thoughts which were circling like crows in her mind. Because of the recent heat wave, the restaurant had been fully booked and she'd been rushed off her feet all day. The lobster salad and summer pudding had sold out, and there had been a run on the cocktail of the month—an innocuous-tasting strawberry punch with a definite kick to it.

But now there was only one person left, a wafer-thin blonde who was lingering over her third glass of wine. Not that Ellie was counting. Well, actually, she was. She just wanted the woman to hurry up so that she could finish her shift in peace. Her head was pounding and she was exhausted—probably because she hadn't slept a wink last night. She'd just lain on her narrow bed, staring up at the ceiling—wide-eyed and restless and thinking about what had happened. Or rather, what hadn't happened. Telling herself that it was insane to get herself worked up about one kiss with a man who shouldn't really have been kissing her.

He was a billionaire Greek who was *way* off limits. She didn't know him, he hadn't even taken her on a date and yet… She licked her lips, which had suddenly grown very dry. Things had got pretty hot, pretty quickly, hadn't they? She could still recall his hands cupping her breasts and making them ache. She remembered wriggling with frustration as he pushed her up against the wall—his rock-hard groin pressing flagrantly against her. For a few seconds she'd thought he was going to try and have sex with her right there, and hadn't part of her wanted that? It might have been insanely wrong and completely out of character—but in the darkness of the summer night, she had wanted him more badly than she'd ever wanted anyone. She'd seen a side of herself she didn't recognise and didn't like very much. She bit her lip. A side like her *mother*?

The blonde was still looking at her with the expression of a hungry bird who had just noticed a worm wriggling up through the soil. 'So he *is* your boyfriend?' she prompted.

'No,' said Ellie quickly. 'He's not.'

'But you were kissing him.'

Nervously, Ellie's fingers slid along the frosted surface of the wine bottle before she recovered herself enough to shove it back in the ice bucket. She glanced around, terrified that another member of staff might have overheard, because although The Hog was famously laid-back and didn't have rules just for the sake of it—there was one which had been drummed into her on her very first day… And that was: you didn't get intimate with the guests.

Ever.

Awkwardly, she shrugged. 'Was I?' she questioned weakly.

The blonde's glacial eyes were alight with curiosity. 'You know you were,' she said slyly. 'I was having a cigarette behind that big tree and I spotted you. Then I saw him walk you back to the hotel—you weren't exactly being discreet.'

Briefly, Ellie closed her eyes as suddenly it all made sense. So that was the brief flare of light she'd seen from behind the tree trunk and the sense that somebody was watching them. She should have done the sensible thing and left then. 'Oh,' she said.

'Yes, *oh*. You *do* know who he is, don't you?'

Ellie stiffened as a pair of lake-blue eyes swam into her memory and her heart missed a beat. *Yes, the most gorgeous man I've ever seen. A man who made me believe all the fairy-tale stuff I never believed before.* 'Of course I do. He's…he's…'

'One of the world's richest men who usually hangs out with supermodels and heiresses,' said the blonde impatiently. 'Which makes me wonder, what was he doing with you?'

Ellie drew back her shoulders. The woman's line of questioning was battering her at a time when she was already feeling emotionally vulnerable, but surely she didn't have to stand here and take these snide insinuations—guest or no guest. 'I don't really see how that's relevant.'

'Don't you? But you liked him, didn't you?' The blonde smiled. 'You liked him a lot.'

'I don't kiss men I don't like,' said Ellie defensively, aware of the irony of her remark, considering it was over a year since she'd kissed *anyone*.

The blonde sipped her wine. 'You do realise he has a reputation? He's known as a man of steel, with a heart to match. Actually, he's a bit of a *bastard* where women are concerned. So what have you got to say to that...' there was a pause as she leant forward to peer at Ellie's name badge '...Ellie?'

Ellie's instinct was to tell the woman that her thoughts about Alek Sarantos were strictly confidential, but the memory of his hands moving with such sweet precision over her body was still so vivid that it was hard not to blush. Suddenly it was easy to forget that at times he'd been a demanding and difficult workaholic of a guest, with an impatience he hadn't bothered to hide.

Because now all she could think about was the way she'd responded so helplessly to him and if he hadn't pulled away and done the decent thing, there was no saying what might have happened. Well, that wasn't quite true. She had a very good idea what might have happened.

She chewed on her lip, remembering the chivalrous way he'd told her to go home and the way she'd practically begged him not to leave her. Why *shouldn't* she defend him?

'I think people may have him all wrong,' she said. 'He's a bit of a pussycat, actually.'

'A pussycat?' The blonde nearly choked on her wine. 'Are you serious?'

'Very,' said Ellie. 'He's actually very sweet—and very good company.'

'I bet he was. He'd obviously been flirting with you all week.'

'Not really,' said Ellie, her cheeks growing pink again. What was it with all this blushing? 'We'd just chatted and stuff over the week. It wasn't until...' Her voice trailed away.

'Until?'

Ellie stared into the woman's glacial eyes. It all seemed slightly unreal now. As if she'd imagined the whole thing. Like a particularly vivid dream, which started to fade the moment you woke up. 'He asked me to join him for a drink because it was his last night here.'

'And so you did?'

Ellie shrugged. 'I don't think there's a woman alive who would have turned him down,' she said truthfully. 'He's...well, he's gorgeous.'

'I'll concur with that. And a brilliant kisser, I bet?' suggested the blonde softly.

Ellie remembered the way his tongue had slipped inside her mouth and how deliciously intimate that had felt. How, for a few brief moments, she'd felt as if someone had sprinkled her with stardust. It had only been a kiss, but still... 'The best,' she said, her voice growing husky.

The blonde didn't answer for a moment and when eventually she did there was an ugly note in her voice. 'And what would you say if I told you he had a girlfriend? That she was waiting for him back in London, while he was busy making out with you?'

Ellie's initial disbelief was followed by a stab of disappointment and the dawning realisation that she'd behaved like a fool. What did she think—that someone like Alek Sarantos was free and looking to start a relationship with someone like *her*? Had she imagined that he was going to come sprinting across the hotel lawn to sweep her off her feet—still in her waitress uniform—just like in that old film which always used to make her blub? Hadn't part of her hoped he hadn't meant it when he'd said *goodbye*—and that he might come back and find her?

A wave of recrimination washed over her. Of course he wasn't coming back and *of course* he had a girlfriend. Someone beautiful and thin and rich, probably. The sort of woman who could run for a bus without wearing a bra. Did she really imagine that *she*—the much too curvy Ellie Brooks—would be any kind of competition for someone like that?

And suddenly she felt not just stupid, but *hurt*. She tried to imagine his girlfriend's reaction if she'd seen them together. Didn't he care about loyalty or trampling over other people's feelings?

'He never said anything to me about a girlfriend.'

'Well, he wouldn't, would he?' said the blonde. 'Not in the circumstances. It's never a good move if a man mentions his lover while making out with someone else.'

'But nothing happened!'

'But you would have liked it to, wouldn't you, Ellie? From where I was standing, it looked pretty passionate.'

Ellie felt sick. She'd been a few minutes away from providing a live sex show! She wanted to walk away. To start clearing the other tables and pretend this conversation had never happened. But what if the blonde went storming into the general manager's office to tell her what she'd seen? There would be only one route they could take and that would be to fire her for unprofessional behaviour. *And she couldn't afford to lose her job and the career opportunity of a lifetime, could she? Not for one stupid kiss.*

'If I'd had any idea that he was involved with someone else, then I would never—'

'Do you often make out with the guests?'

'Never,' croaked Ellie.

'Just him, huh?' The blonde raised her brow. 'Did he say why he was keeping such a low profile?'

Ellie hesitated. She remembered the way he'd smiled at her—almost wistfully—when the little boy with the cut knee had flung his arms around her neck. She remembered how ridiculously *flattered* she'd felt when he insisted on that drink. She'd thought they'd had a special bond—when all the time he was just *using* her, as if she were one of the hotel's special offers. Angrily, her mind flitted back to what he had told her. 'He's been working day and night on some big new deal with the Chinese which is all top secret. And he said his staff had been nagging him for ages to take a vacation.'

'Really?' The blonde smiled, before dabbing at her lips with a napkin. 'Well, well. So he's human, after all. Stop looking so scared, Ellie—I'm not going to tell your boss, but I will give you a bit of advice. I'd stay away from men like Alek Sarantos in future, if I were you. Men like that could eat someone like you for breakfast.'

Alek sensed that something was amiss from the minute he walked into the boardroom but, try as he might, he couldn't quite put his finger on it. The deal went well—his deals always went well—although the Chinese delegation haggled his asking price rather more than he had been anticipating. But he pronounced himself pleased when the final figure was agreed, even if he saw a couple of members of the delegation smirking behind their files. Not a bad day's work, all told. He'd bought a company for peanuts, he'd turned it around—and had now sold it on for a more than healthy profit.

It wasn't until they all were exiting the boardroom when the redhead who'd been interpreting for them sashayed in his direction and said, 'Hello, pussycat,' before giving a fake growl and miming a clawing action.

Alek looked at her. He'd had a thing with her last year and had even taken her to his friend Murat's place in Umbria. But it seemed she hadn't believed him when he'd told her that theirs was no more than a casual fling. When the relationship had fizzled out, she'd taken it badly, as sometimes happened. The recriminatory emails had stopped and so had the phone calls, but as he met the expression in her eyes he could tell that she was still angry.

'And just what's that supposed to mean?' he questioned coolly.

She winked. 'Read the papers, tiger,' she murmured, before adding, 'Scraping the barrel a bit, aren't you?'

And that wasn't all. As he left the building he noticed one of the receptionists biting her lip, as if she was trying to repress a smile, and when he got back to his office he rang straight through to his male assistant.

'What's going on, Vasos?'

'With regard to…?' his assistant enquired cautiously.

'With regard to *me*!'

'Plenty of stuff in the papers about the deal with the Chinese.'

'Obviously,' Alek said impatiently. 'Anything else?'

His assistant's hesitation was illuminating. Did he hear Vasos actually *sigh*?

'I'll bring it in,' he said heavily.

Alek sat as motionless as a piece of rock as Vasos placed the article down on the desk in front of him so that he could scan the offending piece. It was an innocuous enough diary article, featuring a two-year-old library photo, which publications still delighted in using—probably because it made him look particularly forbidding.

Splashed above his unsmiling face were the words: Has Alek Sarantos Struck Gold?

His hands knuckled as he read it.

One of London's most eligible bachelors may be off the market before too long. The Midas touch billionaire, known for his love of supermodels and heiresses, was spotted in a passionate embrace with a waitress last weekend, following candlelit drinks on the terrace of his luxury New Forest hotel.

Ellie Brooks isn't Alek's usual type but the shapely waitress declared herself smitten by the workaholic tycoon, who told her he needed a vacation before his latest eye-wateringly big deal. Seems the Greek tycoon takes relaxation quite seriously!

And, according to Ellie, Alek doesn't always live up to his Man Of Steel nickname. 'He's a pussycat,' she purred.

Perhaps business associates should keep a saucer of milk at the ready in future...

Alek glanced up to see Vasos looking ill at ease, nervously running his finger along the inside of his shirt collar as he gave Alek an apologetic shrug.

'I'm sorry, boss,' he said.

'Unless you actually wrote the piece, I see no reason

for you to apologise. Did they ring here first to check the facts before they went to press?' snapped Alek.

'No.' Vasos cleared his throat. 'I'm assuming they didn't need to.'

Alek glared. 'Meaning?'

Vasos looked him straight in the eye. 'They would only have printed this without verification if it were true.'

Alek crumpled the newspaper angrily before hurling it towards the bin as if it were contaminated. He watched as it bounced uselessly off the window and the fact that he had missed made him angrier still.

Yes, it was true. He had been making out with some waitress in a public place. He'd thought with his groin instead of his brain. He'd done something completely out of character and now the readers of a downmarket rag knew all about it. His famously private life wasn't so private any more, was it?

But worst of all was the realisation that he'd taken his eye off the ball. He'd completely misjudged her. Maybe he'd been suffering from a little temporary sunstroke. Why else would he have thought there was something special about her—or credited her with *softness* or *honesty*, when in reality she was simply on the make? The reputation he'd built up, brick by careful brick, had been compromised by some ambitious little blonde with dollar signs in her eyes.

A slow rage began to smoulder inside him. A lot of good his enforced rest had done him. All those spa treatments and massages had been for nothing if his blood pressure was now shooting through the ceiling. Those solemn therapists telling him he must relax had been wasting their time. He must be more burnt out than he'd thought if he'd seriously thought about having sex with some little nobody like her.

His mood stayed dark for the remainder of the day, though it didn't stop him driving a particularly hard bargain on his latest acquisition. He would show the world that he was most definitely *not* a pussycat! He spent the day tied up with conference calls and had early evening drinks with a Greek politician who wanted his advice.

Back in his penthouse, he listened moodily to the messages which had been left on his phone and thought about how to spend the evening. Any number of beautiful women could have been his and all he had to do was call. He thought of the aristocratic faces and bony bodies which were always available to him and found himself comparing them with the curvaceous body of Ellie. The one whose face had inexplicably made him feel…

What?

As if he could trust her?

What a fool he was. A hormone-crazed, stupid fool. Hadn't he learnt his lesson a long time ago? That women were the last species on the planet who could be trusted?

He'd spent years building up a fierce but fair persona in the business world. His reputation was of someone who was tough, assertive and professional. He was known for his vision and his dependability. He despised the 'celebrity' culture and valued his privacy. He chose his friends and lovers carefully. He didn't let them get too close and nobody ever gave interviews about him. Ever. Even the redhead—supposedly broken-hearted at the time—had possessed enough sense to go away and lick her wounds in private.

But Ellie Brooks had betrayed him. A waitress he'd treated as an equal and then made the mistake of kissing had given some cheap little interview to a journalist. How much had she made? His heart pounded because he hadn't even had the pleasure of losing himself in that soft body of hers. He'd mistakenly thought she was *too sweet* and then she'd gone and sold him down the river. He'd behaved decently and honourably by sending her chastely on her way and look at all the thanks he'd got.

His mouth hardened in conjunction with the exquisite aching in his groin.

Maybe it wasn't too late to do something about that.

CHAPTER THREE

I'M SORRY, ELLIE—but we have no choice other than to let you go.

The words still resonating painfully round in her head, Ellie cycled through the thundery weather towards the staff hostel and thought about the excruciating interview she'd just had with the personnel manager of The Hog. Of *course* they'd had a choice—they'd just chosen not to take it, that was all. Surely they could have just let her lie low and all the fuss would have died down.

Negotiating her bike along the narrow road, she tried to take in what they'd just told her. She would be paid a month's salary in lieu of notice, although she would be allowed to keep her room at the hostel for another four weeks.

'We don't want to be seen as completely heartless by kicking you out on the street,' the HR woman had told her with a look of genuine regret on her face. 'If you hadn't chosen to be indiscreet with such a high-profile guest, then we might have been able to brush over the whole incident and keep you on. But as it is, I'm afraid we can't. Not after Mr Sarantos made such a blistering complaint about the question of guest confidentiality.

My hands are tied—and it's a pity, Ellie, because you showed such promise.'

And Ellie had found herself nodding as she'd left the office, because, despite her shock, hadn't she agreed with pretty much every word the manager had said? She'd even felt a bit sorry for the woman who had looked so uncomfortable while terminating her employment.

She couldn't *believe* she'd been so stupid. She had behaved inappropriately with a guest and had then compounded her transgression by talking about it to a woman who had turned out to be a journalist for some low-end tabloid. A journalist! Clutching on to the handlebars with sticky palms, she stared fixedly at the road ahead.

And that had been at the root of her sacking, apparently. The fact that she had broken trust with a valued client. She had blabbed—and Alek Sarantos was *seething*. Apparently, the telephone wires had been practically smoking when he'd rung up to complain about the diary piece which had found its way into a national newspaper.

The day was heavy and overcast and she heard the distant rumble of thunder as she brought her bike to a halt outside the hostel which was home to The Hog's junior staff. Ellie locked her bike to the railings and opened the front door. Next to one of the ten individual doorbells was her name—but not for very much longer. She had a month to find somewhere new to live. A month to find herself a new job. It was a daunting prospect in the current job market and it looked as if she'd gone straight back to square one. Who would employ her now?

A louder rumble of thunder sounded ominously as she made her way along the corridor to her small room.

The day was so dark that she clicked on the light and the atmosphere was so muggy that strands of her ponytail were sticking to the back of her neck. The day yawned ahead as she filled the kettle and sat down heavily on the bed to wait for it to boil.

Now what did she do?

She stared at the posters she'd hung on the walls— giant photos of Paris and New York and Athens. All those places she'd planned to visit when she was a hot-shot hotelier, which was probably never going to happen now. She should have asked about a reference. She wondered if the hotel would still give her one. One which emphasised her best qualities—or would they make her sound like some kind of desperado who spent her time trying it on with wealthy guests?

Her doorbell shrilled and she gave a start, but the sense that none of this was really happening gave her renewed hope. Was it inconceivable to think that the big boss of the hotel might have overridden his HR boss's decision? Realised that it had been nothing but a foolish one-off and that she was too valuable a member of staff to lose?

Smoothing her hands over her hair, she ran along the corridor and opened the front door—her heart clenching with an emotion she was too dazed to analyse when she saw who was standing there. She blinked as if she'd somehow managed to conjure up the brooding figure from her fevered imagination. She must have done— because why else would Alek Sarantos be outside *her* home?

A few giant droplets of rain had splashed onto the blackness of his hair and his bronze skin gleamed as if someone had spent the morning polishing it. She'd forgotten how startlingly blue his eyes looked, but now she could see something faintly unsettling glinting from their sapphire depths.

And even in the midst of her confusion—*why was he here?*—she could feel her body's instinctive response to him. Her skin prickled with a powerful recognition and her breasts began to ache, as if realising that here was the man who was capable of giving her so much pleasure when he touched them. She could feel colour rushing into her cheeks.

'Mr Sarantos,' she said, more out of habit than anything else—but the cynical twist of his lips told her that he found her words not only inappropriate, but somehow insulting.

'Oh, please,' he said softly. 'I think we know each other well enough for you to call me Alek, don't you?'

The suggestion of intimacy unnerved her even more than his presence and her fingers curled nervelessly around the door handle she was clutching for support. Now the rumble of thunder was closer and never had a sound seemed more fitting. 'What…what are you doing here?'

'No ideas?' he questioned silkily.

'To rub in the fact that you've lost me my job?'

'Oh, but I haven't,' he contradicted softly. 'You managed to do that all by yourself. Now, are you going to let me in?'

Ellie told herself she didn't have to. She could slam the door in his face and that would be that. She doubted he would batter the door down—even though he looked perfectly capable of doing it. But she was curious about what had brought him here and the rest of the day stretched in front of her like an empty void. She was going to have to start looking for a new job—she knew that. But not today.

'If you insist,' she said, turning her back on him and retracing her steps down the corridor. She could hear him closing the front door and following her. But it wasn't until he was standing in her room that she began to wonder why she had been daft enough to let him invade her space.

Because he looked all wrong here. With his towering physique and jewelled eyes, he dominated the small space like some living, breathing treasure. He seemed larger than life and twice as intimidating—like the most outrageously alpha man she had ever set eyes on. And that was making her feel uncomfortable in all kinds of ways. There was that honeyed ache deep down in her belly again and a crazy desire to kiss him. Her body's reaction was making her thoughts go haywire and her lips felt like parchment instead of flesh. She licked them, but that only made the aching worse.

The kettle was reaching its usual ear-splitting crescendo just before reaching boiling point and the great belches of steam meant that the room now resembled a sauna. Ellie could feel a trickle of sweat running down her back. Her shirt was sticking to her skin and her jeans were clinging to her thighs and once again she became horribly aware of her own body.

She cleared her throat. 'What do you want?' she said.

Alek didn't answer. Not immediately. His anger—a slow, simmering concoction of an emotion—had been momentarily eclipsed by finding himself in the kind of environment he hadn't seen in a long time.

He looked around. The room was small and clean and she had the requisite plant growing on the windowsill, but there was a whiff of institutionalisation about the place which the cheap posters couldn't quite disguise. The bed was narrower than any he'd seen in years and an unwilling flicker of desire was his reward for having allowed his concentration to focus on *that*. But he had once lived in a room like this, hadn't he? When he'd started out—much younger than she was now—he'd been given all kinds of dark and inhospitable places to sleep. He'd worked long hours for very little money in order to earn money and get a roof over his head.

He lifted his eyes to her face, remembering the powerful way his body had reacted to her the other night and trying to tell himself that it had been a momentary aberration. Because she was plain. *Ordinary.* If he'd passed her in the street, he wouldn't have given her a second glance. Her jeans weren't particularly flattering and neither was her shirt. But her eyes looked like silver and wavy strands of pale hair were escaping from her ponytail and the ends were curling, so that in the harshness of the artificial light she looked as if she were surrounded by a faint blonde halo.

A *halo*. His mouth twisted. He couldn't think of a less likely candidate for angelic status.

'You sold your story,' he accused.

'I didn't *sell* anything,' she contradicted. 'No money exchanged hands.'

'So the journalist is clairvoyant, is that what you're saying? She just guessed we were making out?'

She shook her head. 'That's not what I'm saying at all. She saw us. She was standing behind a tree having a cigarette and saw us kissing.'

'You mean it was a set-up?' he questioned, his tone flat.

'Of course it wasn't a set-up!' She glared at him.

'You think I deliberately arranged to get myself the sack? Rather a convoluted way to go about it, don't you think? I think being caught dipping your fingers in the till is the more traditional way to go.'

He raised his eyebrows in disbelief. 'So she just *happened* to be there—'

'Yes!' she interrupted angrily. 'She did. She was a guest, staying at the hotel. And the next day she cornered me in the restaurant while I was serving her and there was no way I could have avoided talking to her.'

'You still could have just said *no comment* when she started quizzing you,' he accused. 'You didn't have to gush and call me a pussycat—to damage my business reputation and any credibility I've managed to build up. You didn't have to disclose what you'd overheard when you'd clearly been *listening in to my telephone conversation.*'

'How could I help but listen in, when you broke off to take a call in front of me?'

He glared at her. 'What right did you have to repeat *any* of it?'

'And what right do you have to come here, hurling all these accusations at me?'

'You're skirting round the issue. I asked you a question, Ellie. Are you going to answer it?'

There was an odd kind of silence before eventually she spoke.

'She told me you had a girlfriend,' she said.

He raised his eyebrows. 'So you felt that gave you the right to gossip about me, knowing it might find its way into the press?'

'How could I, when I didn't know what her job was?'

'You mean you're just habitually indiscreet?'

'Or that you're just sexually incontinent?'

He sucked in an angry breath. 'As it happens, I don't have a girlfriend at the moment and if I did, then I certainly wouldn't have been making out with you. You see, I place great store on loyalty, Ellie—in fact, I value it above everything else. While you, on the other hand, don't seem to know the meaning of the word.'

Ellie was taken aback by the coldness in his eyes. She had made a mistake, yes—but it had been a genuine one. She hadn't set out to deliberately tarnish his precious reputation.

'Okay,' she conceded. 'I spoke about you when maybe I shouldn't have done and, because of that, you've managed to get me the sack. I'd say we were quits now, wouldn't you?'

He met her gaze.

'Not quite,' he said softly.

A shiver of something unknowable whispered over her skin as she stared at him. There was something unsettling in his eyes. Something distracting about the sudden tension in his hard body. She stared at him, knowing what he was planning to do and knowing it was wrong. *So why didn't she ask him to leave?*

Because she *couldn't*. She'd dreamed about just such a moment—playing it out in her mind, when it had been little more than a fantasy. She had wanted Alek Sarantos more than she had thought it possible to want anyone and that feeling hadn't changed. If anything, it had grown even stronger. She could feel herself trembling as he reached out and hauled her against him. The angry expression on his face made it seem as if he was doing something he didn't really want to do and she felt a brief flicker of rebellion. How dare he look that way? She told herself to pull away, but the need to have him kiss her again was dominating every other consideration. And maybe this was inevitable—like the thunder which had been rumbling all day through the heavy sky. Sooner or later you just knew the storm was going to break.

His mouth came down on hers—hard—and the hands which should have been pushing him away were gripping his shoulder, as she kissed him back—just as hard. It felt like heaven and it felt like hell. She wanted to hurt him for making her lose her job. She wanted him to take back all those horrible accusations he'd made. And she wanted him to take away this terrible aching deep inside her.

Alek shuddered as he heard the little moan she made and he told himself to tug her jeans down and just *do* it. To give into what they both wanted and feed this damned hunger so that it would go away and leave him. Or maybe he should just turn around and walk out of that door and go find someone else. Someone immaculate and cool— not someone all hot and untidy from cycling on the hottest day of the year.

But she was soft in his arms. So unbelievably soft. She was like Turkish Delight when you pressed your finger against it, anticipating that first sweet, delicious mouthful. He pulled his lips away from hers and slowly raised his head, meeting a gaze which gleamed silver.

'I want you,' he said.

He saw her lips tremble as they opened, as if she was about to list every reason why he couldn't have her and he guessed there might be quite a long list. And then he saw something change—the moment when her eyes darkened and her skin started to flush. The *what-the-*

hell? moment as she looked at him with naked invitation in her eyes.

'And I want you, too,' she said.

It was like dynamite. Like nothing he'd ever known as he drove his lips back down on hers. A kiss which made him feel almost savage with need. It went on and on until they were both breathless, until he drew his mouth away from hers and could suck in a ragged breath of air. Her eyes were wide and very dark and her lips were trembling. With a sense of being slightly out of control, he tugged open her shirt to reveal the spill of her breasts and stared at them in disbelief.

'Theo,' he said softly. 'Your breasts are magnificent.'

'A-are they?'

'They are everything I dreamed they would be. And more.'

'Have you been dreaming about my breasts?'

'Every night.'

He drew a finger over one generous curve and he heard her moan as he bent to touch his lips to the same spot. And that was when she chose to press her palm over the tight curve of his denim-covered buttock, as if tacitly giving him her permission to continue.

He groaned as he straightened up to kiss her again and once he'd started he couldn't seem to stop. It was only when she began to writhe frustratedly that he tugged off the elastic band so that her pale hair spilled free, and suddenly she managed to look both wholesome and wanton. She looked...like a *woman*, he thought longingly. Soft and curving; warm and giving.

His hands were shaking as he stripped her bare, then laid her down on the narrow bed as he removed his own clothes, his eyes not leaving her face. With shak-

ing hands he groped for his wallet and found a condom.
Thank God. Slipping it on as clumsily as if it had been
his first time, he moved over her, smoothing back her
thick hair with hands which were still unsteady. And
as he entered her a savage cry was torn from his throat.

He moved inside her and it felt pretty close to heaven.
Sweet heaven. He had to keep thinking about random
stuff about mergers and acquisitions to stop himself
from coming and it seemed like an eternity until at
last her body began to tense beneath him. Until she
stiffened and her back arched and, inexplicably—she
started to cry.

Only then did Alek let go himself, although the salty
wetness of her tears against his cheek gave him a moment of disquiet. Outside, the thunder seemed to split
the sky. The rain began to teem down against the window. And his body was torn apart by the longest orgasm of his life.

CHAPTER FOUR

Ellie turned the sign to Closed and started clearing away stray currants and dollops of frosting from the glass counters which lined the cake shop. She stacked cardboard boxes, swept the floor and took off her frilly apron.

And then she went and stood at the back of the little store, and wept.

The tears came swiftly and heavily and she tried to think of them as cathartic as she covered her face with her hands. But as they dripped through her fingers all she could think was: *How had this happened? How had her life suddenly become a living nightmare?*

She knew she'd been lucky finding work and accommodation at Candy's Cupcakes so soon after leaving the hotel. She'd been doubly lucky that the kindly Bridget Brody had taken a shine to her, and not cared about her ignominious sacking. But it was hard to focus on gratitude right now. In fact, it was hard to focus on anything except the one thing she couldn't keep ignoring. *But you couldn't make something go away, just because you wanted it to—no matter how hard you wished it would.* Her feet were heavy as she made her way up to the small, furnished apartment above the shop, but not nearly as heavy as her heart.

The mirror in the sitting room was hung in a position you couldn't avoid, unless you walked into the room with your eyes shut, which was never a good idea with such uneven floorboards. The healthy tan she'd acquired while working in the garden restaurant of The Hog had long since faded. Her face was pasty, her breasts were swollen and her skin seemed too loose for her body. And she'd lost weight. She couldn't eat anything before midday because she kept throwing up. She hadn't needed to see the double blue stripes on the little plastic stick to confirm what she already knew.

That she was pregnant with Alek Sarantos's baby and didn't know what she was going to do about it.

Slumping down in one of the overstuffed armchairs, she stared blankly into space. Actually, that wasn't quite true. There was only one thing she *could* do. She had to tell him.

She had to.

It didn't matter what her personal feelings were, or that fact that there had been a deafening silence ever since the Greek billionaire had walked out of her bedroom, leaving her naked in bed. This was about more than *her*. She knew what it was like not to have a father and no real identity. To feel invisible—as if she were only half a person. And that wasn't going to happen to her baby. She hugged her arms tightly around her chest. *She wouldn't allow it to happen.*

But how did you tell someone you were having his baby when he had withdrawn from you in more ways than one as soon as he'd had his orgasm?

Her mind drifted back to that awful moment when

she'd opened her eyes to find Alek Sarantos lying on top of her in the narrow bed in the staff hostel. His warm skin had been sticking to hers and his breathing sounded as if he'd been in a race. On a purely physical level, her own body was glowing with the aftermath of the most incredible sexual experience of her life—although she didn't exactly have a lot to compare it with. Her body felt as if she were floating and she wanted to stay exactly where she was—to capture and hold on to the moment, so that it would never end.

But unfortunately, life wasn't like that.

She wasn't sure what changed everything. They were lying there so close and so quiet while the rain bashed hard against the windows. It felt as if their entire lives were cocooned in that little room. She could feel the slowing beat of his heart and the warmth of his breath as it fanned against the side of her neck. She wanted to fizz over with sheer joy. She'd had a relationship before—of course she had—but she had never known such a feeling of completeness. Did he feel it, too? She remembered reaching up to whisper her fingertips over his hair with soft and rhythmical strokes. And that was the moment when she read something unmistakable on his face. The sense that he'd just made the biggest mistake of his life. She could see it in his eyes—those compelling blue eyes, which went from smoky satisfaction through to ice-cold disbelief as he realised just where he was. And with whom.

With a wince he didn't even bother disguising, he carefully eased himself away from her, making sure the condom was still intact as he withdrew. She remembered the burning of her cheeks and feeling completely out of her depth. Her mind was racing as she thought how best to handle the situation, but her experience of men was scant and of Greek billionaires, even scanter. She decided that coolness would be the way to go. She needed to reassure him that she wasn't fantasising about walking up the aisle wearing a big white dress, just because they'd had sex. To act as if making love to a man who was little more than a stranger was no big deal.

She reminded herself that what they'd done had been driven by anger and perhaps it might have been better if it had stayed that way. Because if it hadn't suddenly morphed into a disconcerting whoosh of passion, then she might not be lying there wishing he would stay and never leave. She might not be starting to understand her own mother a bit more and to wonder if this was what *she* had felt. Had she lain beside her married lover like this, and lost a little bit of her heart to him, even though she must have known that he was the wrong man?

She remembered feigning sleepiness. Letting her lashes flutter down over her eyes as if the lids were too heavy to stay open. She could hear him moving around as he picked up his clothes from the floor and began pulling them on and she risked a little peep from between her lashes, to find him looking anywhere except at her. As if he couldn't bear to look at her. But she guessed it was a measure of how skewed her thinking was that she was still prepared to give him the benefit of the doubt.

'Alek?' she said—casual enough to let him know she wouldn't mind seeing him again, but not so friendly that it could be interpreted as pushy.

He was fully dressed by now—although he looked dishevelled. It was strange to see the powerful billionaire in *her* room, his shirt all creased from where it had been lying on the floor. He was running his fingers through his ruffled hair and his skin gleamed with the exertion of sex, but it was his eyes which got to her. His eyes were cold. Cold as ice. She saw him checking in his pocket for his car keys. Or maybe he was just checking that his wallet was safe.

'That was amazing,' he said, and her suddenly happy heart wanted to burst out of her chest, until his next words killed the dream for ever.

'But a mistake,' he finished with a quick, careful smile. 'I think we both realise that. Goodbye, Ellie.'

And then he was gone and Ellie was left feeling like a fool. He didn't even slam the door and for some reason that only added to her humiliation. As if the quiet click as he shut it behind him was all he could be bothered with.

She didn't move for ages. She lay in that rumpled bed watching the rain running in rivulets over the window, like giant tears. Why had she cried afterwards? Because it had been so perfect? And that was the most stupid thing of all. It *had*. It had felt like everything her faintly cynical self had never believed in. He'd made her feel stuff she'd never felt before. As if she was gorgeous. Precious. Beautiful. Did he do that with everyone woman he had sex with? *Of course he did.* It was like tennis, or playing poker. If you practised something often enough, you got very accomplished at doing it.

She went straight to shower in the shared bathroom along the corridor in an attempt to wash away her memories, but it wasn't that easy. Vivid images of Alek seemed to have stamped themselves indelibly on her mind. She found herself thinking about him at inconvenient times of the day and night and remembering the way he had touched her. And although time would probably have faded those memories away she'd never had a chance to find out because her period had been late.

What was she talking about? Her period hadn't been *late*. It just hadn't arrived and she was normally as regular as clockwork. Waves of nausea had begun striking her at the most inopportune times and she knew she couldn't keep putting it off.

She was going to have to tell him. Not next week, nor next month—but now.

Firing her ancient computer into life, she tapped in the name of the Sarantos organisation, which seemed to have offices all over the world. She prayed he was still in London and as the distinctive blue logo flashed up on the screen, it seemed he was. According to the company website, he'd given a speech about 'Acquisitions & Mergers' at some high-profile City conference, just the evening before.

Even if she'd known his home address—which of course she didn't—it made much more sense to go to his office. She remembered him telling her that he always stayed late. She would go there and explain that she had something of vital importance to tell him and—even if it was only curiosity—she was certain he would listen.

And if he didn't?

Then her conscience would be clear, because at least she would have tried.

Wednesday was her day off and she travelled by train to London, on another of the sticky and humid days which had been dominating the English summer. Her best cotton dress felt like a rag by the time she left the train at Waterloo and she had a nightmare journey on the Underground before emerging close to St Paul's cathedral.

She found the Sarantos building without too much difficulty—a giant steel and glass monolith soaring up into the cloudless blue sky. Lots of people were emerging from the revolving doors and Ellie shrank into the shadows as she watched them heading for the local bars and Tube. How did the women manage to look so cool in this sweltering heat, she wondered—and how could they walk so quickly on those skyscraper heels they all seemed to wear?

She walked into the reception area, where the blessed cool of the air conditioning hit her like a welcome fan. She could see a sleek woman behind the desk staring at her, but she brazened it out and walked over to one of the squidgy leather sofas which were grouped in the far corner of the lobby, sinking down onto it with a feeling of relief.

A security guard she hadn't seen until that moment walked over to her.

'Can I help you, miss?'

Ellie pushed her fringe out of her eyes and forced a smile. 'I'm just waiting for my…friend.'

'And your friend's name is?'

Did she dare? And yet, wasn't the reality that in her belly was growing a son or daughter who might one day be the boss of this mighty corporation? She sucked in a deep breath, telling herself that she had every right to be here.

'His name is Alek Sarantos,' she blurted out, but not before she had seen a wary look entering the guard's eyes.

To his credit—and Ellie's surprise—he didn't offer any judgement or try to move her on, he simply nodded.

'I'll let his office know you're here,' he said, and started to walk towards the reception desk.

He's going to tell him, thought Ellie as the reality of her situation hit her. *He's going to ring up to Alek's office and say that some mad, overheated woman is waiting downstairs for him in Reception.* It wasn't too late to make a run for it. She could be gone by the time Alek got down here. She could go back to the New Forest and carry on working for the owner of Candy's Cupcakes—who wasn't called Candy at all—and somehow scrape by, doing the best she could for her baby.

But that wasn't good enough, was it? She didn't want to bring up a child who had to *make do.* She didn't want to have to shop at thrift stores or learn a hundred ways to be inventive with a packet of lentils. She wanted her child to thrive. To have new shoes whenever he or she needed them and not have to worry about whether there was enough money to pay the rent. Because she knew how miserable that could be.

'Ellie?'

A deep Greek accent broke into her thoughts and Ellie looked up to see Alek Sarantos directly in front of her with the guard a few protective steps away. There was a note of surprise in the way he said her name, and a distinct note of unfriendliness, too.

She supposed she ought to get to her feet. To do something rather than just sit there, like a sack of potatoes which had been dumped. She licked her lips and tried to smile, but a smile was stubbornly refusing to come. And wasn't it crazy that she could look at someone who was glaring at her and *still* want him? Hadn't her body already betrayed her once, without now shamefully prickling with excited recognition—even though she'd never seen him looking quite so intimidating in an immaculately cut business suit?

Keep calm, she told herself. *Act like a grown-up.*

'Hello, Alek,' she said, even managing what she hoped was a friendly smile.

He didn't react. His blue eyes were cool. No. Cool was the wrong temperature. Icy would be more accurate.

'What are you doing here?' he questioned, almost pleasantly—but it didn't quite conceal the undertone of steel in his voice and she could see the guard stiffen, as if anticipating that some unpleasantness was about to reveal itself.

She wondered what would happen if she just came out and said it. *I'm having your baby. You're going to be a daddy, Alek!* That would certainly wipe that cold look from his face! But something stopped her. Something which felt like self-preservation. And pride. She couldn't afford to just *react*—she had to *think*. Not just for herself, but for her baby. In his eyes she'd already betrayed him to the journalist and that had made him go ballistic. She couldn't tell him about impending fatherhood when there was a brick-house of a guard standing there, flexing his muscles. She ought to give him the opportunity to hear the news in private. She owed him that much.

She kept her gaze and her voice steady—though that wasn't particularly easy in the light of that forbidding blue stare. 'I'd prefer to talk to you in private, if you don't mind.'

Alek felt a sudden darkness envelop his heart as the expression on her face told him everything. He tried to tell himself that it was the shock of finding her here which had sent his thoughts haywire, but he knew that wasn't true. Because he'd thought about her. Of course he had. He'd even wondered idly about seeing her again— and why wouldn't he? Why wouldn't he want a repeat of what had been the best sex he could remember? If only it had been that straightforward, but life rarely was.

He remembered the way he'd lain there afterwards, with his head cradled on her shoulder as he drifted in and out of a dreamy sleep. And her fingers—her soft fingers—had been stroking his hair. It had felt soothing and strangely intimate. It had kick-started something unknown inside him—something threatening enough to freak him out. He had felt the walls closing in on him—just as they were closing in on him right now.

He tried to tell himself that maybe he was mistaken— that it couldn't possibly be what he most feared. But what else could it be? No woman in her situation would turn up like this and be so unflappable when challenged— not unless she had a trump card to play. Not when he'd left her without so much as a kiss or a promise to call her again. Somehow he sensed that Ellie had more pride than to come here begging him to see her again. She'd been strong, hadn't she? An equal in his arms and out of them, despite the disparity of their individual circumstances.

He noted the shadows on her face, which suddenly seemed as grey as her eyes, and thought how *drained* she looked. His mouth tightened and a flare of anger and self-recrimination flooded through him. He was going to have to listen to her. He needed to hear what she had to say. *To find out whether what he dreaded was true.*

His mind raced. He thought about taking her to a nearby coffee shop. No. Much too public. Should he take her upstairs to his office? That might be easier.

Easier to get rid of her afterwards than if he took her home. And he had no desire to take her home. He just wanted her out of his life. To forget that he'd ever met her. 'You'd better come up to my office.'

'Okay,' she said, her voice sounding brittle.

It felt bizarre to ride up in the elevator in silence but he didn't want to open any kind of discussion in such a confined space, and she seemed to feel the same. When the doors opened she followed him through the outer office and he looked across at Vasos.

'Hold all my calls,' he said—catching the flicker of surprise in his assistant's eyes.

'Yes, boss.'

Soon they were in his cool suite of offices, which overlooked the city skyline, and he thought how out of place she looked, with her flower-sprigged cotton dress and pale legs. And yet despite a face which was almost bare of make-up and the fact that her hair was hanging down her back in that thick ponytail—there was still something about her which made his body tense with a primitive recognition he didn't understand. Even though she looked pasty and had obviously lost weight, part of him still wanted to pin her down against that leather couch, which stood in the corner, and to lose himself deep inside her honeyed softness. His mouth flattened.

'Sit down,' he said.

'There's no need.' She hesitated, like a guest who had turned up at the wrong party and wasn't quite sure how to explain herself to the host. 'You probably want to know why I've turned up like this—'

'I know exactly why.' Never had it been more of an ordeal to keep his voice steady, but he knew that psychologically it was better to tell than to be told. To remain in control. His words came out calmly, belying the sudden flare of fear deep in his gut. 'You're pregnant, aren't you?'

She swayed. She actually swayed—reaching out to grab the edge of his desk. And despite his anger, Alek strode across the office and took hold of her shoulders and he could feel his fingers sinking into her soft flesh as he levered her down onto a chair.

'Sit down,' he repeated.

Her voice was wobbly. 'I don't want to sit down.'

'And I don't want the responsibility of you passing out on the floor of my office,' he snapped. But he pulled his hands away from her—as if continuing to touch her might risk him behaving like the biggest of all fools for a second time. He didn't want the responsibility of her, full stop. He wanted her to be nothing but a fast-fading memory of an interlude he'd rather forget—but that wasn't going to happen. Not now. Raising his voice, he called for his assistant. 'Vasos!'

Vasos appeared at the door immediately—unable to hide his look of surprise as he saw his boss leaning over the woman who was sitting slumped on a chair.

'Get me some water.' Alek spoke in Greek. 'Quickly.'

The assistant returned seconds later with a glass, his eyes still curious. 'Will there be anything else, boss?'

'Nothing else.' Alek took the water from him. 'Just leave us. And hold all my calls.'

As Vasos closed the door behind him Alek held the glass to her lips. Her eyes were suspicious and her body tense. She reminded him of a stray kitten he'd once brought into the house as a child. The animal had been a flea-ridden bag of bones and Alek had painstakingly brought it back to full and gleaming health. It had been something he'd felt proud of. Something in that cold mausoleum of a house for him to care about. And then his father had discovered it, and…and…

His throat suddenly felt as if it had nails in it. *Why remember something like that now?* 'Drink it,' he said harshly. 'It isn't poison.'

She raised her eyes to his and the suspicion in them had been replaced by a flicker of defiance.

'But you'd probably like it to be,' she answered quietly.

He didn't answer—he didn't trust himself to. He blocked out the maelstrom of emotions which seemed to be hovering like dark spectres and waited until a little colour had returned to her cheeks. Then he walked over to his desk and put the glass down, before positioning himself in front of the vast expanse of window, his arms crossed.

'You'd better start explaining,' he said.

Ellie stared up at him. The water had restored some of her strength, but one glance at the angry sizzle from his blue eyes was enough to remind her that she was here on a mission. She wasn't trying to win friends or influence people, or because she hoped for a repeat of the passion which had got her into this situation in the first place. *So keep emotion out of it*, she told herself fiercely. *Keep to the plain and brutal facts and then you can deal with them.*

'There isn't really a lot to explain. I'm having a baby.'

'We used a condom,' he iced back. 'You know we did.'

Stupidly, that made her blush. As if discussing contraception in his place of work was hopelessly inappropriate. But while it might be inappropriate, it was also *necessary,* she reminded herself grimly. And she was not going to let him intimidate her. It had taken two of them to get into this situation—therefore they both needed to accept responsibility.

'I also know that condoms aren't one hundred per cent reliable,' she said.

'So. You're an expert, are you?' He looked at her with distaste. 'Perhaps there are other men to whom you've taken this tale of woe. How many more in the running, I wonder—could you tell me my position on the list, just so I know?'

Ellie clenched her fists as a wave of fury washed over her. She didn't *need* this—not in any circumstances but especially not now. She made to rise to her feet, but her legs were stubbornly refusing to obey her brain. And even though at that moment she wanted to run out of there and never return, she knew that flight was an indulgence she simply couldn't afford.

'There's nobody else in the running,' she spat out. 'Maybe you're different, but I don't have sex with more than one person at the same time. So why don't you keep your unfounded accusations to yourself? I didn't come here to be your punchbag!'

'No? Then what did you come for?' The brief savagery of his dark features realigned themselves into a quizzical expression. 'Is it money you want?'

'Money?'

'That's what I said.'

Ellie's anger intensified but somehow that seemed to help, because it was giving her focus. It was making her want to fight. Not for herself, but for the tiny life growing inside her. Because *that* was what was important. *That* was the reason she had come here today, even though she'd known it was going to be an ordeal. *So think before you answer. Don't make cheap retorts just for the sake of trying to score points. Show him you mean business. Because you* do.

'I'm here to give you the facts,' she said. 'Because I thought it was your right to have them. That you needed to be aware that there were consequences to what happened that afternoon.'

'A little dramatic, isn't it? Just turning up here like this. Couldn't you have called first to warn me?'

'You think I should have done that? Really?' She tipped her head to one side and looked at him. 'I didn't have your number because you deliberately didn't give it to me, but even if I'd managed to get hold of it—would you have spoken to me? I don't think so.'

Alek considered her words. No, he probably wouldn't, despite his faintly irrational desire to see her again. Through Vasos, he would have demanded she put everything down in an email. He would have kept her at an emotional distance, as he did with all women. But he was beginning to realise that the whys and wherefores of what had happened between them were irrelevant. Didn't matter that she'd broken a cardinal rule and invaded his workspace. There was only one thing which mattered and that was what she had just told him.

And this was one reality he couldn't just walk away from. He asked the question as if he were following some ancient male-female rule book, but if his question sounded lifeless it was because deep down he knew the answer. 'How do I know it's mine?'

'You think I'd be here if it wasn't? That I'd be putting myself through this kind of aggravation if it was someone else's baby?'

He tried telling himself that she might be calling his bluff and that he could demand a DNA test, which would have to wait until the child was born. And yet, once again something told him that no such test would be needed, and he wasn't sure why. Was it the certainty on her pale face which told him that he was the father of her child, or something more subtly complex, which defied all logic? He could hear the door of the prison swinging shut and the sound of the key being turned. He was trapped. Again. And it was the worst feeling in the world. He remembered that distant fortress and his voice sounded gritty. Like it was coming from a long way away. 'What do you want from me?'

There was a pause as those shadowed grey eyes met his.

'I want you to marry me,' she said.

CHAPTER FIVE

WITH NARROWED EYES, Alek looked at her. 'Or what?' he questioned with soft venom. 'Marry you or you'll run blabbing to your journalist friend again? This would be a real scoop, wouldn't it? Pregnant With the Greek's Child.'

Meeting the accusation on his face, Ellie tried to stay calm. She hadn't meant to blurt it out like that—in fact, she hadn't really been planning to say that at all. She had meant to tell him that she was planning to have the baby and would respect whatever decision he made about his own involvement. She had intended to imply that she wasn't bothered one way or another—and she certainly wasn't intending to control or manipulate what was happening.

But something had happened to her during the awkward conversation which had just taken place in the alien surroundings of his penthouse office. With the air-conditioning freezing tiny beads of sweat to her forehead and her cotton dress clinging to her like a dishcloth she had felt worse than ugly. Surrounded by the unbelievable wealth of Alek's penthouse office suite, she had felt *invisible*.

She thought about all the women she'd seen leaving the building—clipping along in their high-heeled shoes with not a hair out of place. Those were the kind of women he dealt with on a daily basis, with their air of purpose and their slim, toned figures. Where did she fit into that world, with her cheap dress and a growing belly and a feeling that she had no real place of her own?

Because she didn't have any real place of her own. This was *his* world and neither she nor her baby belonged in it. How long before he conveniently forgot he had sired a child in a moment of ill-thought-out passion? How long before he married someone classy and had legitimate children who would inherit everything he owned, while her own child shrank into the shadows, forgotten and overlooked? Didn't she know better than anyone that unwanted children usually stayed that way? *She knew what it was like to be rejected by her own father.*

And that was her light-bulb moment. The moment when she knew exactly what she was going to ask for. Her ego didn't matter and neither did her pride, because this was more important than both those things. *This was for her baby.*

'I'm not threatening to blackmail you,' she said quietly. 'I've told you until I was blue in the face that the whole journalist thing was a stupid mistake, which I don't intend on repeating. I just want you to marry me, that's all.'

'That's all?' he echoed with a cruel replica of a smile. 'Why?'

'Because you're so charming, of course,' she snapped. 'And so thoughtful and—'

'Why?' he repeated, a note of steel entering his

voice—as if he suspected that behind her flippancy she was teetering perilously on the brink of hysteria.

'Isn't it obvious?' With an effort she kept her gaze steady, but inside her heart was pounding so loudly she was certain he must be able to hear it. 'Because I want my baby to have some kind of security.'

'Which doesn't need to involve marriage,' he said coldly. 'If the baby really is mine, then I will accept responsibility. I can give you money. A house.' He shrugged. 'Some baubles for yourself, if that's what you're angling for.'

Baubles? *Baubles?* Did he really think her so shallow that he thought jewels might be her motivation? 'It isn't,' she said, her cheeks growing pink, 'just about the money.'

'Really? Woman claims money isn't her sole motivation.' He gave a cynical laugh. 'Wow! That must be a first. So if it isn't about the money—then what *is* it about?'

Distractedly, she rubbed at her forehead. 'I want him—or her—to know who they are—to have a real identity. I want them to bear their father's name.'

She saw the darkness which passed over his face like a cloud crossing the sun.

'And I might not have the kind of name you would want to associate with your baby,' he said harshly.

'What's that supposed to mean?'

But Alek shook his head as the old familiar shutters came slamming down—effectively sealing him off from her questions. Because marriage was a no-no for him—right at the very top of things he was never going to do. And although he'd shaken off his past a long time ago—he could never entirely escape its long tentacles. They reached out and whipped him when he wasn't expecting it. In the darkness of the night they sometimes slithered over his skin, reminding him of things he'd rather forget.

His parents' marriage had been the dark canker at the heart of his life, whose poison had spilled over into so many places. The union between a cruel man and a woman he despised so much that he couldn't even bear to say her name. His mouth hardened. Why the hell would *he* ever want to marry?

Alek's success had been public, but he'd managed to keep his life private. He had locked himself within an emotional shell in order to protect himself and he rarely let anyone get close. And hadn't that been another reason for his anger with Ellie? Not just because her indiscretion had tarnished his hard-won business reputation, but because she'd broken his foolishly misplaced trust in her.

'Maybe I'm not great husband material,' he told her. 'Ask any of the women I've dated and I'm sure they'd be happy to list all my failings. I'm selfish. I'm intolerant. I work too hard and have a low boredom threshold—especially where women are concerned.' He raised his eyebrows. 'Shall I continue?'

She shook her head, so that her ponytail swung from side to side. 'I'm not talking about a real marriage. I'm talking about a legal contract with a finite time limit.'

His eyes narrowed. 'Because?'

'Because I don't want my baby to be born illegitimate—I'm illegitimate myself. But neither do I want to spend the rest of my life with someone who doesn't even seem to like me. I'm not a complete masochist—'

'Just a partial one?' he put in mockingly.

'I must have been,' she said bitterly, 'to have had sex with you.'

'Pretty amazing sex, though,' he said, almost as an aside.

Deliberately, Ellie pushed that thought away, even though just the mention of it was enough to start her body tingling. Yes, it had been amazing. It had started out in anger but it had turned into something else. Something passionate and all consuming, which had completely blown her away. Had he felt it, too—that incredible connection? Or was she doing that thing women were so good at doing? Believing something to be true because you *wanted* it to be true.

'It doesn't matter now what the sex was like,' she said slowly. 'Because the only thing that matters now is the baby.'

He flinched as she said the word. She could see his jaw harden so that it looked as if it were carved from granite.

'Cut to the chase and tell me exactly what you're proposing,' he said.

The combination of heat, emotion and a lack of food was making her feel dizzy but Ellie knew she mustn't crumple now. The thought of having Alek in her life didn't exactly make her want to jump for joy—but it was still better than going it alone.

'We have a small wedding,' she said. 'No doubt your lawyers will want to draw up some kind of contract and that's fine by me.'

'Good of you,' he said sardonically.

'We don't even have to live together,' she continued. 'You just acknowledge paternity and provide support for the future. The baby gets your name and a share of your inheritance.' She shrugged, because the words sounded so bizarre. A few short weeks ago she'd been thinking no further than her next promotion and here she was talking about *paternity.* 'And after the birth, we can get ourselves a no-blame divorce. I think that's fair.'

'Fair?' He gave a short laugh. 'You mean I'm to play the tame benefactor? Sitting on the sidelines, just doling out money?'

'I'm not intending to be greedy.'

He narrowed his eyes. 'And you don't think people are going to be suspicious? To wonder why we aren't living together and why I haven't spent any time with the mother of my baby?'

'Given the way you've reacted to the news, I was assuming that being given a get-out clause would be your dream scenario.'

'Well, don't,' he snapped. 'Don't ever *assume* anything about me, Ellie. That was the first mistake you made. I am not a "pussycat" as you seem to think, not by any stretch of the imagination.'

'Don't worry. I've changed my mind about that!'

'I'm pleased to hear it.' His gaze raked over her, lingering almost reluctantly on her belly. 'I didn't plan a baby and I certainly didn't want marriage. But if these are the cards fate has dealt me—then these are the cards I'm going to have to play. And I play to win.'

She pushed her fringe out of her eyes. 'Is that supposed to be a threat?'

'Not a threat, no. But you haven't yet heard my side of the bargain.' Alek stared at her mutinous face. He knew what he had to do. No matter how much it flew in the face of everything he believed in, he was going to have to make sacrifices for his child in a way nobody had ever done for him. He was going to have to marry her. Because it was far better to have her by his side as his wife, than to leave her free to behave like a loose cannon, with his child helpless and without his protection.

His heart clenched. 'If you want my ring on your finger, then you're going to have to act like a wife,' he said. 'You will live with me—'

'I told you that wasn't—'

'I don't care what you told me,' he interrupted impatiently. 'If we're going to do this, we're going to do it properly. I want this wedding to mimic all the traditions of what a wedding should be.'

'M-mimic?' she echoed, in confusion. 'What do you mean?'

'Can't you guess?' His mouth twisted into a bitter smile. 'We will pretend. You will wear a white dress and look deep into my eyes and play the part of my adoring bride. Do you think you can manage that, Ellie?'

Ellie's stomach began to rumble and she wondered if he could hear it in the strange silence which had descended. It seemed a long time since she'd eaten that apple on the train. In fact, it seemed a long time since she'd done anything which felt remotely *normal*. One minute she'd been waiting tables and the next she was standing discussing marriage with a cold-eyed billionaire who was telling her to pretend to care about him. Suddenly she felt like a feather which had found itself bouncing around on a jet stream.

'You want to make it into some sort of farce,' she breathed.

'Not a farce. Just a performance credible enough to convince the outside world that we have fallen in love.'

'But why?' she questioned. 'Why not just treat it like the contract we both know it is?'

He flexed his fingers and she saw the whitening of his knuckles through the deep olive skin.

'Because I want my child to have *memories*,' he said harshly. 'To be able to look at photos of their mother and father on their wedding day, and even if they are no longer together—which obviously, we won't be— then at least there will be the consolation that once we were an item.'

'But that's…that's a lie!'

'Or just illusionary?' he questioned bitterly. 'Isn't that what life is? An illusion? People see what others want them to see. And I don't want my child hurt. Let him believe that once his parents loved one another.'

Ellie watched his face become ravaged by a pain he couldn't hide. It clouded the brilliance of his blue eyes and darkened his features into a rugged mask. And de- spite everything, she wanted to reach out and ask him what had caused him a hurt so palpable that just wit- nessing it seemed intrusive. She wanted to put her arms around him and cradle him.

But he looked so remote in his beautifully cut suit, with its dark fabric moulding his powerful limbs and the white shirt collar which contrasted against his gleaming skin. He looked so proud and patrician that he seemed almost *untouchable*, which was pretty ironic when you thought about it. She cleared her throat. 'And when should this *marriage* take place?'

'I think as soon as possible, don't you? There's some- thing a little in your face about a bride who is so *obvi- ously* pregnant. I'll have my lawyers draw up a contract and you will move into my London apartment. We can discuss buying you a property after the birth.'

Ellie felt as if her old life was already fading. As if she'd been plucked from obscurity and placed in the spotlight of Alek's glamorous existence and she was suddenly beginning to realise just how powerful that spotlight could be. But when she stopped to think about it, what did she imagine would happen next? That she'd carry on selling cupcakes while wearing his ring on her finger? 'I suppose so,' she agreed.

His blue gaze raked over her. 'You've lost weight,' he observed.

'I get sick in the mornings, but it usually wears off by mid-afternoon.'

'Yet you're expecting to carry on working?'

'I'll manage,' she said stubbornly. 'Most women do.'

'And after the birth—what then? Will your baby take second place to your career?'

'I can't say what will happen,' she said quietly. 'All I do know is that a child shouldn't have to take second place to anything.'

They stared at one another and for a moment Ellie thought he was actually going to say something *nice*, but she was wrong.

'You're going to have to update your wardrobe if you're to make a convincing bride, but that shouldn't be a problem. As the future Mrs Sarantos, you'll get unlimited access to my credit card. Does that turn you on?'

Ellie glared as she met his sardonic smile. 'Will you please stop making me sound like some kind of gold-digger?'

'Oh, come on, Ellie,' he said, and briefly some of the

harshness left his voice. 'Didn't you ever learn to make the best out of a bad situation?'

She felt a twist of pain as she turned away. Didn't he realise he was talking to the queen of the positive spin? That she'd spent her life trying not to be influenced by a mother who was steeped in bitterness and regret. And hadn't she vowed that her own life would be different? That she would make something of herself? She would be strong and most of all...*independent*. And now here she was, tying herself to a cold and unfeeling man because she needed security.

But that didn't matter. None of it did. She was going to do whatever it took to give her baby a better life than the one she'd known.

Her heart clenched.

Even if it meant marrying someone who seemed to despise her.

CHAPTER SIX

ELLIE'S NEW LIFE began the minute Alek agreed to marry her and it felt like waking up in a parallel universe.

No more travelling across London, or a sticky train journey home to the New Forest. He didn't do public transport, did he? And neither would the woman who was carrying his child. A sleek limo was ordered to take her home, but not before Alek insisted she eat something. Her attempts to tell him she wasn't hungry fell on deaf ears and he sent Vasos out for warm bread, tiny purple grapes and a rich chickpea spread, which Ellie fell on with a moan of greed. She ate the lot and looked up to find him studying her.

'You're obviously not looking after yourself properly,' he said repressively. 'Forget working out your notice and move up here straight away. It makes perfect sense.'

'I can't leave Bridget in the lurch. She's been very kind to me. I'll need to give her a month's notice.'

He hadn't been happy about that, just as he hadn't been happy when she'd refused the wad of banknotes he'd tried to press on her for any *expenses*.

'Please don't try to give me money in the street, Alek,' she hissed. 'I'm not some kind of hooker. And while we're on the subject, I'm going to want my own room when I move into your apartment.' The look of surprise on his face had been almost comical. 'And that's a requirement,' she added tartly. 'Not a request.'

It was late when the car eventually dropped her off in the New Forest—too late to speak to Bridget, but Ellie's plan of telling her boss the following day was blown when Bridget walked into the shop with an expression Ellie had never seen before. The fifty-something widow who had treated her like the daughter she'd never had looked as if she was about to burst with excitement.

'Sweet saints in all heaven—why didn't you tell me?' Bridget demanded, her Irish accent still discernible, even after three decades of living in England.

'Tell you what?' questioned Ellie, her skin prickling with an instinctive dread.

'That you're going to be married! And to a handsome Greek, no less! My, but you're a secretive one, Miss Brooks.'

Ellie gripped the glass counter, forgetting the smudgy marks her fingers would leave behind. 'But how—?' She swallowed as she asked a question to which she already knew the answer. 'How did you find out?'

'How do you think?' questioned Bridget, followed by a quick demonstration of her explosive laugh. 'I got a call from the man himself late last night. He woke me out of a deep sleep, but he's so full of the Greek blarney that I told him I didn't mind a bit! He said he needs you at his side and he's offering to compensate me so that you can leave early. Why, I can get ten shop assistants for the money he's giving me—and still have plenty left over for the extension for the tea room! He's a very generous man, Ellie—and you're a very lucky woman.'

Ellie felt sick. Lucky? She felt about as lucky as someone who'd just tossed their winning lottery ticket onto a roaring fire. But she wasn't stupid. Bridget didn't care about her giving a full four weeks' notice, because Alek's offer had wiped out all other considerations. What price was friendship or loyalty in the face of all that hard cash? Was that what made him so cynical? she wondered—knowing everything had a price tag and if he paid enough, he could get exactly what he wanted?

'I've got a girl coming in from the village tomorrow,' continued Bridget chattily. 'It's all sorted.'

Ellie wondered how her boss would react if she told her the truth. *We've only had sex the once and we weren't supposed to see each other again. He's only marrying me because there's a baby on the way.*

But what good would that do? Why disillusion someone for the sake of it? Surely it would be best to repay Bridget's kindness by letting her think this was what she really wanted. Oughtn't she at least act out the fairy tale—even if she didn't believe in it herself?

'It's very sweet of you to be so understanding, Bridget,' she said.

'Nonsense. It's an absolute pleasure to see you so settled and happy. Come round to the cottage tonight and we'll have a slap-up meal, to celebrate.'

After work, Ellie went upstairs to her little flat and, sure enough, there was a text message waiting on her phone.

I've sorted things out with your boss. Car arriving for you at eleven tomorrow morning. Make sure you're ready to leave. Alek.

If she'd thought it would make any difference, she might have been tempted to ping back a stinging reply, but Ellie was too tired to try. Why waste energy fighting the inevitable?

She packed up her meagre wardrobe, then went round to Bridget's hobbit-sized cottage for a vegetarian goulash. Afterwards, as she walked home in the warm summer evening, she looked up at the star-spangled sky with a feeling of wistfulness. She was going to miss the beauty of the forest—with all those cute ponies which wandered around and then stood in the middle of the road, regularly bringing all the traffic to a standstill as they swished their feathery tails. She'd always dreamed she might one day live in a big city, but never in circumstances like this. Her future lay ahead like a big uncharted map, and she felt scared.

Yet the sleep she fell into was deep and she was startled awake by the sound of a car horn beeping from beneath her open window. She staggered out of bed and hastily pulled on a robe. She had overslept and the driver was obviously here.

Except that it wasn't the driver. Ellie waited until the sickness had passed before poking her head out of the window, her breath catching in her throat when she saw Alek himself. He was leaning against a dark green sports car and it was just like the first time she'd seen him—when he'd been off duty in the spa hotel and she'd been trying very hard not to stare.

Dark shades covered his eyes and faded jeans clung to the muscular contours of his long legs. His shirt-sleeves were rolled up to display powerful forearms and his hair glinted blue-black in the bright sunshine.

Liquid desire began to unfold in the base of her belly—warm and unwanted and much too potent.

'Oh,' she said coolly, because she didn't want to feel this way when she looked at him. She wanted to feel *nothing.* 'It's you.'

Lifting up his shades, he narrowed his eyes against the bright light. 'I've had better greetings,' he said drily. 'Why don't you open the door and I'll come up and collect your stuff?'

'There's a key on the top ledge,' she said, withdrawing her head and grabbing some clothes as she headed for the bathroom. By the time she emerged, washed and dressed—he was standing in the middle of her sitting room, not looking in the least bit repentant.

She slammed her soap bag onto the table and turned on him, her growing temper fuelled by the arrogant look on his face. 'How dare you ring up my boss and offer her money to release me from my contract, when I told you I wanted to work out my notice?' she demanded. 'Does it give you a kick to be so *controlling*?'

'If you can give me a single valid objection,' he drawled, 'other than the mild wounding to your ego—then I'll listen. But you can't, can you, Ellie? You've been sick every morning and you look like hell, but you still want to carry on. Not the greatest advertisement for a cake shop, is it—unless you're trying to drive away the customers?' He glanced down at the two battered suitcases which were standing in the middle of the floor. 'This all you've got?'

'No, there are several Louis Vuitton trunks next door,' she said sarcastically.

He picked them up as easily as if they were full of

feathers, rather than the entire contents of her world. 'Come on. The car's waiting.'

She took the keys downstairs to the shop, where Bridget was showing the new assistant all the different cupcakes. The Strawberry Shortcake and the Lemon Lovely. The Chocolate Nemesis and the bestselling Cherry Whirl. It was farewell to a simple life and a great leap into a sophisticated unknown, and Ellie's chest felt tight with emotion as the Irishwoman hugged her, before waving her off in the shiny car.

The car roof was down and the noise of the traffic made conversation difficult but that was a relief because Ellie had no desire to talk and, besides, what would she say? How did you start a conversation with a man you barely knew in circumstances such as these? Staring out of the window, she watched as trees and fields gave way to tall buildings which shimmered in the summer sunshine like distant citadels.

Their journey took them through South Kensington, a place she'd once visited on a school trip. Thirty-five boisterous children had spent the morning in the Natural History Museum and afterwards had been allowed to descend on the museum shop. Ellie had used all her pocket money to buy her mother an expensive little bar of soap in the shape of a dinosaur. But the gift had failed to please. Apparently, it had reminded her—yet again—of all the things which were missing in her life. Ellie remembered her mother staring at the tiny bar as if it had been contaminated. Her voice had been bitter, her face contorted with a rage which was never far from the surface. *If your father had married me, you could have afforded to buy me something which was bigger than a walnut!*

And wasn't that memory reason enough to be grateful that Alek wasn't washing his hands of his responsibilities? Despite his authoritarian attitude, he was stepping up to the mark and shouldering his share of the life they had inadvertently created. He wasn't planning to never pay a penny towards his baby's upkeep, or never bother keeping in touch, was he? She stole a glance at his rugged profile. He wasn't *all* bad. And following on from that wave of appreciation came another, which was rather more unwelcome, especially when his thigh tensed over the accelerator. He was so unbelievably *hot* and she hadn't really stopped to think about what the reality of that might be, when she was closeted together with him in his apartment. Could desire be switched off, like a tap? Or would close contact only increase her awareness of just how gorgeous the father of her unborn child was?

Alek lived in Knightsbridge and his apartment was everything Ellie had expected and more, although nothing could have prepared her for its sheer size and opulence. Even the relative luxury of The Hog paled into insignificance when compared to each high-ceilinged room which seemed to flow effortlessly into the next. Squashy velvet sofas stood on faded silken rugs and everywhere you looked were beautiful objects. On a small table was a box inlaid with mother-of-pearl and a small gilded egg studded with stones of emerald and blue. She blinked at it as it sparkled brightly in the sunshine. Surely those stones weren't *real*? She wanted to ask, but it seemed rude—as if she were sizing up the place and trying to work out its worth. But it wasn't the value so much as the beauty which took her breath away. Everywhere she looked were paintings of places she'd longed to visit—upmarket versions of the posters she'd had hanging in her room at the hostel. Leafy streets in Paris and iconic churches in Rome, as well as the unbelievable architecture of Venice reflected in the dappled water of the canals.

She looked at them longingly. 'Your paintings are amazing.'

'Thank you.' He inclined his head—the tone of his voice altering slightly, as if her comment had surprised him. 'It's something of a hobby of mine. You are fond of art?'

She bit back the defensive remark which hovered on her lips. Did he think someone who worked in the service industry was incapable of appreciating art, or that you had to be wealthy to enjoy it? 'I enjoy visiting galleries when I get the chance,' she said stiffly. 'Though I've never seen stuff like this in someone's home.'

But then she'd never been in a home like this. She walked over to one of the windows which framed a stunning view of the park and when she turned round it was to find him watching her, his blue eyes giving nothing away.

'I take it you approve?'

'How could I not?' She shrugged, trying not to be affected by the intensity of that sapphire gaze. 'It's remarkable. Did you design it yourself?'

'I can't take any of the credit, I'm afraid.' His smile was bland. 'I had someone do that for me. A woman called Alannah Collins.'

Ellie nodded. Of course he did. Men like Alek didn't choose their own wallpaper or spend ages deliberating where to position the sofas. They paid for someone else to do it. Just as he paid shop owners to release their staff early from a contract. He could do what the hell he liked, couldn't he? All he had to do was to take out his chequebook. 'She's a very talented designer,' she said.

'She is.' He narrowed his eyes. 'So I take it you'll be able to tolerate living here for a while?'

'Who knows?' she answered lightly. 'We might be wanting to kill each before the week is out.'

'We might.' There was a heartbeat of a pause. 'Or we might find infinitely more satisfying ways to sublimate our…frustrations. What do you think, Ellie?'

His words were edged with mockery but there was a very real sense of sexual challenge sparking beneath that cool stare, and of course she was tempted by that look.

But even stronger than temptation was Ellie's overwhelming sense of *disorientation* as he flirted with her. Seeing him in his fancy home made it hard to believe the circumstances which had brought her here. Had he really arrived at her humble room in the staff hostel and then had sex with her on that single bed? It seemed like a muddled dream to remember him pulling urgently at her clothing, like a man out of control. She remembered the anger on his face and then the sudden transformation as his rage had given way to a passion which had left her crying in his arms afterwards.

But men could feel passion in the heat of the moment and then turn it off once their appetite had been satisfied, couldn't they? She didn't know a whole heap about sex, but she knew that much and she had to remember that she was vulnerable as far as Alek was concerned. They might have come together as equals that day, but they weren't really equals. She might soon be wearing his wedding ring but that was only a symbol.

It didn't *mean* anything. It certainly didn't mean any of the things a wedding band was *supposed* to mean. She needed to keep her emotional distance. She *had* to, if she wanted to protect herself from getting hurt.

'Just to be clear.' She met the blue gleam of his eyes. 'I meant what I said about wanting my own room. So if you're thinking of trying to persuade me otherwise, I'm afraid you'll be wasting your time.'

He gave a wry smile. 'On balance, I think I agree with you. I'm beginning to think that sharing a room with you would only complicate an already complicated situation.'

Ellie felt a wave of something very feminine and contrary flaring through her as she followed him from the huge reception room. Couldn't he at least have *pretended* to be disappointed, rather than appearing almost *relieved*? With difficulty she dragged her gaze away from his powerful back and forced herself to look at all the different things he was showing her. The plush cinema with its huge screen. The black marble fittings in the shamelessly masculine kitchen. The modern dining room, which didn't look as if it was used very much—with tall silver candlesticks standing on a beautiful gleaming table. On the wall of his study, different clocks were lined up to show the time zones of all the world's major cities and his desk contained a serious amount of paperwork. He explained that there was a swimming pool in the basement of the building, as well as a fully equipped gym.

The bedroom she was allocated wasn't soft or girly—and why would it be?—but at least it was restful. The bed was big, the view spectacular. The en-suite bathroom had snowy towels and expensive bottles of bath oil and she thought about how perfect everything looked. And then there was her. Standing there in her jeans and T-shirt, she felt like a cobweb which had blown onto a line of clean washing.

'Do you like it?' he questioned.

'I can't imagine anyone not liking it. It's beautiful.' She ran her fingertip along a delicate twist of coloured glass which served no useful purpose other than to capture the light and reflect it back in rainbow rays. 'I just can't imagine how a baby is going to fit in here.'

His gaze followed the line of her fingers. 'Neither can I. But I wasn't planning on having a baby when I bought this place.'

'You didn't think that one day you might have a family of your own? I don't mean like this, obviously—'

'Obviously,' he interrupted tightly. 'And the answer is no. Not every man feels the need to lock himself into family life—particularly when so few families are happy.'

'That's a very cynical point of view, Alek.'

'You think so? Why, was your own childhood so happy?' His gaze bore into her. 'Let me guess. A cosy English village where everyone knew each other? A cottage with roses growing around the door?'

'Hardly.' She gave a short laugh. 'I didn't meet my father until I was eighteen and when I did I wished I hadn't bothered.'

His eyes had narrowed. 'Why not?'

It was a story she wasn't proud of. Correction. It was one she was almost ashamed of. She knew it was illogical, but if you were unloved, then didn't that automatically make you unlovable? *Didn't the fault lie within her?* But she pushed that rogue thought away as she had been trying to do for most of her adult life. And there was no reason to keep secrets from Alek. She wasn't trying to impress him, because he'd already made it clear that he no longer wanted her. And if you moved past that rather insulting fact—didn't that mean she could be herself, instead of trying to be the person she thought she *ought* to be?

'I'd hate to shock you,' she said flippantly.

His voice was dry. 'Believe me, I am not easily shocked.'

She watched as the filmy drapes moved in a cloud-like blur at the edges of the giant windows. 'My father was a businessman—quite a successful one by all accounts—and my mother worked as his secretary, but she was also his...' She shrugged as she met his quizzical expression. 'It sounds so old-fashioned now, but she was his mistress.'

'Ah,' he said, in the tone of a man addressing a subject on which he was already an expert. 'His mistress.'

'That's right. It was the usual thing. He set her up in a flat. He bought her clothes and in particular—underwear. They used to go out for what was euphemistically known as "lunch," which I gather didn't make her very popular back at the office. Sometimes he even managed to get away for part of a weekend with her, though of course she was always on her own at Christmas and during vacations. She told me all this one night when she'd been drinking.'

'So what happened?' he questioned, diplomatically ignoring the sudden tremble in her voice. 'How come you came along?'

Caught up in a tale she hadn't thought about in a long time, Ellie sat down heavily on the bed. The Egyptian cotton felt soft as she rested her palms against it and met the cool curiosity in Alek's eyes. 'She wanted him to divorce his wife, but he wouldn't. He kept telling her

that he'd have to wait for his children to leave home—
again, the usual story. So she thought she'd give him a
little encouragement.'

'And she got pregnant?'

'She got pregnant,' she repeated and saw the look
on his face. 'And before you say anything—I did not
set out to repeat history. Believe me, the last thing I
wanted was to recreate my own childhood. What happened between us was—'

'An accident,' he said, almost roughly. 'Yes, I know
that. Go on.'

She'd lost the thread of what she'd been saying and it
took her a couple of seconds to pick it up again. 'I think
she mistakenly thought that he'd get used to having a
baby. That he might even be pleased…evidence of his
virility…that kind of thing. But he wasn't. He already
had three children he was putting through school and a
wife with an expensive jewellery habit. He told her…'

Ellie's voice tailed off. She remembered that awful
night of her birthday when her mother had seen off the
best part of a bottle of gin and started blubbing—telling
her stuff which no child should ever hear. She had buried it deep in the recesses of her own mind, but now it
swam to the surface—like dark scum which had been
submerged too long.

'He told her to get rid of it. Or rather…to get rid
of me,' she said, her bright, pointless smile fading as
her mother's words reverberated round her head. *And
I should have listened to him! If I'd known what lay
ahead, I damned well would have listened to him!* 'I
think she thought he'd change his mind, but he didn't.
He stopped paying the rent on my mother's apartment
and told his wife about the affair—thus effectively cur-

tailing any thoughts of blackmail. Then they moved to another part of the country and that was the end of that.'

'He didn't keep in contact?'

'Nope. It was different in those days, before social media really took off—it's easy to lose touch with someone. There was no maintenance—and my mother was too proud to take him to court. She said she'd already lost so much that she wouldn't give him the satisfaction of seeing her begging. She said we would manage just fine, but of course—it's never that simple.'

'But you said you saw him? When you were eighteen?'

Ellie didn't answer for a moment, because this territory was not only forbidden—it was unmarked. She wondered whether she should tell him—but how could she not? She hadn't talked about it with anyone before because she didn't want to look as if she was drowning in self-pity, but maybe Alek had a right to know.

'I did see him,' she said slowly. 'After my mother died, I tracked him down and wrote to him. Said I'd like to meet him. I was slightly surprised when he agreed.' And slightly scared, too, because she'd built him up in her head to be some kind of hero. Maybe she'd been longing for the closeness she'd never had with her mother. Perhaps she had been as guilty as the next person of wanting a fairy tale which didn't exist. The big reunion which was going to make everything in her life better.

'What happened?'

She narrowed her eyes. 'You really want to know?'

'I do. You tell a good story,' he said, surprisingly.

She wanted to tell him that it wasn't a *story*, but when she stopped to think about it—maybe it was. Life was a never-ending story—wasn't that how the old cliché went? She cleared her throat. 'There was no psychic connection between us. No sense that here was the person whose genes I shared. We didn't even look alike. He sat on the other side of a noisy table in a café at Waterloo station and told me that my mother was a conniving bitch who had almost ruined his life.'

'And that was it?' he asked after a long moment.

'Pretty much. I tried asking about my half-sister and half-brothers and anyone would have thought I'd asked him for the PIN number for his savings account, from the way he reacted.' He had stood up then with an ugly look on his face, but the look had been tinged with satisfaction—as if he'd been *glad* of an excuse to be angry with her. She remembered him knocking against the table and her untouched cappuccino slopping everywhere in a frothy puddle. 'He told me never to contact him again. And then he left.'

Alek heard the determinedly nonchalant note in her voice and something twisted darkly in his gut. Was it recognition? A realisation that everyone carried their own kind of pain, but that most of it was hidden away? Suddenly her fierce ambition became understandable—an ambition which had been forced into second place by the baby. He felt a pang of guilt as he recalled how cavalier he'd been about her losing her job. Suddenly, he could understand her insistence on marriage—a request which must have been fuelled by the uncertainty of her own formative years. Not because she wanted the cachet of being his wife, but because she wanted to give her own baby the security she'd never had.

But recognising something didn't change anything. He needed to be clear about the facts and so did she—and the most important fact she needed to realise was that he could never do the normal stuff that women seemed to want. He might be capable of honouring his responsibility to her and the baby—but, emotionally, wasn't he cut from exactly the same cloth as her father? Hadn't he walked away from women in the past—blind to their tears and their needs?

Ellie Brooks wasn't his type, but even if she were he was the last man she needed. She needed his name on a birth certificate and she needed his money, and he could manage that. *Neh.* A bitter smile curved his lips. He could manage that very well. But if she wanted someone to provide the love and support her father had never given her, then he was the wrong person.

She had pushed the heavy fringe away from her eyebrows. Her face was pale, he thought. And now that she no longer had those generous curves, there was a kind of fragility about her which gave her skin a curious luminosity. And suddenly, all his certainties seemed to fade away. He forgot that it was infinitely more sensible to keep his distance from her as he was overcome by a powerful desire to take her in his arms and offer her comfort.

He swallowed, his feelings confusing him. And angering him. He didn't *want* to be in thrall to anyone, but certainly not to her. Because he recognised that Ellie possessed something which no woman before her had ever possessed. *A part of him.* And didn't that give her a special kind of power? A power she could so easily abuse if he wasn't careful.

He walked quickly towards the door, realising that he needed to get the hell out of there. 'You'd better unpack,' he said abruptly. 'And then we need to sit down and discuss the practicalities of you living here.'

CHAPTER SEVEN

WITH A SPEED which left her slightly dazed, Alek took over Ellie's life. He organised a doctor and a credit card. He filled in all the requisite forms required for their upcoming wedding and booked the register office. But it quickly dawned on Ellie that the most important *practicality* of living with the Greek tycoon was an ability to be happy with her own company.

'I work long hours,' he told her. 'And I travel. A lot. You'll need to be able to amuse yourself and not come running to me because you're bored. Understand?'

Biting back her indignation at being spoken to as if she were some kind of mindless puppet, Ellie told herself that snapping at him was only going to make a difficult situation worse. Bad enough that he prowled around the place looking like a sex god, without taking him to task over his patronising comments. She was trying very hard to give him the benefit of the doubt—telling herself that perhaps he didn't mean to be quite so insulting. That he was a powerful man who was clearly used to issuing orders which he expected to be obeyed. And at first, she did exactly that.

During those early days in his Knightsbridge penthouse, she was still too disorientated by the speed at which her life had changed to object to his steamrollering approach to life. She was introduced as his fiancée to the confusingly large number of staff who worked for him both in and outside his organisation and she tried to remember everyone's name.

There were cleaners who moved noiselessly around the vast apartment—like ghosts carrying buckets—and a woman whose job was to keep his fridge and wine cellar stocked. There was the doctor who insisted on visiting her at home—unheard of!—and told her she should take it easy, and these instructions she followed to the letter. She made the most of her free time. She realised it was the first time she'd ever had a prolonged break—or enjoyed a guilt-free session of relaxation—and she concentrated on settling into her new habitat like a cuckoo finding its way round a new and very luxurious nest.

But the baby still felt as if it weren't happening, even though she was now in possession of a glossy black and white photo showing what looked like a cashew nut, attached to the edge of a dark lake. And when she looked into the icy beauty of Alek's eyes, it was hard to believe that the tiny life growing inside her was somehow connected with him. Would he love his baby? she found herself wondering. Was he even *capable* of love?

He's capable of sex, prompted a whispering voice inside her head—but determinedly she blocked out the thought. She wasn't going to think of him that way. She just wasn't.

The friendly concierge in the lobby gave her a street map and she started exploring Kensington and Chelsea, as well as the nearby park, where the leaves on the trees were showing the first hints of gold. She began visiting the capital's galleries with enough time on her hands to really make the most of them, which she'd never had before.

Each morning, Alek left early for the office and would return late, a pair of dark-rimmed reading glasses giving him a surprisingly sexy, geeky look as he carried in the sheaf of papers he'd been studying in the car. He would disappear into his room to shower and change and then—surprisingly—disappear into the kitchen to cook them both dinner. An extensive repertoire of dishes began to appear each evening—one involving aubergine and cheese, which quickly became Ellie's favourite. He told her that he'd learnt to cook at sixteen, when he'd been working in a restaurant and the chef had told him that a man who could feed himself was a man who would survive.

His skill in the kitchen wasn't what she had been expecting and it took some getting used to—sitting and politely discussing the day's happenings over dinner, like two people on a first date who were on their best behaviour. It was like being in some kind of dream. As if it were all happening to someone else.

It was just unfortunate that Ellie's body didn't feel a bit dreamlike, but uncomfortably real. Her reservations about living with him had been realised and she was achingly aware of him. How could she not be? His presence was impossible to ignore. Much as she tried to deny it, he was her every fantasy come to life. Worse still, she'd had a brief taste of what lovemaking could be like in Alek's arms, and it had left her hungry and wanting more. And daily exposure to him was only reinforcing that hunger.

She saw him first thing when he was newly showered

and dressed, with his dark hair slicked back and his skin smelling of lemon. She saw him sitting at the breakfast bar, sliding heavy gold cufflinks through one of his pristine shirts—and her heart would give a powerful contraction of blatant longing. Did he know that? Did he realise that inside she was berating herself for having insisted on a stupid no-sex rule? Had she imagined a hint of amusement dancing in the depths of those sapphire eyes when he looked at her? As if he was enjoying some private joke at her expense—silently taunting her with the knowledge that he could cope with sensual deprivation far better than her.

It was weekends which were hardest, when his failure to leave for the office left a gaping hole in the day ahead, along with the distraction of having him around without a break. This was when breakfast became a more awkward meal than usual. Was she imagining him staring at her intently, or was that just wishful thinking on her part? Had he deliberately left a button of his silk shirt unbuttoned, so that a smooth golden triangle of skin was revealed? Ellie would feel her breasts tingling with a hateful kind of hunger as he slid a jar of marmalade across the table towards her. She remembered what he'd said about faking affection for the wedding photos. No. She definitely wasn't going to have a problem with that.

On the third weekend, she was as edgy as an exam candidate and glad to get out of the apartment for Alek's suggested trip to the Victoria and Albert. It was a museum she'd longed to visit again, even though this time the statues were wasted on her. She kept looking at the carved and stony features of various kings and dignitaries and comparing them unfavourably with the beautiful features of the man by her side. Afterwards, they walked to an open-air restaurant for a late lunch and she had to fight to quash her stupid desire to have him touch her again. She thought about their wedding and their wedding night, and wondered how she was going to cope with *that*.

This time next month I'll be his wife, she thought. *Even though both of us seem determined not to talk about it.*

The sun was dipping lower in the sky as they walked back across the park, but when she got back to the apartment she found herself unable to get comfortable. Her feet were aching and she was wriggling around restlessly on the sofa.

She didn't know what she was expecting when Alek walked across the room and sat down next to her, lifting her bare feet into his lap and beginning to massage each one in turn. It was the first time he'd touched her in a long time and, despite her thoughts of earlier, her instinctive reaction was to freeze, even though her heart had started hammering. Could he hear its wild beat or maybe even see it, beneath her thin T-shirt? Was that why he gave that slow half-smile?

But her initial tension dissolved the instant the warm pad of his thumb started caressing her insole and once she realised that this wasn't a seduction but simply a foot massage, she just lay back and enjoyed it. It felt like bliss and she found herself thinking how ironic it was that all his money couldn't buy something as good as this. Did he realise how much she loved the thoughtful gesture, even though she'd done her best to conceal her squirming pleasure from him? Was he aware that small kindnesses like these were the dangerous blocks which made her start building impossible dreams?

The following Monday, she was drinking ginger tea at the kitchen table when he glanced up from his newspaper and narrowed his eyes.

'About these new clothes you're supposed to be buying,' he said.

'Maternity clothes?'

'Not quite yet. I meant pretty clothes,' he said. 'Isn't that what we agreed? Something to make you look the part of a Sarantos bride. Not long to go now.'

'I know that.'

'You haven't shown very much interest in your wedding so far.'

'It's difficult to get enthusiastic about a ceremony which feels fake.'

He didn't rise to the taunt. 'I thought you'd be itching to get your hands on my chequebook.'

'Sorry to disappoint you,' she said in a hollow voice, thinking about the foot massage. Didn't he realise that something that simple and intimate was worth far more to her than his money? Of course he didn't. It suited him much more to imagine her salivating over his credit card.

He put his newspaper down. 'Well, there's no point in putting it off any longer. I can arrange for Alannah to take you shopping and you can choose your wedding dress at the same time, if you like. You'll find she has a superb eye.'

'You mean I don't?'

He frowned. 'That wasn't what I said.'

'But that's what you implied, isn't it? Poor little Ellie—snatched up from rural Hampshire with no idea how to shop for clothes which might make her believable as the wife of the powerful Greek!' She stood up quickly—too quickly—and had to steady herself. 'Well,

I'm perfectly capable of buying my own clothes—and my own wedding dress. So why don't you give me your precious credit card and I'll see if I can do it justice? I'll go out this morning and just spend, spend, spend like the stereotypical gold-digger you're so fond of portraying!'

'Ellie—'

She stalked off into her room and slammed the door very noisily, but when she came out again sometime later it was to find him still sitting there—the pile of newspapers almost completely read.

'I thought you were going into the office this morning,' she said.

'Not any more,' he said. 'I'm taking you shopping.'

'I don't want you to...' Her voice faltered, because when his blue eyes softened like that, he was making her feel stuff she didn't want to feel.

'Don't want me to what?'

She didn't want him standing on the other side of a curtain while she tried to cram her awkward-looking body into suitable clothes. She didn't want to see the disbelieving faces of the sales assistants as they wondered what someone like him was doing with someone like her. Shopping for clothes was a nightmare experience at the best of times, but throwing the arrogant Alek into the mix would make it a million times worse. 'Hang around outside the changing room,' she said.

'Why not?'

She shrugged. Why not tell him the truth? 'I'm self-conscious about my body.'

He poured himself a cup of coffee. 'Why?'

'Because I *am*, that's why.' She glared at him. 'Most women are—especially when they're pregnant.'

His gaze slid over her navel, his expression suggesting he wasn't used to looking at a woman in a way which wasn't sexual. 'I should have thought that my own reaction to your body would have been enough to reassure you that I find it very attractive indeed.'

'That isn't the point,' she said, unwilling to point out that lately he hadn't shown the slightest interest in her body, because wouldn't that make her seem *vulnerable*? 'I'm not willing to do a Cinderella transformation scene with you as an audience.'

He opened his mouth and then, shutting it again, he sighed. 'Okay. So what if I act as your chauffeur for the day? I'll drive you to a department store and park up somewhere and wait. And you can text me when you're done. How does that sound?'

It sounded so reasonable that Ellie couldn't come up with a single objection and soon she was seated beside him in the car as he negotiated the morning traffic. She was slightly terrified when he dropped her off outside the store, but she'd read enough magazines to know that she was perfectly entitled to request the services of a personal shopper. And it didn't seem to matter that she was wearing jeans and a T-shirt or that her untrimmed fringe was flopping into her eyes like a sheepdog—because the elegant woman assigned to her made no judgements. She delicately enquired what Ellie's upper price limit was. And although Ellie's instinct was to go for the cheapest option, she knew Alek wouldn't thank her for shopping on a budget. He'd once drawlingly told her that it was the dream of every woman to get her hands on his credit card, so why disappoint him? Why not try to become the woman that he and his fancy friends would obviously expect her to be?

She quickly discovered how easy shopping was when

you had money. You could buy the best. You could complement your outfits with soft leather shoes and pick up a delicate twist of a silk scarf which echoed the detail in a fabric. And expensive clothes really could transform, she decided. The luscious fabrics seemed to flatter her shape, rather than highlight her defects.

The shopper persuaded her into the dresses she usually rejected on the grounds that jeans were more practical, and Ellie found she liked the swish of the delicate fabrics brushing against her skin. She bought all the basic clothes she needed and then picked out a silvery-white wedding gown which did amazing things for her eyes as well as her figure. On impulse, the personal shopper draped a scarlet pashmina around her shoulders—a stole so fine it was almost transparent, and it was that addition which brought glowing life to her skin. Ellie stared at herself in the long mirror.

'It's perfect,' she said slowly.

By the time she emerged from the store wearing some of her purchases, she felt like a new woman.

She saw Alek's face change as she approached the car, accompanied by two doormen who were weighed down with armfuls of packages. His arm brushed over her back with proprietary courtesy as he held open the car door for her and she stiffened, because just that brief touch felt as if he'd branded her with the heat of his flesh. Was that why he stiffened, too? Why his eyes narrowed and a nerve began to work at his temple? She thought he might be about to touch her again—and wasn't she longing for him to do just that?—but some car had begun sounding its horn and the noise seemed to snap him out of his uncharacteristic hesitation.

He didn't say much as they drove to Bond Street, not

until they were standing in front of a jeweller's window which was ablaze with the glitter of a thousand gems. And suddenly he turned to her and his face had that expression she'd seen once before, when all the cool arrogance which defined him had been replaced by a raw and naked hunger.

His finger wasn't quite steady as it drifted a slow path down over her cheek and he must have felt her shiver in response, because his eyes narrowed.

'You look…different,' he said.

'I thought that was the whole point of the exercise?' she said, more archly than she had intended. 'I have to look *credible*, don't I, as the future Mrs Sarantos?'

'But you don't, Ellie—that's the thing.' He gave her an odd kind of smile. 'You don't look credible at all. Not with that uptight expression on your face. It's not the look one might expect from a woman who is just about to marry one of the world's most eligible bachelors. There's no real joy or pleasure there, and I think we might have to remedy that. Shall we make a statement to the world about our relationship, *poulaki mou*? To show them we really do mean business?'

And before Ellie realised what was happening, he was kissing her. Kissing her in full view of the traffic and the security guard and all the upmarket shoppers who were passing them on the pavement. He had wrapped his arms tightly around her and was making her feel as if he *owned her*. The man who was so famously private was making a very public declaration. And even though her heart was pounding with joy, suddenly she felt like a possession. A woman he was putting his stamp on. *His* woman; *his* property.

She tried keeping her lips clamped shut to prevent

his tongue from entering her mouth—to let him know that she was *not* a possession. That he couldn't just pick her up and put her down when he felt like it. But there was only so much resistance she could put up when he was this determined. When he was splaying his fingers over the bare skin of her back and making it tingle. His hard body was so close that a cigarette paper couldn't have come between them, and, beneath her delicate new bra, her breasts were growing heavy.

His lips were still brushing against hers and her eyelids fluttered to a close. She thought how crazy it was that so many emotions could be stimulated by a single kiss. Did he realise that she found being in his arms satisfying in all kinds of ways? Ways which were about so much more than sex? She felt safe and secure. Like nothing could ever hurt her while Alek was around. And it was his strength rather than his sensuality which finally melted the last of her reservations. She kissed him back with fervour and passion and, in the process, completely forgot where she was. Her hands reached up to frame his head and she moaned softly as she circled her hips against him, so that in the end it was Alek who pulled back—his eyes smouldering with blue fire.

'Oh, my,' he said softly, and a distinctive twang of North Atlantic entered his gravelly Greek accent. 'Maybe I should have kissed you back at the apartment, if I'd known that this was the reaction I was going to get.'

His words broke the spell and Ellie jerked away with a bitter feeling of self-recrimination. She had allowed herself to be seduced again when this was nothing but a game to him. A stupid, meaningless game. He had kissed her to make a point and she wasn't sure if it had been a demonstration of power, or just payback time for

her expensive new wardrobe. But either way, she was
going to get hurt if she wasn't careful. Badly hurt. She
rose up on tiptoe in her new leather pumps, placing her
lips to his ear.

'What was that all about?' she hissed.

'Want me to draw a diagram for you?' he murmured
back.

'That won't be necessary.' She moved her mouth
closer to his ear, tempted to take a nip at its perfect
lobe. 'Sex just *complicates* matters. That was the deal—
remember?'

'I think I might be prepared to overlook the deal in
view of the response I just got.'

'Well, I wouldn't—and there's something you'd better understand, Alek.' She swallowed, trying to inject
conviction into her voice. 'Which is that I wouldn't
go to bed with you if you were the last man standing.'

He tipped his head back so that she was caught in the
crossfire of his eyes, the darkened blue hue backlit by
the definite glitter of amusement. He lifted his fingertip
to her mouth and traced it thoughtfully along the line of
her lips. 'I don't think that's entirely true, do you, Ellie?'

'Yes,' she said fiercely, resisting the urge to bite his
finger, afraid that if she did she might just start suck-
ing it. 'It's true.'

He took her hand in his and she wanted to snatch
it away like a sulky child. But the doorman was still
watching them and she knew that if she was to play the
part of fiancée convincingly, then she had no choice
other than to let him carry on stroking her fingers like
that and pretend it wasn't turning her on.

'Let's go and buy your wedding ring,' he said.

CHAPTER EIGHT

THE RING WAS a glittering band of diamonds and the silvery shoes which matched her wedding dress had racy scarlet soles. Ellie touched her fingertips to her professionally styled hair, which had been snipped and blow-dried. She looked like a bride, all right, but a magazine version of a bride—untraditional and slightly edgy. The silver dress and scarlet pashmina gave her a sophisticated patina she wasn't used to and projected an image which wasn't really *her*. But the unfamiliar sleekness of her appearance did nothing to subdue the butterflies which were swarming in her stomach. They'd been building in numbers ever since she and Alek had said their vows earlier, with Vasos and another Sarantos employee standing as their only witnesses.

Strange to believe they were now man and wife—and that fifty of Alek's closest friends were assembling at the upmarket restaurant they'd chosen to stage their wedding party. And if it felt like a sham, that's because it was.

And yet...

Yet...

She stared down at her sparkling wedding band. When he'd kissed her so passionately in Bond Street—

hadn't that felt like something? Even though she'd tried telling herself that he'd only done it to make a point, that hadn't been enough to dull her reaction to him. She had nearly gone up in flames as sexual hunger had overpowered her and a wave of emotion had crashed over her with such force that she'd felt positively weak afterwards. It was as if the rest of the world hadn't existed in those few minutes afterwards, and wasn't that… *dangerous*?

The peremptory knock on her bedroom door broke into her thoughts and she opened it to find Alek standing there—broodingly handsome in his beautifully cut wedding suit, with a tie the colour of storm clouds.

'Ready?' he questioned.

She told herself she wasn't waiting for him to comment on her appearance—but what else would account for the sudden plummeting of her heart? She'd blamed pre-wedding jitters for his failure to compliment her the first time he'd seen her in her wedding dress. But now that they were man and wife, surely he could have said *something*. Had she secretly been longing for his eyes to light up and him to tell her that she made a halfway passable bride? Or was she hoping he'd make another pass at her, only this time she might not get so angry with him? She might just let him carry on…and they could consummate their marriage and satisfy the law, as well as their hungry bodies.

She swallowed. Yes. If the truth be known, she had wanted exactly that. From the time they'd returned from that shopping trip right up to the brief civil ceremony this morning, she'd been like a cat on a hot tin roof. She'd been convinced he would try to renegotiate the separate bedrooms rule, but she had been wrong. Despite her feisty words, he must have known from the way she'd responded to his kiss that she'd changed her mind. That all he needed to do was to kiss her one more time and she would be his. But Alek wasn't a man whose behaviour you could predict. It felt as if he had been deliberately keeping his distance from her ever since. Skirting around her as if she were some unexploded device he didn't dare approach. Even when he'd put the ring on her finger this morning in front of the registrar, she had received nothing more than a cool and perfunctory kiss on each cheek.

She gave him her best waitress smile. 'Yes, I'm ready.'

'Then let's go.'

She felt sick with nerves at the thought of meeting all his friends, especially since the only person she'd invited was Bridget, who wasn't able to attend because the new assistant still wasn't confident enough to be left on her own. Ellie picked up her handbag. She'd thought about inviting some of her New Forest friends, but how to go about explaining why she was marrying a man who was little more than a stranger to her? Wouldn't one of her girlfriends quickly suss that it was odd not to be giggling and cuddling up to a man you were planning to spend the rest of your life with? No. She didn't want pity or a well-meaning mate trying to talk her out of what was the only sensible solution to her predicament. She was going to have to go it alone. To be at her sparkling best and not let any of her insecurities show. She was going to have to make the marriage look as real as possible to *his* friends—and surely that wasn't beyond her capabilities to play a convincing part in front of people who didn't know her?

'Remind me again who's going,' she said as their car began to slip through the early evening traffic.

'Niccolò and Alannah—property tycoon and interior designer,' he said. 'Luis and Carly—he's the ex world champion racing driver and she's his medic wife. Oh, and Murat.'

Ellie forced a smile. Didn't he know any *normal* people? 'The Sultan?'

'That's right. And because of that, security will be tight.'

'You mean, I'll be frisked going into my own wedding party?'

He'd been staring out of the window and drumming his fingertips over one taut thigh and Ellie wished he'd say something equally flippant—anything to dispel this weird *atmosphere* between them. But when he spoke it was merely to resume a clipped tally of the guest list. 'There are people flying in from Paris, New York, Rome, Sicily—'

'And Greece, of course?' she prompted.

He shook his head. 'No. Not Greece.'

'But…that's where you come from.'

'So what? I left there a long time ago, and rarely visit these days.'

'But—'

'Look, can we just dispense with the interrogation, Ellie?' he interrupted coolly. 'I'm not really inclined to answer any more questions and, anyway, we're here.'

'Of course,' she said, quickly turning her head to look out of the window.

Alek felt a pang of guilt as he saw her silvery shoulders tense up. Okay, maybe he *had* been short with her but she needed to realise that being questioned like that wasn't his idea of fun. His mouth flattened. But what had he expected? Wasn't this what happened when you spent prolonged time with a woman? They felt it gave them the right to chip away at things. To quiz you about stuff you didn't want to talk about, even when you made it clear that a subject was deliberately off limits.

He'd never lived with anyone before Ellie. He'd never given a home to a second toothbrush, nor had to clear out space in his closet. Even though they had their own rooms, sometimes it felt as if it were impossible to get away from her. And the stupid thing was that he didn't want to get away from her. He wanted to get closer, even though instinct was telling him that was a bad idea. She was a constant temptation. She made him want her all the time, even though she didn't flirt with him. And wasn't even *that* a turn on? She was there in the morning before he left for work, all bright-eyed and smiling as she sat drinking her ginger tea. Just as she was there at night when he got home, offering to pour him a drink, telling him that she'd started experimenting with cooking and would he like to try some? She'd asked him for tips on how to cook the aubergine dish and he had found himself leaning dangerously close to her while she stirred something in a pot, tempted to kiss the bare neck which was a few tempting inches away from him. Slowly and very subtly her presence was driving him mad. Mostly, it was driving him mad because he wanted her—and he had no one to blame but himself.

That hot-headed kiss outside the jewellers had been intended as nothing more than a distraction. If he was being honest, it had also been intended as an arrogant demonstration of his sexual mastery. To show her that he was boss and always would be. But somehow it had backfired on him. It had reactivated his desire and now he was stuck with a raging sexual hunger which kept him awake most nights, staring at the ceiling and imagining all the different things he wanted to do to her.

He knew there was nothing stopping him from acting on it. From stealing into her room when darkness had fallen. From pulling back a crisp sheet and finding her, what...naked? Or wearing some slinky little nightgown she might have bought at the same time as the killer heels and new clothes. Those occasional longing looks and accidental touches had reinforced what he'd already known...that she wanted him as much as he wanted her. Physically, at least. He was confident enough to know he could be inside her in minutes if he put his mind to it, tangling his fingers in the soft spill of her pale hair and staring down at her beautiful pale curves.

And then what?

He felt another unwanted and unfamiliar stab of his conscience, which was enough to kill his desire stone-dead. Make her fall in love with him? Break her heart as he had broken so many in the past and leave her bitter and upset? Some good that would do when Ellie, above all others, was someone he needed to keep onside. She was carrying his baby and he needed her as a friend, not as a lover.

Because something inside him had changed. He'd imagined he would feel nothing about the new life growing inside her and that he would feel disconnected from her pregnancy. But he had been wrong. Hadn't his heart clenched savagely in his chest the first time he'd seen her fingertips drift almost reflectively over her still-flat belly?

With a fascination which seemed beyond his control, he had found himself watching her when she wasn't looking. When she was curled up in an armchair reading a book and making his life seem almost...*normal*. He'd never had normal before. And hadn't he been filled with an unbearable sense of longing for the family life which had been nothing but a dark void during his own childhood? Hadn't he started wondering again whether he could give this child what he'd never had himself? And one thing was for sure: he could not break the heart of his child's mother...

The car stopped outside the restaurant and as she draped the scarlet shawl around her shoulders he found he couldn't look away. He wanted to pull her into his arms and kiss all that shiny lipstick away from her beautiful lips, but why start the evening on a false promise?

'You look...great,' he said neutrally as the driver opened the limousine door for her.

'Thanks.'

Ellie's fingers tightened around the gilt chain of her handbag. First he'd shot her down in flames and then he'd told her she looked *great*? Was that the best he could do? Why, she'd had more praise from her science teacher at school—and she was hopeless at science. Cautiously, she stepped onto the pavement, balancing carefully on her high heels, thinking how unlike the Ellie of old she must look with enough diamonds glittering on her finger to have bought her an apartment outright.

She was grateful for the armour of her expensive new clothes in a room where every other woman looked amazing—but it wasn't that which made her feel suddenly wistful. All the wives and girlfriends looked so *happy*. Did she? Did she look how a new bride was supposed to look—all dewy-eyed and serene? She wondered if anyone guessed that inside she felt as if she were clinging onto this strange new reality by the tips of her fingers.

But sometimes you built things up in your head and they weren't nearly as bad as you'd feared. The woman who'd designed Alek's apartment—Alannah—turned out to be a lot less scary than Ellie had imagined. Maybe because she was married to Niccolò da Conti, a stunningly handsome man who seemed to command almost as much attention as Alek and who clearly adored his wife.

Some of the guests were more memorable than others. Ellie stood for ages talking to Luis and Carly and discovered they were all friends going back years. When the sultan arrived—last—Ellie was overcome with nerves because she'd never met a royal before and might not have bought such high heels if she'd thought about having to curtsey in them. But Murat was charming and quickly put her at her ease, and his Welsh wife was lovely.

Ellie watched the exalted group of men joshing and laughing with one another and as she listened to their wives eagerly discussing their social calendars she tried not to feel like the outsider in their midst.

'Let me see your ring, Ellie,' said Alannah, catching hold of Ellie's hand and peering down at the glittering band. 'Gosh, it's beautiful. Those diamonds look almost blue—they're so bright.' She raised her eyes and smiled. 'So tell us about Alek's proposal—was it romantic?'

Ellie wished she'd anticipated this perfectly understandable question so that she could have prepped an answer. She didn't know how honest to be. She didn't know how much he'd already told them. She knew that apart from the faint swell of her breasts, there was no outward sign of her pregnancy. Maybe some of the women had already guessed the reason why the world's most reluctant groom had put a ring on her finger, but for some reason she didn't want to tell them. Not right now. Couldn't tonight be her fantasy? Couldn't she play the part of the shiny-eyed new bride and pretend, just this once?

So she curved a smile—and found it was stupidly easy to let her voice tremble with excitement as she allowed herself to be caught up in the memory. 'He kissed me in Bond Street and almost stopped the traffic.'

'Really?' Alannah smiled. 'Not *another* "get a room" moment from the famously private Alek Sarantos? Didn't I read something about him kissing you while you were working as a waitress?'

A sudden lump in her throat was making words difficult and Ellie just nodded. She wondered if Alek ever thought about that moment of passion beneath the starry sky. That split second of thoughtlessness, setting off the domino effect which had brought them to this moment. Did he regret it?

Yet as she glanced over to see him deep in conversation with Murat, she found that she *couldn't* regret what had happened, because sometimes your feelings defied logic. Something incredible had happened when she'd lain with him and she couldn't seem to scrub that memory away. He could be arrogant and cold, but there was something about him which drew her to him like a magnet, no matter how hard she tried to resist. It might be senseless to care about him, but did that mean it was wrong? Could you stop yourself from falling in love with someone, even if you knew it was a mistake?

She saw him smile at something Murat said and he responded by gesturing expansively with his hands in a way an Englishman would never do. She'd never been to Greece, but in that moment he seemed to sum up everything about that sun-washed land with its ancient history and its passions.

Yet that side of his life remained a mystery to her. He'd clammed up when she'd mentioned his birthplace on the way here. He had snapped and changed the subject and done that not very subtle thing of letting her know who had all the power in this relationship. How much did she really know about the father of her baby? She stared down at the slice of lime which was bobbing around in her tonic water. Probably as much as she knew about her own father.

But she pushed the troublesome thoughts away and tried to enter into the spirit of the evening. She nibbled on a few canapés and stood beside Alek as he made a short speech about love and marriage, with just the right touch of lightness and solemnity.

And that was the bit she found hardest. The moment when she wanted to shake off the hand which was resting lightly on her shoulders, because it was kick-starting all kinds of reactions. It was making her want to feel that extraordinary *connection* with him again. To lie with him and feel him deep inside her. To wonder why the hell she'd insisted on separate rooms—not realising that denial would only feed the hunger she felt for him.

She spoke to all the guests with just the right amount of interest and pretended she was Ellie the trainee hotel manager again—chatting away with smiling attention.

People were never terrifying if you got them on a one-to-one basis, no matter how initially intimidating they were. She met a judge, a Hollywood actress and a Spaniard named Vicente de Castilla, whose buccaneering appearance was attracting plenty of covert glances. But gorgeous as Vicente was, there was only one man who commanded Ellie's attention and she knew exactly where he was at any given point in the evening. He seemed to command all her attention and it was difficult not to stare. Beneath the fractured rainbow light of the chandeliers, his hair gleamed like jet. At one point he slowly turned his head to look at her, his blue eyes blazing as they held her in their spotlight. And she turned away, feeling curiously *exposed*...stiffening slightly when he came to stand beside her, sliding his arm around her waist with easy possession. As if he touched her like that all the time, when they both knew he didn't touch her at all.

She knew it was done to add authenticity to their marriage. She *knew* his touch meant nothing, but unfortunately her body didn't. It was sending frantic messages to her brain. It was making her want more. It was making her wish it were all real. That he'd married her because he loved her and not because there was a baby on the way.

Quickly excusing herself, she made her way to the restroom where Alannah was standing in front of the mirror, brushing her long black hair.

'Enjoying your wedding party?' she questioned.

Ellie pulled out a convincing smile as she met the other woman's denim-blue eyes. 'It's wonderful. Such a gorgeous place. And all Alek's friends seem lovely and very welcoming,' she added.

Alannah laughed. 'You don't *have* to say that—but thanks very much all the same. We're just all very happy for him, that's all. Nobody thought he would ever settle down. I expect you know that he's never really committed to anyone before? Mind you, Niccolò was exactly the same. They just need to find the right woman,' she said, pulling open the door and wiggling her fingers in a little wave of farewell.

Ellie watched the door swing closed again.

The right woman.

If only they knew. Would they all be choking into their champagne if they realised that the newlyweds were about as far apart as two people could be?

But *she* had been the one who insisted on having separate rooms, hadn't she? She'd been the one who had thought that keeping distance between them would help protect her against emotional pain. And it didn't. Because she found herself wanting Alek no matter how hard she tried not to want him.

She gazed at her reflection, thinking that her appearance betrayed nothing of her turmoil. The silvery silk dress gleamed and her professionally blow-dried hair fell in a soft cascade over her shoulders. She didn't look like herself, and she didn't feel like herself either. All she could feel was a longing so powerful that it felt like a physical pain. It might be crazy but she wasn't going to lie…and the truth was that she wanted Alek.

She closed her eyes.

She wanted more than that single encounter which had resulted in this pregnancy. She wanted something slow and precious because everything else had happened so *fast*. She'd become pregnant after that one time. She had demanded marriage and moved in with him. She'd attended doctor's appointments, taken care of herself and tried to keep busy. But she wasn't a cardboard cut-out. She still had feelings—feelings she'd tried to put on ice, only somewhere along the way they had started to melt.

So what was she going to do about it? Was she brave enough to go after what she really wanted and to hell with the consequences? Did she dare risk pain for another moment of passion?

Picking up her handbag, she walked out into the corridor where Alek's shadow fell over her and instantly she froze.

'Oh,' she said, attempting a smile. 'You startled me.'

Alek felt a pulse hammering away at his temple as he stared at her. She was close enough to touch and it was distracting. *Theos*, but it was distracting. Her hair was tumbling down over her shoulders and she had that slightly untouchable beauty of all brides. But all he could think about was the creaminess of her skin and the scent of something which smelt like roses, or cinnamon. Maybe both. He felt his throat thicken. 'I was looking for you.'

'Well…here I am,' she said, and as she met his eyes her lips parted. 'What exactly do you want?'

Alek went very still. He saw the darkening of her eyes and heard the dip of her voice, but it was more than that which told him what was on her mind. He'd been around enough women to realise when they were sending out messages of sexual availability—it was just that he hadn't been expecting it with Ellie. Not tonight. He knew that she considered the wedding a farce. That they hadn't been honest with anyone, least of all themselves. Nobody knew the real reason for this wedding, but he'd justified not telling his friends about the baby by remembering what the doctor had said—that there was a slightly higher risk of miscarriage until after the twelve-week mark. And something about those cautionary words had made him realise how much he wanted this baby—for reasons he didn't care to fathom. He realised that the life she carried inside her *mattered*. Should he tell her that? Should he?

But suddenly he wasn't thinking about the baby and neither, it seemed, was she. He could almost *see* the invitation glinting from her eyes and although he wanted her more badly than he'd ever wanted anyone—one last stab of conscience told him to hang fire. That the most sensible option would be if they ended the night as they'd begun it. Separately.

But sometimes the right decision was the wrong decision when it went against everything your body was crying out for. The ache in his groin was unbearable as he reached for her hand, which was trembling, just like his.

He studied the sheen of her fingernails before lifting his head in a clashing of eyes. 'I want you,' he said unsteadily. 'Do you have any idea how much?'

'I think I'm getting the general idea.'

'But I'm not going to do this if it's not what *you* want.' He stared at her intently. 'Do you understand?'

'Alek.' One of the silvery straps of her dress slipped off one shoulder and she pushed it back again with fingers which were trembling and her grey eyes looked wary. As if she was suddenly out of her depth. As if the words she was about to say were difficult. 'You... you're an experienced man. You must know how much I want you.'

He shook his head. 'I know that your body wants me and that physically we're very compatible. But if you're going to wake up in the morning with tears all over my pillow because you're regretting what happened, then I'll back off right now and we'll act like this conversation never happened.'

There was silence. A silence which seemed to go on for countless minutes.

'I don't want you to back off,' she whispered at last.

His heart pounded and his body grew hard. He raised her hand to his lips and although the now faint voice of his conscience made one last, weak appeal, ruthlessly he brushed it aside. 'Then let's get home,' he said roughly. 'So I can take you to bed.'

CHAPTER NINE

ALEK FELT AS if he wanted to explode but he knew he had to take it slowly.

He and Ellie had left the party almost immediately—smiling through the rose petals and rice showering down on their heads. But the journey home had been tense and silent, in direct contrast to their teasing banter at the wedding reception. He hadn't trusted himself to touch her and maybe Ellie had felt the same because she'd sat apart from him, her shoulders stiff. The tension in the car had grown and grown until it had felt as if he was having difficulty breathing. *And wasn't he terrified that she'd changed her mind?*

Her face had been paler than usual as they'd ridden up in the elevator. The space had seemed to close in on them until the ping announcing their arrival at the penthouse had broken into the silence like the chime of a mighty bell. He'd convinced himself that she *had* changed her mind as he'd unlocked the door to his apartment. But it seemed she hadn't. *Oh.* She…had…*not*—and the minute the door had closed behind them they had been all over each other.

Their first kiss had been hungry—almost clumsy. They'd reached blindly for each other in the hall as some ornament had gone crashing to the ground, and he'd ended up pushing her up against the wall with his hand halfway up her dress until he'd realised that he hadn't wanted to do it to her like that. Not on her wedding night. Not after last time. He wanted to show her he knew the meaning of the word *consideration*. He wanted to make love to her slowly—very slowly. And so she had allowed him to lead her to his bedroom where now she stood, looking around her with a slightly nervous expression on her face.

'I suppose this must be the scene of a thousand seductions?'

'A rather inflated estimate,' he responded drily. 'You don't want me to lie to you? To say you're the first woman I've brought here?'

She gave a funny little smile. 'No, of course not.'

'I haven't asked you about any of *your* former lovers, have I?'

'No, that's right. You haven't.'

He wondered what he was trying to do—whether he was trying to sabotage things before they'd even got started. Why the hell hadn't he just told her that in her silvery gown she eclipsed every other woman he'd ever known? That she was beautiful and soft and completely desirable? With a small growl of anger directed mainly at himself, he pulled her into his arms and kissed her again and he heard the gasping little sound she made as she caught hold of his shoulders. He kissed her for a long time, until she started to relax—until she began to press herself against his body and the barrier of their clothes suddenly seemed like something he couldn't endure for a second longer. He led her over to the bed and sat her down on the edge, before getting down on his knees in front of her.

'What are you doing?' she joked weakly as he began to unstrap one of her shoes. 'You've already made the proposal.'

He lifted his gaze; his expression mocking. 'I thought it was you who did the proposing?'

'Oh, yes.' She tipped her head back and expelled a breath as he started rubbing the pad of his thumb over her instep. 'So I did.'

He removed both shoes and peeled off her silvery wedding dress before laying her back on the bed and kicking off his shoes and socks. He lay down next to her, pushing the hair from her face and brushing his lips over hers, taking his time. 'You are very beautiful,' he said.

'I'm—'

He silenced her with the press of his forefinger over her mouth. 'The correct response is, thank you, Alek.'

She swallowed. 'Thank you, Alek.'

'But I'm afraid of hurting you.'

She reached her hand up to brush a strand of hair off his forehead and suddenly her face looked very tender. He felt his heart clench.

'Because of the baby?' she asked softly.

He nodded, still wary around that shining tenderness which instinctively put him on his guard. 'Because of the baby,' he repeated.

'The doctor said it was okay.' She leant forward and kissed him. 'But that maybe we should avoid swinging from the chandeliers.'

'I don't have any…chandeliers,' he said indistinctly, but suddenly the flirting word games of foreplay became swamped by a far more primitive need to possess. Refocusing his attention, he began to explore her properly—touching the coolness of her flesh above her stocking tops as she began to make soft little sounds of pleasure. Did she feel his uncharacteristic hesitation as his fingers tiptoed upwards? Could she hear the loud pounding of his heart? Did she know that suddenly— ridiculously—this felt completely new?

'It's no different from how it was before,' she whispered. 'I'm still me.'

He kissed her again. But it *was* different. She was like a ship carrying a precious cargo. His baby. He swallowed as his finger trailed over her navel and he could tell she was holding her breath, expelling it only when he eased his hand beneath the elastic of her panties and cupped her where she was warm and wet.

'Oh,' she said.

His mouth hovered over hers. 'Oh,' he echoed indistinctly as, blindly, he reached for his belt and suddenly she was unbuttoning his shirt, making a low sound of pleasure as she slipped it away from his shoulders. And he stopped thinking. He just gave himself up to every erotic second. There was a snap as he released her bra and her breasts tumbled into his eager hands. He felt the slide of her bare thigh against his as she used her foot to push his trousers down his legs. He could smell the musky aroma of her sex as he peeled off her panties and threw them aside.

Their eyes met in a long moment and he felt shaken by the sudden unexpected intimacy of that.

He slid the flat of his hand over her hip. 'I don't want to hurt you—'

She bit her lip, as if she was about to say something

controversial but had thought better of it at the last moment. 'Just make love to me, Alek,' she said with a simple sincerity which tore through him like a flame.

Slowly he eased himself inside her, uttering something guttural in Greek, which wasn't like him. But none of this was *like* him. He'd never felt this close to a woman before, nor so aware of her as a person rather than as just a body. It rocked him to the core and, yes, it intimidated him, too—and he didn't like that. He wasn't used to being out of control. To feeling as if he were putty in a woman's hands. He groaned. Maybe not putty. Because putty was soft, wasn't it? And he was hard. Ah, *neh*. He was very hard. Harder than he could ever remember. And if he wasn't careful, he was going to come too soon.

This is sex, he told himself fiercely. *Sex which you both want. So treat it like sex.* Breaking eye contact, he buried his face in her neck as he began to take command, each slow and deliberate thrust demonstrating his power and control. He smiled against her skin when she moaned his name and smiled some more when she began to gasp in a rising crescendo. 'Oh, yes...*yes*!'

He raised his head and watched as she came. Saw her tip her head back and her eyes close. He saw her body shudder and heard the disbelieving little cry which followed. And then he saw the first big fat tear which rolled down her cheek to be quickly followed by another, and he frowned. Because hadn't she cried last time—and wasn't the deal supposed to be that this time there were no tears? No regrets. His mouth twisted. No nothing—only pleasure.

'Alek,' she whispered and he could no longer hold

back—letting go in a great burst of seed which pumped from his body as if it was never going to stop.

He must have fallen asleep, and when eventually he opened his eyes again he found her sleeping, too. Rolling away, he stared up at the ceiling, but although his heart was still pounding with post-orgasmic euphoria he felt confusion slide a cold and bewildering trail across his skin.

He glanced around the room. Her wedding dress lay on the floor along with his own discarded trousers and shirt. His usually pristine bedroom looked as if someone had ransacked it and he found himself remembering the ornament breaking in the hall—a priceless piece of porcelain shattered into a hundred pieces which had crunched beneath his feet.

What was it about her which made him lose control like that? He turned his head to look at her again—a pale Venus rising from the crumpled white waves of the sheets. His gaze shifted to her belly—still flat—and his heart clenched as he thought about the reality of being a father.

The fears he'd been trying to silence now crowded darkly in his mind. What if certain traits were inherited rather than learnt? Wasn't that one of the reasons why he'd always ruled out fatherhood as a life choice, not daring to take the risk of failing as miserably at the task as his own father had done?

She began to stir and opened her eyes and he thought how bright and clear they looked, with no hint of tears now.

'Why do you cry?' he asked suddenly. 'When I make love to you?'

Ellie brushed her fringe out of her eyes, more as a

stalling mechanism than anything else. His question suggested a layer of intimacy she hadn't been expecting and that surprised her. This was supposed to be about sex, wasn't it? That was what she thought his agenda was. The only agenda there could possibly be—no matter what her feelings for him were. If she suddenly came out and told him the reason she'd cried was because he made her feel *complete*, then wouldn't he laugh, or run screaming in the opposite direction? If she told him that when he was deep inside her, it felt as if she'd been waiting her whole life for that moment, wouldn't it come over as fanciful, or—worse—needy? If she told him she was crying for all the things she would never have from him—like his *love*—wouldn't that make her seem like just another woman greedily trying to take from him something she knew he would never give?

She told him part of the truth. 'Because you are an amazing lover.'

'And that makes you cry?'

'Blame my hormones.'

'I suppose I should be flattered,' he drawled. 'Though, of course, that would depend on how experienced you are.'

She pushed her hair out of her eyes and narrowed her eyes. 'Are you fishing to find out how many lovers I've had before you?'

'Is it unreasonable of me to want to know?'

She sat up and looked down at his dark body outlined against the tumbled bedding. 'I've had one long-term relationship before this and that's all I'm going to say on the subject, because I think it's distasteful to discuss it, especially at a time like this. Is that acceptable?'

'Completely acceptable would be for there to have

been no one before me.' He smiled, but it was a smile tinged with intent rather than humour. 'And since I intend to drive the memory of anyone else from your mind for ever, you'd better come back over here and kiss me right now.'

His hand starfished over her breast and, even though his questioning was unfair and his attitude outrageously macho, Ellie couldn't seem to stop herself from reacting to him. She wondered what he'd say if she told him he'd banished every other man from her mind the first time he'd kissed her. Would he be surprised? Probably not. Women probably told him that kind of thing all the time.

It hadn't been her plan to have him parting her legs again quite so soon, and certainly not to cry his name out like a kind of prayer as he entered her a second time. But she did. And afterwards she was left feeling exposed and naked in all kinds of ways, while he remained as much of an enigma as he'd always done.

She lay there wrapped in his arms and although his lips pressing against her shoulder were making his words muffled, they were still clear enough to hear.

'I'm thinking that we ought to start sleeping together from now on—what about you?' he said. 'Because it would be crazy not to.'

It was a strangely emotionless conclusion to their lovemaking and Ellie didn't know why she was so disappointed, because he was only behaving true to form. But she made sure her smile didn't slip and show her disappointment. She kept her expression as neutral as his. He wanted to treat sex as simply another appetite to be fed, did he?

Well, then, so would she.

She lay back against the pillow and coiled her arms around his neck. 'Absolutely crazy,' she agreed huskily.

CHAPTER TEN

HER WEDDING RING no longer mocked her and neither did the closed door of Alek's room. Because Ellie now shared that room, just as she shared the bed within and the man who slept in it.

Pulling on a tea dress, Ellie began to brush her hair. To all intents and purposes, she and Alek now had a 'full' marriage. Ever since the night of their wedding—when they'd broken the sexual drought—they had been enjoying the pleasures of the marital bed in a way which had surpassed her every expectation.

He could turn her on with a single smile. He could have her naked in his arms in seconds. Even when she told herself she ought to resist him—in a futile attempt to regain some control over her shattered equilibrium—she would fail time and time again.

'But you can't resist me, *poulaki mou*,' he would murmur, as if he guessed exactly what she was trying to do. 'You know you really want me.'

And that was the trouble. She did. She couldn't seem to stop wanting him, no matter how much she tried to tell herself that she was getting in too deep. And if sometimes she lay looking wistfully at the ceiling after he'd made love to her, she made sure it was while Alek was asleep. She tried to stop herself from caring for him too much—and certainly to hide her feelings for him. Because that wasn't what he wanted. This was as close to a business arrangement as a personal relationship could be.

But her life had changed in other ways, too. They started going out more as a couple, so that at times the marriage felt almost authentic. He took her to the theatre, which she loved. They watched films and ate in fancy restaurants and explored all the tiny backstreets of the city. They drove down to the south coast, to visit Luis and Carly in their amazing house which overlooked a beautiful river.

And yet, despite the increased richness of their day-to-day existence, it was difficult to get to know the real man behind the steely image, despite the external thaw between them. He could do that thoughtful stuff of massaging her feet when she was tired, but if his fingers hadn't been made of flesh and blood she might have thought she was being administered to by some sort of robot. Sometimes it felt as if she didn't know him any better than when that list of his likes and dislikes had been circulated to staff at The Hog before his arrival. She still wasn't sure what motivated him, or what made him sometimes wake her in the night when he'd had a dream which had clearly been a bad one. She would turn to find his eyes open but not really seeing, his body tense—suspended between the two worlds of sleeping and waking. But when she gently shook him awake, his face would become guarded and he would deflect her concerns with something sensual enough to send any questions scuttling from her mind.

He was a master at concealing the real man who

lay beneath; adept at avoiding questions. His cool blue eyes would narrow if she tried to probe more deeply; his gaze becoming one of sapphire ice. *Don't push me*, those eyes seemed to say. But that didn't stop Ellie from trying, even though he would deflect her questions by sliding his hand beneath her skirt and starting to make love to her. He'd leave her breathless and panting as all her questions dissolved and nothing was left but the pleasure he gave her, time after time. And she didn't give up. She just lowered her sights a little. She stopped expecting big revelations and just concentrated on the little ones.

And every time she discovered something about him, it felt like a major victory—like another little missing bit of the jigsaw. In those sleepy moments after making love, he told her about how he'd worked his way up from being a kitchen boy in Athens, to owning an entire chain of restaurants. He told her about working on a fancy vineyard in California, so that he knew all about the wine trade. He made a wistful face when he described his friend Murat's beautiful country of Qurhah and told her how big the stars looked when you were out in the middle of the desert. He explained how life was just one great big learning experience and everything he knew, he had taught himself.

And one thing she was learning faster than any other was that it wasn't so easy to put the brakes on her own emotions. She wasn't sure if it was her fluctuating hormones which were changing her feelings towards her Greek husband, or just that sex had removed the protective shield from her heart. No matter how hard she tried, she couldn't seem to stop herself from caring for him in a way that went bone-deep. Her heart was stubbornly refusing to listen to all the logic her head tried to throw at it.

Yet she *knew* what happened to women who were stupid enough to love men who didn't love them back. She'd watched her mother's life become diminished because she had wanted something she was never going to have. She'd wasted years on bitterness and resentment, because she'd refused to accept that you couldn't make another person do what you wanted them to.

And that was not going to happen to her.

She wouldn't let it.

Smoothing down the folds of her tea dress, she walked into the kitchen to find Alek seated at the table, a half-full coffee pot beside him as he worked his way through a stack of financial newspapers. He glanced up as she walked in, his eyes following her every step, like a snake bewitched by a charmer. She had become used to his very macho appraisal of her appearance and, with a certain amount of guilt, had grown to enjoy it.

He put the newspaper down as she sat down opposite him and his eyes glinted as she reached for the honeypot.

'I enjoyed licking my favourite honey last night,' he murmured.

Her eyes widened. 'Alek!'

'Are you blushing, Ellie?'

'Certainly not. It's just the steam from the coffee making me hot.'

'Would you like to come to Italy?' he questioned.

Ellie dropped the little wooden spatula back in the pot. 'You mean, with you?' she said.

'Of course with me. Unless you had someone else

in mind?' He smiled and gave a lazy shrug. 'We can treat it as a kind of honeymoon, if you like. I thought we could go to Lucca. I have business in Pisa and I can go there afterwards while you fly home. And Lucca is an extraordinarily pretty city. They call it the hidden gem of Tuscany. It has an oval piazza instead of a square one and a tower with trees growing out of the top. Lots of dark and winding streets and iconic churches. You've never been there?'

She shook her head. 'I've never been anywhere apart from a day trip to Calais with my mother.'

'Well, then.' He raised his eyebrows. 'Didn't you once tell me how much you longed to travel?'

Yes, she'd told him that, but that had been when she'd still had ambition burning big in her heart. When travelling had been part of her work plan and independence had been a believable dream which seemed to have fallen by the wayside since she'd discovered she was pregnant. She thought of Italy—with its green hills and terracotta roofs. All those famous churches and marble statues she'd only ever seen in pictures.

Wouldn't it be good to go on an unexpected honeymoon for some sunshine and culture—even if it was the most unconventional honeymoon in the history of the world? And yet, just the fact that Alek had suggested it brightened her mood. Wasn't this a bit of a breakthrough from her enigmatic husband? Could she possibly make it a *real* honeymoon—as if they were people who genuinely cared about one another, rather than two people who were just trying to make the best of a bad situation?

She began to spread the thick, golden honey on her

toast and smiled at him. 'I'd like that,' she said. 'I'd like that very much.'

'*Thavmassios*. We will fly the day after tomorrow.'

Two days later their flight touched down in Pisa where Alek had arranged for a car to take them to Lucca. The drive took less than an hour and they arrived in the late afternoon, when all the shops were closed and the place had a drowsy feel about it. Ellie looked up at the high city walls and thought she'd never seen anywhere more beautiful. Alek had rented an old-fashioned apartment overlooking a sheltered courtyard, where geraniums tumbled brightly from terracotta pots. The wooden frame of their bed was dark and worn and the sheets were crisp and scented with lavender.

She knew that they weren't like other traditional honeymooners, and yet as he closed the apartment door behind them Ellie was filled with something which felt awfully like *hope*. She thought: *We're in a city where nobody knows us. Two strangers blending with all the other strangers*. Mightn't there be a chance that here the man she had married would let his mask slip for once, when there was only her to see?

They made love, unpacked and showered and then Alek took her out to dinner in a garden shimmering with candlelight where they ate the local delicacy of *tortelli lucchese*—a bright yellow stuffed pasta, topped with a rich ragu sauce. Afterwards, they sat beneath the star-spangled sky and drank their coffee—their fingers linking together on the table, and for once it felt real. As if they really were genuine honeymooners and not just a pair of actors acting out the parts. When he took her home, she put her arms around his neck and kissed him passionately and he picked her up and carried her to the bedroom with a look on his face which made her tremble.

The following morning Ellie awoke alone. For a minute she lay there as sensual memories of the previous night filtered into her mind, then she pulled on a robe, splashed cold water over her sleepy face and went off to find Alek. He was sitting on their balcony with breakfast laid out on the small table and the aroma of coffee vying with the powerful scent of jasmine.

'Where did all this come from?' she questioned as she looked at the crisp bread, the buttery pastries and the rich red jam.

'I got up early and you looked much too peaceful to wake. I went for a walk around the city walls and called in at the *panificio* on the way back.' He poured out two cups of coffee and pushed one across the table and smiled. 'So what would you like to do today?'

And suddenly—she had no idea what caused it—the perfect scene before her began to disintegrate. It was like tugging at a tiny nick on a delicate piece of fabric which suddenly ripped open. It all seemed so *false*. There was Alek—looking ruggedly handsome in an open-necked white shirt and dark trousers, his blue eyes gleaming like jewels. Yet his polite distance made her feel as if she were just another item to be ticked off on his agenda. His smile seemed more automatic than genuine and she found herself resenting his control and his inbuilt detachment. *This has nothing to do with reality*, she thought, as a feeling of rebellion began to bubble up inside her.

She sat down and looked at him. 'Actually, I'd like to talk about the baby.'

He stilled. 'The baby?'

'That's right. Our baby. You know. The one we never talk about.' She paused and laid her hand over her stomach. 'Because although it's growing inside me, we never discuss it, do we? We always seem to skirt around the subject. I mean, I go to the doctor and report back with a clean bill of health—and you manage to look pleased. And once or twice you've even come with me and you nod your head in all the right places, but you still act like nothing's happening, or as if it's happening to someone else. As if none of this is real.'

A shuttered look came over his face and he shrugged. 'I suppose we could sit around having hypothetical discussions about what we're going to do and how we're going to react when the baby arrives, but why bother when it's impossible to predict?'

'So you just want to ignore it until it happens?'

His eyes became hooded and suddenly he didn't look quite so detached. 'Isn't that what I've just said?'

And Ellie heard the distortion in his words—the crack of bitterness he couldn't quite hide. She saw the way his body had grown hard and tense and wondered what had caused it. And she wondered why she didn't have the guts to come right out and ask him, and keep on asking him until he finally gave her an answer. What was she so afraid of? Scared that if she unlocked his secrets, she'd discover something to kill off the dormant hope which lingered so foolishly in her heart? Surely it was better to know and to face up to the truth, no matter how grim it was... Better that than building dreams which were never going to materialise.

'You know, through all the time we've been together, you've never spoken about your childhood,' she said.

'Apart from a throwaway comment about never having used public transport because your father owned an island.'

'And why do you think that is?' he questioned. 'If somebody doesn't want to talk about something, there's usually a reason why.'

'You've never told me anything about your family,' she continued stubbornly. 'Not a single thing. I don't even know if you've got any brothers or sisters—'

'I don't.'

'And you've never mentioned your parents.'

Unsmilingly, he looked into her eyes. 'Maybe that's because I don't want to.'

'Alek.' She leant forward. 'You need to tell me.'

'Why?' he snapped.

'Because this baby is going to share your parents' genes. Your father—'

'Is dead,' he said flatly. 'And believe me, you'd better hope that our baby doesn't share many of his genes.'

A shiver ran down her spine. 'And what about your mother?'

For a moment there was silence. 'What about her?'

Ellie was unprepared for the savage note in his voice or the bunching of his powerful shoulders. Everything about his reaction told her she was entering dangerous territory—but she knew she couldn't let up. Not this time. If she backtracked now she might win his temporary approval, but then what? She would simply be signing up to a life of half-truths. Bringing up a baby in a world of ignorance, where nothing was what it really seemed. Because knowledge was power. *And wasn't the balance of power in this relationship already hopelessly unequal?*

'Is she still alive?'

'I don't know,' he snapped, his voice as cold as ice. 'I don't know a damned thing about her. Do you want me to spell it out for you in words of one syllable, Ellie? She walked out on me when I was a baby. And while I'm known for my amazing sense of recall—not even I can remember that. Are you satisfied now?'

Ellie's head was spinning. *His mother had walked out on him.* Wasn't that the worst thing that could happen to someone? Hadn't she read somewhere that it was better to be abused than abandoned, and wondered at the time if that was true? She supposed you could always challenge your abuser—but if you were deserted, wouldn't that leave you with no choice except to feel empty and bewildered? She imagined a tiny baby waking up one morning crying for his mother—only that mother never came. How would that feel, to miss the comfort of a maternal embrace and never know it again? Even if the bond wasn't strong, a cuddle would still feel like safety to a helpless infant. On some primitive and subliminal level—would that make it impossible for you to put your trust in a woman afterwards? Would that explain his coldness and his lack of real intimacy, no matter how many times they had sex?

'What…what happened?'

'I just told you.'

'But you didn't.' She met his gaze, determined not to be cowed by the fury sparking from those cold blue depths. 'You only gave me the bare facts.'

'And didn't it occur to you that maybe that's all I wanted to give you?' Pushing back his chair, he got up from the table and began to pace around the veranda like a man in a cell. 'Why don't you learn when enough is enough?'

She'd never seen him so angry and a few weeks ago Ellie might have backed down, but not any more. She wasn't someone who was trying to win his affection or keep the peace, no matter what. She was a mother-to-be and she wanted to be the best mother she possibly could be—and that meant decoding her baby's father, even if he didn't want her to. Even if it pushed them further apart, it was a risk she had to take.

'Because it's not enough,' she said stubbornly.

'What difference does it make that a woman walked out of a house on a Greek island over thirty years ago?'

'It makes all kinds of difference. I want to know about *her*. I want to know whether she was artistic, or good at math. I'm trying to join up all the dots, Alek— to imagine what kind of characteristics our baby might inherit. Maybe it's extra important to me because I don't know much about my own father. If things were different, I'd have learnt the answers to some of these questions already.'

Alek stared at her as her passionate words broke into the quiet Italian morning. Her own upbringing hadn't been much of a picnic but, despite all that, her mother had stuck by her, hadn't she? Ellie hadn't been rejected by the one person you were supposed to be able to rely on. Behind her the jasmine and miniature lemon trees made her look like a character in a painting. In her silky robe she looked fresh and young, and nothing could disguise the flicker of hope in her eyes. Did she think there was going to be some fairy-tale ending, that he could soothe everything over and make everything okay with a few carefully chosen words?

His jaw tightened. Maybe he *should* tell her the truth. Let her understand the kind of man he really was—and why. Let her know that his emotional coldness wasn't something he'd just invented to pass the time. It had been ground into him from the start—embedded too deeply for him to be any other way. Maybe knowing that would nip any rosy dreams she was in danger of nurturing. Show her why the barriers he'd erected around himself were impenetrable. *And why he wouldn't want them any other way.*

'There were no custody visits or vacations,' he said. 'For a long time, I knew nothing about my mother. Or indeed, any mother. When you grow up without something, you don't even realise you're missing it. Her name was never mentioned in front of me, and the only women I knew were my father's whores.'

She flinched at his use of the word and he saw her compose her face into an expression of understanding. 'It's perfectly reasonable not to like the women who supplanted your mother—'

'Oh, please. Quit the amateur psychology,' he interrupted, pushing his fingers impatiently through his hair. 'I'm not making a prudish judgement because it makes me feel better. They *were* whores. They looked like whores and acted like whores. He paid them for sex. They were the only women I came in contact with. I grew up thinking that all females caked their face in make-up and wore skirts short enough for you to see their knickers.' And one in particular who had invited a boy of twelve to take her knickers down so that she could *show him a good time.*

Did she believe him now? Was that why she was biting her lip? He could almost see her mind working overtime as she searched for something to say—as if trying to find a positive spin to put on what he'd just told her. He could have saved her the trouble and told her there was none.

'But…you must have had friends,' she said, a touch of desperation in her voice now. 'You must have looked at *their* mothers, and wondered what had happened to yours.'

'I had no friends,' he said flatly. 'My life was carefully controlled. I might as well have had a prison as a house. I saw no one except for the servants—my father liked childless, unmarried servants who could devote all their time to him. And if you have nothing with which to compare, then no comparisons can be made. His island was remote and inaccessible. He ran everything and owned everything. I lived in a vast complex which was more like a palace and I was tutored at home. I didn't find out anything about my mother until I was seven years old and when I did—the boy who told me was beaten.'

He stared into space. Should he tell her that the boy's injuries had been so bad that he'd been airlifted to the hospital on the mainland and had never returned? And that the boy's parents—even though they had been extremely poor—had threatened to go to the police? Alek had only been young but he remembered the panic which had swirled around the complex as a result. He remembered the fearful faces of his father's aides, as if the old man really *had* overstepped the mark this time. But he'd wriggled out of it, just as he always did. Money had been offered, and accepted. Money got you whatever it was you wanted. It bought silence as well as sex—and another catastrophe had been averted. *And hadn't he done that, too? Hadn't he paid off Ellie's contract with the Irishwoman with the same ruthlessness which his father would have employed?*

He saw the distress on her face and tried to imagine how this must sound through her ears. Incredible, probably. Like one of those porn films his father's bodyguards used to watch, late into the night. He wondered if he stopped the story now, whether it would be enough to make her understand why he was not like other men. But she had demanded the truth and perhaps she would continue to demand it. To niggle away at it, as women invariably did. He realised that for the first time in his life he couldn't just block her out, or refuse to take her calls. To fade her into the background as if she had never existed, which was what he'd always done before. Whether he liked it or not, he was stuck with Ellie Brooks, or Ellie Sarantos as she was now. And maybe she ought to learn that it was better not to ask questions in case you didn't like the answers.

'Anything else you want to know?' he demanded. 'Any other stone you've left unturned?'

'What did the boy tell you about your mother?'

'He told me the truth. That she'd left in the middle of the night with one of the island's fishermen.' He leant back against the intricate wrought-iron tracings of the balustrade. Somewhere in the distance he could hear a woman call out in Italian and a child answered. 'It was convenient that she chose a lover with his own boat, for there would have been no other way of her leaving the island without my father knowing about it. But I guess her main achievement was in managing to conduct an affair right under his nose, without the old man finding out. And the fact that she was prepared to risk his rage.' His mouth twisted. 'She must have been quite some woman.'

He felt a pain he hadn't felt in a long time. A hot, unwelcome pain which excluded everything else. It stabbed at his heart like a rusty knife and he wished he'd told her to mind her own business, but now he was on a roll and somehow he couldn't stop—pain or no pain. 'My father was completely humiliated by her desertion and determined to wipe away all traces of her. Something he found surprisingly easy to accomplish.' He looked into her bright eyes and then he said it. He'd never admitted it before. Never told anyone. Not the therapist he'd half-heartedly consulted when he'd been living in New York, not any of his friends, nor the women who'd shared his bed in the intervening years and tried to dig away to get at the truth. No one. Not until now. He swallowed as the bitterness rose up inside him like a dark tide. 'I never even saw a photo of her. He destroyed them all. My mother is a stranger to me. I don't even know what she looks like.'

She didn't gasp or utter some meaningless platitude. She just sat there and nodded—as if she was absorbing everything he'd told her. 'But…didn't you ever think about tracking her down and hearing her side of the story?'

He stared at her. 'Why would I want to find a woman who left me behind?'

'Oh, Alek. Because she's your mum, that's why.' She got up and walked across the sun-dappled balcony until she'd reached him. And then she put her arms tightly around his back and held him, as if she never wanted to let him go.

He felt her fingers wrapping themselves around

him—like one of those speeded-up documentaries of a fast-growing vine which covered everything in seconds. He tried to move away. He didn't need her softness or her sympathy. He didn't need a thing from her. He had learnt to live with pain and abandonment and to normalise them. He had pushed his memories into a place of restricted access and had slammed the door on them…what right did she have to make him open the door and stare at all those dark spectres? Did she get some kind of *kick* out of making him confront stuff that was dead and buried?

He wanted to push her away, but her soft body was melting against his. Her fingers were burying themselves in his hair and suddenly he was kissing her like a man who had finally lost control. Losing himself in a kiss as sweet as honey and being sucked into a sensation which was making him feel…

He jerked away from her, his heart pounding. He didn't want to *feel* anything. She'd stirred up stuff which was better left alone and she needed to learn that he was not prepared to tolerate such an intrusion. She'd done it once, but it would not happen again. With an effort, he steadied his breath.

'I don't really want to provide some sort of erotic floor show for the surrounding apartments,' he said, his voice cold as he walked over to the table and poured himself a glass of juice. 'So why don't you sit down and eat your breakfast, before we start sightseeing? You wanted to travel, didn't you, Ellie? Better not waste this golden opportunity.'

CHAPTER ELEVEN

IT WAS NOT a successful honeymoon.

Yes, Lucca was completely gorgeous, and, with her brand-new sun hat crammed down over her hair, Ellie accompanied Alek to every iconic destination the beautiful city had to offer. She saw the tower with the trees growing from the top and drank cappuccino in the famous oval piazza. They visited so many churches that she lost count, and ate their meals in leafy squares and hidden courtyards. There were marble statues in beautiful gardens, where roses grew beside lemon trees. And when the sun became too fierce there were shady streets to walk down, with the rich smell of leather purses and handbags wafting out from the tiny shops which lined them.

But a new *froideur* had settled over Alek. It didn't seem to matter that her first instincts on meeting him had been correct—and that on some level they *were* kindred spirits. They'd both known pretty awful childhoods but had just chosen to deal with them in different ways. And yes, she'd managed at last to extract the truth about his past. She now knew him better…but at what price? It hadn't made them closer, or brought them together in some magical kind of way.

It was as if the confidences she'd forced him to share had ruptured the tentative truce which had existed between them. As if he'd closed right down and shut her out—only this time she sensed there was no going back. No chink of light coming from behind the steely door he had retreated behind. The anger had gone and in its place was a consideration and cool courtesy which made him seem even further away. He spoke to her as if he were her doctor. Was she too hot? Too tired? A little hungry, perhaps? And she would assure him that she felt absolutely fine, because what was the alternative?

But she didn't feel fine. She felt headachey and out of sorts—with a kind of heaviness which seemed to have entered her limbs and which she put down to the new tension which had sprung up between them. She understood now why he was emotionally distant, but she still didn't know how to solve it.

Vasos called several times from London but instead of saying something like, *sorry, but I'm on my honeymoon*—Alek took every call and spent as much time as possible on it. Or so it seemed to Ellie. She would be left sitting on the terrace, her book stuck on the same page while he spoke in a torrent of Greek she couldn't understand.

She stared at the unread pages of her novel. Had she thought this was going to be easy? Had she been naive enough to think that extracting information about his painful childhood might make him warm and open towards her? If she'd known that the opposite would be true, she might have thought twice before quizzing him about the mother who had deserted him. She slammed the book shut. No wonder he was so closed off. So lacklustre about *their* baby.

Feeling queasy, she glanced up to see him standing

framed by the miniature orange trees which grew on their leafy terrace and frowning as he slid his cell phone back into his pocket.

'That was Vasos,' he said.

'Again?'

'The new deal on the Rafael building seems to be nearing completion earlier than planned and the architect is flying into London later this evening.'

'And let me guess.' Her voice was light. 'You need to get back?'

'I'm afraid I do. My business in Pisa will have to wait.' His frown deepened as he seemed to look at her properly for the first time. 'You're sweating, Ellie. Are you okay?'

No, she was not okay. She felt hot and dizzy and disillusioned. Maybe it was time to stop grabbing at rainbows and settle for reality.

'I'm fine,' she said tightly. 'I'd better go and pack.'

Something dark and unwanted rose up inside him as Alek watched her go, her shoulders tight with tension. Something which clutched at his heart and made it twist with pain. *Damn her*, he thought. Why hadn't he slapped her down? Why hadn't he refused to answer all those intrusive questions which had done nothing but open up a dark can of worms?

And yet now that he had pushed her away, the sense of relief he'd been anticipating hadn't happened. They'd been doing that thing of sleeping on opposite sides of the bed—their breathing sounding unnaturally loud in the darkness of the night—each knowing the other was awake and yet not speaking. *Because they had nothing left to say.*

Was it some cruel twist of fate which had left him

feeling so lost without the softness of her arms around him? A taunting reminder of just how empty and alone rejection could make you feel. And yet wasn't it better this way? For him to do the rejecting rather than risk being pushed away for a second time?

When she returned from packing, he thought her face looked almost translucent beneath the brim of her straw hat, which she had worn during most of the trip. The Italian sun had barely touched her skin and her grey eyes seemed shadowed, and even though he knew he ought to say something he could think of nothing which would fall easily into the empty silence. She was quiet all during the journey back to London and the moment their plane touched down and he turned on his phone, it began to vibrate with a flurry of calls. And deep down, wasn't he glad to have the opportunity to lose himself in the infinitely more straightforward problems of work? Far better than having to confront the silent reproach or the lip she kept biting as if she was trying to hold back tears. He had the car drop her off at the apartment while he went straight to the office.

'You don't mind?' he questioned.

She gave an unconvincing laugh, as if she recognised the question for what it was—a meaningless platitude. 'And if I do? Would you be prepared to put your precious work aside and spend the afternoon with me, if I asked you to?'

'Ellie—'

'I'll take that as a no,' she said with another brittle smile. 'Anyway, I want to have a lie-down. I'm tired.'

After he'd gone she closed the bedroom curtains and, switching her phone to Silent, left it in her handbag on the far side of the room. But she could hear it vibrating like a persistent fly as she lay on the bed drifting in and out of an uncomfortable doze—too lazy to get up and switch it off completely.

By five o'clock she forced herself to get up and saw there were three missed calls from a number she didn't recognise. Muzzily, she took a shower but her mood was still flat as she pulled on a pair of linen trousers and a T-shirt. She was drinking a glass of water when the doorbell rang.

Touching her fingertips to her belly, she went to answer the door to find a blonde woman standing on the step—someone she didn't recognise but who looked oddly familiar.

'Can I help you?' questioned Ellie.

'You don't remember me?'

Ellie shook her head. 'Should I?'

'Probably. I knew you before you were married. I was staying at The Hog when you were working there. Remember now?'

And suddenly the mist cleared. Of course. It was the journalist. The sneaky blonde who had asked those questions which Ellie had stupidly answered, and which had ended up with her getting the sack. She looked into the woman's glacial eyes.

'I've got nothing to say to you,' said Ellie.

'Maybe not. But you might be interested in what I have to say to you.'

'I don't think so.' She started to close the door. 'My husband doesn't like journalists and neither do I.'

'Does your husband realise he has a brother?'

Sweat broke out on her forehead as Ellie leant against the door. She thought about what Alek had told her about his childhood. And amid all the pain and the heartbreak of his upbringing, he hadn't mentioned his father having any more children. *But maybe his mother had gone on to have more children. If he'd never met her, he wouldn't actually know, would he?* 'You're lying,' she croaked.

'Why would I lie? Actually, he has a *twin* brother. Yeah, I thought you'd be interested.'

Yes, she was interested but that didn't stop Ellie from shaking her head, because the dramatic words seemed to make no sense. 'But if what you say is true, how come you know and he doesn't?'

The woman shrugged. 'His brother asked me to track him down and speak to him. He wanted to know whether Alek would be receptive to a meeting. The first part wasn't difficult but the second part was, because I could never get close enough to ask him. Men like Alek Sarantos are never easy to get close to. He doesn't do interviews and he's not the kind of man who drinks alone in bars, so trying to pick him up was never going to work. And as you say, he doesn't like journalists.'

'Are you surprised?'

'Nothing surprises me any more,' said the woman cynically. 'That's why I couldn't believe my luck when I saw him with you that night. A waitress who was way out of his league and you were making out like two teenagers at a school disco! I thought I had the perfect opportunity to smoke him out, and I was right.'

'Smoke him out?' echoed Ellie in horror.

'Sure. Put a woman into a man's life and immediately you've got another way in.'

'You're disgusting.'

'No, honey. I'm just doing my job.' The journalist

leant forward and tucked a business card into Ellie's free hand. 'Why don't you tell him to call me?'

After she'd gone, Ellie shut the door, leaning back against it and trying very hard to steady her breathing.

A brother.

A *twin* brother.

How could that be? Did Alek know about this explosive fact and was this just one more thing he had deliberately omitted to tell her? She felt so spaced out that she couldn't seem to take it in. Had the journalist being doing what journalists did so well…inventing a story to try to get some sort of reaction? Her heart was pounding and a weird kind of pain was spearing through her and she wasn't sure how long she stood there, only that she couldn't stay there. She couldn't let Alek come home from work and find her slumped there like a zombie.

She forced herself to dress, but the silky tea dress seemed only to mock her. She remembered the day she'd gone shopping, when she'd felt so proud of herself. So stupidly proud. As if managing to run up a massive bill on a man's credit card all by herself was some sort of mega achievement. She remembered how easy she'd found it to spend his money. For all her feisty words, was she really any different from the other women who adored his wealth? He hated gold-diggers. He seemed to hate women in general and now she could understand why.

Never had that famous saying seemed more appropriate.

Give me the child until he is seven and I will give you the man.

Wasn't that just the truth?

Alek had spent the first years of his life deserted by

his mother and left alone with a cruel father. Was it any wonder that he'd locked his emotions away and thrown away the key?

She got more and more nervy as time wore on but when eventually Alek arrived home and walked into the sitting room, she thought how weary he looked. She'd been intending to break it to him gently but maybe something in her expression alerted him, because he frowned the minute he saw her.

'What's wrong?'

She'd been racking her brain to come up with the right way of telling him, but maybe there was no *right* way. There were only facts. She couldn't protect him from what she was about to tell him, no matter how much she wanted to.

'You remember that journalist who wrote the diary piece about us?'

He tensed. 'I'm not likely to forget her.'

'Well, she was here today.'

He scowled. 'How the hell did she find out where I lived?'

'I don't think that's really the issue here.'

'No?' His mouth twisted. 'Well, my privacy *is* an issue, something which I thought you might have realised by now. What did you tell her this time?' He gave a bitter laugh. 'Did you give her a blow-by-blow account of your husband's tragic childhood?'

'I would *never*—'

'Or maybe you thought you'd announce the baby news.' His words cut over hers. 'Even though we agreed not to say anything before the twelve weeks is up?'

'Actually, she was the one with the news.' She hesitated and then drew a deep breath. 'She told me that you've got a brother.'

His eyes narrowed. 'What the hell are you talking about?'

'Actually, a twin brother.' She licked her lips. 'You didn't know?'

'I don't know what you're talking about,' he said coldly.

'He asked her to contact you, to see if you'd be receptive to a meeting.'

I do not have a brother!' he thundered.

'Alek…' But her words were forgotten as her body was racked by the most piercing pain Ellie had ever felt. Hot knives were chasing through her belly and stabbing deeper and deeper. All the strength was draining from her legs. Shakily, she reached out to grab the edge of the window seat as Alek strode across the room, his face criss-crossed with concern as he caught hold of her.

But she didn't want his concern. She just wanted something to stop the pain. Not just the one in her belly—but the one in her heart.

'Go away!' she mumbled, lashing out at him ineffectively—but she could see something else in his eyes now. Something which scared her. Why was he looking like that? And why had his face gone so white? Following the direction of his gaze, she saw the shocking scarlet contrast of blood as it began to drip onto the polished gleam of the wooden floorboards.

And that must have been when she passed out.

CHAPTER TWELVE

ALEK FELT THE clench of pain around his heart—icy-cold and constricting. He couldn't breathe. He couldn't think. He was powerless to help her and even if he'd been capable of helping her—it seemed he wasn't going to get the chance to try. Ellie didn't want him in the ambulance with her, or so one of the paramedics told him, a faintly embarrassed look on his face as he didn't quite dare look him in the eye.

For the first time in his adult life, Alek discovered the feeling of powerlessness. He couldn't insist on doing things *his* way, or overrule what was happening by the sheer force of his personality or financial clout. He was being forced to accept the bitter facts. That Ellie was sick and their baby's life was in danger. That she was being rushed through the London streets with blue lights flashing and sirens blaring and she didn't want him anywhere near her.

A bitter taste stained his mouth.

Who could blame her?

He drove to the hospital as quickly as he could but his usual unerring sense of direction failed him and he found himself lost in the maze of hospital corridors, until a kindly nurse took pity on him and showed him the way to the unit. His heart was in his mouth as he approached that white and sterile place. And still they wouldn't let him see her.

'But I'm her husband,' he said, wondering if the words sounded as fake as they felt. What right did he have to call himself her husband? Was that why the ward sister was fixing him with a disapproving look? Had Ellie blurted out the truth to her in a moment of weakness, begging the nurses not to allow him anywhere near her—this man who had brought her nothing but pain?

'The doctor is with her right now.'

'Please…' His voice broke. It sounded cracked and hollow. Not like his voice at all. But then he'd never asked anyone for anything, had he? Not since those air-conditioned nights in his father's miserable fortress of a house, when he'd lain awake, the pillow clasped tightly over his head but too scared to cry. To the background sound of the night herons which had called across the island, he had silently begged an uncaring god to bring his mother back to him. And then, just like now, events had been completely outside his control. Things didn't happen just because you wanted them to. He saw now that maybe the reason he'd always turned his back on relationships was because, ultimately, he was unable to control them and that control had become his security in an uncertain world. His heart slammed against his ribcage. Or maybe it was just because, until Ellie, he'd never had a real relationship with anyone.

He looked into the ward sister's eyes. 'How is she?'

'She's being stabilised right now.'

'And…the baby?'

His voice cracked again. He hadn't expected that question to hurt so much, nor for it to mean as much as it did. When had been the critical moment that this unborn life had crept into his heart and taken residence there? The world seemed to tip on its axis as the woman's face assumed an expression of careful calm—as if she was attempting to reassure him without raising false hopes. He guessed she must have been asked that question a million times before.

'I'm afraid it's too early to say.'

He could do nothing but accept her words and he nodded grimly as he was shown into a waiting room which looked onto an ugly brick wall. There was a stack of old magazines on a chipped table and—all too poignantly—a little heap of plastic bricks piled in one corner, presumably for any accompanying children to play with.

Children.

He hadn't wanted any of his own—that had always been a given. He hadn't wanted to risk any child of his having to go through what he had gone through. But now, suddenly, he wanted this baby so bad. He wanted to nurture the child that the baby would grow into.

I will never abandon my baby or hurt or punish him, he thought fiercely. *He will know nothing but love from me—even if I have to learn how to love him from scratch.*

He closed his eyes as the minutes ticked by. Someone brought him a cup of coffee in a plastic cup, but it lay untouched in front of him. And when eventually the doctor came into the waiting room with a ward sister beside him—a different one this time—he sprang to his feet and felt the true meaning of fear. His hands were clammy and cold. His heart was pounding in his chest.

'How is she?' he demanded.

'She's fine—a little shocked and a little scared, but she's had a scan—'

'A scan?' For a second he felt confused. He realised that he'd been thinking in Greek instead of English and the word sounded alien to him.

'We needed to check that the pregnancy is still viable, and I'm delighted to tell you that it is.'

'Still *viable*?' he repeated stupidly.

'The baby is fine,' said the medic gently as if he were speaking to a child. 'Your wife has had a slight bleed, which is not uncommon in early pregnancy—but she's going to have to take it easy from now on. That means no more rushing around. No horse riding.' He smiled gently, as if to prepare him for some kind of blow. 'And no sex, I'm afraid.'

They took him to Ellie's room, where she lay on the narrow hospital bed, looking almost as white as the sheets. Her eyes were closed and her pale fringe was damp with sweat, so that her dark, winged eyebrows looked dramatic against her milky brow.

She didn't stir and, mindful of the doctor's words, he sat down noiselessly in the chair beside the bed, his hand reaching out to cover hers. He didn't know how long he sat there for—only that the rest of the world seemed to have retreated. He measured time by the slow drip of the intravenous bag which was hooked up to her arm. And he must have been looking at that when she eventually woke up, because he turned his head to find her grey eyes fixed steadily on him. He tried to read the expression in them, but he could see nothing.

'Hi,' he said.

She didn't answer, just tugged her hand away from

his as she tried to sit up, reaching down to touch her belly, her gaze lifting to his in agonised question.

'The baby?'

He nodded. 'It's okay. The baby's fine.'

She made a choked kind of sob as she slumped back against the pillows, her mouth trembling in relief. 'I didn't dream it, then.'

'Dream what?'

'Someone came.' She licked her lips and paused, as if the effort of speaking was too much. 'They were putting something cold on my stomach. Circling it round and round. They said it was going to be okay, but I thought...'

He felt completely inadequate as her words tailed off and he thought: *You have only yourself to blame. If you hadn't pushed her away, if you hadn't tried to impose your own stupid rules, then you would be able to comfort her now. You'd be able take her in your arms and tell her that everything was going to be all right.*

But he couldn't do that, could he? He couldn't make guarantees he couldn't possibly keep. Promises she'd never believe. All he could do was to make sure she had everything she needed.

'Shh,' he said in as gentle a voice as he'd ever used and she shut her eyes tightly closed, as if she couldn't bear to meet his gaze any longer. 'The doctor says you're going to have to take it easy.'

'I know,' she said as tears began to slide from beneath her lashes.

They kept her in overnight and she was discharged into his care the following day. She tried refusing his offer of a wheelchair, telling him that she was perfectly capable of walking to the car.

'They said to take it easy,' she told him tartly. 'Not to spend the next six months behaving like an invalid.'

'I'm not taking any chances,' came his even response, but his tone was underpinned with steel. 'And if you won't get in the wheelchair, then I shall be forced to pick you up and carry you across the car park—which might cause something of a stir. Up to you, Ellie.'

She glowered but made no further protest as he wheeled her to the car, and she didn't say anything else until they were back at the apartment, when he'd sat her down on one of the squashy sofas and made her the ginger tea she loved.

She glanced up as he walked in with the tray. Her expression was steady and very calm. She drew a deep breath. 'So what are you intending to do about your brother?'

His throat constricted. She'd gone straight for the jugular, hadn't she? 'My brother?' he repeated as if it were the first time he'd ever heard that word. As if he hadn't spent the past twenty-four hours trying to purge his mind of its existence. 'It's you and the baby which are on my mind right now.'

'You're avoiding the subject,' she pointed out. 'Which is par for the course for you. But I'm not going to let this drop, Alek. I'm just not. Before I went into hospital, we discovered something pretty momentous about your—'

'I don't have a brother,' he cut in harshly. 'Understand?'

Frustratedly, she shook her head. 'I understand that you're pig-headed and stubborn! You might not like the journalist, or the message she left—but that doesn't mean it isn't true. Why would she lie?'

He clenched his hands into fists and another wave

of powerlessness washed over him, only this he could do something about. 'I'm not prepared to discuss it any further.'

She shrugged, a look of resignation turning her expression stony. 'Have it your own way. And I'm sure you'll understand that I'm no longer prepared to share my bed with you. I'm moving back into my own bedroom.'

Alek flinched. It hurt more than it should have done, even though it came as no big surprise. Yet something made him want to try to hang on to what they had—and briefly he wondered whether it was a fear of losing her, or just a fear of losing. 'I know the doctor advised no sex, but I can live with that,' he said. 'But that doesn't mean we can't sleep together. I can be there for you in the night if you need anything.'

She stared at him as if he'd taken leave of his senses. 'I can call you if I *need* anything, Alek.'

'But—'

'The charade is over, Alek,' she said. 'I'm not sleeping with a stranger any more.'

He looked at her in disbelief. 'How can we possibly be strangers, when you know more about me than anyone else?'

'I only know because I wore you down until you told me—and it was like getting blood from a stone. And I understand why. I realise how painful it was for you to tell me, and that what happened to you is the reason you don't do intimacy. I get all that. But I've also realised that I *want* intimacy. Actually, I crave it. And I can't do sex for sex's sake. I can't do cuddling up together at night-time either. It's too confusing. It blurs the boundaries. It will make me start thinking we're getting closer, but of course we won't be and we never will.'

'Ellie—'

'No,' she said firmly. 'It's important that I say this, so hear me out. I don't blame you for your attitude. I understand why you are the way you are. I think I can almost understand why you don't want to stir up all the emotional stuff of reuniting with the brother you say you don't have—I just can't live with it. If I were one hundred per cent fit, I think I'd be able to get you to change your mind about wanting to stay with me until after the baby is born. Because I think we both recognise that's no longer really important, and I hope you know me well enough to realise that I'll give you as much contact with your child as you want.' She gave a sad sort of smile, like someone waving goodbye to a ship they knew they would never see again. 'Ideally, I'd like to go back to the New Forest and find myself a little cottage there and live a simple life and look after myself. But obviously I can't do that, because the doctors won't let me and because you're based in London.'

'Ellie—'

'No. Please. Let me finish. I want you to know that I'm grateful to be here and to know you're looking out for me and the baby, because this is all about the baby now. And only the baby.' Her voice was trembling now. 'Because I don't ever want to get physically close to you again, Alek. I can't risk all the fallout and the potential heartbreak. Do you understand?'

And the terrible thing was that he did. He agreed with every reasoned word she'd said. He accepted each hurtful point she made, even though something unfamiliar was bubbling inside him which was urging him to challenge her. To talk her round.

But he couldn't. One of the reasons for his outstand-

ing achievements in the world of commerce was an
ability to see things as they really were. His vision was
X-ray clear whenever he looked at a run-down business, with the intention of turning it around to make
a profit. And he realised that he must apply the same
kind of logic now. It was what it was. He had destroyed
any kind of future with the mother of his child and he
must live with her decision and accept it. She was better off without someone like him, anyway. A man who
couldn't do feelings. Who was too afraid to try.

A pain like a cold and remorseless wind swept
through him.

'Yes, I understand,' he said.

CHAPTER THIRTEEN

SO WHY WAS he so damned restless?

Alek stared out of his office window and drummed his fingers impatiently on his desk. Why couldn't he accept a life which—despite having a pregnant wife living in his apartment—was still tailored to fit his needs? He told himself that things weren't *really* that different. Why should it bother him so much that he and Ellie were now back in separate rooms?

He still went to work each morning just the way he'd always done, although Ellie had taken to sleeping late these days instead of joining him for tea before he went to the office. At least, he was assuming she was sleeping. She might have been wide awake, doing naked yoga moves as the sun rose for all he knew. Or submerging her rapidly growing bump beneath a bath filled to the brim with sensual bubbles. He had no idea what went on behind her bedroom door once it was closed, although he'd fantasised about it often enough. Hell, yes.

He wondered if his frustration showed in his face. Whether he'd given himself away the other morning, when he'd unexpectedly seen her padding back from the kitchen clutching a mug of ginger tea as he'd been about to take an early morning conference call. Her hair had been tumbling in glorious disarray around her shoulders and the floaty, flowery robe she wore had managed to conceal her changing shape while somehow emphasising it. Her skin had been fresh and her eyes bright, despite the earliness of the hour. She'd looked more like a teenager than a woman of twenty-five and he'd felt a pang of something like regret. Just the day before, the doctor had given her a glowing bill of health. Mother and baby were ticking all the right boxes, and Alek told himself that at least something good had come out of all this.

But wasn't it funny how you always wanted what you hadn't got? Why else would he be craving more of her company and wishing she'd linger longer over dinner? Wanting her to say something—anything—other than make those polite little observations about what kind of day she'd had. He'd made quite a few concessions to fit in with her pregnancy, but even they hadn't softened her resolve. Hadn't he eaten his words and joined that wretched antenatal class, where they were expected to lie on the floor—puffing like a bunch of whales? Yet still she kept her distance. He felt a stab of conscience. Wasn't that how he used to be with her? And wasn't he discovering that he didn't much like being pushed away? And in the meantime, he was aching for her. Aching in ways which were nothing to do with sex.

He'd been brooding about it all week and not coming up with any answers about how he could change things, when on Saturday night she looked at him across the dinner table with an odd expression on her face.

'I want you to know,' she said in the careful way people did when they'd been practising saying something, 'that if you decide you want to start seeing other... women, I shan't mind.'

His fork fell to his plate with a clatter. His heart pounded. Rarely had he been more shocked. Or outraged. 'Say that again,' he breathed.

'You heard me perfectly well, Alek. I'm just asking you to be discreet about it, that's all. I don't particularly want—'

'No, wait a minute.' Ruthlessly he cut across her words in a way he'd avoided doing of late, leaning across the table and glaring at her. 'Are you telling me that you *want* me to start dating other women?'

Ellie didn't reply, not immediately. She fiddled around with her napkin for just long enough to hang on to her composure—telling herself that this was the only solution. She couldn't keep him chained up like a tame lion. 'I don't know if *want* is the right word—'

'Maybe you want to watch?' he suggested crudely. 'Perhaps that's one of your fantasises. Does the thought of me having sex with somebody else turn you on, Ellie?'

'Don't be so disgusting!' she snapped, feeling her cheeks growing hot. 'That's not what I meant at all and you know it.'

'Do I?' he demanded furiously. 'What am I supposed to think, when you give me your blessing to have sex with someone else, while you're still living under my roof?'

She glared back. 'I wasn't giving you my *blessing*. I'm trying to be fair!'

'Fair?' he echoed, furiously.

'Yes, fair.' She took a shaky sip of water. 'I know you're a virile man with a healthy sexual appetite and

I shouldn't expect you to have to curtail that, just because...'

'Because you no longer want me?'

Ellie swallowed as she met the accusation spitting from his blue eyes. Oh, if only. If only it were as simple as that. 'It's not that I don't want you.'

'You just take masochistic pleasure in us sleeping apart? In me lying wide-eyed for most of the night knowing you're in the room next door?'

'I told you before. I can't do fake intimacy. And I didn't start this conversation to discuss the reasons why I won't sleep with you.'

'Then why *did* you start it?'

'Because I'm trying to be kind.'

'Kind?' He stared at her incredulously. 'How does that work?'

'I'm just suggesting that if you want to relieve your frustrations, then feel free—but please be discreet about it. I just don't want it in my face, that's all.'

There was silence for a moment while he stared down at his clenched fists and when he looked up again, there was something in his eyes she didn't recognise.

'Why not you?' he questioned simply. 'When you're the only woman I want? When we both know that if I came round to the other side of that table and started kissing you, you'd go up in flames—the way you always do when I touch you.'

'So why don't you?' she challenged. 'Why don't you take control, as you're so good at doing? Take the choice away from me?'

He shook his head and gave a short laugh. 'Because that would make it too easy. A short-term fix, not a long-term solution. You have to be with me because you want to, Ellie—and not just because your body is reacting to something I do to you.'

She stared at her napkin. She stared at her water glass. But when she looked up, she shook her head. 'I can't,' she said. 'It would be insane to even try. We're planning a divorce before too long and I want to acclimatise myself to the situation. I'm trying to get used to the separate lives we've agreed to lead.'

For a minute there was silence.

'And what if I told you I don't want separate lives, or a divorce?' he said at last. 'That I wanted to start over, only this time to do it differently? We'll take it as slow as you like, Ellie. I'll court you, if that's what you want. I'll woo you with flowers. I won't take business calls when we're away. I'll do whatever it takes, if you just give me another chance.'

His bright eyes bored into her and for a moment Ellie couldn't speak, because she got the feeling that Alek didn't often ask questions like that. And hadn't she sometimes dreamt of a moment like this—even though she'd told herself it would never happen? But it *was* happening. He was sitting there and saying things she'd longed to hear and temptation was tugging at her—because Alek in a peace-making mood was pretty irresistible. His blue eyes were blazing and his lips were parted, as if already anticipating her kiss—and didn't she want to kiss him so badly? She could go into his arms and they could just lose themselves in each other, and...

And what?

How long before domesticity bored him? Before the emotional demands *she would inevitably make* became too tedious for him to bear? Because he still didn't do communication, did he? Not about the things that really mattered. He was still denying that he had a brother. He was only talking this way because he was bargaining with her. Because it was probably frustrating the life out of him that she wasn't falling into his arms with gratitude.

She shook her head. 'I can't.'

'Why not?'

She realised that his pride was going to be hurt—and maybe that wasn't a bad thing. But she needed to show him that this was about more than pride. She had to summon up enough courage and strength to present him with a few harsh home truths.

'Because I can't contemplate life with a man who keeps running away.'

'Running away?' he echoed and she heard the anger building in his voice. 'Are you accusing me of cowardice, Ellie?'

'It's up to you to make the diagnosis, not me.' She stared at the little vase of blue flowers which sat at the centre of the table. She thought how delicate the petals were. How most things in life were delicate, when you stopped to think about it. She lifted her gaze to his, trying not to react to his anger. 'When you told me all about your family—about your mother walking out on you and the effect it had on you—I could understand why you never tried to get in touch with her. I understood that you'd taken your pain and turned it into success and that it was easier to turn your back on the past. But you're an adult now, with the world at your fingertips—the most successful man I've ever met. You're intelligent and resourceful and yet you've just heard that you've got a brother and you're acting like nothing's happened!'

His dark head was bent and there was silence, and when at last he looked at her she flinched from the pain she saw written in his eyes.

'Not just a brother,' he said. 'I think I could have dealt with that. But a twin brother? Do you know what that means, if it's true? Have you thought about it, Ellie? She didn't have another baby with another man. She had one who was exactly the same age. *She took him with her and left me behind.* I was the one she rejected. I was the one she didn't want. How do you think that makes me feel?'

'I don't think it makes you *feel* anything,' she whispered back. 'Because you're blocking out your feelings, the way you've always done. You're ignoring it and pretending it isn't there and hoping it will go away. But it won't go away. It will just fester and fester and make you bitter. And I don't want a man like that. I want someone who can face up to reality. Who can accept how it's making him feel—even if it hurts—and who isn't afraid to show it.'

She leant forward and her voice was fervent. 'The stuff you imagine is always worse than the real thing,' she said. 'I know that. When I met my father—all the dreams I'd nurtured about us becoming one big happy family were destroyed the moment he pushed the table away and my cappuccino spilt everywhere. And of course I was upset. But afterwards I felt…well, free, I suppose. I could let go of all those foolish fantasies. Because it's better to deal with reality, than with dreams. Or nightmares,' she finished as she rose to her feet. She looked into his face and saw the pain which was written there. Such raw and bitter pain that it made her instinctively want to reach out and comfort him.

But she knew she couldn't rid him of his nightmares. She couldn't *fix* Alek. He had to do that all by himself.

CHAPTER FOURTEEN

HE DIDN'T TELL her he was leaving until the morning of his departure, when Ellie walked into the kitchen and saw him drinking coffee, a leather bag on the floor beside his feet. He turned as she entered the room and, although his hooded eyes gave nothing away, his powerful body was stiff with tension. A trickle of apprehension began to whisper down her spine.

'You're going away on a business trip?' she questioned.

He shook his head. 'I'm going to Paris.'

Fear and dread punched at her heart in rapid succession. Paris. The city of romance. She looked down. An overnight bag. The fear grew. 'You've decided to take me up on my offer?' she breathed in horror.

He frowned. 'What offer?'

'You're seeing someone else?'

His brow darkened. She saw a pulse flicker at his temple. 'Are you crazy? I'm going to meet my brother. I phoned the journalist and spoke to her. She gave me his details and I emailed him. We're having lunch at the Paris Ritz later.'

Ellie's heart flooded with a complex mixture of emotions. There was relief that he hadn't taken her up on her foolish suggestion and joy that he'd taken the step of arranging to meet his brother. But there was disappointment, too. He was facing up to his demons—but he hadn't stopped to think that she might like to be involved, too. She was curious to meet her baby's uncle, yes—and wasn't it possible she could be a support to her husband if she was there at his side? She took an eager step towards him, but the emphatic shake of his head halted her.

'Please don't,' he said. 'Elaborate displays of emotion are the last thing I want to deal with right now.'

It wasn't an unreasonable reaction in the circumstances, but that didn't stop it from hurting. Ellie's arms hung uselessly by her sides as she pursed her lips. Yet, why *should* he accept her comfort or her help when she'd spent weeks pushing him away?

She nodded. 'Good luck,' she said quietly, though never had she wanted to kiss him quite so much.

She spent the day trying not to think about what might be happening in France. She told herself that Alek wouldn't ring and she was right. Every time she glanced at her phone—too often—there were no texts or missed calls and the small screen remained infuriatingly blank. She'd been due to meet Alannah for lunch, but she cancelled—afraid she would end up doing something stupid, like crying. Or even worse, that she would blurt out the whole story. And she couldn't do that. It wasn't her story to tell. She'd already broken Alek's confidence once and to do so again—wittingly this time—would be unforgivable.

She tried to keep herself occupied as best she could. There was a subtle nip to the air, so she slipped on a jacket and walked across a park with leaves showing the distinct bronzed brushstrokes of autumn. She went shopping for food in the little deli she'd discovered, which was hidden unexpectedly in a narrow road behind the smart Knightsbridge shops, and she bought all the things she knew Alek liked best to eat.

But no matter what she did, she couldn't clear her mind of nagging questions which couldn't be answered until he arrived home. Though it occurred to her at some point that he might not want to tell her anything. He was naturally secretive and that wouldn't necessarily have changed. Discovering something about his past wasn't necessarily going to transform him into someone who was comfortable with disclosure.

She went to bed at around eleven and it was sometime later that she heard the sound of a key in the lock and a door quietly closing. Her throat dried. He was home. She could hear him moving around, as if he didn't want to wake her, but as the footsteps passed her door she called out to him.

'Alek.'

The footsteps halted. The floor creaked and there was silence.

'Alek?' she said again.

The door opened and a powerful shaft of light slanted across the room to shine on her bed, like a spotlight. She blinked a little in the fierce gleam and sat up, pushing her hair out of her eyes. She tried to search his face, but his eyes were in shadow and all she could see was his powerful body silhouetted against the bright light.

'Are you okay?' she said.

'I didn't want to wake you.'

'Won't you…come in?' Her voice gave a nervous wobble as she switched on the bedside lamp. 'And tell me what happened.'

She'd been half expecting him to refuse, to coolly inform her that he'd tell her everything—well, maybe not quite everything—in the morning. That would be much more characteristic of the Alek she knew. But he didn't. He walked into the room and sat down on the edge of the bed, only she noticed he kept his distance—as if ensuring that he was nowhere within touching range. And stupidly—because it wasn't very appropriate in the circumstances—she found herself wishing she were wearing some provocative little excuse for a nightie, instead of an oversized T-shirt which had nothing but comfort to commend it.

'So,' she said nervously. 'What happened?'

Alek looked at the way she was biting her lip. At the shiny hair spilling over her shoulders and the anxiousness she couldn't quite keep from her eyes. He thought that she loved him, but he couldn't be sure. His mouth hardened. How could you tell if a woman really loved you? He had no baseline to work from.

'We met,' he said. 'And after a while he showed me some photos. The first—' His voice cracked slightly. 'The first photos I'd ever seen of her.'

She nodded. Swallowed. 'What were they like?'

He tipped his head and looked up at the ceiling. 'She was very beautiful—even in the later shots. She had this thick black hair and the most amazing blue eyes.'

'Like yours, you mean?'

He gave a wry smile as he looked at her again. 'That's right. Just like mine.' It had been beyond strange to see the physical evidence of somebody he'd only ever heard about in the most negative terms. A woman in a cotton dress, glinting at the sun—her face filled with an unmistakable sadness.

'And what was your brother like?'

Ellie's words broke into his thoughts and Alek

opened his mouth to answer but the most articulate person in the world would've had difficulty expressing the conflicting feelings which had torn through him when he'd seen his twin brother for the first time.

'He looks like me,' he said, at last.

'Your twin brother looks like you? You don't say!'

And unexpectedly, he began to laugh—her quip doing the impossible and taking some of the heat out of the situation. He thought about how he'd felt when he'd walked into the famous hotel and seen a black-haired man with a face so scarily like his own, staring back at him from the other side of the restaurant. He remembered the overpowering sense of recognition which had rocked him and momentarily robbed him of breath.

'His name is Loukas but his eyes are black,' he said. 'Not blue.'

And that had been the only physical difference he'd been able to see, although after the second bottle of wine Loukas had told him about the scars which tracked over his back, and what had caused them. He'd told him a lot of stuff. Some of which was hard to hear. Some he'd wanted instantly to forget. About a mother who had been a congenitally bad picker of men, and the sorry way that had influenced her life. About his poverty-stricken childhood—so different from Alek's, but not without its own problems. Dark problems which Loukas had told him he would save for another day.

'Had he been trying to find you for a long time?' Ellie whispered.

He shook his head. 'He only discovered that I existed last year, when his…our…mother died.'

'Oh, Alek.'

He shook his head, unprepared for the rush of emotion, wanting to stem it, in case it made him do what he'd been trying very hard not to do all day. He cleared his throat and concentrated on the facts.

'She left behind a long letter, explaining why she'd done what she'd done. She said she knew she couldn't live with my father any more—that his rages and infidelities were becoming intolerable. She had no money and no power—she was essentially trapped on his island. She thought he would blight the lives of all three of us if she stayed, but she also knew that there was no way she could cope with two babies. And so she…she chose Loukas.'

She nodded, not saying anything and for a moment he thought she wasn't going to ask it, but of course she asked it. This was Ellie, after all.

'How did she choose?'

Another silence. 'She tossed a coin.'

'Oh.' Her voice was very quiet. 'Oh, I see.'

He gave a bitter laugh. He wasn't a man given to flights of fancy but he'd vividly imagined that moment just before she'd walked out of the house for good. He'd wanted his brother to lie; to invent a fairy story. To tell him that she'd chosen Loukas because he had been weaker, or because she thought that Alek would fare better because he was two minutes older and a pound heavier. Or because Loukas had cried at the last minute and it had torn at her heartstrings. But no. It was something much more prosaic than that. His fate and the fate of his brother being decided by a coin spinning in the air, until it landed on the back of her hand and she covered it with her palm. What had she thought as she'd lifted her hand to see which boy would be going with her, and which boy would be left behind? Did she find it easy to walk away from him?

'My mother flipped a coin and I lost out,' he said.

Another silence. A much longer one this time.

'You know she did it because she loved you?' she said suddenly. 'You do realise that?'

He raised his head, barely noticing the salty prickling at the backs of his eyes. 'What the hell are you talking about?'

'She did it because she loved you,' she repeated, more fiercely. 'She must have done. She must have been out of her head with worry—knowing that she could barely look after one baby, let alone two. And if she'd taken you both, he would have come after you. He definitely would. She must have thought your father would be glad to have been left with one son, and that he'd love you as best he could. But he couldn't. He just couldn't—for reasons you'll probably never know. But what you have to do, is to stop thinking that because of what happened you're unlovable—because you aren't. You need to accept that you're very lovable indeed, if only you'd stop shutting people out. Our baby is going to love you, that's for sure. And I've got so much love in my heart that I'm bursting to give you—if only you'll let me. Oh, darling. Darling. It's all right. It's all right. Oh, Alek—come here.' Her eyes began to blur. 'Everything's going to be all right.'

She put her arms around him and he did what he'd been trying not to do all day, which was to cry. He cried the tears he'd never cried before. Tears of loneliness and pain, which eventually gave way to the realisation that he was free at last. Free of the past and all its dark tentacles. He had let it go and Ellie had helped him do that.

His hand was shaking as he smoothed the pale hair away from her face and looked at her.

'You would never do that,' he said.

She turned her head slightly, so that she could kiss the hand which was still cupping the side of her face. 'Do what?'

'Leave our baby.'

She turned her head back, biting her lip, her grey eyes darkening. 'I don't want to judge your mother, or to compare—'

'That wasn't my aim,' he said quietly. 'I'm just stating a fact and letting myself be grateful for that fact. I've given you a hard time, Ellie, and a lot of women might have lost patience with me before now. Yet you didn't. You hung on in there. You gave me strength and showed me the way.'

His question shimmered on the air as she looked into his eyes.

'Because I love you,' she said simply. 'You must have realised that by now? But love sometimes means having to take a step back, because it can never flourish if there are darknesses or secrets, or things which never dare be spoken about.'

'And I love you,' he said, his free hand reaching out to lie possessively over the bump of their unborn child. A lump rose in his throat as he felt the powerful ripple of movement beneath. 'I love you and our baby and I will love you both for ever. I will nurture and care for you both and never let you down. Be very certain of that, *poulaki mou*. I will never let you down.'

He could taste the salt from her own tears as he kissed her and did what he'd been wanting to do for so long. He lay down beside her and put his arms around her, gathering her close against his beating heart.

EPILOGUE

'SO WHAT'S IT LIKE, being back?' Ellie's words seemed to float through the warm night air towards her husband. 'Is it weird?'

Shining brightly through the unshuttered windows, the moon had turned the room into a fantasy setting of indigo and silver. Over their heads whirled a big old-fashioned fan and the sheets were rumpled around their gleaming bodies. The faint scent of sex hung in the air and mingled with the tang of the lemons squeezed into the water jug which stood beside the bed.

Ellie turned onto her side and looked at Alek, who lay beside her with his arms stretched above his head, looking a picture of blissful contentment.

This journey to Kristalothos was one they'd waited a while to make, until both of them were certain they were ready. A trip to the island home of Alek's childhood—a place which symbolised so much of the darkness and horror of his past—was never going to be at the top of their bucket list. In fact, Ellie had been surprised when Alek had first suggested it because although their life had been hectic, it was pretty close to perfect. The birth of their son two years previously had put the seal on their happiness and Ellie had been...

She swallowed.

Frightened that going back would test their happiness and threaten to destroy it? Scared he might go back to being the secretive Alek of old who had locked her out of his heart—or that the reality of confronting his past might bring renewed bitterness?

Yes, she had thought all those things—and more. But she'd quashed her fears and entered into his plans with enthusiasm, because she'd sensed it was something he'd needed to do. Hadn't she been the one who'd insisted you had to face your fears instead of running away from them? And perhaps there was some truth in the idea that you could never go forward until you were properly at peace with your past.

After much discussion, they had decided to leave their little boy behind in England. Young Loukas—their adored son, who they'd named after Alek's twin brother and who had given them so much more than joy. It was the tiny tot more than anything who had been responsible for Alek's growing ability to show emotion. Because children loved unconditionally and Alek had learnt to do the same. He had learnt that real love knew no boundaries and sometimes Ellie just sat watching him play with their little boy and her heart swelled up with so much pride and affection.

But a lively two-year-old was not an ideal companion for a cathartic trip which might be emotionally painful, which was why they'd left him behind with Bridget—who had become his honorary grandmother.

Ellie and Alek had chartered a boat from Athens, which had taken them out to his childhood island home of Kristalothos, with the vessel making a foamy trail through the wine-dark sea as they journeyed. They had arrived on a spring morning, when the wild flowers were massed over the gentle hills and the sea was crystal clear as it lapped gently against the fine white sand.

As he had looked around him with slightly dazed eyes, Alek had told her the place had changed beyond recognition. Some of the changes he'd discovered when he was making plans for their trip but seeing them with his own eyes had really driven home the fact that nothing ever stayed the same. A Greek-born hotelier named Zak Constantides had bought his father's old fortress and razed it to the ground, putting in its place a boutique hotel, which was fast becoming as famous as his iconic London Granchester.

But Alek had chosen to rent a villa instead of staying there and Ellie was glad, because she didn't want to spend a single night on the spot where a young boy had spent so many miserable years.

She leant across the rumpled bed and stroked her fingertips over his bronzed cheek, and her touch seemed to stir him from his pensive mood. He smiled as he reached for her and thought about her question.

What was it like being back?

Reflectively, he stroked her hair. 'It is a bit weird,' he admitted. 'But it doesn't hurt. Not any more. And I'm glad I came, because it was something I needed to do. Another ghost laid to rest. I like the fact that Zak's hotel has brought work and prosperity to the island and that the place is no longer ruled by fear and oppression.'

'I'm glad, too,' she said, wriggling up closer.

'But I'm glad of so many things,' he said. 'Mainly for my beautiful wife and my equally beautiful son, who provide me with the kind of contentment I never thought existed.' He tilted her chin with the tip of his finger, so

he could see the gleam of her eyes in the moonlight. 'I'm
even glad that I've got a brother, although—'

'Although Loukas has his own demons,' she finished slowly.

'Yes, he does. But it isn't Loukas I'm thinking about
at this moment, *poulaki mou*. It's you.' He rolled on top
of her, his fingers playing with the tumble of her hair as
he felt the softness of her body beneath him. 'Because
without you I would have nothing. I am who I am because of you, Ellie. You made me confront things I'd
spent my life avoiding. You made me look at myself,
even though I didn't want to. I've learnt...'

'What have you learnt?' she questioned softly as his
voice tailed off.

He shrugged. 'That it's better to face up to the truth
rather than to block it out. And that feelings don't kill
you—even the very toughest ones. Everything that's
worth knowing, you have taught me and I love you for
that, Ellie Sarantos—and for a million reasons more besides.' He gave a mock glower of a frown. 'Even though
you have stubbornly refused to let me announce that
particular piece of information to the world.'

He traced a thoughtful finger over the angled line of
her collarbone. He had wanted to go through a second
marriage ceremony—a big glitzy occasion at the Greek
Cathedral in London, intended as a mark of his love for
her because he felt she'd been short-changed last time.
For a while Ellie had been agreeable—even consulting
a wedding planner and hearing about the rival merits of
a string quartet versus an old-fashioned bouzouki band
for the reception. Until one morning at breakfast, she'd
told him she didn't need declarations or lavish gestures.
That it was enough to know he cared, and in the pri-

vate moments of their precious relationship his heartfelt words of love meant more than a truckload of confetti.

And wasn't that another aspect of her personality which made him love her so much? That the things she cared about weren't the *things* which so many people strived for. She didn't need to put on a show or make some kind of statement. She didn't need to prove anything. Diamonds she could take or leave, and, although she wore silky tea dresses because she knew he liked them, she was happiest in a pair of jeans and a T-shirt. She was still Ellie—the same straightforward, uncomplicated woman he'd first fallen for—and he wouldn't want her any other way.

He reached for her breasts and cupped them and she made a purring little sound in the back of her throat, because she liked it. *Theos*, but he liked it, too. But then he liked everything about his soft and beautiful wife.

'Shall I make love to you now?' he questioned.

She touched her fingertips to the dark shadow of his jaw and followed it up with the slow drift of her lips. 'Oh, yes, please,' she whispered.

They were in the place of his birth, but they could have been anywhere. A place which had once symbolised darkness and heartbreak, but not any more. Because Ellie made everywhere feel like the home he'd never really had. Ellie breathed life into *his* life. He bent his head and kissed her as the night herons gathered around the lapping bay outside their window.

* * * * *

Claimed for Makarov's Baby

CHAPTER ONE

IT DIDN'T MEAN ANYTHING. It was just a means to an end.
A few words and a signature on a piece of paper and
then afterwards...

Erin swallowed as the silky white dress brushed
against her bare ankles. Afterwards she would be able
to create a better future. A different kind of future. Most
of all, she would be secure—and wasn't that the whole
point of this? That she would be *safe*.

But she could feel her palms growing clammy as she
clutched the bouquet of flowers her groom had insisted
she buy—'It will add authenticity...'—and wondered
if her bright, forced smile would add the same kind of
authenticity. She doubted it. As she walked towards the
registrar's desk her face was reflected back in a mirror—
a face almost as white as her dress. Beside her stood a
man—a kind man and a dear friend whom she must pretend to love, at least until the ceremony was over. And
that was the hardest part of all.

Because she didn't believe in love. She'd tried it once
and it had only reinforced what she'd already known.
That love was for fools, and hadn't she been the biggest
one of all? She'd picked the worst kind of man. A man
who was not worthy of love.

Of anyone's love.

The two witnesses were sitting quietly and the registrar was smiling, too, but Erin was certain she could see suspicion in the smart middle-aged woman's eyes. Did she guess? Did she have any kind of inkling that Erin Turner was about to break the law for the first time in her life?

Beside her, Chico reached out and curled his fingers around her wrist, giving it a comforting squeeze as the registrar began to speak.

'You are here to witness the joining in matrimony of Chico and Erin…'

There was a pause as Erin heard a door behind her open and the sound of footsteps, but her heart was thumping too loudly to care who had just walked in. Her smile felt as brittle as glass. Her hand was now so slippery that she was afraid of dropping the flowers. And then the question was being asked. The question she had practised not reacting to over and over again.

'If any person present knows of any lawful impediment to this marriage, he or she should declare it now.'

She watched the registrar give a quick nod—as if this particular query always got the same silent response—when suddenly a voice shattered the quiet of the institutional room.

'*Da.* I do.'

For a split second Erin froze and then she whirled round as she heard the Russian accent, her head refusing to believe what her heart and her body were telling her. That it was nothing but a mistake—a mistake with especially bad timing.

And then she was caught and captured—lasered by the brilliance of a pair of icy blue eyes—and Erin's heart plummeted, for this was no mistake. This was real. As real as the silk flowers which stood on the registrar's desk. As real as the sudden thunder of blood to her heart. Like a fizzing firework thrown into the blackest night, Dimitri Makarov was dominating the room with his unique blend of sex appeal and power, just as he always did.

Her fingers bit into the fleshy stems of her flowers as she stared at him. He was wearing a silvery-grey suit which emphasised his powerful build, and the artificial light from the cheap chandelier had turned his hair to molten gold. Prestige and privilege pulsated from every pore of his muscular body as he flicked his icy gaze over her.

But something about him was different. Gone was the bloodshot glow which had sometimes marred the beauty of those spectacular eyes. And gone, too, was the faint stubble which had habitually darkened his jaw and made him look slightly disreputable. This man was clean-shaven and his eyes were bright and clear and... *penetrating*.

'Dimitri,' Erin breathed.

'*Da*. The very same,' he said, his voice mocking her, but the look on his face sent a shiver down her spine. 'Pleased to see me, Erin?'

He knows, thought Erin.

He knows.

She told herself that he couldn't possibly know. It was over six years since she'd last seen him, when he'd made it clear how little she had meant to him. His attitude towards her had been insulting and dismissive—reminding her all too clearly that she'd only ever been a minion in his life. Somebody he could just shove aside when she got too close. And that was what had happened, wasn't it? She'd got way too close.

She thought of Leo and why she was here. Of everything she was fighting for, and she forced a smile onto her lips. Because if she showed the slightest sign of weakness, Dimitri would leap on it.

And devour her.

'This is rather bad timing,' she said lightly.

'I disagree. The timing could not have been better.'

'I'm just about to get married, Dimitri. To Chico.'

'I don't think so.' His gaze flicked over Chico, who was standing with his mouth gaping open and a distinct look of alarm in his eyes.

'Is there a problem?' asked the registrar pleasantly, but Erin could see her glancing at the telephone which sat on the desk beside the silk flowers, as if convincing herself that a line to the outside world lay within easy reach.

'A problem of a purely emotional nature,' answered Dimitri smoothly as he began to walk towards Erin.

Erin stiffened as he closed the space between them and even as her body started going into some sort of automatic meltdown at his approach the irony of his words did not escape her. Was Dimitri Makarov really claiming something to be of an *emotional nature*—when he was about as familiar with emotion as a shark was to sitting around a fire and warming its fin?

'Miss Turner?' said the registrar, fixing Erin with a questioning look, as if she was eager for the unexpected floor show to be over.

But it wasn't over. It was nowhere near over. Because Dimitri had now reached her and his tall shadow was enveloping her, like a stifling cloud which seemed to have sucked all the air from her lungs. She told herself to stop him—to scream out her protest or shove at that broad chest with one indignant hand—but she seemed powerless to do anything. And suddenly it was too late, because he was pulling her against him and his hands were wrapped around her back as he held her close. Trapped against his body, she could feel his fingers imprinting themselves on the thin silk of her wedding dress and it felt as if he were touching her bare skin. With a shuddered breath she lifted her face to his, to the icy glitter of his eyes, which studied her for a long moment before he bent his head to kiss her.

Erin could sense the contempt underpinning his action, but that didn't stop her lips from opening automatically beneath his, or her body starting to tremble the moment he touched her. Weakly, she recognised that this was not a kiss driven by affection or lust, but a mark of possession—a stamp of ownership. Yet it was a kiss too potent to resist and stupidly—even now—it made her start longing for the things she was never going to have.

He was pulling her closer, bringing her up against the proud jut of his hips and the unmistakable hardness at their centre, which was hidden from everyone in the room but her. She thought how...*outrageous* it was for him to push his erection against her quite so blatantly when there were other people around, but that didn't stop her from reacting to it, did it—from wanting him deep inside her? She could feel the melting heat of desire and the betraying prickle of her breasts as she tried to stop her body from pushing so insistently against his. Her breathing was shallow as it mingled with the warmth of his and she felt the moist flicker of his tongue, which promised so much pleasure. Oh, why was it Dimitri and only Dimitri who could ever make her feel this way? she thought despairingly.

Fleetingly, she wondered if Chico would do anything to stop what was happening—but what could he do, even if he was that kind of man? How could he tell Dimitri to back off when they were about to commit a crime? That this was nothing but a sham marriage, so that Chico could get his work permit.

She felt the bouquet slide from her nerveless fingers to the ground and she was afraid she might do the same when, suddenly, Dimitri terminated the kiss. His shadowed features tensed as he drew away from her—but not before his eyes had glittered out a warning and Erin knew exactly what that warning meant. She had worked for him for years. She knew how his mind worked—at least, some of the time—and the message in their icy blue depths was as clear as day. *Leave this to me*, they said, and something inside her rebelled.

Did he really think he could waltz back into her life and start taking over, after all the grief he'd given her in the past? Because Dimitri was a man who *took*, she reminded herself grimly. Who took and took and never gave anything back. And he wasn't going to take anything else from her. Not any more. There were good reasons why he was no longer in her life—and even better ones why it should stay that way.

'How *dare* you?' she spat out, her voice shaking. 'What the hell do you think you're playing at?'

'You know exactly what I'm *playing* at, Erin.'

'You can't do this,' she said, meeting his gaze with a rebellious tilt of her chin. 'You can't.'

'No?' His pale eyes glittered in response. 'Just watch me.'

'Would someone mind explaining exactly what is going on?' asked the registrar, her polite tone not quite hiding her growing irritation. 'We have a number of weddings following yours and this unexpected interruption is—'

'There isn't going to be any wedding,' said Dimitri softly. 'Is there, Erin?'

They had all turned to look at her. Chico. The two witnesses. The registrar. But the only face Erin could see was Dimitri's and the icy challenge in his eyes. And suddenly it wasn't so easy to be rebellious. Suddenly, her certainties began to crumble as she recognised the glint of danger in the Russian's eyes.

She opened her mouth—so dry that it felt like parchment—before shutting it again with a snap. She looked at the faint frown on Chico's brow. Was he perceptive enough to know that if he dared confront Dimitri, he risked everything—that it would be like a centipede preparing to do battle with a lion? Or had the Russian effectively humiliated him by kissing his bride-to-be in full view of everyone, thus silencing any objections for ever?

But none of this mattered. Not really. Only Leo mattered and she didn't dare put his livelihood at risk. A mother being dragged in front of the courts for participating in a sham marriage could not really be deemed a fit mother. Imagine the shame and the terror and the very real threat of a fine—or even jail. Her mouth set into a determined line, because nothing like that was ever going to impact on her beloved son. Wasn't she only doing this to guarantee him a secure future and the feeling of safety which had always eluded her?

'I'm afraid it does look as if we might have to postpone the wedding,' she said, as apologetically as she could—though nothing in her vocabulary seemed a suitable response for such a bizarre situation. What could she say? She looked around nervously, like a stage compère facing a hostile audience. 'Dimitri is—'

'The only man she really wants—as her public capitulation has just proved,' said the Russian with cool arrogance and an even more arrogant smile, which only emphasised the rage in his eyes. 'Isn't that right, Erin?'

And now she saw something more than danger in his eyes. She saw the dark flicker of knowledge and Erin's heart twisted with pain. He *did* know! He *must* know. Had he somehow found out about Leo?

Her instinct was to get away from him and she wondered what would happen if she just picked up the skirts of her long dress and ran as fast as her feet could take her. The anonymous grey of the autumnal London day would swallow her up, leaving Dimitri far behind. She could take her wedding dress back to the same thrift shop from which she'd bought it. She could pick up Leo from school herself and tell him that Mummy wasn't going away on holiday after all and that they wouldn't be moving to a big house in the country.

If she ran away from him, she could cope—somehow. True, none of her immediate problems would have been solved, but she felt as if she could deal with anything as long as it wasn't beneath the Russian's unforgiving scrutiny and the fear of what he might or might not know.

But he had placed his hand at the small of her back— a light but proprietorial gesture which somehow managed to send out conflicting reactions of desire and dread. And she knew she wouldn't be running anywhere, any time soon.

'I'm sure this kind of thing happens all the time,' he said smoothly. 'The bride getting cold feet when she realises she's making a big mistake.'

The registrar put her pen down. 'Perhaps you would all like to leave the building,' she said quietly, 'and sort out your problems somewhere else?'

'My sentiments entirely. Do you happen to have a room we could use to talk in private?' questioned Dimitri in a pleasant tone which didn't quite conceal the steely note of determination. And then he smiled and it was like the moon appearing from behind a dark cloud. 'Please?'

The registrar looked up at him, her disapproving expression melting away beneath the sensual impact of that unexpected smile.

'There is somewhere you can use,' she said grudgingly. 'But please don't be long.'

'Oh, we won't be long. It won't take long for me to say what I need to say,' said Dimitri softly, his hand still at the small of Erin's back. 'That I can promise you.'

'Come with me, then.'

They all followed the registrar out into the corridor and the two witnesses who'd been plucked from the street shrugged their shoulders and headed for the exit, probably to the nearest pub. Erin saw the shell-shocked expression on Chico's face as Dimitri ushered her past and her feelings of powerlessness only increased.

The registrar was opening the door to a featureless-looking room, but now that some of the initial shock was leaving her system Erin started to recover some of her equilibrium. *Remember why you were doing this*, she reminded herself fiercely. *There were good, solid reasons why you did what you did.*

And out there stood a confused man who had never been anything but a good friend to her.

Pulling away from Dimitri, she glared at him. 'I have to go and talk to Chico. I have to explain what is happening,' she said, even though she wasn't entirely sure herself. 'Wait here for me.'

But he caught hold of her wrist, his fingers vice-like against the frantic hammering of her pulse. 'Okay, speak to him if you must—but make it brief. And just make sure you come back, Erin,' he said, his voice cold. 'Because if you try to run away I will find you. Be in no doubt about that.'

She pulled away from him and went to find Chico, trying to explain why there wasn't going to be a wedding, her heart twisting with distress as she saw his face crumple. But by the time she returned to the featureless room where Dimitri was waiting, her distress had turned into anger and she was shaking with rage as she shut the door behind her. 'You had no right to do that!' she flared.

'I had every right,' he said. 'And you know it. And what is more—you didn't fight me very hard, did you? If you don't want a man near you, then you shouldn't kiss him as if you want him to do it to you right then and there.'

'You bastard.'

'Is that what I am, Erin?'

'You know you are!'

'Shouldn't you think very carefully about applying that *particular* word as an insult?'

His loaded words precipitated something—it must have been shock—for why else would her teeth have started chattering so violently? She made one last attempt at rebellion. *He has no real hold over you*, she told herself fiercely. *He's not your guardian or your keeper, or your boss.* 'I'm going now,' she said, meeting his eyes with a defiant stare. 'I want to go home.'

He laughed very softly and the sound filled her with dread.

'Please don't be delusional,' he said. 'We both know you aren't going anywhere—at least not until you and I have had a little talk. So sit down.'

Part of her wanted to object to the masterful way he sat her down on a nearby chair, but in truth she was grateful because her knees felt as if they might give way at any minute. But any feeling of gratitude was soon forgotten when she looked into the determined set of his face. She'd forgotten just how ruthless he could be. How he moved people around as if they were pawns on his own personal chessboard. As his secretary she'd been granted the rare gift of immunity to his whims, because once he had liked her and respected her.

Once.

Sitting huddled in her too-big wedding dress, she stared up at him. 'Now what?'

'Now you tell me all about your Brazilian lover,' he drawled. 'Is he hot between the sheets?'

'He isn't…' She hesitated, wondering how much he already knew. 'Chico isn't my lover—as I suspect you may have worked out for yourself, since he's gay.'

His mouth twisted. 'So it isn't a love match?'

'Hardly.'

'You're marrying a gay man,' he said slowly. 'Who I suspect is paying you for the privilege. Maybe he needs a visa, or a work permit.' His icy eyes glittered. 'Am I right, Erin?'

Did her face give her away? Did guilt wrap itself around her features so that he was able to give the smug smile of someone who'd just had his hunch confirmed?

'And that—as we both know—is against the law,' he continued softly.

Shaking herself out of her stupor, she glared at him, telling herself that attack was the best form of defence. 'Is that why you turned up out of the blue today, to point out the finer points of the law?' She willed herself not to show fear even though inside her heart was pumping like a piston. *Brazen it out*, she told herself. *Just brazen it out*. 'Is that what this is all about, Dimitri—are you about to report me to the authorities?'

Suddenly, his face changed and Erin knew that when he spoke his voice would be different, too. It would be steely and matter-of-fact instead of mocking and casual. He was bored with playing games and was about to cut to the chase. She knew him much too well.

'But you already know the answer to that question, Erin. You've known since the moment you turned round and saw me. You just haven't had the guts to come out and admit it.' In the featureless room with the blinds drawn down to block out the outside world, his eyes glittered like shards of blue ice. 'Or maybe you were intending to keep my son hidden from me for ever— was that your plan?'

CHAPTER TWO

DIMITRI SAW ALL the colour drain from Erin's face and felt a beat of something which felt very close to satisfaction. He watched as she leaned her head back against the wall—as if the weight of her head were too much for that slender neck to support—and looked at him warily, her green eyes slitted. He didn't know what had hurt the most. No, not hurt. He didn't do hurt. Mentally, he corrected himself. What had *angered* him most. The fact that she hadn't told him, or the fact that she had lied to him, when once he would have counted Erin Turner as about the only truly honest person he'd ever known. She was still trying to lie—he could see it in the sudden whitening of her face and the way she was nervously licking her lips. He found himself thinking that she would make a useless poker player.

'Your son?' she said, as if it were a word she'd never heard before.

Her disingenuous question sealed his rage and Dimitri tensed, not daring to respond until he had his emotions under control, because not once in all his turbulent thirty-six years could he ever recall feeling such anger. Not even towards his cheating mother or crooked father. Instinct made him want to lash out at her. To haul her towards him and hurl his accusations straight into her lying face. To ask why *she*—of all people—would have betrayed him. But he had been successful for long enough to know that it was far more effective to hide the edge of anger beneath the velvet cloak of smoothness, even if Erin was one of the few people who would know how angry he really was.

'Oh, come on, Erin,' he said silkily. 'Please don't try to assume the role of innocent, because it insults my intelligence. You should have had an answer to this question by now because you must have been expecting that I would turn up and ask it at some point. Or did you really think I would never find out? Maybe not this year, or even next—but surely you must have anticipated that one day I would be confronting you like this to ask you about your son. *My* son.'

He thought she looked like a textbook study of guilt. She was looking from side to side, like an animal which had been cornered, and it was difficult for Dimitri to reconcile himself with this new version of her. The white-faced woman in the ill-fitting wedding gown was nothing like the Erin he'd known. The smart and straightforward woman who had worked by his side for years, ever since she'd left secretarial college. Who, unlike every other woman on the planet, had never flirted with him and had thus earned his grudging respect. She was the person who'd been given unprecedented access to all areas of his life and affairs. The one person he had trusted above all others. And yes, sleeping with her that one time had been a mistake. Definitely. It had quickly become apparent that things could never be the same between them afterwards—but even so how dared she keep the consequences of that night from him for all these years?

How dared she?

'You aren't going to deny it, are you, Erin?' he continued mockingly. 'Because you can't.'

Her lips opened and she shivered and, powered by an instinct he wasn't sure he recognised, Dimitri removed his jacket and draped it around her narrow shoulders. The suit's grey jacket swamped her and made her complexion look even more waxy than it had been before and his mouth hardened. Was she opening those green eyes as wide as a kitten and thinking he would take pity on her? Because if that was the case—she was wrong.

Very wrong.

There was a tap on the door and a woman poked her head in, before mouthing *sorry* apologetically and withdrawing again.

'Let's get out of here,' he said coldly.

He half lifted her out of the chair and ushered her outside, where a cold blast of autumnal air cut right through her and Erin was aware of people turning to stare as if the tall, molten-haired man were abducting the shivering bride. Instantly, a sleek black limousine purred to a halt in front of them and Dimitri opened up the door and bundled her inside. Sliding onto the seat beside her, he gave a peremptory tap on the window and the car began to move away.

'Where are we going?' she questioned, looking around her in alarm. 'Where are you taking me?'

'Cut the dramatics,' he snapped. 'We need to have a conversation, so it's your place or mine. Up to you.'

His words were greeted with the expression of someone who had just been offered a choice of two poisons to drink, for she bit her bottom lip, bringing a little colour to its plump fullness. And suddenly Dimitri found himself remembering the way he'd kissed her in the register office—a kiss born out of rage and a desire to take control. A kiss intended to show young Chico exactly who was boss—as if any such demonstration were really needed. But it hadn't worked out quite as he'd intended, had it? He hadn't meant it to kick-start his libido, but it had. And despite his rage and disbelief, it was as much as he could do not to kiss her again. To pull her into his arms and feel that ripe, young body close to his, opening up like a flower. He'd forgotten just how instantly she went up in flames the moment he touched her. How her fairly commonplace exterior hid a powerful sexuality, which was both unexpected and surprising.

He could see her swallowing—the movement rippling down that swanlike neck of hers. And he could hear the note of anxiety which had entered her voice.

'Why can't we just have the conversation here?'

'I think you know the answer to that, Erin. Apart from wanting complete privacy—and my driver speaks perfect English as well as Russian—I don't think I trust myself to be in such a confined space with you when we are discussing something which I'm still having difficulty getting my head round.' His voice lowered into a harsh rasp. 'Discovering that I have a son and that you have kept him hidden from me for all these years is bad enough and I might be tempted into doing something which I might later regret. So you'd better make up your mind about where we're going, or I'll be forced to make the decision for you.'

Erin pulled the jacket closer around her shoulders—grateful for the warmth but wishing that the expensive cloth were not permeated with Dimitri's distinctive scent. She was trapped—in every which way. She didn't want to take him to the home she shared with Leo and her sister, Tara. Not because she was ashamed of the rather humble dwelling. No, the truth was more worrying than that. She was terrified of him seeing Leo. Afraid he might just take command and grab the child—stealing him away from her and thinking he was perfectly entitled to. Because mightn't she attempt something similar if the situation were reversed? If she'd discovered that someone had kept her flesh and blood hidden from her like some kind of guilty secret for all these years?

A feeling of despair washed over her as she contemplated what lay ahead, knowing that further lies and evasion were pointless. And besides, hadn't this been a long time coming? How many times over the years had she picked up the telephone to tell him about the blue-eyed little boy who was his spitting image? Hadn't her heart sometimes burned with the pain of denying her boy access to his father? Until she had forced herself to remember the truth about the man and his appalling lifestyle.

She remembered the hours he'd spent in nightclubs and bars and casinos, gambling away millions of rubles as if they were nothing but loose change, in a vodka- or whisky-induced haze. She remembered all the women who had passed through his bed—the ones with the tiny dresses and tottering heels who exuded a dangerous kind of glamour, along with the occasional flash of their knickers. She certainly didn't want her son growing up to think those kind of women were the norm. Who was to say that the seedy world Dimitri inhabited wouldn't corrupt her golden-haired boy and introduce him to some unspeakable future?

She remembered his coldness towards her the morning after she'd slept with him—his shocked face when he'd opened his eyes and seen who was lying beside him. With her brown hair and narrow build she must have seemed like a different species from the blowsy women he usually bedded. No wonder he hadn't been able to wait to get away from her.

'We'd better go to your place, I suppose,' she said, her voice filled with resignation.

His mouth hardened as he rapped on the window and spoke to the driver in his native tongue, and the car took a left, travelling towards the dockland area of the city.

Erin waited for his interrogation to begin, but when Dimitri took a phone call and began what was clearly a business conversation in his native Russian, she was momentarily perplexed. Until she remembered that his ability to switch on and off was legendary. And he was manipulative—that was one of the reasons he was so frighteningly successful. Right now, he would have realised that by leaving her to stew he would only increase her feelings of insecurity and put him in an even stronger position. His clever mind would be carefully stockpiling a series of questions, but he would ask them only in his time, and on his terms.

And really, there was only one question which she was going to have difficulty answering...

The car took them to his skyscraper apartment overlooking the river and Erin was filled with a horrible feeling of déjà vu as they walked into the magnificent marbled foyer, with its forest of tall, potted palms—behind which sat one of the burly porters who were all ju-jitsu trained. Sometimes she used to come here to take dictation if her boss was getting ready to go abroad, and it was a place she had always liked—a coldly magnificent apartment which was worlds away from her own rented home. She'd liked the river view and the fact that you could push a button and the blinds would float down, or another button would send music drifting out from one of the many speakers. She'd liked pretty much everything about it until the night when she'd overstepped the mark. When she'd offered him comfort during the one time she'd seen Dimitri looking vulnerable.

And he'd responded by taking her virginity on his vast dining-room table, tearing off her panties like a man possessed and making that almost *feral* moan as he drove deep inside her.

She could see the porter looking her up and down as she stepped out of the revolving door in her badly fitting white dress, with Dimitri's jacket hanging around her shoulders. Briefly, she felt like some sort of crazy woman, especially when he propelled her into the waiting elevator at great speed.

'Hurry up,' he said as he pressed the button for the penthouse elevator. 'I don't want my reputation being trashed by being seen with a woman in a second-hand wedding dress.'

'I didn't think it was possible for your reputation to sink any lower!'

Pale eyes swept over her. 'You might be surprised how out of touch you are,' he said mockingly.

'I doubt it,' she spat back.

But as the elevator gathered speed Erin knew she had to forget the past and concentrate on the present.

She had to think about the situation as it *was*, not what it used to be. If only she hadn't allowed her feelings for him to ruin everything. If only she hadn't started entertaining romantic fantasies about him—when she knew better than anyone that grand passion brought with it nothing but disillusionment.

She bunched up the material of her white dress as he unlocked his apartment and stood aside to let her pass, and she couldn't work out whether to be happy or sad when she noticed that very little had changed. The vast, wooden-floored entrance hall still provided the perfect backdrop for all the Russian artefacts which were everywhere. The Fabergé eggs he collected were displayed in a casual grouping, which only seemed to emphasise their priceless beauty. There was one in particular which she used to love—a perfect golden sphere studded with emeralds and rubies, which seemed to mock her now as it sparkled in the autumn sunlight.

'Come with me,' he said, as if he didn't trust her to be out of his sight for a second.

He walked into the main reception—a room dominated by a panoramic view over the river and the glittering skyscrapers which housed much of the city's wealth. Yet it was the room itself which drew the eye as much as the view. He had always kept bonsai trees—exquisite miniature trees which experts came in weekly to tend. Sitting on a polished table was a Japanese Acer—its tiny leaves the bright red colour of a sunset. Erin stared at it with the delight of someone encountering an old friend. How she had always loved that little tree.

But as she glanced up from the vibrant leaves she saw in Dimitri's eyes the unmistakable flicker of fury.

'So. Start explaining,' he bit out.

Her knees had suddenly gone wobbly and she sat down on one of the leather sofas, even though he hadn't asked her to—terrified of appearing weak when she knew it was vital to stay strong. She looked up into his face and tried to keep her voice steady. 'I don't think it needs very much of an explanation, do you? You are as aware of the facts as I am. We spent that night together...'

Her words trailed off because it still felt faintly unbelievable that she'd ended up in his bed, when he could have had any woman on the planet. And yes, she'd found him attractive—in the way that you sometimes looked at the ocean and were rendered speechless by its power and beauty. Erin certainly hadn't been immune to the carved symmetry of Dimitri's proud Russian features, or the hair which gleamed like dark gold. There probably wasn't a woman alive who wouldn't have looked twice at his powerful body or admired his clever mind or the way a rare flash of humour could sometimes lighten his cold face. But she had never let her admiration show, because that was unprofessional—and she was pragmatic enough to know that she was the kind of woman he would never find attractive, even if she hadn't been his secretary.

She had worked for him for years. He'd plucked her from a lowly job within his organisation—mainly, she suspected, because she didn't go into instant meltdown whenever he came into the room. She had trained herself not to be affected by his sex appeal and a charisma undimmed by his haughty arrogance. She'd tried to treat him as she would treat anyone else, with dignity and respect. She had been calm and capable in the face of any storm—he'd told her that often enough. Soon he'd started giving her more and more responsibility until gradually the job had begun to take over her life, so that she'd had little left of her own. Maybe it was always that way when you worked for a powerful oligarch, with fingers in so many pies that he could have done with an extra pair of hands. She'd lost count of the times when she'd had to take a call from him during a dinner date, or miss the second half of a film because Dimitri had been flying in from Russia and needed her.

And she'd liked that feeling of being needed, hadn't she? She'd liked the fact that such a powerful man used to listen to *her*—plain, ordinary Erin Turner. Maybe her ego was bigger than she'd given it credit for. Maybe it was that same ego which was responsible for allowing her feelings to slip from the consummate professional to being a woman with a stupid crush, despite her increasing awareness of the murkier side of her boss's life. She began to nurture feelings about him which were unaffected by his gambling and clubbing and drinking and women. And those feelings began to grow.

She used to watch in mild horror from the sidelines as he played the part of the wild oligarch as if it were going out of fashion—as if he'd needed to prove something to the world, and to himself. There had been luxury yachts and private jets stopping off at Mediterranean fleshpots and Caribbean islands—always with some supermodel hanging on to his arm like a limpet. He'd mixed with empty-eyed men with faces even harder than his own. His hangovers had been legendary. He'd been…reckless—embracing life in the fast lane with a hunger and a speed which had seemed to be getting more and more out of control. Even his trusted bodyguard, Loukas Sarantos, had ended up resigning in frustration as Erin had looked on in despair. She remembered ringing up Loukas in desperation after he'd left—and the terrible bust-up in Paris which had followed.

Had it been her growing feelings for Dimitri which had made her start watching out for him, above and beyond the call of duty? Why she'd gone round to his apartment one dark and rainy night, a stack of papers beneath her arm—worried because he hadn't been answering his phone and she'd been imagining the worst?

She remembered that her hand had been shaking as she'd rung the doorbell and had started shaking even more when he'd answered the door wearing nothing but a tiny towel, his bronzed body still damp and gleaming from the shower. Erin had been so relieved to see him that she'd been struck dumb, until it had dawned on her that he was almost naked. And that his face was dark and unsmiling.

'Yes?' he said impatiently. 'What is it, Erin?'

Even now she could remember the hard pounding of her heart. 'I've…er… I've brought some papers for you to sign.'

He frowned as he began to walk towards the dining room and made an impatient indication that she follow him. 'Couldn't they have waited until the morning?'

Faced with the sight of her powerful and very sexy boss wearing nothing but a tiny towel was playing havoc with her breathing, but Erin remembered looking at him very steadily as she put the papers down on the table.

'Actually, I was worried about you.'

'And what precisely were you worried about?'

'You haven't been answering your phone.'

'So?'

Painfully aware of his proximity and the heat of

his body, Erin was struck dumb. She'd planned to say something on the lines of wishing he wouldn't keep such dangerous company, but the only thing she could think of right then was the danger of being alone with him like this.

She wondered if something in her expression gave away the desire which was shooting through her. Or whether it was the way she nervously licked her lips which made his body tense like that. His eyes seemed drawn to the involuntary movement of her tongue and then he nodded, like someone doing a complicated mathematical puzzle and coming up with a totally unexpected answer.

'Oh, I see,' he said, his lips curving into a predatory smile. 'And there was me thinking you were the one woman who was immune to my charms, Erin.'

She didn't even get a chance to object to his arrogance because without warning he gave a low laugh and pulled her against him—his lips covering hers in a hard kiss, as if he was trying out a new kind of sport. And Erin dissolved because she'd never been kissed like that before. Never. Within seconds of that kiss, she was so aroused that she barely noticed that the towel had slipped from his hips. It was only when her hand slipped down his back to encounter the rocky globe of a bare buttock that her eyes snapped open as she stared into his.

'Shocked?' he drawled.

'N-no.'

'I think you want me,' he said unevenly as he began to unbutton her jacket. 'Do you want me, *zvezda moya*?'

Did the sun rise every morning?

Of *course* she wanted him.

Erin gasped with hunger and delight as he pulled the navy jacket impatiently from her shoulders and un-clipped the matching pencil skirt so that it slid to the ground.

She thought he might carry her into the bedroom, the way he'd done so often in her wilder fantasies. But instead he laid her out on the dining-room table—like some kind of sacrificial offering—and things happened very quickly after that. He started tearing hungrily at her underwear and she was shocked by how much she *liked* that, writhing her hips in silent hunger as she urged him on. She had vague memories of him put-ting on a condom and making some remark about how aroused she was making him feel. And then he thrust deep inside her and it wasn't a dream, or a fantasy—it was really happening.

She had been a virgin, but he didn't mention it—and neither did she. She wasn't even sure he'd noticed. And it hadn't hurt the way people warned you it might—maybe because she wanted him so much. All she knew was that she'd never seen Dimitri looking quite so out of control. As if the universe could have exploded around them and he wouldn't have paid it a blind bit of attention.

She remembered that first urgent thrust—as if he'd wanted to lose something of himself deep inside her. And hadn't she felt exactly the same? As if her whole life had been spent in preparation for that moment. She remembered the way she'd shuddered with pleasure, or-gasming not once, but twice, in rapid succession. And he had laughed—softly and triumphantly—running his fingertip over her trembling lips and telling her that she handled better than any of his cars.

'Yes, we spent the night together,' he said impatiently, completing her sentence, and Erin blinked as Dimitri's voice shattered her erotic memories. She came back to the present with a start—to the cheap wedding dress and the unforgiving coldness of his face as he paced around his vast apartment.

'We had a night of sex which should never have happened,' he continued harshly. 'I thought we both decided that. That it had been a mistake.'

Erin nodded. That was what he had said the morning after, and she'd felt there had been no choice but to agree. What else could she have done—clung to his naked body and begged him to stay with her and do it to her all over again? Told him that she wanted to care for him and save him, and keep him safe from the awful world he inhabited? She remembered the bedcovers falling away from her breasts and the sombre look which had come over his face. The way he'd suddenly got out of bed, as if he hadn't been able to wait to get away from her. His final words had killed off any hopes she might have had for a repeat. 'I'm not the kind of man you need, Erin,' he'd said abruptly. 'Go and find yourself someone nice and kind. Someone who will treat you the way you should be treated.'

After that, dignity had seemed the only way forward, especially when he'd left the country the next day and kept communication brief and unemotional during the weeks which had followed.

'And we used a condom,' he said, his brow furrowing and his lips flattening into a scowl. 'I always do.'

His words seemed intended to remind her that she was just one of many and Erin looked at him, her clasped hands feeling sticky as she buried them within the folds of her wedding dress. 'I know we did,' she said.

'I never wanted a child,' he added bitterly.

She knew that, too. He'd made no secret of his thoughts about marriage and childhood. That marriage was an expensive waste of time and some people were never cut out for parenthood. Was that one of the reasons why she'd balked at telling him about her pregnancy—terrified he would try to prevent her from having his baby? She remembered going round to his apartment, sick with dread at the thought of blurting out her momentous news—and what she had found there had made her turn around and never go back…

But his condemnatory words were bringing something to life inside her and that something was a mother's protective instinct. She thought of Leo's innocent face—all flushed and warm after his evening bath—and a feeling of strength washed over her. 'Then pretend you don't have a child,' she said fiercely. 'Pretend that nothing has changed, because I have no intention of forcing something on you which you don't want. You can walk away and forget you ever found out. Leave me with our son and don't let it trouble your conscience. Leo and I can manage perfectly well on our own.'

Erin saw something which almost looked like *pleasure* flickering in his icy eyes and she remembered that dissent was something he was used to dealing with. Something he seemed almost to *enjoy*. Because dissent implied battle and Dimitri Makarov always won the battles he fought.

'You can manage perfectly well?' he questioned softly.

'Yes,' she said, aware on some level that she was walking into a trap, but not knowing exactly where that trap lay.

'So how come I found you standing in a cheap wedding dress, about to break the law?'

She licked her lips but didn't answer.

'Why, Erin?'

'I had my reasons.'

'And I want to hear them.'

She hesitated, knowing she could procrastinate no longer. 'Leo and I live with my sister. She owns a café in Bow.'

'I know that.'

Had her face registered her shock and surprise? 'How could you possibly know that?'

'I had some of my people investigate you.'

'You had *what*? Why?' She could hear her voice beginning to tremble. 'Why would you do something like that?'

'Because of the child, of course.' His pale eyes narrowed into icy shards. 'Why else?'

'How did you find out about Leo?'

'The means are irrelevant,' he snapped. 'Just accept that I did. Now, where were we?'

Her heart sinking, she stared at him, knowing that she was trapped. 'Leo goes to a local school and he's doing very well, but…'

He bit out the words like bullets. 'But what?'

She tried to keep the fear from her voice. The fear that she wasn't doing the best for the golden child who had inherited so many of his father's qualities.

'He's good at sport and there just aren't the facilities where we live. The nearest park is a good bus ride away and Tara and I are often too busy working in the café to take him. You remember Tara? She's my sister.'

'I remember,' he said tightly.

She drew in a deep breath, hoping to see some softening or understanding on the granite features, but there was none. And suddenly she wanted him to understand that there were reasons why she'd agreed to the marriage today. Good reasons. 'Chico comes from a rich family in Brazil and wants to stay in England. He offered me a large sum of money to marry him, so that he could get a work permit. I was planning on using the money to resettle. To…to take Leo to the countryside and live somewhere with a garden. Somewhere he could kick a ball around and get plenty of fresh air and exercise. I… I want him to have that kind of life.'

Still his face showed no sign of reaction as he walked over to the large fireplace and pressed a bell recessed into the wall beside it. Moments later, a young woman appeared—a beautiful, cool blonde. Of course she was blonde. Every woman in the Russian's life, bar Erin, was fair—sporting every shade in the spectrum from spun gold to moonbeam pale, because Dimitri needed blondes in the same way other men needed to breathe. Her flaxen hair was cut into a soft bob and her high cheekbones marked her out as Slavic, so it came as no surprise when Dimitri spoke to her in Russian. She glanced briefly over at Erin and nodded, before turning on her high-heeled shoes and leaving the room again.

Still Dimitri said nothing and in a way his silence was far more intimidating than if he'd continued to subject her to a barrage of angry questions. Would she ever be able to convince him that she'd tried to act in everyone's best interests?

Erin was surprised when the blonde returned a few minutes later, carrying a pair of jeans and a cashmere sweater over her arm. She walked across the room and, placing them on the table in front of her, she smiled.

'I think they will fit you,' she said, her cut-glass English accent seeming to contradict the fluent Russian she'd used moments before. 'But I have a belt you can use if the jeans are too big.'

'*Spasiba*, Sofia,' growled Dimitri, watching as the blonde left the room with that same confident wiggle.

Erin stared at the clothes. 'What are these for?'

'What do they look like they're for? Sofia is lending you some of her own clothes,' he said. 'Put them on. I'm taking you home and I want as few people as possible seeing you. A woman leaving my apartment wearing a wedding dress would be bound to get the press excited, and I make a point of steering clear of the newspapers these days.'

Erin narrowed her eyes. Was that why he hadn't featured in any of his famous post-nightclub shots with a half-clothed woman in tow recently? Was he getting better at hiding his seedy lifestyle?

She felt like refusing his autocratic demand to wear someone else's clothes but she was cold now and she was starting to shiver. Maybe it was reaction. 'Okay, I'll put the jeans on,' she said, from between chattering teeth. 'But I don't need you to take me home afterwards. I'm perfectly capable of catching the bus.'

'I don't think you quite understand the situation, Erin,' he said coldly. 'Unless you are trying to be coy, thinking I might take pity on you and let you go. Because that's not going to happen. So let me spell it out for you, so that you get the message loud and clear.' His eyes glittered like early-morning sun on ice. 'I am taking you home so that I can meet my son.'

CHAPTER THREE

'YOU CAN'T,' SAID Erin fervently as the limousine gathered speed, and she turned to look at Dimitri, who was sitting like some granite-faced sentry in the back seat beside her. Sofia's designer jeans were indeed too big but the baby-blue sweater hugged her nicely and now she was warmer she felt more in control. She made one last attempt to appeal to the Russian's better nature, even if deep in her heart she knew he didn't have one. 'You can't just turn up out of the blue and introduce yourself to a six-year-old boy and tell him you're his long-lost father.'

'Just watch me,' he said grimly.

Erin heard the harsh note in his voice and was reminded of his fierce reputation. Not that he had minded. He always maintained that a fierce reputation kept fools at a distance and for a long time she had been flattered by that statement and its implication. Because *she* had been one of the few people he'd allowed to get close to him—and hadn't that made her think she meant more to him than she actually did? Oh, the foolish longings of a rich man's secretary!

'Think about it, Dimitri,' she said quietly.

'What do you think I've been doing?' he demanded.

'I've done nothing but think about it since I was first shown a photograph of the boy.'

'And when was that?'

'Seven days ago,' he snapped.

She nodded, determined not to let him sweep her aside with the force of his anger, knowing she had to fight her little boy's corner here. For his sake. For all their sakes. 'Leo doesn't know you—'

'And whose fault is that?'

A wave of remorse washed over her and suddenly her decision didn't seem quite so clear-cut. Because Dimitri *did* seem different. The clear-eyed man in the pristine suit was light years away from the stubble-jawed and hungover man who used to arrive at the office demanding strong coffee. 'Mine,' she admitted. 'But I did it with the best intentions.'

'I don't care about your intentions, Erin,' he said, his voice dipping. 'I just care about what is mine. And this child is my flesh and blood, too, not just yours.'

His unashamed possessiveness sent a ripple of alarm through her and Erin recognised that once a piece of information was out there, you couldn't get it back. And you couldn't control the outcome, either. Dimitri was here and—judging from the grim expression on his face—he was here to stay.

'If you really care about him,' she said, 'then you must take it slowly. Imagine how it would feel if you suddenly exploded into his life without warning.'

'You should have considered that before, shouldn't you?'

The car drew up in front of a set of red traffic lights and a man on a bike raced past them, using the inside lane. Erin listened to the blare of horns which greeted the cyclist's action as she thought how best to get Dimitri to see sense. He liked facts, didn't he? Hard, cold facts. *So present them to him.*

She sucked in a deep breath. 'You always used to say you had no desire to be a father.'

'Given the choice,' came his flat response. 'Which I haven't been.'

'And what if that's still true? You might meet him and wish you never had. It might reinforce all the worst things you ever thought about fatherhood. And if that were the case, wouldn't it be hard for you to walk away and even harder for him to pretend that the meeting had never happened?'

Dimitri's lips tightened as her words struck an unwanted chord, thinking how well she knew him—better perhaps than anyone else. What if he met the child, but could not meet the boy's expectations? What if the boy wanted love from him—real love—and commitment? Could he take that risk, knowing that he could provide none of those things?

'What are you suggesting?' he demanded.

She met his gaze without flinching. 'I don't know you any more. I have to be sure that you're no longer the man you used to be. You have to convince me that you've changed. I don't want Leo mixing with gamblers or heavy drinkers, or witnessing a stream of women parading their bodies in front of him.'

His mouth twisted. 'You mean you want to vet me?'

'Can you blame me?' she retorted. 'But we also need to discuss what to say to him. If you're going to meet Leo after all this time, we need to present a united front.'

Dimitri felt his body tense as she stated her demands.

As if what *she* wanted was the only thing which mattered. There was no sense of remorse that she'd kept this information from him for so long, was there? Not a flicker of it...

Anger bubbled up inside him and suddenly he felt the need to lash out. Without thinking, he caught hold of her arms—thinking how slim they felt beneath the borrowed sweater. She jerked her head back in surprise so that the light caught the cheap, fake pearls which were woven into her hair. Her lips were parted, her green eyes were dark and, although her face was wary, he realised that she still wanted him. That in the midst of everything, there was desire. Of course there was. No female remained immune to him for long. He could feel sexual hunger pulsating in the air around them as his gaze flickered to the twin thrust of her nipples pinpointing against the soft wool of the sweater. He thought how easy it would be to burrow his hands beneath. To caress those hard little nubs with the skill which could sometimes make a woman come, just by doing that. For a nanosecond he was tempted beyond measure, his fingers longing to creep over those tiny mounds and play with them.

Until he remembered that this was the woman who had deliberately concealed his son from him. Who had written him out of her life as if he no longer existed. How could he possibly desire a woman like that? Abruptly, he dropped his hands, wondering if she was aware that disappointment was written all over her face as he did so. A flicker of triumph coursed through him as she bit her lip and he took a moment to enjoy her obvious frustration.

'So what were you planning to do after your wedding?' he questioned. 'Were you coming back here to the café with your new husband to parade your shiny new ring for all to see?'

'No. We'd...we'd planned to spend a long weekend at a hotel in the country. Chico took my suitcase down there yesterday.'

'For your *honeymoon*?' he scorned.

'I suppose you could call it that. It was intended to make our marriage seem more authentic to the authorities, that was all.'

'So Leo knows about the wedding?'

There was silence for a moment. 'Of course he does,' she said. 'He likes Chico. We were... We were all going to live together in a lovely house in the country.'

'A fake marriage to a gay man—with separate rooms, I presume?' he said. 'How the hell was that supposed to work?'

'We would have *made* it work,' she defended. 'I was thinking about Leo's future. About giving him the financial security I could never guarantee him!'

'What kind of example is that to set for a child?' he demanded bitterly, because he was discovering a nerve which was still raw, even after all these years. 'Basing your life on lies and deception?'

Nervously, she glanced out of the window. 'I don't want to talk about it any more. At least, not now,' she said, her voice growing strained. 'Because we're nearly there.'

He followed the direction of her gaze to the grey, treeless streets outside. 'And will my son be there?'

She flinched a little, as if it hurt to hear him use the possessive phrase. Well, *tough*, he thought grimly. She was going to have to get used to a lot more than that.

'No. He'll still be at school. He won't be back for a couple of hours.'

Dimitri flexed his fingers as he forced himself to think about practicalities, because he could see that she was right. He couldn't just burst in, unannounced—and although it went against his every instinct, he could see that the process should be gradual. Yet his discovery about the boy could not have come at a worse time, because he was due to travel to Jazratan tomorrow, for some delicate end-stage negotiations with the Sheikh of that oil-rich land. It was a deal which had been a long time in the making, and Saladin Al Mektala was not a man whose presence you could postpone. But Dimitri recognised suddenly that this discovery was more important than any deal—and the realisation surprised him almost as much as the unexpected twist of his heart when he thought of his unknown son. Because he was a man who put business above everything— who never allowed his personal life to intrude on his material ambitions.

He glanced at Erin, but she wasn't looking at him. Her head was bent and the fake pearls were glinting in her dark hair. He guessed he could start getting to know Leo when he returned from his desert trip, but he was reluctant to let her out of his sight. What if she disappeared while he was away, taking Leo with her? If she was determined for him not to meet his son, he wouldn't put it past her. He wouldn't put anything past her.

Unless… Restlessly, he tapped his finger against one taut thigh as he began to sift through all the options which lay open to him and the germ of an idea came to him. It wasn't perfect, but it was simple—if he could persuade her to accept it. His mouth hardened, knowing he would make her accept it, whether she liked it or not.

'So if the wedding is off and you were due to go away for the weekend, then Leo won't be expecting you home?' he said.

'N-no,' she answered uncertainly, as if sensing a trap.

'Then listen to me very carefully, Erin—because this is what you are going to do. You will go and pack yourself another bag.'

She stilled. 'What for?'

'Think about it. You said that you needed to get to know me and that we needed to present a united front when I meet Leo—so that's exactly what we're going to do. As it happens, I'm booked to go to Jazratan this weekend to stay at the royal palace—'

'Not with the horse-mad Sheikh?'

Her instant recall of his business dealings made him give a reluctant nod of satisfaction. 'That's the one.'

'You're not still trying to buy some of his oil wells?'

'Indeed I am. And I am this close…' he held up his thumb and forefinger, with a distance of an inch between them '…to succeeding. Which is why the trip cannot be cancelled—and why you will be accompanying me.'

'Me?' Her voice was a squeak as her hands tightened into balled fists. 'Why on earth would I come with you to Jazratan?'

'Why not? It will provide us with the space we need. I'll have to run it past the Sheikh's advisors first, but I can foresee no problem. You were the best secretary I've ever had and you've worked on some of the negotiations with me in the past. I can say that I want you beside me if and when I sign the biggest deal of my life.'

She stared at him. 'Are you...*out of your mind*?'

Abruptly, his mood seemed to change. Gone was the element of negotiation and in its place was a steely determination she recognised only too well.

'No, I am not out of my mind,' he iced back. 'I am trying to work out a solution and I am fighting every instinct I possess not to go in there and tell that little boy the truth. To tell him that not only is his mother a liar, but that she has kept me completely out of the loop. I don't think the courts look very favourably on that kind of behaviour these days. A mother denying her child access to his father is seen as selfish, not noble—and gone are the days when a father has no rights. So are you going to accept my suggestion, Erin—or are you going to waste time by arguing with me, when we both know I always get what I want in the end?'

Yes, he did.

Always.

Erin tried to get her head around his words. *Accompany him to Jazratan, to stay in a desert palace?*

He couldn't force her...yet if she turned him down, her refusal to cooperate would surely impact on Leo. Her gaze strayed to his stony profile and she saw a nerve flickering at his temple—an indication he had reached the limit of his patience, a quality for which he had never been renowned. And she knew he was right. There was no point in fighting him. Because he *would* win.

'It seems I have no choice,' she said.

He smiled, but the smile didn't touch his eyes. 'That is possibly the first sensible thing you've said all day,' he said. 'So go and get your stuff together and explain to your sister that there's been a change of plan.' He pulled a card from his pocket and handed it to her. 'This is my private number. She can contact you via this should the need arise while we're away.'

Erin took the card from him as the limousine drew up at the end of her road and thoughts of escape overwhelmed her as she reached for the door handle. What if he turned up at the appointed time and she and Leo weren't there—he would have to leave for Jazratan without her, wouldn't he?

But almost as if he'd read her mind, he reached out and caught hold of her and Erin could feel her pulse rocketing as his fingers curled over her wrist.

'This is going to happen, make no mistake. So don't keep me waiting and don't even think about running away,' he said softly. 'You have precisely one hour and then my car will return for you. Do you understand?'

Erin was still shaking as she watched him drive away, taking a moment to compose herself as she pushed open the door of the Oranges & Lemons café, which her sister had named after a famous nursery rhyme about the church bells of London. It was a bright and cheerful place, decorated with framed paintings of the fruits done by local children, and usually Erin enjoyed that first explosion of colour whenever she walked in. But today all she could think about were a pair of icy eyes and the harsh words Dimitri had spoken to her.

Her sister, Tara, was polishing glasses behind the counter and she looked up in surprise when she saw her, blinking behind her owl-like glasses.

'Erin! What on earth are you doing here? You look terrible,' she added before lowering her voice, even though there were hardly any customers around. 'Did something happen? Did it…' She hesitated, her face twisting with a funny kind of expression. 'Did the wedding all go off as planned?'

'No,' said Erin flatly. 'It didn't.'

Tara stared. 'Whose clothes are you wearing?'

For a minute Erin didn't know what her sister was talking about and then looked down and realised she was wearing another woman's sweater and a pair of jeans which didn't fit her properly. 'It's a long story,' she said and then, stupidly, her voice began to wobble and for one awful moment she thought she was about to cry. She swallowed, because she wasn't going to do that. She mustn't do that. Staying calm needed to be her focus, not making stupid displays of unnecessary emotion. She drew a deep breath and tried to make her voice sound as bland as if she were announcing what was showing on TV that night. 'Dimitri Makarov turned up.'

Tara's face blanched. 'He actually *turned up*?'

'That's right. He—'

'For God's sake.' Tara put the glass down with a hand which was far from steady. 'Come round here and sit down. I'll make you a coffee.'

'I don't want any coffee.' But Erin walked behind the bar all the same and noticed that Tara was making her a cup anyway. She watched her grinding beans and driving steam into the small cup, and forced herself to take a sip of the espresso which was pushed firmly along the counter towards her.

'So, what happened?' asked Tara.

Briefly, Erin explained—though it sounded like the plot of an old film as she recounted how Dimitri had stormed in to halt the wedding, before taking her back to his place to lay down the law.

'He did that?' questioned Tara shakily.

'He did.' Erin's voice was grim. 'He wants to see Leo. He wants to get to know him.' And suddenly it wasn't quite so easy to stay focused. Suddenly, it was all too easy to see how problematic this was going to be. 'He's coming back in an hour and he wants me packed and ready.'

'Packed and ready for what?'

'You're not going to believe me if I tell you.'

'Try me.'

Erin wriggled shoulders which were stiff with tension. 'He's taking me to Jazratan. It's a country in the Middle East—one of the richest of the desert states, as it happens. He thinks we ought to get to know each other better before he's introduced to Leo.'

Tara frowned. 'And what's that supposed to mean?'

'I *don't know*.' Beads of sweat broke out on Erin's brow and she brushed them away with the back of her hand. She told herself she didn't have to do anything she didn't want to. But that was the trouble. With Dimitri it wasn't that simple—nothing ever was. Whenever she looked at him she started thinking about things which were forbidden. Things she was never going to have. Things she didn't even believe in. And she'd made that mistake once before. She'd thought she'd been in love when she'd woken up in his bed that morning and look where it had got her. His look of shock and horror had stripped away all her stupid delusions. Her *grand passion* had gone the way of all grand passions—it had burnt itself out before it had even had the chance to get started. It had reinforced everything she'd always known about letting your heart rule your head—and no way was she going to repeat that mistake. Her life hadn't been easy since she'd handed in her notice—but at least she hadn't had to live with the unbearable pain of heartbreak.

She pushed away her cup before looking up at her sister with bewildered eyes. 'The only thing I can't work out is how he found out about the wedding.'

There was a pause, and when Tara spoke it was in a voice Erin didn't recognise.

'I told him.'

For the second time that day Erin's heart felt as if it had been crushed by an iron fist. For a moment she just sat there frozen with shock, before her breath exploded from her mouth. 'You told him?' she echoed. 'You told Dimitri about the wedding? *You?*'

'Yes,' said Tara.

'What, you just tracked him down and phoned him up and announced that he had a son?'

'He was easy enough to find—he owns half of London, for heaven's sake! Getting through to him was the tricky part but once I mentioned your name, he took the call straight away. But I didn't say anything about Leo, I promise you that, Erin. I just told him you were getting married. I didn't breathe a word about his son.'

'Then how come he knew he had one?'

'*I don't know!*' snapped Tara. 'And before you say anything else—I'm glad I did it. Yes—glad!'

Erin felt sick. Her sister was the closest person she had, next to Leo—the person she would have trusted most in the world—and she had betrayed her to the man she feared most. She had unleashed a powerful secret without knowing where it would take them.

'Why would you be glad about something like that?' she questioned dully.

'You know why,' said Tara softly. 'Because you were

breaking the law by marrying Chico so that he could get a work permit and I was worried about the fallout if that ever got out. Because Dimitri might have changed—and shouldn't you at least give him the chance to show you whether he has? But mainly because Leo...'

Her words tailed off and Erin's head jerked back, anger and hurt blending together to form a potent cocktail of emotion as she stared at her sister.

'Because Leo what?' she questioned coldly.

Tara swallowed. 'Leo deserves to know who his father is. He *does*, Erin. Don't you ever feel guilty that he doesn't even *know*?'

'*Of course I do!*' Erin's hissed words were so fervent that they startled her as much as they evidently startled Tara. 'But life isn't black and white. You know exactly why I did it. I didn't want my son to be brought up in the kind of world which Dimitri inhabits.'

'I didn't hear you objecting when you worked for him.'

Erin didn't answer. No, that much was true. Because she'd loved her job and had been dazzled by the trust he'd placed in her. So she'd turned a blind eye to all the whispers and rumours about the Russian oligarch. Even when her eyes had been opened to the kind of man he really was, even when the scales had fallen away and she'd seen the dark soul at his core, it hadn't made any difference. And wasn't that the worst part of all—that she had wanted to reach out to help clear that darkness away instead of running as fast as she could in the opposite direction? What a fool she'd been. Because all that had happened was that her altruism had been misinterpreted by a man who didn't seem to know what kindness was—and had ended up with them having sex. Sex which had meant nothing to him.

'And he's been getting some very good press lately,' continued Tara. 'I'm sure I read that he's built a laboratory to investigate childhood diseases, somewhere in Russia. In fact, I think he's set up some sort of charitable foundation in his name. Maybe he's a reformed character.'

Erin kicked the tip of her white wedding shoe against the counter and for once Tara didn't object. 'Leopards don't change their spots,' she said flatly. 'Everyone knows that.'

'Maybe they don't,' said Tara quietly. 'But even leopards can adapt—otherwise you wouldn't find them living in zoos.'

'I hate zoos,' said Erin, sliding down from the stool and staring at her sister. 'And I still can't believe you told him.'

'I did it because I love you,' said Tara simply. 'And one day you might even thank me for it.'

With an angry shake of her head, Erin went upstairs to the room she shared with Leo. She'd done her best to smarten it up, with pale walls and rows of books which she encouraged her clever son to read—but the cramped dimensions reminded her that this way of living couldn't continue indefinitely. Her gaze lingered on the framed photos of Leo at various milestones in his life—from chubby and very demanding infant right up to his first day of school, last year. She studied that one the hardest, her eyes scanning his innocent little face— so full of hope and happiness—and her heart clenched with a sense of having completely messed things up.

Kicking off her shoes, she changed into her own

clothes, wondering how she must have appeared to Dimitri after all these years. Had she changed much? She stared into the mirror. Of course she had. Even the most liberal of observers would have described her appearance as bizarre, and nobody had ever accused Dimitri of being liberal.

Her green eyes were fringed with more make-up than usual and her hair was still woven into a complex updo, studded with the fake-pearl pins which she'd bought from the cash-and-carry to try to emphasise her bridal status. All that time spent angsting over her decision and all the trouble she'd gone to, trying to look like a pukka bride—and it had all been over before it had even begun. Viciously, she tugged the pins out, one by one, until her long brown hair floated free and her thoughts were spinning as she began to brush it.

She had to get a grip. She had agreed on a course of action and she was going to stick to it, with as little fuss and emotion as possible. She would accompany the Russian to Jazratan and pretend to be his secretary. The two of them would talk candidly about Leo and maybe Dimitri would realise that having a child just wouldn't fit into his lifestyle. That there was a good reason why he'd never wanted any children of his own.

And was it a terrible thing to admit that a part of her hoped that would be the case? Because wouldn't that be easier all round? No uneasy meetings. No thoughts about the future. No sizzling sexual chemistry. She put the hairbrush down and gave her reflection a defiant stare.

She would handle it.

She had to.

CHAPTER FOUR

FROM WITHIN THE shadowed interior of the car, Dimitri fixed his gaze on the café opposite. He had been tempted to go inside, to discover what his son's world was really like, but had decided against it—despite his uncanny ability to blend into the background when required. His mouth thinned. Russian men were taught from an early age how to lose themselves in the shadows and he had always managed it better than most, despite his distinctively powerful build and the pale blue eyes he had been told were unforgettable.

He could see Tara standing behind the counter, slicing cheese and making sandwiches. He had met Erin's sister only once before, years ago, and she hadn't seemed to approve of him. Maybe that was why he had been so surprised to receive her phone call. She hadn't been particularly friendly as she'd haltingly explained that Erin was getting married the following week. When he'd asked her outright why she was bothering to tell him, she had refused to be drawn further, but her attitude hadn't bothered him. He was used to women disliking him if they felt he'd taken advantage of them, or, in this case, of their beloved sister. But the fact remained that he had done nothing he was ashamed of. He had taken Erin to bed because she had been practically begging him to and because the chemistry between them had been so explosive that night. Who would ever have guessed that his unassuming little secretary would have been so damned *hot*? Or that she had given him the best sex of his life?

But while her allure had surprised him, he had decided against a repeat performance because he remembered the way she'd made him feel when he had opened his eyes to see her lying beside him. He remembered feeling uncomfortable as her shining gaze had met his. Because this was Erin. Erin who knew him better than any other woman. Not someone he'd picked up in a nightclub or at a party, but the woman he spent most of his waking hours with. He had felt naked in more ways than one as she had smiled at him dreamily and something unfamiliar had stabbed at his heart. For the first and only time in his life he had realised he couldn't get away with his usual smooth and meaningless post-conquest dialogue. He had broken the rule of a lifetime of mixing work with pleasure and he should have known better.

But Tara's news about her sister's impending wedding had been underpinned with a note in her voice which had alerted his interest. He began to wonder why she'd told him something so seemingly innocuous, when, presumably, legions of his ex-lovers were going off and getting married all the time. There had been something dark and secretive in her tone. Something which had made him pick up the phone to speak with the security firm he had little need of these days.

'Just take a quiet look at a woman called Erin Turner and see what she's up to,' Dimitri had suggested to the head of the firm.

He remembered the expressionless look on the man's

face when he had walked into his office a few days later with an envelope which contained a clutch of photos. Photos of a child who looked just like him.

Forcing the memory away, he saw Erin standing in the doorway of the café and watched his driver get out of the car to take her suitcase from her. Dimitri watched as she approached and, inexplicably, his heart began to pound.

She had removed most of the heavy eye make-up she'd been wearing for the wedding and, without the elaborate pearl-studded wedding hairstyle, she looked more like the Erin of old. Her faded jeans were unremarkable and so were her beat-up sneakers. She was wearing a forgettable little waterproof jacket, with some ugly fake fur around the collar, and her long brown hair was tied back in a ponytail, which blew wildly in the strong autumn wind.

His groin grew heavy with lust and Dimitri was irritated by his own reaction, because he didn't understand it. She was ordinary. Some people might have said that she made no effort to attract a man. She didn't dress to impress—clothes had never been high on her list of priorities, even when she'd occupied the prestigious position of being his secretary. So why the sudden urge to crush her lips beneath his and to press himself down on that narrow-hipped body? Was it simply a case of anger being a potent aphrodisiac—or was he remembering that her forgettable looks had been forgotten when she'd come alive in his arms?

The driver opened the door and she got in beside him, a chill breeze accompanying her. He wondered if he was imagining her faint look of disappointment when she saw him sitting in the shadows.

'Hoping I might have changed my mind and left you alone?' he questioned silkily.

Clear green eyes met his. 'Yes,' she said quietly. 'Actually, I was.'

'Sorry to disappoint you, *milaya moya*,' he said sarcastically, and his jaw tightened. 'What time does he get home?'

A look of anxiety crossed her face as she glanced down at her watch. 'Soon. In fact, very soon. We ought to get going.'

Dimitri hesitated as a wave of something he didn't recognise washed over him with a fierce kind of power.

'No,' he said. 'Not yet.'

'He mustn't see me,' she said and suddenly her voice sounded urgent. 'He mustn't.'

'He won't,' he clipped back, impatient now. 'If he looks at anything, it will be at the car, not the passengers. If you're that worried, you can slide down the seat so that you're completely out of view.'

'But why?' she questioned. 'Why risk it?'

Why indeed? Even Dimitri was perplexed by his own reaction. Was it just to convince himself it was true—because he was the kind of man who liked to see the evidence with his own eyes? Or because his love of risk wasn't as deeply buried as he'd thought?

He stretched his fingers out and then bent them so that the knuckles cracked and it sounded almost deafening in the close confines of the car. 'We'll wait five minutes,' he said. 'And if he hasn't appeared by then, we'll go.'

He could feel her tension rising as the minutes ticked by. He could see it in the stiff set of her shoulders and he felt a grim kind of pleasure as she began to shift nervously in her seat. Now might she understand how it felt to be powerless?

'Please, Dimitri,' she said.

But then something in her posture changed—softened—it was like a flower opening to the sun. Following the direction of her gaze, he looked out of the window as a little boy ran along the road with an unknown woman trying to keep up behind him, carrying a plastic lunch box in one hand and a flapping piece of paper in the other.

Dimitri froze as he caught a glimpse of the boy's pale eyes and dark golden hair and bizarrely found his mind flashing back to his own childhood. He remembered the professional photo his parents used to insist on being taken every year on his birthday—stiff-looking portraits where nobody was smiling. There hadn't been a lot to smile about, despite the wealth and the lavish home and the servants.

But this little boy...

His heart clenched.

This little boy was *laughing* as he pushed open the door and disappeared inside the café. His features looked so like Dimitri's own and yet they were completely different—transformed by a wave of sheer happiness.

Dimitri swallowed, but that did nothing to shift the dryness in his throat. He had expected to feel nothing but distance when he first saw the child—and hadn't part of him *wanted* that? He knew how much easier it would be if he could just turn his back and walk away from them both. Erin would doubtless be delighted to see the back of him. And even more delighted not to have to endure two days in a strange country with a man who was still so angry with her. He could speak to his bank and arrange to have the child funded until he was eighteen. If he performed well at school or showed some of his father's natural acumen, there was no reason why he shouldn't be given a role within Dimitri's organisation. And if he proved himself worthy, there was no reason why one day he shouldn't inherit some—maybe all—of Dimitri's vast fortune, for he had never planned for himself the traditional route of marriage and fatherhood.

So why was that impartial assessment not happening? Why was there a stab of something deep in his heart which he couldn't quite define? A feeling of pride and possessiveness, like the day when he'd picked up his first super-yacht—only this was stronger. Much, much stronger.

His breathing wasn't quite steady as he pressed a button recessed in the armrest and the car pulled away.

Erin breathed out a sigh of relief as the café began to retreat into the distance. For one awful moment she'd thought that Leo might see her. Come running over and ask why Mummy was back so early and what was she doing in the big, shiny car with that strange man.

She snatched a glance at Dimitri's profile.

'Thank you,' she said quietly.

'For what?' he demanded.

'For not speaking to him.'

He gave a short and bitter laugh. 'What did you expect me to do—rush up and introduce myself? Hi, Leo, I'm your long-lost daddy!'

'Is that what you wanted to do?'

Dimitri didn't answer. His instinct was to tell her that

it was none of her damned business what he wanted to do. But even he could see that it was.

He studied the pale oval of her face and the green eyes, which were surveying him so steadily. 'No, it's not what I wanted,' he said flatly. 'What I really wanted was to convince myself that it was all some kind of bad dream. That I would look at him and realise there had been some kind of mistake—that you just happen to have a penchant for lovers with hard bodies and high cheekbones and that I was just a number in a possible list of fathers.'

'But now?' she said.

His lips hardened and all the arguments which he might have brought against another woman could not, he realised, be applied to Erin. Because the accusation that she had deliberately fallen pregnant in order to trap him could never be levelled against her. She had not come sniffing around his vast fortune—demanding marriage or regular payments for his son. On the contrary, she had done the exact opposite.

'I don't know,' he said suddenly, in as rare and as honest an admission of confusion as he had ever made—something he could only attribute to the shock of being confronted by his own flesh and blood. 'For while the logical part of my brain continues to tell me I have no desire for a child of my own—there is another part...a part which is more powerful. The part programmed by nature to perpetuate the species. To carry my own, unique genes forward into the future.'

Her face contorted, as if she'd just bitten into something very sour.

'Is that all he is to you, Dimitri—a product of your gene pool?'

'How else do you expect me to react?' he demanded. 'You have given me no opportunity to get to know him. You deny me even the knowledge of his existence. What did you imagine I would feel when I found out, Erin? Only, I was never expected to find out, was I, you cold-hearted little bitch? You would have kept it from me until I had drawn the last breath from my body.'

She flinched. 'I don't want this to deteriorate into a slanging match.'

'At this precise moment I don't particularly care what you want, but you *will* hear me out,' he said icily. 'Do you think I approve of the way you've reared my son? To see him making his home in a place like that?'

'Externals aren't everything,' she flared back defensively. 'And at least I managed to bring him up to be happy and healthy.'

'But you could have done much more than *manage*,' he argued. 'You could have come to me for help. A man who was in a position to help you properly—so that you wouldn't have to struggle bringing up my son in an apartment over a *café* and having to make a sham marriage because you needed money.'

His words brought Erin to her senses. What was she *doing*, letting him browbeat her like this? She knew enough of Dimitri to realise that he would take control in any situation if she let him, because that was his default setting. And she couldn't afford to let him. Not over this.

'You know exactly why I didn't come to you,' she said quietly.

'Because I never wanted children?'

'That was one of the reasons. I…' She halted, suddenly at a loss. *What has Tara done?* she thought bitterly. *What serpent has she unleashed here?*

She swallowed as the enormity of her actions came crashing home in a way it had never done before. Or maybe she had just never allowed herself to think about it properly. She tried putting herself in his shoes and imagining how she would feel if the situation were reversed. Like him, she would be spitting mad and hurt and angry. Had her action of not telling him been motivated simply out of protectiveness for Leo, or had she also been protecting her own vulnerable heart?

Yes.

Yes, she had.

His dark world was not one she wanted her son growing up in. She wanted Leo to remain sunny and innocent—not be dark and complicated like his father. Yet as she looked into Dimitri's proud face she thought she saw a flash of something she didn't recognise in the depths of those icy eyes. Something almost…vulnerable. She gave herself a little shake, telling herself that it was a trick of the light. Because that was a mistake she'd made before. The Russian didn't do vulnerable. He did hard and inviolate and proud.

But none of those facts impacted on the way she was currently feeling—an emotion which felt uncomfortably close to guilt.

'I should have told you,' she said slowly.

He gave the ghost of a smile, as if another small battle had been won. 'Why didn't you?'

Erin shook her head. It was difficult to think straight when he was this close. Tara had told her that she'd rung Dimitri because there was the possibility that he might have changed. *But what if he hadn't?* What if his world was as dark and dangerous as before? And suddenly the truth came blurting out—the memory having the power to hurt her, even now.

'But I did try to tell you. Don't you remember?'

His eyes narrowed and he shook his head. 'When?'

'I came round to your home one Saturday morning, because I felt it best to tell you away from the office. It was just over two months since we'd slept together.' She paused to let her words sink in. 'I suppose it was my own fault. If I'd waited until midday, you might have been alone.'

She had been scared, naïve, foolish, hopeful. It had been ten weeks since she'd spent the night with him. Ten weeks since he'd taken her virginity without realising and then acted as if nothing had happened. He had gone away to Russia on business and then on to the United States. She had suspected that he was deliberately putting distance between them. The weeks had drifted by and her contact with him had been limited to the strictly impersonal. To telephone calls and emails. Clearly he regretted that momentary lapse, which had started with an unexpected kiss and had ended with him thrusting into her over his dining-room table.

She thought at first that her period was late because of the stress and the emotion of having broken the professional boundaries by sleeping with her boss. But her aching breasts were not so easy to ignore. And then she'd missed a second period and had done the test— sitting on the floor of her bathroom and staring at it in disbelief. She knew straight away that she had to tell Dimitri, but she had been so confused. And frightened. She'd blocked out thoughts of how he might react, but one thing she had known above all else was that she wanted to keep this baby. And that her feelings for her boss were secondary to that one fundamental truth.

But Dimitri was away travelling and she was aware she couldn't tell him something like that over the phone, or by email. Apart from anything else, she was terrified it might be intercepted or overheard. On escalating tenterhooks, she waited until he flew in and phoned to say he would be back in the office first thing Monday. She tried to blot out the fact that a new distance seemed to have entered his voice, and that he sounded cool when he spoke to her. And that was when she'd known that she couldn't wait a moment longer and she couldn't tell him at work. She would go round to his apartment and tell him face-to-face, because there was never going to be anything like a 'perfect' time to break the news that she was carrying his baby.

She had—foolishly, in retrospect—gone to a lot of trouble with her appearance that morning. She'd washed her hair and applied a little more make-up than usual. She'd put on a dress, because, she remembered, it had been a sunny spring day—but it hadn't been as warm outside as it had looked from the window of her apartment, and she remembered her bare legs being covered in goosebumps. Afterwards she'd wondered whether she had stupidly been hoping for some romantic conclusion to her news. That he would sweep her into his arms and look down at her with shining eyes, and tell her that it was all going to be okay.

Of course she had.

But he had taken ages to answer the door and, when he had, he had been bad-tempered, sleepy and half naked, his icy eyes narrowed and bloodshot, and his hard jaw shadowed with growth.

'What is it, Erin?' he questioned impatiently, zip-ping up his jeans with a slight wince. 'Can't it wait?'

She had walked into his apartment, noting the gen-eral scene of disarray which greeted her. There was an empty champagne bottle lying on the floor and an-other which was half drunk—standing on the same table where he had taken her virginity. Now was probably not the right moment to tell him that he was going to be a daddy, but what choice did she have? Tell him on Monday—trying desperately to squeeze in the unwel-come news between wall-to-wall meetings?

It took her a moment or two to notice the various items of female underwear strewn around the room be-cause she was too busy ogling the lurid cover of what looked like a porn film. She remembered colour flood-ing to her cheeks as she recalled the picture of a woman wearing very little other than a leather thong and wield-ing some sort of whip, with a scary look in her eyes. Erin had little experience of men and what they got up to in their leisure time, but even she could work out what had been going on.

And it was then that a woman had appeared from the bedroom, making Erin feel like the biggest fool in the world, because the woman was completely naked. Her long blonde hair was mussed, her eyes all smudged with mascara and her large breasts jiggled provocatively as she walked into the reception room—completely ig-noring Erin—and pouted at Dimitri.

'Aren't you coming back to bed, *lyubimiy*?'

The fact that she was obviously Russian had only made it worse—if it was possible for such a situation to get any more dire than it already was. Erin saw the expression on Dimitri's face—a mixture of irritation at being interrupted and an unmistakable look of lust, which had automatically darkened his eyes.

'Go back to bed and I'll be there in a minute,' he said, before fixing Erin with an enquiring look. 'So what is it, Erin? What do you want?'

'I...' Erin had been at a loss; her words tailing off until the blonde had wiggled her way back towards the bedroom and she had been momentarily transfixed by the retreating sight of her pale, globe-like buttocks.

'Look.' He paused, as if searching for the right words to say, but of course there *were* no right words. 'I think we both know what happened that night was a mistake and if you were hoping for some kind of repeat—'

'No! No, of course I wasn't,' she said, forcing some stupid, meaningless smile onto her lips as she realised there was only one direction she could contemplate taking. 'I came here to hand in my notice.'

Was that *relief* she saw on his face? Was it?

'You're sure about that?'

Erin nodded. And the fact that he didn't try to talk her out of it spoke volumes. She had fooled herself into thinking she was his indispensable ally—the woman he couldn't do without. And yet she was so wrong. She had become an *embarrassment*, she recognised. The frumpy secretary he'd stupidly bedded in a mad moment when he hadn't been thinking straight. Had he been afraid that she was going to start mooning around after him at the office and becoming a sexual nuisance? Was that why he had uncharacteristically absented himself from England for so long?

'I'd like to leave immediately, if that's okay with you,' she said, as briskly as possible. 'I can easily find someone to step in for me.'

His eyebrows had winged upwards. 'You mean you've had a better offer?'

'Much better,' she lied.

He smiled slightly, as if he understood that. But she guessed he did. Dimitri understood ambition and power and climbing the ladder towards the ever-higher pinnacle of success—it was feelings he was bad at.

But he had made a stab at expressing regret—even if he had done it badly.

'I want you to know that I've…' He shrugged his shoulders and smiled. 'Well, I've enjoyed working with you these past years.'

The easiest thing to have done would have been to have withdrawn gracefully before he probed any further and worked out for himself that there was no other job. Murmured something polite before she walked away for good, so that she could leave on amicable terms. But Erin cared about Dimitri, no matter how much she told herself he didn't deserve it. She had looked into his haunted and sleep-deprived eyes and, although she found herself wishing she could take his unknown pain away, deep down she knew she couldn't save him. He was the only person who could do that. *But didn't she owe him her honesty—if not about her future, then surely about his own? To give him a few home truths, in a way which few other people would ever have dared. To tell him that he might not have a future if he didn't start changing.*

'And I've enjoyed working for you, for the most part,' she said quietly. 'Actually, I used to admire and respect you very much.'

His eyes narrowed, as if he had misheard her. He knitted together the dark eyebrows which contrasted so vividly with the deep gold of his hair. '*Used* to?'

'Sorry to use the past tense,' she said, not sounding sorry at all. 'But it's hard to admire someone who is behaving like an idiot.'

'An *idiot*?' he echoed incredulously.

It hadn't been easy to continue, but she had forced herself to finish what she'd started. 'What else would you call someone who lives the way you do?' she demanded. 'Who goes from day to day on a knife edge, taking all kinds of unnecessary risks? How long do you think your body will survive on too much booze and not enough sleep? How long before your lifestyle impacts on your ability to make razor-sharp business decisions? You're not indestructible, Dimitri—even if you think you are.'

She curled her lips in disgust as she shot the messy room one last withering look—though if he'd been a little more perceptive he might have noticed the distress in her eyes, which had made her start sobbing her heart out the moment she got home to her lovely apartment.

She remembered raising her head from one of the tear-soaked cushions and looking around the luxury home which Dimitri's generous salary had enabled her to rent, knowing that this kind of lifestyle would soon be a thing of the past. Because she wasn't rich and she shouldn't pretend otherwise. She had simply worked for a rich man and now she carried his child beneath her heart while he looked at her with impatient eyes—eager to get back to one of the sexiest women she had ever seen.

'You came round to my apartment and gave me a piece of your mind,' said Dimitri slowly, his voice breaking into her thoughts and bringing Erin right back to the present. To the luxury car heading towards the city and the man whose icy eyes were boring into her. She looked deep into their pale glitter.

'And found you with another woman,' she said.

Dimitri nodded. Yes, she had found him with another woman. Someone whose face he couldn't even remember, let alone her name. There had been a lot of women like that. One beautiful blonde merging into another, like a blurred and naked merry-go-round whirling through his life and his bedroom.

But he did remember the look of disgust on Erin's face and his instinctive fury that she should dare to judge him. What right did *she* have to judge him? She had made out that she was some paragon of virtue—but she hadn't been so damned virtuous when her nails had been raking his naked back and urging him into her sticky warmth, had she? She had certainly blown her goody-two-shoes image right out of the sky *that* night.

But even though he'd told himself he didn't care what Erin Turner thought about him—he'd found himself thinking about the things she'd said. And there had been a lot of time to consider them during those fruitless months spent seeking a replacement secretary who came even close to her abilities.

His mind cleared as he stared into the clear green light of her eyes.

'And that was enough to prevent you from telling me you were pregnant, was it?' he demanded. 'A simple case of sexual jealousy—because you found me with another woman?'

Erin didn't say anything. Not at first. He made her sound unreasonable—as if she'd simply acted out of pique because her pride had been hurt. But it hadn't just been about the naked blonde. Of much greater concern had been his chaotic lifestyle *which might not have changed*. And if that was the case, she would protect

Leo from him with every last breath in her body. She had agreed to spend a weekend with him because she'd been in a position of weakness, but she was not going to be cowed into behaving like a victim. So why not tell him the truth? She had nothing left to lose...

'There was nothing *simple* about it,' she said. 'I didn't want my child to be part of your world.'

His blue eyes were like ice. 'And you were to be the judge and the jury?'

She shrugged. 'Why not? Nobody else ever dared tell you the truth—or if they did, you didn't bother listening to them. Loukas Sarantos told you often enough, before he left your employment.' And suddenly she realised that something else about him was different, and she screwed up her face in confusion as she remembered the eternal shadowy presence which had never been far from his side. 'Where's your bodyguard?' she asked. 'You never go anywhere without a bodyguard.'

'Not any more.' A faint smile lifted the edges of his lips. 'Surprised, Erin?'

'A little.' She nodded. 'Actually, more than a little. What happened?'

He shrugged. 'After Loukas left I could never find anyone else I could bear to have around me 24/7—you know that. And then you left, too.'

Her word fell like a stone into the silence which followed. 'And?'

He glanced out of the window at the stop-start traffic. 'And I realised I was sick of the press dogging my every move and everyone standing on the sidelines waiting for me to tip over the edge.' He turned back to her again. 'So I decided to tie up a few loose ends—

actually, more than a few. I cleaned up my act and be-came Mr Respectable.'

'You?' she echoed. 'Respectable?'

He gave another mirthless smile. 'An image you probably find as difficult to process as much as I do the thought of you as a mother.'

'Touché.' She sighed, wishing she had some kind of magic wand to wave. But if she did, what would she wish for? That she'd never met him? If she wished for that, then she wouldn't have Leo—and she couldn't bear that. 'So what now?' she questioned.

There was a pause as his gaze flicked over her.

'My car is going to drop me off at my office and then it will take you out to the airport, to one of the hotels there. I've had Sofia book you into a suite.'

She looked at him blankly. 'A hotel?'

'Of course. We're flying out first thing and it makes sense for you to be close to the airport. You're masquer-ading as my secretary, Erin—where else would you go? You can't stay home—and you surely weren't expect-ing to spend the night with *me*?'

His sarcastic words stung her and made a dull rush of colour stab at her cheeks, but the worst thing of all was that they touched on the truth. *Had* she thought he would be taking her back to that elegant, bonsai-filled apartment of his where there were more than enough spare bedrooms? Maybe she had—when the truth of it was that since he'd kissed her so coldly yet so passion-ately in the register office, he hadn't come near her.

She tried to mirror the faint cruelty of his smile. 'Don't be ridiculous, Dimitri,' she said. 'I'm not a com-plete sucker for punishment.'

CHAPTER FIVE

IT WAS A long time since Erin had stayed in a five-star hotel. Not since she'd worked for Dimitri, when luxury had been the norm. When she'd taken for granted the valets and bellboys and meals which arrived on silent trolleys concealed by heavy silver domes.

Dimitri's car had dropped her off at the Heathrow branch of the Granchester hotel chain, which was tucked away only ten minutes' drive from Heathrow. True, her suite didn't have the greatest view in the world but the bathroom was every woman's fantasy. After stripping off all her clothes, she lost herself in a world of scented bubbles and dried her hair and was just padding around in the oversized towelling robe, when the doorbell rang.

At first she thought it might be the soup and salad she'd ordered from room service, but instead she found Dimitri's assistant, Sofia, standing there, her arms laden down with glossy bags and shoe boxes.

'Dimitri said you'd need these,' she said as Erin invited her in.

Erin stared at the bags in confusion. 'What are they?'

'Clothes suitable for staying in a country with clothing restrictions a little more rigid than our own.'

Erin nodded. She guessed what Sofia meant was that

her own everyday clothes would be completely unsuitable for a stay in a royal palace. Her ordinary jeans and sweaters and dresses—bought in chain stores or online—would highlight a relative poverty which might reflect badly on Dimitri. If she was supposed to be the secretary to one of the world's richest men, it followed she would need to look the part. Erin watched as Sofia pulled a full-length fitted gown from one of the bags and gave an instinctive little murmur of pleasure.

'How did you know my size?' she questioned as she leaned forward to touch it, her fingertips skating over the exquisitely embroidered silk dress.

'I had a rough idea from the way my jeans fitted you—or didn't fit you!—but it was Dimitri who guessed,' answered Sofia, with a slightly embarrassed shrug.

Erin gave a wry smile. Of course he had guessed. With the amount of women Dimitri had bedded, he could probably work out a woman's measurements to within the nearest centimetre.

Sofia left soon after and Erin picked at a supper she didn't really want, before getting into the largest and softest bed she'd ever seen. Except that she couldn't sleep. She kept thinking back over the things Dimitri had said. The way he'd described himself as Mr Respectable and her natural reluctance to believe him. Or maybe she didn't *dare* believe him. Because how could a red-blooded sinner like him suddenly become a bona fide saint?

The hotel was deathly quiet and she glanced at her watch and grimaced. Three-fifteen in the morning. Picking up the TV's remote control, she put on the rolling news summary. Bright pictures appeared on the giant screen and she lay there listening to the drone of the announcer until she must have dropped off, because she awoke to the sound of her phone ringing.

It was Sofia, telling her that the car was waiting outside to take her to the airport and that Dimitri would meet her there.

'And I hope…' Sofia hesitated. 'I hope you have a lovely vacation in Jazratan.'

'Vacation' wouldn't have been Erin's word of choice as one of Dimitri's powerful jets thundered down the runway and soared up into the cloudless autumn sky. And she didn't feel remotely vacation-like when the plane touched down on Jazratan soil eight hours later. They had exchanged few words during the long flight, but that hadn't stopped her from being uncomfortably aware of his presence. Especially when he'd first seen her in the full-length embroidered dress, which made walking more difficult than usual. The soft silk revealed no flesh whatsoever, but Erin had felt almost naked as those blue eyes burned into her.

She hated the way her body tingled in response, as if it were written into her DNA that she should desire him every time he looked at her with hunger in his eyes…

She'd tried to read a magazine, wondering if he was aware that she wasn't taking in a single word. She found herself ridiculously grateful when he fell asleep and for once his hard face softened. And even though she'd tried not to, it had been impossible not to drink in the carved beauty of his proud features—until one of the stewards had appeared and she'd been forced to hastily avert her gaze.

Her body felt stiff as the aircraft doors were pushed open and her sense of detachment only increased when she saw the deputation of robed figures waiting to greet them. Nervously, she smoothed down her hair, which had already begun to react to the dense blanket of heat which hit them the moment they stepped outside. The burning heat and the vivid blue sky were so different from the drizzle she'd left back at home in England, and she'd never gone away without Leo before. She thought about her son back in London and felt a sudden pang as she turned to Dimitri. The desert sun was gilding his hair into an abundance of deepest gold and she thought his eyes had never looked quite so blue. 'I must ring Leo.'

'I think it had better wait until we have reached the royal palace,' he said. 'There's a certain amount of protocol we need to get through before you start pulling out your cell phone.'

This can't be happening, Erin thought as she was ushered into the first of a convoy of vehicles by the light press of Dimitri's hand at her spine. *I can't be in an air-conditioned car so cold that it feels like travelling in an icebox, while outside there are palm trees and camels carrying men with headdresses billowing behind them as they move across the dusty sands.*

But it *was* happening. Every surreal second of it. People were bowing as the convoy went past—as if they suspected that their royal king might be enclosed in one of the long line of dark vehicles. The car was approaching an enormous domed palace whose golden gates were opening before them. Past stern-faced guards they drove, into vast and formal grounds, studded with marble statues and exotic blooms she'd never seen before. She found herself wondering how on earth the grass could be so green when nothing but dust and desert surrounded them. She wondered what kind of birds she could hear singing in those strange and beautiful trees.

'Excited?' came the accented caress of Dimitri's voice from beside her as they came to a halt.

She turned to look at him, hating the instant thudding of her heart. Why did it have to be *him* who made her body react like this? Why couldn't she have desired some other man to tease her bare breasts with his teeth, as Dimitri had done on that long-ago night she'd never forgotten.

'I don't know if "excited" is the word I'd use,' she answered, trying to sound blasé. 'It will be an interesting experience to see a country I would never normally get the chance to visit—but the thought of being cooped up with you for two days isn't exactly filling me with joy.'

'Oh, really?' he drawled, knotting his silk tie as he glanced towards the palace doors. 'And fascinating as this discussion is, I think we're going to have to take a rain check. Because if you look over there you'll see a man in golden robes heading this way. It seems that the Sheikh of Jazratan has come out in person to greet us.'

'I notice that you have been very preoccupied tonight, my friend.'

Dimitri smiled as he listened to the Sheikh's silken words, for they both knew that the title of 'friend' was completely spurious. The man who said it was too remote and too powerful to have true friends—indeed, Saladin was as friendless as he, for men like them always stood alone.

But that was the way he liked it.

Dimitri watched as yet another fragrant platter of food was placed before him, waiting until the robed male servant had withdrawn, before turning to the hawk-faced king beside him.

'Have I?'

'Mmm.' The Sheikh waved away another servant who was hovering with a water jug. 'I note that you have barely been able to tear your gaze away from your *secretary* all evening.'

Dimitri picked up a jewel-inlaid goblet and sipped from it. 'Is it not always the instinct of a man to look at a woman, particularly when she is the only one present?'

'Indeed it is,' commented Saladin thoughtfully, his eyebrows rising to just below the edge of his white head-dress. 'But she does not fall into the category of your preferred blondes, one of whom I saw pictured with you in the newspapers not a fortnight ago.'

Dimitri gave a thin smile. 'You surprise me, Saladin. I did not have you down as a reader of tabloid newspapers.'

The Sheikh's eyes hardened. 'Ah, but I always do my research. I like to know about the lifestyle of my prospective business partners.'

Dimitri put his goblet down, his heart giving a quick beat—as if sensing that, after so many years of delicate negotiation, the prize was at last within his grasp. But he kept all emotion from his voice. 'Do I take it this means you have agreed to sell me the oil fields?'

A shadow of something imperceptible moved across Saladin's hawklike features.

'I try never to conduct business at mealtimes,' he said smoothly. 'It has been a long day and your secretary is looking somewhat *weary*. I trust that your sleeping arrangements meet with your satisfaction?'

Dimitri stiffened, wondering what Saladin was hinting at. Had he suspected that he and Erin had once been lovers and might have preferred a shared suite rather than the two adjoining ones they'd been allocated? No. He felt the flicker of a pulse at his temple. One unplanned night all those years ago did not put them in the category of *lovers*. It had been nothing. Nothing but a blip. He drank some more pomegranate juice. And yet he had never been able to completely forget that night, had he? It had been too easy to recall the way he'd felt as he had thrust deep inside her. The memory of her slim-hipped body and tiny breasts was curiously persistent. It was forbidden fruit at its sweetest.

He saw Saladin watching her and felt a responding shimmer of something which felt decidedly *territorial*. The mother of his child was sitting between Prince Khalim of Maraban and the ambassador of nearby Qurhah, looking almost as if she had been born to eat from jewelled platters, in the sumptuous opulence of a state banqueting room.

It was an image he found difficult to reconcile, because this was not the Erin he knew. She had always been such a *back room* type of person, content to apply herself industriously at the office and fade into the fixtures and fittings. Unlike other members of his staff, she had never hankered after the glamour of the high-profile parties and events he was regularly invited to.

Had he thought she might seem out of her depth here, in such imposing and opulent surroundings—where chandeliers like cascades of diamonds dangled from the ceilings, and intricate mosaic work made the walls look as if they were fashioned from pure gold? Because if that was the case, then he had been wrong.

Tonight she seemed to have an innate grace about her which he'd never really noticed when she'd been sitting behind a desk, fielding his phone calls. Her wrists were so damned *delicate*, he thought, watching as she lifted a jewel-studded goblet to her lips and sipped from it. The residue of the drink left a faint gleam on her lips and he found himself noticing how perfect they looked.

He narrowed his eyes. What was the matter with him tonight? What was it about her which made her seem so…*bewitching*? Surely it couldn't just be that silvery-green gown, which made her body gleam like a mermaid and brought out the colour of her eyes. He wondered what she was saying to that Qurhahian which had made him throw back his dark head and laugh so much.

At that moment she seemed to sense his eyes on her, because slowly she turned her head and met his steady gaze. And something about the stillness which settled over her made the rest of the room suddenly retreat. The sounds of chatter became muffled and all Dimitri could hear was the sound of his own heartbeat. With a start, he realised that she looked almost *beautiful*.

His fingers tightened around his goblet. Whoever would have guessed that Erin Turner could look so at home in this regal setting? That in spite of the maelstrom of events which had led to her being here, she had somehow maintained an air of calm and dignity, which she was carrying off with aplomb?

He could feel the urgent jerk of his erection and wondered if he was imagining the tightening of her nipples in response to his scrutiny, or whether that was simply his own fantasy running wild. He felt a momentary pang of regret as he realised that he hadn't enjoyed Erin Turner as a woman should be enjoyed. His desire for her had been raw and unfamiliar. A one-off he'd found difficult to understand—both at the time and afterwards. But it had been at a dark time in his life, hadn't it? Just about the time when he'd reached his rock-bottom, and Erin had witnessed every second of it.

He had seen the look of alarm in her eyes when she'd arrived at his apartment that night. A look which had given away to relief when he'd eventually answered the door and she realised that he'd been delayed by nothing more onerous than a shower. He remembered feeling weary—and jaded. He'd spent the previous night in a casino, being fawned over by women wearing nothing but a smattering of sequins, but Erin had looked so young and so *fresh* in that boxy navy work suit that desire had suddenly taken root inside him. And once it had been planted, it had grown like something rampant and uncontrollable.

He had kissed her more as an experiment than anything else—expecting a prim response or even a slap round the face for daring to make a pass at her. But it hadn't turned out that way. She had kissed him back—with a passion which had more to do with enthusiasm than experience, and it had blown him away. He hadn't planned to pull her into his arms and God only knew how they had ended up on his dining-room table, with him ripping off her panties and her urging him on with a gurgle of delighted laughter. He remembered his shuddered shout of pleasure as he had eased himself into her tight and sticky warmth.

But the sex had only been the beginning and he hadn't liked what had come afterwards. Daylight had brought with it disbelief. It had felt *claustrophobic* to wake up in Erin's arms. He had felt uncomfortable beneath that sweet, uncomplicated gaze of hers. His decision to fly unexpectedly to Russia had been dramatic but necessary, because she'd made him feel stuff. Stuff he hadn't wanted to feel—and it was easier to escape from it than to confront it.

A robed servant removed his untouched dessert and replaced it with a cup of mint tea and suddenly Dimitri couldn't wait for dinner to end as he realised he wanted sex with Erin Turner again. His mouth dried. He wanted a replay of what had happened all those years ago, only this time he wanted to do it long and slow.

He shook his head as he tried to fight the hungry demands of his body. Because this was the woman who deceived him. The woman who had decided to play judge and jury and to hide his child from him, without ever giving him the opportunity to show her he'd changed. He thought of another woman who had done something similar and he felt his heart twist with a cold anger.

He realised that the Sheikh was speaking to him and forced himself to listen.

'You must be weary after your travels, Makarov?'

'A little,' Dimitri agreed.

'Then we will retire for the night, since negotiations are better conducted by the light of day, following a good night's sleep and a little exercise.' The Sheikh smiled. 'I believe you ride?'

'Of course,' said Dimitri.

'Then perhaps you would care to join me in the morning?' The Sheikh's eyes gleamed. 'I have two fine new stallions I am keen to show you and to put through their paces.'

Dimitri gave a little click of irritation. 'I would like nothing better but have brought no riding clothes with me.'

'This is of no matter.' The Sheikh gave an impatient wave of his hand. 'I can provide you with something. We are men of similar size, I think. Meet me at eight—before the sun is too high and the desert heat becomes merciless. And in the meantime I shall bid you and your secretary a good night.' The Sheikh rose to his feet and everyone fell silent as he swept from the room, followed by a retinue of servants.

As the chatter recommenced Dimitri stood up and walked round the other side of the table, where Erin was giggling at something the Qurhahian official was saying. Was that what made Dimitri clamp a possessive hand over her arm, or simply that the desire to touch her had become too strong to resist?

'*Zvezda moya*, you have spent many hours travelling today,' he said, seeing the faint clouding of her eyes which she couldn't quite disguise. As if it was hypocritical of him to use the Russian term of endearment, or to whisper his fingertips over her slamming pulse like that. Unseen, he circled his thumb over the delicate skin and he felt her heart pick up even more speed. 'Let us follow the Sheikh's good example and retire for the night.'

Erin nodded as she stood up and said goodnight to the interesting ambassador from Qurhah, who had told her so many interesting things about living in the desert. She would never have guessed in a million years that the way to stop yourself feeling thirsty was to suck on a pebble, or that cacti had so many medicinal uses. In a way she was reluctant to leave the table, but she could hardly sit there all night just because she was terrified about the thought of being alone with Dimitri. Especially after the way he had been ogling her during dinner.

And the way her body had instinctively responded to him. That was what was worrying her more than anything. She'd tried to rationalise it as best she could, but in the end she'd been forced to face the truth. That she still wanted him. She swallowed. But that didn't mean she was going to follow through. Because even though she'd ring-fenced her heart, Dimitri could still mess with her head. He could make her want things she knew were bad for her.

Mainly him.

Walking rigidly alongside him, she attempted to concentrate on her surroundings as they left the banqueting hall, trying to steer her thoughts away from his power and strength. But it wasn't easy. There was a definite *edge* to him tonight. An edge which was all about sex—she guessed that, despite her relative innocence. The hunger in his eyes had been unmistakable as he'd stared at her across the dinner table—and she couldn't deny that the feeling had been mutual. She had been overcome with a breathless need to feel him close to her again. To have him crush his lips down on hers. To let him pin her down onto the mattress and…and…

Erin swallowed.

And it wasn't going to happen.

It *couldn't* happen.

Because sex with Dimitri would weaken her. It would tear down her defences and make her helpless. And she couldn't afford to be helpless. For Leo's sake, she had to stay strong.

He might have changed in many ways. He might no longer be gambling, or drinking or embracing danger with a reckless hunger—but there was no guarantee that his attitude towards women was any different. *Remember the way he treated you.* She certainly hadn't been expecting violins and commitment from him, but after that single night of sex he had been barely able to look her in the eyes. He'd acted as if the whole extraordinary night had never happened.

Her sandals made little sound as they made their way along the marbled corridors. But the magnificent architecture and scented courtyards were wasted on her—just like the wrought-iron lamps which flickered delicate patterns onto the walls. Her mind started picturing her little apartment back home, where everything she held dear was centred. She thought about a little boy sitting at a table, crayoning. She thought about his warm milk and bedtime story and those innocent eyes, which were so like those of his manipulative father, and her heart clenched.

They reached her suite first and stopped outside and Erin felt slightly breathless as she pushed open the door. Inside, low divans were scattered with brocade cushions and the powerful scent of roses wafted through the air.

'Goodnight,' she said, thinking how inadequate that word sounded when all she could think about was that he was close enough to touch. Close enough to kiss. *So go. Go now—before the cool gleam of his eyes entices you any more and the sensual lines of his lips tempt you into doing something you shouldn't.* But her sandaled feet didn't move from the spot.

Dimitri stared at the woman in front of him, conscious of the mixed messages she was sending out, and conscious of his own feelings of confusion. He wanted to remember the web of deceit she had woven and to remind himself that she'd told the same lies as his own, dear mother. But the hungry throb of desire which pulsed through his body was far stronger than his reservations. Part of him hated what he was about to do, but he seemed unable to stop himself from stepping onto the inevitable path of seduction. 'You look beautiful tonight, Erin.'

She looked momentarily nonplussed, as if she wasn't

used to receiving compliments about her looks. 'Thank you,' she said, her voice betraying a hint of nerves. 'I have Sofia to thank for the dress. She has excellent taste.'

'I don't want to talk about Sofia's taste.'

'No,' she said, looking as if she was trying to make herself yawn. 'Actually, it's very late and I want to go to sleep—'

'Are you quite sure about that?' he questioned.

'About…what? About whether I want to go to sleep?'

'About what you really want.' He reached out to touch her cheek. 'See how you shiver when I touch you?'

'Maybe I'm cold.'

'In the desert?'

She licked her lips. 'Dimitri,' she whispered. 'Don't.'

'Don't what? Don't tell it how it is, when I get the distinct feeling that you want me as much as I want you. Don't you? I think you want me to kiss you—and God knows I want that, too. You've driven me crazy all through dinner. I could barely concentrate on a word the Sheikh was saying because I kept looking at you and thinking how much I longed to touch you.'

His words disarmed her and so did the molten look of desire in his eyes—and Erin was already weakened by her own desire and the stupid vulnerability which his passionate words had stirred up. Was that to blame for what happened next—so quickly and so completely that any other action seemed unthinkable? One minute she was staring at him and trying to summon up the strength to walk away and the next she was in his arms and he was kissing her so hungrily that she thought she gasped, or squealed or *something*.

Perhaps the sound reminded him that they were on the Sheikh's territory and the rules governing Jazratan were far stricter than their own, because suddenly Dimitri was levering her into her suite and shutting the door behind them. For a moment she just stared at him with her heart beating wildly beneath the beautiful dress and then he was pushing her up against the wall and kissing her.

One last stab at reason told her to stop him before it was too late, but she simply ignored it, coiling her arms greedily around his neck as he deepened the kiss. Because he was right. Her eyelids flickered to a close as his tongue began to explore her mouth. She *did* still want him.

For years she'd been yearning for his kiss—not the arrogant mark of possession which had taken place in the register office, but this. A *real* kiss.

When she'd lain sleepless, with his baby kicking beneath her heart, she had wanted him to hold her tight like this. In those early years of struggle, when she'd discovered that Leo was allergic to peanuts and she'd felt as if she'd been running round chasing her tail, existing on hardly any sleep and far too much black coffee, she had longed for the comfort of a man's touch.

Dimitri's touch.

And now she had it—and it was all-consuming. He was driving his lips down hard on hers and she was responding in kind, not just because she felt frustrated and empty or because he was irresistible—it went much deeper than that. Because their cells had mingled when their child had formed inside her and Dimitri had awoken her in so many ways. He had taken her virginity and given her an orgasm and made her pregnant, all during one long night of bliss.

His hands were moving over her body, palms undulating over the narrow curves of waist and hips, as if he were discovering them for the first time. She heard his low growl of pleasure as he brought her up against the growing hardness at his groin, mirrored by the molten rush of heat to her sex. He cupped one of her breasts, curling his fingers over the shiny green material, and her nipple pushed insistently against his palm as she teetered on the brink of giving in to the urgent demands of her body. A couple of minutes more and he would be undressing her. He would be kissing his way over her naked body and she would be urging him on, just like last time.

Until the truth hit her like a bucket of ice water as she realised what he was doing. Once again, she was letting him *use* her. She had dressed up for dinner and behaved as impeccably as she knew how and he was responding by behaving as if she were nothing more than a decorative object he could take to bed without conscience. As if she were a piece of clay he could mould to his own desires, never stopping to think that she might have *feelings*—and that he might be trampling all over them.

Tearing her lips away from his, she used all her strength to plant her hands on his shoulders to push him away and he jerked his head back in surprise.

His eyes darkened. 'What's wrong?'

She stepped away from him and the temptation he presented. She could feel the heat of her face and the thunder of her pulse as she glared at him. 'What's wrong? Are you…serious?' she demanded breathlessly. 'Do you really think you can walk back into my life and completely disrupt it—and then expect me to have sex with you, just because you've snapped your fingers?'

'But you want me.'

He said it unequivocally—like someone stating calmly that the sky was blue—and all the anger which had been simmering away inside Erin now came to the boil.

'Oh, I might *want* you,' she agreed. 'My body may have been programmed to react to yours in a way I don't particularly like, but that doesn't mean I'm going to follow through. Because you don't have any respect for women, do you, Dimitri? Not just me, but any woman. You use your undoubted charisma to get them into your bed, but you blaze through their lives without thinking about the consequences. You used me that night because you were in a dark place—and afterwards you just cast me aside, as if I was someone of no consequence. Like I was a *thing*—not a person.'

She shook her head as she struggled to get more breath in her lungs. 'I thought my sister was wrong to tell you about my wedding—but now I can see it was probably the right thing to do. Leo does have the right to know about his father. But that doesn't mean I'm going to act like… like some sort of *convenience* by getting intimate with you. Because that night was a one-off and it was a mistake.'

'Erin—'

'No! You aren't going to change my mind—no matter how hard you try.' Frustratedly she pushed a handful of hair away from her hot face. 'While we're here we can accomplish what we initially set out to do. I will pretend to be your secretary if that's what you want and we can use the time to decide on a way forward best suited to our son. But I don't plan on having sex with you, Dimitri—not now and not ever—so you'd better get that into your stubborn head.'

CHAPTER SIX

DIMITRI'S BODY ACHED and his blood sang with the most unbearable frustration he'd ever experienced. He still couldn't quite believe the way the evening had ended—with Erin refusing to have sex with him, even though her body had been screaming out its objections as she'd pushed him away.

When had a woman ever done that?

Walking over to the unshuttered windows, he stared out at the clear night sky of Jazratan. With no light pollution, the stars were impossibly bright and they shone down over the desert plains like blazing beacons. He had left the bedroom windows open and the scent of the exotic blooms in the palace gardens drifted in to mingle with the heavy fragrance of the roses which perfumed the room. It was over two hours since she'd kicked him out of her suite and yet still he couldn't sleep.

In the old days he might have seen off a shot or three of vodka to chase away the uncomfortable feelings which now gnawed away at the pit of his stomach. If he'd been in a city, he might have ordered a car to drive him to a casino, where he would play cards until daybreak. But it was nearly seven years since he'd drunk vodka or gambled away his money, and so far he hadn't missed either.

Until tonight.

Tonight he would have welcomed the oblivion of something—anything—to blot out these dark thoughts. What he wouldn't give to forget the accusations she'd flung at him, or to work out why they had cut so deep.

Because they were true?

He stared into the sky as a shooting star shot through the inky stratosphere, leaving behind a blurred and silvery trail. *Had* he treated her like a commodity by kicking her out of his apartment the morning after he'd bedded her—or had he simply been protecting her from the kind of man he really was? He hadn't wanted to drag someone like Erin into the seedy world he'd inhabited at the time. He had looked into her shining eyes and known that he couldn't take away any more of her innocence. She deserved better than him.

He'd convinced himself that he was doing her a favour by making it clear that if she wanted to hold on to her job, they must resume their roles of boss and employee. That was why he'd left the country—to give her time to get used to the fact that the sex wasn't going to happen again. And when he'd returned she had come round to his apartment with that strange expression on her face and had found him *in flagrante* with some blonde. He'd thought sexual jealousy had been the motivation behind her decision to resign—and in many ways it had been simpler to let her go. He hadn't wanted to be reminded of the night they'd shared. He hadn't wanted to have to fight off any inconvenient feelings of still wanting her…

But the truth was that he'd missed her. No secretary

he'd employed before or since had been able to equal her. They'd always worked well together—even if sometimes she used to regard him sternly with those catlike eyes of hers. He had allowed Erin Turner a cautious proximity which nobody other than his most favoured bodyguard had been granted. And the irony of it was that he'd never even thought about her in a sexual way before that night. To him she'd just been part of the background—as reliable as the cup of strong coffee she placed on his desk each morning. Sometimes they used to discuss the morning's headlines. Sometimes he used to ask her opinion and, occasionally, act on it. Was it a crazy admission to make that he'd almost *forgotten* she was a woman, until the night when his spirit had been dark and desperate and she had been standing in his doorway in her sensible navy work suit. He had looked at her and suddenly she had been *all* woman.

He thought about her sleeping in the adjoining suite as dawn broke over the Jazratan desert in an explosion of colour—turning the sky an intense shade of rose pink before giving way to gold, then amber. But suddenly his thoughts were far away from the luxurious palace. He thought about the laughing little boy he'd seen running along the London street and his heart clenched with an emotion he didn't recognise.

He showered and shaved, but Erin still hadn't risen when a servant rapped at the door and presented him with a folded pile of riding clothes. Minutes later, he emerged from his dressing room to see that she must have let herself into his suite while he'd been changing. She was staring out at the gardens and she was washed gold with morning sunlight, wearing another of those all-concealing outfits—the ones deemed suitable not to offend the country's notoriously strict dress codes, but which somehow managed to draw attention to the slender curves of her body. She turned round when she heard him enter and, although her face looked bloodless and pale, he couldn't miss the way her eyes darkened when she saw him.

Infuriatingly, he felt his body's own powerful response to her presence but, ruthlessly, he clamped it down. Because it was better this way. In the cold, clear light of morning it was easier to compartmentalise the lust he'd felt for her last night and to squash it. Far better they kept things businesslike and impersonal.

'Ah, awake at last,' he remarked non-committally. 'I trust you slept well?'

Erin met his cool gaze with a feeling of confusion. She had anticipated that this morning's conversation was going to be difficult in view of what had nearly happened last night, and would need careful handling. She had planned to stick to neutrals—to concentrate on the banal and not give in to all the dark thoughts which were jostling for space inside her head. She had intended to forget last night's kiss and all the hungry feelings it had provoked, but the look on Dimitri's face told her she needn't have worried. It seemed that her concerns about having to resist him again were completely unfounded—because he was looking at her as dispassionately as he might look at a speck of dust on his shirt.

Yet the sight of him striding into the room wearing riding gear was doing dangerous things to her heart rate. Why was he dressed in a way which was so unbelievably provocative? The jodhpurs did things to his body which were only just this side of decent, clinging to every sinew of his muscular thighs and hugging his hips like a second skin. A billowing white silk shirt was tucked into the waistband and hinted at the hard torso which lay beneath. Dark leather knee-length boots completed the outfit and Erin could feel her mouth growing dry because suddenly he looked like every woman's fantasy. And she had turned him down…

Was she insane?

She cleared her throat. 'What…what are you doing?'

'Isn't it obvious?' he said, with a touch of impatience in his voice. 'I'm getting ready to go riding with the Sheikh.'

'You didn't mention that last night.'

'Why? Should I have run it past you first?'

'Don't be ridiculous,' she said, unable to quell her natural concerns for him, even though he was stonewalling every remark she made. 'When was the last time you rode?'

'Why?'

She shrugged, but she could feel the familiar flare of fear leaping up inside her.

He seemed so different these days. So cool and in control. A long way from the man who'd never slept— who'd existed on vodka and danger. And now he was putting himself in danger again. He was acting like arrogant, invulnerable Dimitri once more. The man who thought he was charmed—but how long before his charmed life ran out?

She glared at him, resenting the way he was making her feel. *She didn't want to worry about him any more, or fret about him. Those days were over and what he did was none of her business.* But something made her say it anyway. Was it the thought of Leo and something happening to the daddy he would only just be getting to know? Or was the shameful truth that she was getting in much deeper than she'd imagined and the thought of something happening to him more than she could bear?

'It's dangerous.'

'Only if you don't know what you're doing—and I do. I learned to ride in the Russian army on the famous Don horse—the favoured mount of the Cossacks. Remember?' His eyes glinted out a challenge. 'I've been well taught, Erin—you know that—and I respect the might and the power of the horse, ever to be flippant about riding one. I do have *some* redeeming qualities, even if last night you seemed determined to list all my negative ones.'

She bit her lip, wondering if some of the accusations she'd hurled at him had been unduly harsh.

'Last night.' She cleared her throat. 'Those things I said—'

'Were probably things I needed to hear.' His eyes glittered. 'Because most of the things you said were true, and I'm sorry.'

She met his gaze with suspicion and confusion, because contrition was not an emotion she'd ever associated with Dimitri Makarov.

'Oh,' she said, unable to keep the faint note of surprise from her voice. 'Right.'

'I've taken on board that you don't want any intimacy with me, Erin,' he said. 'And with hindsight—I think that may be the best decision.'

Even more confused now, Erin looked at him. 'You do?'

'I do. Last night happened for all kinds of reasons, but I'm grateful to you for stopping it in time. Starting a physical relationship creates its own kind of tension between a couple—particularly when it comes to an end. And I think Leo deserves more than his parents warring.'

Now Erin felt completely wrong-footed. 'You sound...'

Golden-brown eyebrows winged upwards. 'What?'

She shrugged, unsure how much to say and unwilling to threaten this tentative truce. But last night seemed to have opened up a new channel of communication and maybe it was time to start dealing permanently in the currency of truth. She'd seen the trouble subterfuge could cause and if their uneasy partnership of shared parentage was to have any kind of future, then they needed to be honest with each another. And if sex was off the agenda, they could concentrate on the other stuff. The important stuff.

But that didn't stop her from being curious. From wondering what made him tick.

'You make it sound as if you think every physical relationship will end,' she said.

'That's because they do. And if they survive, they are invariably riddled with infidelity. And there's no need to look at me quite so disapprovingly, Erin. I've never made any secret of my cynicism. You should know that better than anyone.'

'I do.' She hesitated. 'It's just I've never known *why*.'

'It wouldn't take a genius to work it out.' His voice roughened. 'Don't they say that the first relationship you observe is the blueprint for your own life?'

'You mean your parents weren't happy?'

'No, they weren't,' he said, but he quickly followed up his answer with another question, as if eager to change the subject. 'Though I suppose your childhood was all milk and honey and picnics on the weekend?'

'Well, that's what my parents were aiming for,' she said, watching as he picked up his riding crop to twist it between his fingers. 'Only, my perfect childhood didn't turn out the way it was supposed to. If ever we had picnics, then the sandwiches were jam and the bread was stale, because there was never enough money to go round.'

'Why not?'

She sighed. 'Because my parents were impossible romantics. They've spent their lives following the demands of their hearts, but never bothered listening to their heads. They live in Australia now. They went there after seeing a documentary on ostrich farming and decided to start up a farm of their own. They were seduced by big blue skies and a hot sun and the idea of being close to the earth—without stopping to think that a little bit of farming experience might be a good idea before they actually channelled all their savings into it.'

His eyes narrowed. 'What happened?'

She shrugged. 'What everyone told them would happen, only they were too stubborn to pay any attention. They lost all their money and the farm was repossessed— and now my mother has had the bright idea of making silver jewellery, at a time when mass-market products are in the ascendancy, so nobody is buying hers. They are currently travelling around New South Wales in a camper van, selling her wares in markets and barely making enough money to make ends meet.'

He was silent for a minute. 'And what do these two impossible romantics think of Leo?' he asked suddenly.

'Do they mind you having a child out of wedlock? Are they close to their grandson?'

She shook her head. 'No, they're not close to him—at least, not geographically. We email and talk via the internet once a week, but it's not quite the same thing. They can't afford to come to England and I was only able to afford to fly out there once. That was…' She hesitated.

His eyes narrowed.

'That was another reason why you decided to marry Chico, wasn't it? So that you could afford to visit them more often?'

'That's right.' His perception surprised her. 'I thought they'd be pleased but they…'

'They what?'

His unfamiliar interest in her personal life was beguiling, but it was making her think about stuff it was better to avoid. Her parents had wanted her and Tara to marry for love because they believed in love. She did not. She believed in providing security and protection for yourself because love was flaky and unreliable. It made people make stupid, random decisions like going off to the other end of the world, fuelled by nothing but a pipe dream, just as they had done.

But once she had believed in love, hadn't she? She had been sucked in by that meaningless fairy tale, just like everyone else. She'd misinterpreted her boss's relaxed attitude towards her and thought it might be something else. Her feelings for him had bubbled away, getting hotter and hotter. By the time he'd kissed her that night in his apartment, all her immunity had gone—and she realised too late that she could never get it back again. Before, she had been Erin his trusted aide…and afterwards?

Afterwards, she had been just another woman he'd bedded. Just another woman he couldn't wait to see the back of, scrabbling around on the floor to locate her scattered underwear. But at least she had one thing to thank Dimitri for. With one stroke he had effectively destroyed the love myth which had been building up inside her. As she'd walked home that morning, wearing last night's clothes, she had vowed she would never be like her parents.

Never.

She shook her head. 'They think that babies should only be the product of love. And even if that patently isn't true—I don't want that kind of love.'

'You don't want love?' he echoed slowly. 'Why not?'

'Because it takes over your life.' She shook her head impatiently. 'I've seen what it does to people—the way my parents allowed it to dominate their lives, so that nothing else really mattered. I've seen it break hearts and cause jealousy. It's nothing but a con. A way of justifying desire, that's all. Now who's the one looking shocked? What's the matter, Dimitri? Do you think all women are programmed to lose their hearts to a man?'

He didn't take the bait. 'Going back to your parents, do they know I'm the father of your child?'

She shook her head. 'No. Nobody does, except Tara.'

'So why not? Why the desire for secrecy? You could have taken the story to the press,' he observed. 'You could have earned yourself a nice little payout without having to resort to a sham marriage.'

'I would never do that,' she said fiercely. 'That kind of cheap publicity is the last thing I would inflict on Leo.'

He regarded her thoughtfully. 'But there was another reason for your discretion, wasn't there, Erin? Because if you'd gone to the press—I would inevitably have found out and that was something you didn't want to risk, did you?'

Erin stared at him as the silence seemed to expand the space between them. She heard the hurt and the anger in his voice, knowing both were justified, and the stab at her conscience was almost more than she could bear. 'You're right,' she said in a low voice. 'I wanted to keep him hidden away from you.'

She hardly dared look at him to see his reaction, but she knew that to avert her gaze would be the act of an emotional coward. She wondered if she had imagined that brief, hard flare of *sadness* in his eyes, when she had been expecting the full force of his anger.

'It's history now,' he said abruptly as he glanced down at his watch. 'It's nearly eight o'clock. Are you coming to watch me ride?'

Erin hesitated. The conversation had left her feeling raw and exposed—but what else was she going to do if he went off to ride with the Sheikh? Sit alone in her suite while crazy thoughts circulated in her head—or take a solitary breakfast while all those silent servants watched her?

'Only if you promise not to take any unnecessary risks.'

'Ah! So you *do* care?' he taunted.

'Only because if you're going to meet Leo, I'd like you to meet him in one piece.'

A sharp rap on the door put an end to any further talk and a robed servant led them through the corridors to the vast stable complex, which was situated on the eastern side of the palace.

The sun was already warm as two grooms led a pair of magnificent stallions out into the yard—one golden and one black. Erin thought they looked like textbook versions of equine perfection with their coats gleaming in the brightness of the morning light. In the far distance she could see the Sheikh making his way towards them, his usual phalanx of servants surrounding him. She noticed that he was wearing his robes, not jodhpurs—and wondered how on earth he could ride in them.

Dimitri moved towards the horses and she watched his every step, wishing she weren't so shockingly aware of his muscular body and the sun gilding his thick hair. She wasn't surprised to see him jump onto the golden horse, which seemed to echo his own colouring, but wondered why the two men briefly shook hands before the king mounted his own ebony stallion. For a few moments she watched as they trotted the horses round and round the yard. Dimitri was clearly trying to gauge the temperament of his mount and even a novice like Erin could see that the animal was powerful and strong. A flicker of apprehension ran down her spine. He'd given her all that spiel about having learned to ride in the Russian army and how brilliant the teaching had been, but he hadn't actually mentioned how long ago it was since he'd last ridden.

She could see the Sheikh leaning across to say something to him and the quick flash of anticipation in Dimitri's eyes made Erin stiffen. Because she knew that look. It was the same look he used to wear when poised on the brink of some monumental deal. The same look which usually heralded a long night spent drinking, or playing cards. It was a reckless look, edged with danger, and it took her right back to a place where she used to be frozen with fear, just wondering what the hell he was going to do next and imagining the worst.

She knew then that he had just accepted a challenge from the Sheikh—who just happened to be one of the world's most accomplished horsemen. *The stupid fool was going to race against a man with way more experience than himself.*

Her first thought was one of anger, because he'd told her he'd changed. He'd said he'd become Mr Respectable and she knew now why she'd found it so hard to believe. Because it wasn't true. Respectable men didn't race a temperamental thoroughbred they'd never ridden before, did they? They didn't take their life in their hands—especially when they hadn't even met the son they'd made so much fuss about meeting.

She wanted to dash over to stop them and she did actually take a step forward before sanity prevailed. Because what good could she do in a land where the king was hell-bent on racing a man desperate to buy some of his oil fields? Did she really think that either Dimitri or Saladin would listen to *her*?

She watched as they lined the two horses up at the edge of the gallops, sensing the excitement in the restless stallions as they strained forward. Suddenly, one of the servants fired a loud starting pistol but barely had Erin recovered from her startled reaction, when the two men took off at a furious pace.

Barely able to breathe, she watched as they galloped past, two gleaming streaks of ebony and gold—their hooves pounding the ground like thunder. The Sheikh was ahead by a margin which was gradually increasing and for a moment she thought that Dimitri was going to do the sensible thing and just let him win. But she hadn't factored in his highly competitive nature. She could see the determination on his face as he pressed his thighs hard into the animal's flanks and she could read the hungry tension in the Russian's body as he crouched over the horse and urged it forward.

He was coming up closer to the man ahead of him, and then closer still. He had almost caught up with the king of Jazratan as they rounded the bend but now both horses were going at a breakneck pace. *Please just let him be safe*, prayed Erin as waves of emotion too complex to comprehend twisted her heart and stomach into knots.

The two men were now almost neck and neck and Erin saw the Sheikh glance over at the Russian as he tightened his own reins. She could see the strain and exhilaration on both their faces as they urged their mounts on. She could see the servants at the finishing line trying to position themselves, crouching down in an attempt to visually work out what was going to be a photo finish.

But as they approached the line the Sheikh's horse reared up as if something had spooked it and to Erin's horror she saw Saladin slipping down the side of the horse, as if in slow motion.

For one heart-stopping moment she thought the king was about to disappear under the pounding hooves to certain death when Dimitri drew close to the frightened animal. Collision seemed inevitable and Erin froze as the Russian reached out, somehow anchoring Saladin to the ebony horse while grabbing the other reins and managing to bring both animals to a shaky halt. Her knees grew weak. She felt the rush of relief, which was quickly replaced by one of anxiety as she saw the look of pain which briefly distorted Dimitri's features as he held on to the Sheikh as if his life depended on it.

And then grooms, servants, bodyguards came running out from the yard towards the two men and all hell broke loose.

CHAPTER SEVEN

'I'VE NEVER SEEN anything so reckless. Or so…so…*stupid*,' said Erin, her voice trembling with rage and fear as she held a golden goblet to Dimitri's parched lips. 'Here. Drink this.'

From his prone position on the velvet divan, Dimitri winced. 'What's in it?'

'Nothing stronger than water. And it's good for you. Which I suppose means you don't want it.'

He winced a little as he shifted his position on the divan. 'Are you angry with me, Erin?'

'Too right I am.' Unwanted emotions were exploding like fireworks inside her and she gritted her teeth as she registered the ashen colour of his face. 'You could have *died* out there!'

'But I didn't.'

'That's not the point,' she said stubbornly.

They were back in the palace after an incident which had clearly rocked all the spectators and left everyone in the palace reeling as they considered how much worse it could have been, if Dimitri hadn't prevented Saladin from falling beneath the hooves of the galloping horse. But the Sheikh had emerged from the incident unscathed and it was Dimitri who was hurt. Dimitri who had winced with pain after the doctor had examined him and ordered a full-body X-ray. With Erin at his side he had been taken to the nearby hospital and given the all-clear, but the bruising was bad and he'd been told to take it easy.

Erin had stuck to his side like glue and accompanied him back to his suite and soon after their arrival Saladin had turned up, still in the same robes he'd worn while riding. His face and hair had been covered in fine dust and he had looked dark and very sombre—but his gratitude had been heartfelt as he'd thanked Dimitri.

'I owe you,' he had said in a low voice. 'I owe you my life. And that means that we are now as brothers. Do you realise that, my friend?' And then he had embraced the Russian with a powerful bear hug, which had made Dimitri wince again, before sweeping out, his retinue following closely behind.

'You told me that you didn't do that whole danger thing any more,' Erin accused as she held the goblet of water to Dimitri's lips and made him drink another mouthful. 'You said you were respectable these days. You made out like you were a changed man. That you didn't drink vodka any more—'

'Which I don't.'

'Or embrace danger just for the sake of it.'

'Which I don't.'

'Oh, really?' She glared at him. 'So what was that all about out there? How long since you've ridden?'

He shrugged. 'I don't remember.'

'So what made you think you could take on one of the most celebrated horsemen in the world and *win*?'

'I *did* win.'

Erin glared. 'Only because the Sheikh nearly fell.'

'Exactly.' Dimitri stretched his long legs in front of him and through his half-closed eyes he subjected her to a mocking stare. 'And if I hadn't stopped to assist him, then I would have won by a much greater margin. We both know that.'

'Why accept the challenge in the first place when anyone else would have defined it as reckless?'

'Because I wanted to,' he said flatly. 'And because I'm doing business with a powerful man who might have considered it a sign of weakness if I had refused, thus putting the deal in jeopardy.'

'Your business deals are more important than your life, are they, Dimitri?'

'They are important,' he said, his voice suddenly cooling. 'They are a quantifiable success, unlike most other things in life.'

There was a soft rap on the door and Erin walked across the room to answer it, frustration simmering away inside her. Who was it this time? Why couldn't they just leave him alone and let him recover?

She didn't know who she expected to find but she was surprised to see a robed woman standing on the threshold—maybe because this was the only other woman she'd seen since she'd arrived in Jazratan. Petite and slender and wearing a silvery veil, which provided the perfect backdrop for her lustrous ebony hair, she was holding a small pot in her hands. Rather surprisingly, her smile was confident and she didn't appear in the least bit shy.

'The Sheikh has sent me,' she said, in the loveliest accent Erin had ever heard. 'To minister to the esteemed Russian who today risked his life to save our beloved monarch.'

Erin's hackles started rising; she couldn't help herself. Was she imagining the gleam in the woman's doelike eyes or the anticipatory curve of her soft smile as she looked over towards where Dimitri lay on the divan? A whisper of apprehension washed over her skin. No, she was not.

'What do you mean, *"minister"*?' she questioned, more sharply than she had intended.

The woman's smile grew serene. 'This rare cream has many healing properties,' she said softly. 'It is made from the fire berries which grow in the foothills of the mountains to the far north of our country and after I have applied it the Sheikh's saviour will feel no more pain, and the bruising on his skin will disappear as if by magic.'

Erin wasn't sure if it was paranoia or just a powerful sense of something territorial, but she knew that *no way* was this gorgeous young creature going to start slapping cream all over Dimitri's chest. A thought occurred to her. It came out of nowhere but for some reason it stuck firmly in her mind and wouldn't seem to budge. Did Saladin realise that she and the Russian weren't having sex—had Dimitri told him that? And was he sending this luscious woman to Dimitri's suite as some primitive way of *thanking* him? Nothing would surprise her about an autocratic king like Saladin, who ruled a country where the opposite sex seemed almost invisible.

Coolly, she removed the pot from the woman's hands and smiled at her. 'Thank you so much for taking the time to bring this, and please convey our deepest gratitude to His Royal Highness,' she said. 'But I think Dimitri would prefer me to *minister* it.'

She closed the door in the woman's startled face and

turned around to see the faintest glint of humour lighting Dimitri's eyes, before he winced again—as if it hurt to attempt to smile.

'You meant it, didn't you?' he said weakly as she began to walk across the room towards him. 'You're going to apply the cream yourself.'

'I did,' she said. 'And I am.'

'Be gentle with me, Erin.'

'Why wouldn't I be?'

'The look on your face does not suggest gentleness.'

Putting the fire-berry potion down on a table beside the divan, she began to unbutton his silky riding shirt, aware that it was clinging like damp tissue paper to the sweat-sheened muscles. She told herself that this was exactly the reason why she had gained a first-aid certificate and remembered the need to remain completely impartial. To treat him as she would treat anyone else requiring medical assistance. But the moment she began to massage the cream into the honed torso, she understood the challenge that impartiality presented. Dimitri's eyes were fully open now and there was a mocking light in their depths, as if they were asking a silent question which she didn't dare interpret—let alone answer.

Her fingers slid over his chest. It was sheer torture to touch him with this near-intimacy, even though she was doing her best to concentrate on the healing aspect and not on how delicious it felt to glide the cream over hard muscle covered by silky skin. But when he shifted his jodhpur-covered groin, it took all her determination not to be distracted by the distinct bulge there. Yet she couldn't look away, could she? She couldn't just stare at the wall. Instead, she focused intently on the bruises he had suffered and not the soft sigh which escaped from between his parted lips.

She continued to massage him, working intently and silently until she saw some of the tension leave his body. She put the pot down and went off to wash the cream from her hands but when she returned to the divan, she stared at his torso with a feeling of disbelief.

'Good grief,' she said faintly. 'Just look at that.'

Erin had spent years working for Dimitri, but she'd never seen that look of genuine astonishment on his face before, as he followed the direction of her gaze. And no wonder—for the bruises had reduced dramatically. The livid purple marks which had stained the golden skin had faded several shades lighter.

His eyes narrowed. 'What the hell happened? Did you wave a magic wand or something?'

She could see the flicker of a pulse at his temple. She saw the gleam of his torso and suddenly her throat grew dry. 'It must have been the potion,' she managed.

His gaze mocked her. 'Is that what it was?'

Erin stood there, knowing she ought to get the hell out of there while she still could, but something was keeping her rooted there—as if her feet had been super-glued to the spot. Her heart began to pound. Was it the *magnificence* of touching his half-naked body after all this time, or just the memory of how it had felt when he was deep inside her? She shook her head slightly, trying to erase the image from her mind, only the image was stubbornly refusing to budge. She swallowed. 'Perhaps you need to rest now.'

'Perhaps I do.'

He stretched out on the divan, his body outlined against the rich velvet and brocade cushions, but she noticed that his eyes were only half closed. She could see the icy glint of blue from between the thick lashes and she felt as if he was observing her. Watching her. Waiting to see what she would do next. She knew she ought to turn and walk away from him. She knew a lot of things, but the thing she knew above everything else was that she wanted to kiss him. To lose herself in his arms and shudder with pleasure. And it wasn't going to happen. She swallowed. There was a whole stack of reasons why intimacy would be a bad thing, and none of those had changed. But she was still standing there, wasn't she? Standing there feeling conflicted while she dug her fingernails into the palms of her hands and longed for what she knew she shouldn't have.

'Can I get you anything else?' she questioned stiffly.

He gave a slow, watchful smile. 'Like what?'

The tension shimmering between them was now so intense that Erin felt as if a single word or movement would shatter it, but his expression gave nothing away. He was a contradiction, she realised. He was stubborn and proud and angry with her for keeping Leo hidden from him, but he still wanted her. She could read it in the smoky smoulder of his blue eyes and the tension in his body. He wanted her, but he wasn't going to act on it. Instinct told her the next step was all down to her. That the ball was in her court. She had turned him down last night and his pride would not allow him to be turned down again. If she wanted him, then she was going to have to reach out to him. Still she hesitated, because wasn't this yet another way of Dimitri exercising his power over her?

'I think you've had enough rehydration and fire-berry potion for the time being, so I'll let you rest,' she said, even though the words felt as if they might strangle her.

But then he smiled again—and that smile changed everything. Something inside her snapped, like a piece of elastic which had been stretched too far, and suddenly she was doing what she'd only dreamed of doing in her most forbidden fantasies. She was leaning over him and brushing her lips over his—like a role reversal of the prince trying to waken the sleeping princess with his kiss.

Only, Dimitri was awake. Wide awake. The smile died on his lips. His calculating gaze lasted only a second before he hooked his hand behind her neck and brought her face back down to his.

She stared into his blue eyes. 'I... I shouldn't have done that.'

'Yes, you should,' he growled. 'And now you're going to do it all over again.'

He smelt of horse and dust and desire, underpinned with the faint scent of fire berries, and Erin trembled as he pulled her close and kissed her. She worried about her weight pushing against his battered body, but he didn't seem to care. He didn't seem to care about anything except deepening the kiss so that she quickly became weak with longing, but she drew her head back when she heard him moan.

'Am I hurting you?' she whispered.

'No.' Grabbing her ponytail as if it was a rope, he tipped her head back so that she was caught in the spotlight of his eyes. 'But I am at something of a disadvantage, since the doctor has suggested I avoid any strenuous movement.' His eyes gleamed. 'And since I am in no position to undress you or to master you—I think you will have to play the dominatrix this time.'

Erin froze. Until her sister had lent her *that* book last year, she hadn't even known what the word 'dominatrix' *meant*. She wondered if he was expecting some kind of souped-up sexual performance from her. Yet here was she—not a virgin, but very nearly. Did she come straight out and tell him that?

'You know,' he said, filling the silence, 'the suggestion wasn't supposed to make your eyes widen with horror. That is not what a man intends when he wants to have sex with a woman.'

'I don't want you to be disappointed.'

His hand still wrapped around her ponytail, he steered her face towards his. 'What are you talking about?'

'I'm not very…experienced.'

'Some men might consider a lack of experience to be a positive advantage.'

'And are you one of those men?'

He shook his head. 'Not now, Erin. I know how much you love to talk, but now is not a good time to discuss my sexual preferences.' His expression changed. 'Because every time you react to one of my remarks, you jerk your head back—causing your hips to slide over mine. And as a result, my erection is getting stronger by the minute—a fact which cannot have escaped you, *zvezda moya*.'

No, of course it hadn't escaped her. She didn't need to be experienced to realise just how aroused he was. She could feel the unfamiliar ridge pressing hard against one of her thighs and she told herself that now was the time for her to get off the divan and suggest putting more distance between them, not less. *Because surely that was what any sane person in her position would do.*

'We aren't supposed to be doing this,' she whispered as the finger which had been at the base of her neck began to slide slowly downwards.

'This?'

She forced herself to say it. To say it as it was and not how she'd like it to be. 'Sex.'

His finger stilled in its tantalising journey towards her breast. 'Do you want to stop?'

She closed her eyes, as if blotting out the distraction of his face could help her come to the right decision, but even that didn't help. She wriggled and shook her head. 'No,' she breathed.

'So stop analysing,' he instructed. 'And take off my clothes.'

Dimitri could feel her trembling as she unclipped the waistband of his jodhpurs and heard her unsteady rush of breath as she eased down the straining zipper. He shifted uncomfortably on the divan, trying to focus on something other than his body, trying to slow down the race of his own desire—because he could never remember sexual desire feeling quite so potent, nor so *dangerous.*

As she began to peel the jodhpurs down over his thighs he forced himself to remember that, for all her supposed sweetness and innocence, he couldn't trust her. He'd put Erin Turner in a different category from any other woman he'd ever known, and he was a fool to have done so. Because she wasn't different. She was exactly the same. Selfish. Calculating. Single-minded. She hadn't even given him a chance to get to know his son, or to see whether he'd changed, because it hadn't suited her to do so. *And because children were nothing but pawns in the lives of women.* How could he have forgotten a truth as fundamental as that?

His anger had made him even more aroused—something he hadn't thought possible—and he enjoyed the darkening of her eyes as he breathed out a series of instructions to her. 'Go over to my wash bag and find my condoms. No, let me put it on—you just concentrate on taking off your dress. Mmm… That's better. Now your panties. And your bra. And then climb on top of me and take me inside you. *Da.* Just like that. Oh, God, Erin—just like that.'

With his hands on her narrow hips and her small breasts positioned perfectly for his delectation, he watched as she came very quickly. And so did he. Too quickly, perhaps. He could have carried on having sex with her for hours and already his desire was returning with an intensity which took his breath away, but he forced himself to roll to the other side of the large divan—as if putting distance between them was the only sensible thing he'd done all day.

'What did you mean?' he asked, when eventually his breathing was steady enough for him to make himself understood. 'When you said you weren't very experienced?'

Her eyes were wary as she looked at him—like a small animal who had inadvertently wandered into a hostile domain—and she shrugged, as if embarrassed.

'It doesn't matter.'

'It does,' he contradicted.

'Because you say so?'

He smiled. 'Precisely.'

She began to play with the ends of her hair. 'You're the only man I've ever had sex with.'

A sudden silence fell between them. Her answer was so unexpected that it took a moment for him to process it.

'Why?' he said, at last.

'Why do you think?' Her words came out in a rush, as if she had been bottling them up for a long time. 'First I was pregnant and then I had a tiny baby who wasn't very fond of sleeping, which meant I kept dozing off at various points during the day and forgetting to wash my hair and my tops always seemed to be stained with milk. That's never really a good look. And then the baby grew into a demanding toddler who was into everything, so that I felt like some kind of maternal health and safety expert trying to keep him out of trouble. I was helping my sister with the café and trying to keep our heads above water and I…' Her words faded away and a shuttered look came over her face, as if she'd said too much and only just realised it. 'There was never really time for men.'

'So if I was your first lover—'

'You *knew* that?'

He gave a faint smile. 'Of course I knew it. I may have often been accused of a lack of sensitivity towards women—but never when it comes to sex.'

Her green eyes looked confused. 'But you didn't… you didn't mention it at the time.'

'And neither did you.' He shrugged. 'That night was supposed to be about pleasure—not an anatomical discussion about why your hymen was still intact.'

Her green eyes spat fire as she pulled the coverlet up over her breasts. 'How *callous* you can be, Dimitri!'

'You think so?' He narrowed his eyes as he looked at her. 'Don't you think that after everything which has happened between us, we now deserve the truth?'

'Even if the truth hurts?'

'But being hurt is a part of life. A big part of it—as is regret,' he said. 'And if you must know, I was angry with myself for having sex with you that night.'

'Angry?' She sounded bewildered. 'Why?'

'Because you were an employee and I liked you that way. I had crossed a line I never intended to cross. And because it is a responsibility when a man takes a woman's virginity.'

'Responsibility?' She repeated the word in horror.

'Of course it is,' he said. 'I didn't want you fixating on me, or clinging to me or deciding that I was the man who was going to make you happy. And I just couldn't work out how it had happened, that was the most frustrating thing. How years of a perfectly satisfying platonic relationship had suddenly erupted into something which was so unbelievably X-rated. So tell me, Erin—since we're being truthful—did you choose me because you were aware of my reputation as a lover and considered me the most suitable candidate to take your virginity? Because you knew that I was the man most likely to give you pleasure?'

She didn't answer straight away and when she did, her voice was shaking. 'You flatter yourself,' she said. 'As well as misjudging me, if you think I could have been that cold-blooded about it. I didn't *choose* you. It just happened.'

'You just *happened* to bring a totally unnecessary batch of paperwork round to my apartment when it could have waited until morning?'

'I was worried about you,' she said. 'Worried sick, if you must know. You seemed to have a permanent hangover and to exist on no sleep. Your bodyguard told me you were living like a vampire. And then he resigned and there was all that trouble in Paris and I didn't trust your new bodyguard one bit. Every time the phone rang I thought it was going to be the hospital telling me you'd been admitted. Or the morgue telling me you were lying on a slab...'

'So you thought a little creature comfort might bring me to my senses?' he mocked as her words tailed off. 'That a taste of the pure and innocent Erin Turner might be enough to make me see the error of my ways?'

'You are hateful, Dimitri.'

'Maybe I am. But I've never pretended to be anything else,' he said, steeling himself against the hurt which was clouding her green eyes and telling himself it was better this way. Because although she'd told him she didn't believe in love, he wasn't sure he believed her. Women were programmed to believe in it, weren't they? Better she didn't start thinking he was someone who was capable of providing her with happiness. Especially not domestic happiness. 'Didn't anyone ever teach you that it's a bad idea to go to a man's apartment late at night, looking so unbelievably sexy?'

'I was wearing my navy work suit and a white shirt!' she protested. 'It was hardly what you'd call provocative.'

'Not intentionally, no.' His voice deepened. 'But you were. I'll never forget the sight of you standing there, all wide-eyed and soaking wet.'

'I didn't know it was going to rain!'

'And I wasn't expecting my secretary to ring the doorbell looking as if she'd just taken part in a wet T-shirt competition.'

He hadn't been planning to kiss her, either. It had been a combination of factors which had made something inside him snap. Her wide-eyed look of concern, which had contrasted with the erotic spectacle of that forbidding suit clinging to her slim body. Her complete obliviousness as to how *sexy* she looked had sealed her fate. He had been existing in such a dark place for so long and in that moment Erin had looked like a beacon of light. He'd given in to impulse and kissed her. And hadn't the way she'd responded driven him wild? He remembered being taken aback that his unassuming secretary should suddenly morph into a little wildcat when he'd taken her in his arms. He remembered telling himself he would stop. Just one more kiss and he would definitely stop...

But he hadn't stopped, had he? He had been unable to prevent himself from plunging into her tight, wet warmth and being the first man ever to possess her. He remembered that he had never come quite so many times in one night. That he seemed to have a permanent hard-on whenever he looked at her. Yet his conscience had troubled him afterwards and *that* in itself was unusual, for he had been brought up to believe that conscience was a waste of time. Had he known on some subliminal level before he'd even kissed her that she was innocent—and didn't that make his subsequent self-contempt seem a little hypocritical?

The only honourable thing he'd done was to make sure he'd used contraception—even if it had subsequently failed. And then he had left the country.

Had he been afraid that desire would overcome him again? That he would become one of those clichéd men who slept with their secretary and she'd end up knowing everything about him, instead of just the lion's share? Or was he just afraid that he would hurt her very badly—and someone like Erin did not deserve to be hurt.

But it seemed that he had been regarding her through rose-tinted spectacles and that she had been perfectly capable of her own brand of deception and lies. Her own brand of hurt.

An uneasy silence had fallen again and he didn't object when she climbed off the divan and bent down to pick up her discarded clothes. He felt more in control when she was away from him and control was vital. Especially now. Because nothing had changed, he reminded himself grimly. She had kept their son hidden from him. She was no friend to him.

The armful of clothes was concealing her naked breasts, but her neck was flushed pink and the dark triangle of hair at the fork of her thighs made his body flood with another powerful wave of lust.

And it wasn't going to happen, he told himself grimly. *There was going to be no more intimacy, no matter how much he wanted it. Because sex with Erin Turner didn't feel anonymous—it made him feel exposed and weak. And he didn't do weak.*

'So what do you think we should do now?' she questioned, her voice breaking into his uncomfortable thoughts.

'Now?' He could hear the uncertainty in her voice and it pleased him. It made him feel in control again—even if he had to shift his body beneath the coverlet to hide his growing erection. 'I shall rest for a while as the doctor instructed—and after that I shall meet with the Sheikh, as was originally planned. I'm sure you can find plenty with which to amuse yourself in the meantime. There is a magnificent library here in the palace, or you could ask one of the servants to show you around the gardens. I believe they are very famous.' He let his heavy eyelids fall and failed to stifle a yawn as he blotted out the unsettling look of distress in her eyes. 'But I am weary now, Erin—so let me sleep.'

CHAPTER EIGHT

How *COULD* SHE?

Erin walked to the edge of the man-made lake which dominated the sheltered grounds at the rear of the palace and stared gloomily at the gleaming water. How could she have done something so fundamentally *self-destructive*? She'd had sex with Dimitri. Despite knowing that it was the action of a fool, she had walked straight into it.

The sun dazzled off the glittering surface of the lake and now and then an exotic bird would swoop down to drink. These gardens were like an oasis—one of the most beautiful places she'd ever visited—yet all Erin could think about was that erotic episode on the divan yesterday, following Dimitri's riding accident.

He'd been so matter-of-fact about it afterwards, displaying a cold-bloodedness she remembered from watching him doing countless business deals. Once that amazing bout of sex was over, he seemed to have retreated from her—physically *and* mentally—just like last time. He hadn't touched her again, had just rolled over and turned his back on her and gone to sleep. And even though she'd told herself that his body was still recovering from the accident on the horse—it had only increased her feelings of mortification.

She had gone back to her own suite, feeling empty and a little bit *cheap*, and the long shower she'd taken afterwards hadn't made her feel much better. But she had done her best to stay calm and tried very hard to keep herself occupied, because activity stopped her brooding and dwelling on what she'd done. She explored the palace library as Dimitri had suggested and made it her personal mission to find her way around the bewildering maze of wide marble corridors which made up the Al Mektala residence. She spent several hours being driven out into the desert—accompanied by the woman who had brought the fire-berry lotion to Dimitri's suite, who actually turned out to be very sweet. And although she had tried to take in the stark beauty of the stark desert sands, unwanted images of Dimitri's ice-blue eyes kept flashing through her mind.

And he hadn't come near her. He hadn't touched her, or kissed her. There had been no silent message which had passed between them to acknowledge their shared intimacy.

Erin kept trying to convince herself that this new stand-off was sensible. More sex would complicate an already complicated situation—she *knew* that. Yet she was finding his behaviour more wounding than any open hostility. He was treating her with all the polite indifference he might have shown to a passing waitress at a cocktail party. As if the man who had kissed her so passionately yesterday morning was nothing but a figment of her imagination. She found herself dressing for their final dinner at the palace with a heavy heart.

When he knocked, she opened the door to find him

wearing a darker than usual suit, which made him look powerful and forbidding.

'I'm having a final meeting with Saladin before dinner, so I'll come back and collect you once it's over,' he said, his hair gleaming molten gold beneath the glittering chandelier. 'Oh, and we will leave for London tomorrow. The jet will be ready for us in the morning. I'm sure you'll be keen to get back.'

'Absolutely.' Erin was determined to match his cool demeanour even though her teeth were gritted behind her smile. 'I'll ring my sister.'

'You spoke to her earlier?'

'Yes.'

'How's Leo?' he asked suddenly.

'He's fine.'

There was a pause. 'He hasn't missed you too much?'

'It's barely been two days.' She hesitated, because this was the closest they'd come to conversation since they'd had sex and she found herself wanting to prolong it. To pretend that everything was normal when nothing felt normal. 'Has the Sheikh come to any decision about selling you the oil fields?'

He finished knotting his tie—a blue silk affair one shade darker than his eyes. 'He says he'll give me his answer this evening. Though I suspect that is simply a formality and his answer will be yes.'

'You sound surprised.'

'I suppose I am—a little. After all these years of one step forward, two steps back—the deal has been much more straightforward than I ever anticipated.'

'Because you saved his life?'

He shrugged. 'Probably.'

She shifted from one foot to the other, aware that her

composure was in danger of deserting her as the reality of returning to London loomed before her. 'What's going to happen when we get back?'

He lifted his dark brows in query. 'In regard to?'

Her heart began to pound. 'Leo, of course. About you...getting to know him.'

He raised his eyebrows. 'You would prefer it if I didn't?'

To Erin's horror his words struck a chord, highlighting a part of herself she didn't like. A selfish, horrible part which made her wish he would just disappear and take with him his ability to inflict pain and hurt on her stupidly vulnerable heart. 'No,' she said, wondering if he could hear the hesitation in her voice. 'That isn't what I want, but...'

'But? You still think I'm unsuitable? I've failed the Erin Turner fit-to-be-a-father test? You think I'll be dragging him to the nearest bar or casino as soon as he's old enough?'

She met the challenge in his eyes, reminding herself that her own feelings weren't the issue here—but those of her son were paramount. And Dimitri needed to know that. He needed to know that she would fight with everything she possessed to protect her little boy from being hurt or disappointed.

'No, I don't think that,' she said. 'You don't seem like that kind of man any more. But there are other considerations, Dimitri.'

'To do with you?'

She shook her head. Did he think she was about to start clinging to him because they'd just had sex? 'No. To do with him. I don't want you coming into his life on a whim. You can't just waltz in and tell him you're his father and decide you don't really like fatherhood—before disappearing again.'

'So what are you suggesting?'

'I'm just asking you to give it a little time before you tell him who you are. In case you want to walk away. I'm giving you an opt-out clause in case you change your mind.' She held up her hand, as if anticipating his objections. 'Because children take up a lot of time. They're demanding. They need love and reassurance and stability—and it's constant. You can't just close the door on them and tell them to go away. You've always lived life on your terms, Dimitri—more than anyone else I've ever known. You might find the responsibilities of parenthood don't suit you, and if that's the case, then that's fine. No one is going to condemn you for that—least of all me. I just don't want you making promises to him. Promises you are unable to keep. Surely you can understand that?'

Their gazes clashed for a moment before he nodded his head.

'Yes, I can understand,' he said as he left her suite and headed towards the Sheikh's private apartments, thinking about everything she'd said and the painful honesty with which she'd chosen her words. He was beginning to understand now that when it came to Leo, she was the one with all the power and it was rare for him to be in the weaker position. Was that why he had stayed away from her since the erotic encounter after his riding accident—because that was *his* way of wielding power? He had known that he could have taken her in his arms at any time and had her gasping with desire within minutes. But something had stopped him. What was it? Something to do with the way she made him feel? As if he were some sort of jigsaw which had been scattered and she was eager to put all the pieces back together again. And he didn't want that. He didn't want anyone *reconstructing* him.

The corridors were cool as he walked towards the Sheikh's private apartments and he could see the outline of the moon beginning to appear in the still blue sky. He thought how ironic it was that for months this had been the one thing he'd wanted above all else. A deal with Saladin Al Mektala. Oil in exchange for diamonds. A foothold in the Middle East at last and a triumph to eclipse all his most recent triumphs.

But suddenly its allure seemed to have faded and all he could think about was the little boy with the golden hair and eyes so like his own. And inevitably those thoughts led back to Erin…

He was shown into a high-ceilinged room which resembled a cross between a library and a study. Oil paintings of magnificent horses lined the walls and priceless artefacts drew the eye like museum pieces. On the Sheikh's desk was a photo of Saladin holding the prestigious Omar Cup, a gleaming chestnut stallion beside him, and Dimitri took a moment to study it.

'That was one of my proudest moments,' said Saladin, his deep voice breaking the silence as he emerged from the shadows of the room, his eyes following the direction of the Russian's gaze.

'But?' said Dimitri, lifting his gaze from the photo and supplying the word which seemed to hang in the air, like the rich incense which scented the room.

The Sheikh's eyes gleamed as he sat down behind the desk and indicated a chair opposite for Dimitri.

'Victory seems irrelevant when you are forced to

face your own mortality as I have had to do,' he said heavily. 'If it had been another man but you racing against me, I might not be here today—for the desert lands breed many enemies who would have been glad to see me disfigured, or to have perished. Who would have enjoyed seeing me fall beneath all the galloping power of those two mighty horses, knowing that I have no living heir and that all my lands would pass into the hands of a distant branch of the family.' The king's black eyes gleamed. 'But then, few men other than you would have accepted my challenge to race, for all kinds of reasons.'

'But how could I resist a challenge from a king?' said Dimitri mockingly.

'Even if doing so caused obvious distress to the beautiful woman accompanying you?'

For some reason it irritated Dimitri to hear Saladin describe Erin as beautiful. He had not brought her here to be gazed at and complimented by a powerful sheikh. 'I do not live my life in accordance with the wishes of others,' he said stiffly. 'I act as I see fit.'

'But your actions placed you in mortal danger.'

Dimitri shrugged. 'To brush with death is inevitable. It is part of life itself.'

Saladin picked up a gleaming golden pen. 'But the timing of such a brush is crucial, don't you think? And this one especially so. It has made me re-examine my life. I wonder if it will make you do the same.' Abruptly, he signed the thick sheet of parchment which lay before him and then looked up. 'The oil fields are yours.'

Dimitri inclined his head. 'Thank you.'

'My lawyers will be in touch. But, Dimitri—'

Dimitri had been about to rise from the chair until

the monarch's unfamiliar use of his first name made him pause.

He raised his eyebrows. 'Majesty?'

The Sheikh paused, as if he was about to start speaking in a language unfamiliar to him. 'I recognise in you someone with demons,' he said softly. 'The demons which seem to plague all successful men. And sometimes the only way to rid ourselves of them is to confront them without fear.'

The Sheikh's words echoed around his head as Dimitri made his way back to his suite. It was a curiously personal remark for a king to make—especially one with the stony reputation of Saladin. Was the bond forged between them over that near-fatal race responsible for such an uncharacteristic statement, and was it true? Dimitri shut the door behind him. *Were* his demons still dominating his life because he had failed to reach out and confront them?

He realised that it was not just Erin's deception which had angered him, or the powerlessness he'd felt about being presented with a fatherhood he had not chosen. It was the fear of fatherhood itself. Would his inability to love or nurture damage that laughing little boy whose life was materially poor but emotionally rich? And Saladin's words came back to him again. Surely he had to *try*.

He went to Erin's suite to take her to dinner and she looked up from the book she was reading. The gleam of the chandeliers shone on her dark hair and the claret silk dress caressed her slender body, and automatically he felt his body stiffen with desire. But desire could cloud your judgement. It could distract you from the things which really mattered—and right now he knew what mattered most.

He stared into Erin's green eyes, knowing how incompatible their two lifestyles were. He hadn't known precisely what it was he wanted, or how he was going to go about the daunting task of discovering fatherhood.

Until now.

The idea hit him with a sudden resolve. A primitive and bone-deep certainty, which seemed to have been inspired by Saladin's words. It felt like a distant call to his own ancestry—yet how could that make any sense when his past was so tainted and warped?

But sometimes instinct could be stronger than reason and there was no waver in his voice as he spoke. 'I want to take Leo to my country,' he said.

The book slipped from her fingers.

'You mean, to Russia?'

Something stirred deep within his heart as he nodded.

'*Da*. To Russia,' he echoed, and saw the uncertainty which clouded her face.

CHAPTER NINE

A DISTANT DOOR slammed and a little boy came running into the room, pulling off his waterproof jacket and shaking his head like a puppy. Raindrops showered down over the worn carpet as Erin stepped forward to take the jacket from her son.

'Hello, darling,' she said, trying to act as normally as possible, but it wasn't easy. How could she act normally when Dimitri was standing there staring at Leo—his blue eyes burning with what looked like a distinct sense of ownership? She thought how out of place he looked in his expensive grey suit, dominating the small room at the back of the café. She wished she'd asked her sister to stay for some moral support, but had decided against it at the last minute. She needed to do this on her own. With Leo. Just the three of them. Swallowing down her anxiety, she replaced it with a bright smile as she looked at her son. 'Darling, I want you to meet a friend of mine.'

Leo, a child who always seemed to be in perpetual motion, stood and stared up at the man with all the unembarrassed curiosity of a child.

'What's your name?'

'Dimitri. And you're Leo.'

'Who told you that?'

'Your mummy did.'

A silent look passed between them.

'Why do you talk in that funny voice?'

'Because I am from Russia.'

'Where's Russia?'

Dimitri smiled. 'It is a vast and magnificent land which straddles both Europe and Asia. We have lots of snow in winter and very beautiful buildings which are like no others you will ever see. I could show you where it is on a map if you would like that.' He lifted his gaze to Erin's. 'Do you have any maps around the place, Erin?'

'I'm sure I can find one,' she said, but her heart was beating very fast and she wasn't sure why.

It turned out to be one of the most bizarre evenings of her life. During occasional moments of wistfulness or vulnerability, she'd sometimes tried to picture Dimitri with his son but had found it impossible to imagine the icy oligarch being warm and loving towards a child. Maybe she had misjudged him, or he was a better actor than she'd thought—because soon Leo was sitting happily up beside him as he pointed out seas and rivers on the map.

She'd told him that he couldn't just swoop into their lives and carry Leo off to Russia—that he had to get to know the little boy first. She just hadn't expected it to go so *well*. And when, a week later, she walked into the room and found two heads of molten gold bent over the table together in silent concentration as Dimitri showed Leo a photograph, a shiver of something like fear whispered over her skin.

Already they were sharing secrets.

Already she was the outsider.

'What's that?' she said, glancing down at the photograph, which showed a beautiful house.

Dimitri raised his head. 'It's a place outside Moscow which I own.'

'That's…nice,' she said, her voice growing uncertain.

He smiled but Erin could see a flicker of triumph in his blue eyes. 'And I think we should take Leo there,' he said.

'Can we go, Mummy?' Leo was asking, a look of excitement on his face. '*Can* we?'

Erin stared into the eyes which glittered so icily above Leo's head and felt a punch of helpless rage. Hadn't he ever heard of consensus? Of running it past her first? Of course not. He didn't negotiate with women, because they always caved in and gave him exactly what he wanted. 'I'm not sure if I can get anyone to cover for me at the café—not at such short notice.'

'I can get you all the cover you need,' he said, with cool assurance. 'Neither you nor your sister need worry about a thing.'

He was just going to throw money at the problem, Erin thought. And there was nothing she could do to stop it. This was going to happen whether she liked it or not.

'In that case, I don't see why not,' she said lightly. 'It's half-term next week, after all.'

Moscow was a city straight out of a fairy tale. As if Walt Disney had met with the local architects and been given a free hand in its design. Intricate buildings were topped with brightly coloured turrets shaped like artichokes. Golden monuments dazzled with giant stars. Statuesque government buildings lined the wide Moskva River, where boats drifted by in slow motion—all seen from the helicopter which had been waiting to whisk them away from the airport.

Despite her reservations about the trip, Erin could feel a growing sense of excitement as she looked around, while Leo was almost incoherent with delight as the bird-like craft whirred over the Russian capital.

'Will it snow?' asked Leo eagerly as he stared up into the clear blue sky. 'Will it? My teacher says it always snows in Russia.'

'Not always,' answered Dimitri. 'It usually starts at the end of October, so we may just miss it.'

Leo scowled. 'But I want snow. I want to build a snowman!'

'In that case...' Dimitri smiled '...we might just have to come back again when it's colder.'

His words made Erin's fingers stiffen as she wound her new pashmina around her neck. She was trying not to fret about how her son would readjust to life in Bow after a trip like this, because how could he fail to be affected by Dimitri's lifestyle? If he'd tasted private jets and helicopters and fast cars, surely it would seem mundane to have to hop on the local bus. If the man organising all this had only to lift his hand for someone to cater to his every whim—as had been demonstrated on every step of their journey—then wouldn't Leo be seduced by that, no matter how hard she'd tried to bring him up to appreciate the simple things in life?

And what about her? Was she also in danger of being affected by the Russian influence and undeniable sex appeal? She'd been so sure of the person she was. Someone who didn't want to believe in love any more. Someone who'd had her fingers burned and her heart bruised when she'd fallen for her oligarch boss all those years ago. She'd convinced herself that she had learned her lesson and would never allow herself to feel like that again.

So why was Dimitri dominating her thoughts like a pop song she couldn't get out of her head? She knew he was no good for her. He'd made it clear he no longer wanted her. He'd had sex with her and then just pushed her away afterwards. He'd rejected her all over again and it hurt. It hurt like hell.

She shot a glance at his profile, at the high slash of his cheekbones and hard set of his lips. The sun was flooding into the helicopter, making him look precious and powerful—as if he'd been dipped in gold.

'Look down there,' said Dimitri, his rich accent breaking into her troubled thoughts. 'We're nearly there.'

They were passing over a huge patch of dark and impenetrable trees before beginning their descent towards the smooth circle of a helipad on the outskirts of the forest. A rush of air came up to meet them and a man on the ground signalled to the pilot—his hair plastered to his head as the craft came rocking to a halt. The blades stopped spinning and Dimitri jumped out, holding up his arms to Leo, while Erin exited the craft with as much grace as possible, glad she'd worn trousers.

A four-wheel drive was waiting and Dimitri took the wheel, speeding along a straight road which looked uncannily quiet after the crowded streets of Moscow. Soon they were entering the forest through a concealed and guarded entrance and passing mansion after mansion, some completely hidden behind high, dense hedges, while others offered a tantalising glimpse of turrets and towers.

Dimitri indicated left and the car swung through a huge pair of electronic gates and Erin peered out of the window. 'What is this place?' she asked.

'It's a private estate and each house is called a *dacha*. In England some people own second homes in the country and this is similar. Many Russians have them. It's where I did most of my growing up.'

'I thought you grew up in Moscow.'

'No. My father was in the city a lot, but my mother preferred it here. They call it Moscow's secret city. Many people think it doesn't exist—that it's just a myth—but as you can see for yourself, it isn't. Just that not everyone knows where to find it, and that's deliberate. It's where the rich live—and play. Where there's no pressure to be modest and no shame in showing off your wealth. They say that security here is tighter than in the Kremlin and very few outsiders are permitted entry. You should count yourself privileged, Erin.'

Privileged? She felt closer to panic, especially when Leo clutched at her hand.

'Look, Mummy—look!'

Erin turned her head to see him pointing towards a stunning art deco house, which Erin recognised immediately. It was the house from the photograph. Up close, the tall house was even larger and more imposing than it had appeared in the glossy photo, and the unusual curved wooden door made it look like something out of a fairy tale.

There were so many questions Erin wanted to ask but there wasn't time because the front door was being opened by a homely-looking woman whose creased face broke into a wide smile when she saw Dimitri. She looked as if she wanted to fling her arms around him but didn't quite dare. And Erin was surprised by one of the most unguarded smiles she'd ever seen on the oligarch's face as he bent his head to kiss the woman's cheeks before speaking to her in rapid Russian.

'This is Svetlana,' he said, 'who used to look after me when I was a little boy, even younger than you are now, Leo. Svetlana—this is Erin, Leo's mother.'

'You are very…welcome,' said Svetlana in halting English, her eyes softening as she looked down at Leo. 'Come inside, little one. You must be tired.'

Automatically, Leo shook his head. 'I'm not tired,' he said.

'Well, that is good!' Svetlana smiled. 'I wonder, do you like gingerbread, Leo? We have much famous gingerbread here in Russia and we like to eat it with hot, sweet tea. It was Dimitri's favourite when he was a little boy. Would you like to try some?'

Expecting continued resistance, Erin glanced down at her son—but he was wearing the same expression he'd had the first time she'd taken him to meet Father Christmas. Was the child who was notoriously picky when it came to food really taking Svetlana's outstretched hand and wandering off with her towards the back of the house as if they'd known each other all their lives? It seemed he was.

For a while she stood listening to the sound of their retreating footsteps until at last they became silent and she was left alone with Dimitri. His hands were on her shoulders as he helped her out of her coat, his fingers brushing softly across her back and making her spine tingle.

'Come with me,' he said and she followed him into a reception room which overlooked the sweeping gardens at the back of the house. It was a breathtakingly impressive room and she looked around it with an undeniable sense of wonder. Who would ever have guessed that such an exquisite place lay in the middle of some random forest?

Fabergé eggs stood on gilded furniture, and a bonsai tree which stood in pride of place on a lacquered Chinese table made her think of his apartment in London. She walked over and stared at the perfectly formed miniature leaves and wondered how on earth he could get experts to come and tend it—all these miles from Moscow. How many apartments and houses and bonsai trees did he actually own? Did they all merge into one, she wondered—so that sometimes he forgot which city he was in? Were the women who passed through his life just as interchangeable as his houses?

She looked up to meet the blue ice of his gaze. 'Is this your real home?'

He gave an oblique smile. 'I visit here maybe three or four times a year—more if the opportunity arises.'

'You maintain a house this size just for the occasional visit?' She looked at him incredulously. 'Why would you do that?'

'Why not? Russians like owning bricks and mortar because they represent security. It is also Svetlana's home,' he added. 'And I owe her a debt of care. Her son tends the gardens here and his wife helps maintain the house.' His gaze drifted over her and lingered on her face. 'But my property empire isn't what's uppermost on my mind at the moment.'

His voice had deepened. It seemed to whisper over

her skin like velvet, but she kept her voice careless. *He's not going to play games with you*, she thought fiercely. *He's just not.* 'Oh?'

His gaze was very steady. 'You may have noticed that I have been a little *cool* towards you.'

She tried not to react. 'Yeah, I've noticed.'

'And you're probably wondering why.'

'Don't worry, Dimitri—I'm not losing any sleep over it.'

He studied the bonsai tree for a moment, before glancing up again. 'I thought it would be better for both of us—and for Leo—if we attempted to keep our relationship platonic. I thought that what happened in Jazratan would be better kept as a one-off. I thought the fewer complications, the better. But maybe I was wrong.'

'Dimitri Makarov wrong?' she questioned sarcastically. 'Gosh. Can I have that in writing?'

'Because despite everything that has happened,' he continued, as if she hadn't spoken, 'and despite the note of caution in my head, there is one factor which outweighs all the others...and that is that I still want you, *zvezda moya*. In fact, I cannot believe how badly I want you.' He smiled. 'And I know enough about women to realise that the feeling is mutual.'

Erin met his eyes, trying to ignore the instinctive rush of heat to her body and to concentrate instead on his arrogant words. *Note of caution?* Had he really said that? Of course he had. Because not only was arrogance one of his faults—he also had a complete inability to recognise it! She drew in a shaky breath. 'Oh, I might want you,' she agreed. 'I'm not enough of a hypocrite to deny that.'

'So?' he questioned, unabashed, the hint of that smile still playing at the edges of his mouth.

Expectation was coming off him in waves which were almost tangible and Erin felt a flare of anger. She recognised that there was an element of negotiation in what he was saying, but it wasn't enough. Not nearly enough. Was she expected to grab at whatever scraps he threw her? To settle for something which sounded like a reluctant afterthought?

'So, nothing! Do you really expect me to accommodate your see-sawing desires just like that?' she demanded, snapping her fingers in the air. 'To behave like an obedient puppet, just waiting for you to pull my strings one minute and then smilingly accept it when you put me back in the box the next?'

His eyes narrowed. 'Why the hell do you have to analyse everything to death?' he gritted.

'Because that's what women do,' she retorted. 'And we file it under self-respect. I may have made mistakes in the past and perhaps I should have acknowledged them sooner, but I'm doing my best to make amends for that now. I'm sorry I excluded you from Leo's life without giving you the opportunity to prove you've changed. That's one of the reasons I've come to Russia with you, even though it's...*difficult*. But there's no way I'm going to be treated like a convenient plaything while I'm here, no matter how many of my buttons you press. So if you'd please show me my room, I'd like to go and unpack.'

His face was a picture, Erin thought. A mixture of disbelief and fury as he muttered something decidedly angry in Russian before turning away and stomping towards the grand staircase. But his discomfiture was small consolation for the aching in her body and the even greater aching in her heart.

CHAPTER TEN

IT WAS THE first time in a long time that Erin had been given a room she could call her own. She'd shared a cramped bedroom with Leo since the day she'd first brought him home from hospital and was used to tip-toeing around and condensing her stuff into the small-est possible space while fighting a losing battle against clutter. But Leo was now ensconced in his own cosy set of rooms just along the corridor and playing with every remaining toy from Dimitri's childhood, which had been dragged down from the attic by Svetlana's son.

Following her explosive row with Dimitri, he had taken himself off to his study and shut the door very firmly behind him. It had been left to Svetlana to take her and Leo on a guided tour of the house, showing them the countless rooms, the beautiful gardens and finally the indoor swimming pool, which gleamed in-vitingly and made Leo squeal with delight. Erin felt her heart plummet. She hated swimming at the best of times and was dreading her son's next inevitable demand, when Dimitri walked into the pool complex.

'Do you like swimming, Leo?'

Erin's heart pounded as she looked up to meet the cool blue gaze, but there was no mockery or flirtation there. The briefest of smiles and a cursory nod were his only acknowledgement to her, before he crouched down to his son's level.

'He doesn't swim,' she said quickly.

'In that case, I can teach him.'

She didn't even get a chance to say that Leo had brought nothing suitable to wear in the water, because it seemed that swimming trunks and armbands were readily available and had already been purchased from a nearby department store. It made Erin realise that, behind the scenes, Dimitri must have been making plans for his son's arrival before she'd even agreed to the trip and that made her feel odd. Manipulated, almost. But she didn't have the heart to spoil Leo's fun and her guilty secret was that she enjoyed watching Dimitri put himself out for someone else in a way she'd never seen him do before. And wasn't the shameful truth that she also enjoyed looking at that powerful body in a pair of clinging swim-shorts, despite her intention to avert her gaze whenever he levered himself out of the water?

Water highlighted his masculinity. It gleamed and highlighted the golden skin and emphasised the honed contours of his powerful physique. It made her body sizzle with desire and she couldn't work out a way to stop it. And the most infuriating thing was that she could have had him. She could have had him on her first night here, and yet she had turned him down.

By the third day, Leo was not only becoming confident in the water—he was behaving as if he'd spent his whole life living in a luxurious *dacha*. He listened to Dimitri's firm house rules and obeyed them. He knew that the swimming pool was out of bounds unless there was an adult present and in the meantime he made friends with Svetlana's grandson, Anatoly—who was a year older. Erin watched from the sidelines, aware that there was a lot of Dimitri in her son which she'd never seen before. Or never *allowed* herself to see. With the large grounds at his disposal, a playmate and a football, he was able to enjoy the kind of healthy freedom which wasn't readily available in London.

She told herself she was grateful to Dimitri for his hospitality, but his polite and non-committal behaviour towards her was starting to drive her insane. Yet this was what she had actually *asked* for, so she was hardly in a position to complain about it. Was it simply a case of wanting what she couldn't have? Like when you tried to cut down on sugar and it left you craving something sweet.

Dimitri wasn't sweet. He was the antithesis of sweet. He was hard and strong and ruthless. But here he was showing a side of himself she'd never seen before. She'd never imagined he could be so *gentle*, or that his cold face could warm into such a breathtaking smile when he interacted with his little boy.

Suddenly, she felt like someone who had been left out in the cold. As if *she* were the outsider.

After dinner on the third night she'd gone to her room and shut the door behind her with a heavy sigh. She should have felt, if not exactly happy, then at least *content*. It had been another successful day. Dimitri had taken them deep into the forest in the crisp cold, and they'd all been worn out with fresh air and exercise. Leo was fast asleep next door and, although supper had been civilised and delicious, Dimitri had been called to the telephone soon afterwards and had excused himself.

He had shut himself in his study and showed no sign of coming out and so Erin had come upstairs to bed.

She began to unbutton her cardigan, wondering how he would react if she went and found him and told him she'd changed her mind. That she no longer cared about being treated like a plaything if only he would kiss her again. She hung the cardigan over the back of the chair and pulled a face at her washed-out reflection in the mirror. But that would be the action of an idiot, wouldn't it? Long-term pain for short-term gain.

She'd just put on her nightdress when there was a knock at the door and, thinking it might be Leo, she sped over to answer it, her bare feet making no sound on the silky antique rug. But it wasn't Leo; it was Dimitri who stood there and she despaired at the predictability of her reaction as the breath dried hotly in her throat.

'Is it Leo?' she questioned.

'No, Erin—it isn't Leo.' He glanced over her shoulder. 'You weren't in bed?'

'Not yet.' She was grateful for the darkness, which hid her sudden blush. And for the nightdress, which concealed her rapidly hardening nipples. 'I was just about to turn in.'

'May I come in?'

She didn't ask him why and that was her first mistake. Her second was not to move away when he shut the door behind him. To get as far away from the intoxicating closeness of his body as the dimensions of the room would allow.

She tried to match the studied politeness he'd been showing her all day, but suddenly she noticed a new restlessness in his eyes. A certain tension in his powerful body. 'What is it that you want, Dimitri?'

She was trying to sound matter-of-fact but she failed miserably and something about the thready quality of her voice made his eyes narrow.

'I've come to say some things which I should have said a long time ago.'

She looked at him. 'What kind of things?'

Dimitri met the question in her green eyes and hesitated, because what he was about to do did not come easily to him. He had grown up in a world where explanations were never given, where feelings were buried so deeply that you could almost fool yourself into thinking they didn't exist. And he had carried on that same sterile tradition into his own adult life. *Never explain* had been his motto. People could take him as they found him and if they didn't like him, then tough. There were plenty more eager to fall into line, because power made people eager to please you.

But not Erin. Erin was different. She did what she thought was right—no matter at what cost to herself. And she was the mother of his child. She deserved his respect—he realised that now. And maybe she also needed to know some of the things he was fast discovering about himself.

'I understand now why you kept Leo from me for so long,' he said.

Her eyes were wary. 'You do?'

He nodded. 'Why would you want an innocent child being corrupted by someone who saw life through the bottom of a glass, as I did? Whose idea of fun was being the last person left in the casino after he'd emptied his wallet? Who revelled in the sense of danger, as much as the thrill of risk? I don't blame you for cutting me out of his life, because that's what any good mother would do and you are a fantastic mother,' he said slowly. 'And our son is beautiful. He's just beautiful, Erin.'

Erin didn't know what she'd been expecting, but this hadn't even featured on her list of possibilities. And the crazy thing was that the things he'd said made her want to cry. She found herself wishing he'd come and found her a long time ago to tell her he had cleaned up his act and then he could have met Leo a whole lot sooner. She thought of all those wasted years which they could never get back and suddenly she didn't want to risk a moment's more regret.

She blinked away the incipient tears which were pricking at the backs of her eyes. 'Kiss me,' she whispered.

'Erin—'

'Shut up,' she interrupted and in the midst of her hunger and heartache she realised that she was one of the few people he would *allow* to interrupt him like that. 'Just shut up and kiss me, Dimitri. Please.'

He moved forward and cupped her face in his hands and suddenly he was driving his mouth down onto hers, his tongue coaxing her lips apart as he began to explore her with an urgency which made her feel weak. She wondered if it was her self-imposed embargo on sex which made this kiss seem so...*profound*, or because it was underpinned by a distinct air of reconciliation?

She didn't know and, right now, she didn't care. The only thing she cared about was the way he was touching her—running the flat of his hand down over her flower-sprigged nightdress.

'Is this what the English call a passion-killer?' he questioned drily as he peeled off her long nightdress.

'Why?' She shivered as the cool air hit her heated skin. 'Is it working?'

'Are you kidding? It's the sexiest piece of clothing I've ever seen,' he growled as he picked her up and carried her over to the bed.

She helped him undress—her inexperience forgotten in the midst of her excitement at revealing the powerful body. She traced her fingers experimentally over his hair-roughened thighs, feeling stupidly pleased by his exultant shiver and the little groan of satisfaction he made. And wasn't that the thing about Dimitri—that somehow, despite everything, she always felt like his equal in bed?

The sheets felt cool against her naked body but Dimitri was all welcoming warmth as the mattress dipped beneath them. Tilting her chin, he looked at her for one long, wordless moment before slowly lowering his mouth to kiss her.

He wrapped his arms around her—his powerful legs entwining with hers and his fingers stroking her skin, so that at first she shivered and then relaxed. It felt so good to be here with him like this. Unbearably good. She found herself praying that he wouldn't hurt her—before vowing that she wouldn't ever *allow* herself to get hurt.

His hands moved to her hips, urging her even closer, and her nipples grew hard against his chest. She could feel the heavy weight of his erection pushing against her belly and her face grew hot. The blood in her veins seemed to be growing thicker. She could feel the molten heat between her legs and when he slid his fingers there, she writhed with pleasure—moving her body against him in a silent message of invitation.

'You like that, don't you, *milaya moya*?' he whispered and when she nodded eagerly, he whispered into her ear. 'Then *tell* me.'

'I…love it,' she whispered shakily. 'You know I do.'

Somehow he found a condom but his hands were unsteady as he slid it on, before entering her with such exquisite precision that Erin gasped.

He moved slowly at first—as if he had all the time in the world. And wasn't that exactly what it felt like? That for once there were no constraints, or questions. That she could simply enjoy this for what it was.

She was aware that his eyes were open and she felt confident enough to hold his gaze as each thrust took her higher. Every time he moved it increased her pleasure—tightening it, notch by delicious notch. And just when it became almost unbearable her orgasm hit her in waves so powerful that it felt as if it were tearing her body apart. Her fingers tightened around him as he shuddered inside her with a ragged groan of his own.

It seemed like ages before he withdrew and Erin had to fight the urge to claw at him—wanting to bring him back inside her. She turned to look at him. His eyes were closed and he appeared to be sleeping—and she knew him well enough to realise that he'd probably like her to turn over and go to sleep, too. She remembered once overhearing him saying to his friend Ivan: *The trouble with women is that they ask too many questions.*

For a long time she had tried to abide by his pre-ferred diktat, because she'd wanted to be the perfect secretary. She had questioned him only when abso-lutely necessary—but those days were gone. Even if the intimacy they'd just shared didn't give her any rights—surely the fact that they had a son between them allowed her the luxury of asking questions for once. Wasn't it time he told her stuff—instead of mak-ing out that it was presumptuous of her to dare ask?

'Dimitri?'

'Mmm?'

'I want to ask you something.'

He opened his eyes. 'Must you?'

She ignored that, positioning herself more comfortably on the pillows so that she was in the direct line of his cool gaze. 'You know when you were going off the rails?'

'What about it?'

'You just never told me why. What made you do it?'

'Does there have to be a reason, Erin?'

'I don't know. You tell me.'

He was so quiet for a moment that Erin wondered whether he was just going to ignore her question, when suddenly he started talking.

'It was a combination of factors,' he said. 'I was living in London—and that was the world I was inhabiting at the time.'

She rested her chin on his chest and looked up at him. 'What kind of world was that?'

He shrugged. 'The world of success—and excess. My company was doing better than I could have ever dreamed. Suddenly, I had more time. More money. More everything, really. Whatever I touched seemed to turn to gold. My stocks were touching the stratosphere. Women were throwing themselves at me—'

'How unbearable that must have been.'

'At first I can't deny that I enjoyed it,' he said, skating over her sarcasm. 'But it doesn't take long for an appetite to become jaded. For too much to become not nearly enough. Suddenly, nothing ever seemed to *satisfy* me. I tried gambling, and then vodka. But nothing seemed to do it. Nothing could take away...'

His voice trailed off as if he'd said too much but Erin was onto it in an instant.

'Take away what?'

'It doesn't matter.'

'It *does* matter,' she said stubbornly.

His voice hardened. 'The discoveries I had made. The ones which made oblivion seem like a good idea.'

'What kind of discoveries?' she persisted.

'Erin, is this really relevant? We've just had some pretty amazing sex…' he trailed his finger down over her torso until it came to rest comfortably in her belly button '…and now you're ruining it by hurling all these questions at me.'

'How can talking ruin what's just happened?' She pushed his finger away. 'And it *is* relevant. It isn't just prurient curiosity on my part, if that's what you're thinking. It's about a need to know more about my son's heritage—so I don't have to look at him blankly when he asks me the questions he will one day inevitably ask. Because I want to be able to tell Leo the truth from now on.'

'I don't think these are the kind of things you'd want to tell an innocent young boy,' he said bitterly.

'But I'm a grown woman,' she said. 'You can tell me.'

Dimitri stared into her green eyes, thinking how cat-like they looked against her flushed skin. Her dark hair was tumbling over her tiny breasts and every instinct in his body was urging him to block her questions and make love to her again. But some of her words were stubbornly refusing to shift. Didn't matter how much he wanted them to go away; they weren't going to. Because she was right. As the mother of his child didn't she *deserve* to hear the truth?

He gave an expansive flick of his hand—as if to draw attention to the dimensions of the huge room in which they lay. 'You can see for yourself how privileged my background was. I was the only son of a hugely successful businessman and his devoted wife.' He gave a bitter laugh. 'Or that's what I thought I was—until the whole pack of cards came tumbling down.'

For once she was silent, but he felt her grow very still beside him.

'I discovered that my life was nothing but an illusion based on lies and deception,' he said. 'It was all smoke and mirrors and nothing was as it seemed. My father wasn't the respectable businessman I'd always thought. His respectability was just a front for his underworld dealings. He made the bulk of his money from drugs and gambling, and from human trafficking and misery.'

He could see her eyes widening in shock, but he forced himself to continue—as if suddenly recognising the burden of having kept this to himself for all these years. Because wasn't that another legacy of criminality—that the secrets it created tainted everyone around with the sense of nothing being as it should be?

'My relationship with him wasn't good. He was the coldest man I've ever encountered. Sometimes I used to wonder if it was just something inside him which made him so distant—or whether it was something to do with *me*. I wondered why he sometimes looked through me as if I was invisible, or worse. As if he actually *hated* me.' He paused. 'It took a long time for me to discover why.'

'Why?'

He could hear her holding her breath.

'Because he wasn't actually my father,' he said

slowly. 'I was the cuckoo child. A product of a passionate liaison between my mother and the family gardener.'

'Your mother had an affair with the *gardener*?'

He nodded and waited while she processed this piece of information.

'And what was he like? This gardener.'

Dimitri frowned. He had been anticipating judgement—not understanding. Was it that which made him stray deeper into the memory—into the dark place he usually kept locked and bolted?

'A striking man,' he said slowly. 'Tall and muscular, with tawny hair and blue eyes. I remember how much the maids used to idolise him and how women turned to look at him whenever he walked by. But most of all, he was kind. I didn't realise that men could be kind. It never occurred to me to question why he used to spend so much time with me—way more than my father ever did. It didn't even occur to me until much later that whenever I looked at him, it was like looking in the mirror. But afterwards I wished he'd said something—something to acknowledge that I was his. But he never did.' He saw how wide her green eyes had grown. 'Shocked, Erin?'

'Not half as shocked as you must have been.' She seemed to choose her next words with care. 'But if your other father knew you weren't his child, then why did he stay with your mother? Why didn't he just divorce her and cut his losses?'

'And lose face?' Dimitri gave a hollow laugh. 'Admit that some *labourer* had succeeded where he had failed? No. That wasn't the way he operated. My mother's punishment was to remain in a loveless marriage. Locked in a relationship based on fear with a man who despised her. And I think she felt the same way about me. I can

certainly never remember her being warm towards me.'
He sucked in a breath. 'Maybe she didn't dare show me
affection because she knew it would enrage my father.
Or maybe she saw me as a constant reminder of what
she had done. Maybe I represented the failure she'd
made of her life and her relationships.'

'And the gardener? What happened to him?'

There was a long silence before he shrugged. 'One
morning he just wasn't there any more. I remember it
was winter and the front door was open and I went looking for my mother. I found her in the forest, in the little
shed where he used to keep his tools. She was curled up
on the floor crying her eyes out, half mad with grief.'

'And did you...' Erin's hand crept over his and
squeezed it. 'Did you ever meet up with him again?
Did you ever form some kind of relationship and make
peace with the past?'

His eyes were icier than she'd ever seen them—and
that was saying something about a man who could do
every degree of ice.

'No,' he said abruptly. 'Although I tried. After my
mother died I attempted to track him and that was when I
discovered that he had been executed some years before.'

'Executed?'

'Killed by a single bullet to the head in a Moscow
alleyway. It was, as they say in the business, a professional hit.'

'And you think...' She licked her lips. 'You think
your father was behind it?'

'I'm no longer a gambling man,' he said, but she saw
the awful knowledge written in his eyes.

Erin squeezed his hand tighter as she began to understand why he'd wanted to escape from the reality of

his past. Because he had said himself that everyone was a product of their own experience. And Dimitri's was darker than most. His was the kind of past which kept psychiatrists in business. A mother who didn't show her love and a cold-hearted crook who hated you because you weren't his son. A crook who had probably ordered an execution, thus effectively cutting off any opportunity for reconciliation between Dimitri and his real father. Was it any wonder that he'd gone off the rails quite so spectacularly?

She rested her head against his shoulder, even though she wanted to do so much more. She wanted to hug him tightly and tell him everything was going to be all right. She wanted to cover his golden face with kisses and tell him she was there for him and would always be there for him, if only he would let her. But some instinct stopped her. She reminded herself that she didn't *do* emotional stuff like that and, more important, neither did he. Yet it was hard to restrain her instinct to reach out to him and it left her feeling confused.

She told herself that what she was feeling was just natural sympathy after hearing a particularly grim story. Except that it wasn't—because it felt like something more. Something which she'd tried to convince herself was the biggest con in the world and one she was never going to fall for again.

She swallowed as she turned her face away from his.

It felt uncomfortably like love.

CHAPTER ELEVEN

NOW WHAT?

Dimitri glanced across the room to where Leo was teaching Erin how to play the popular card game of P'yanitsa. A game the boy hadn't known how to play until earlier that week, but he was a quick learner—and now he was playing it as well as any Russian. Dimitri felt a stir of pride whisper over him as he studied the bent head of dark gold—so like his own—as once again the question nagged at him.

What was he going to do about the problem of a small boy and a woman who talked more than was comfortable?

His eyes moved to the woman in question as he watched Erin smiling as Leo scooped up a handful of cards with a triumphant whoop. To look at her now— you would never have guessed that a few hours ago he had been deep inside her while the rest of the house still slept. She had ridden him as he had shown her how he liked to be ridden, his hands on either side of her hips as he had positioned her to make penetration even deeper. And afterwards she had choked out her sigh as his tongue had slid down over her and he'd tasted her flesh.

'You must learn to be a good sport, darling,' she was saying softly. 'And to play fair.'

Play fair. It wouldn't have been the lesson Dimitri would have focused on. In fact, up until a week ago, he would have said the opposite—that playing fair never got you anywhere. That in the big, harsh world out there, it was dog eat dog. But now he could see that you shouldn't teach a child to cut corners, or to operate ruthlessly. He understood that you needed to show them how to do things right in order for them to live right. Just because his own childhood had been messed up, that was no reason for him to try to impose his own cynicism on someone else.

And Erin had shown him that—by example rather than preaching. She was patient and understanding with Leo—pretty much every minute of every day—and Dimitri knew with a heavy certainty that he could never be the instrument to drive the two of them apart. His heart pounded. Because hadn't that been a consideration when he'd first found out about Leo—thinking he might be able to lure the boy away using the power of his wealth and influence? He'd planned to show the child that he could have more fun in penthouses and private jets than he ever could living in the cramped quarters above his aunt's café. But that option wasn't on the cards any more—and it made him uncomfortable to think he could have ever entertained such a ruthless strategy.

He stared out of the window, where the grey skies were heavy with snow and the occasional stray flake drifted past like a white feather. But experience told him that the snow would not fall tonight and it looked as if Leo wouldn't get his snowman, no matter how hard he wished for it. Tomorrow they were flying back to England because half-term was almost over and Dimitri knew he needed to come to some sort of decision about what was going to happen.

He waited until Leo had gone through his bedtime routine and, once he'd been embraced in a sleepy bear hug, Dimitri went downstairs to wait for Erin in the library while she read a bedtime story.

He lit a fire, which crackled magnificently—the light from the flames flickering over the rows of books which lined the room, while Shostakovich played in the background. He spoke to Svetlana and soon two crystal flutes were standing beside a bottle in an ice bucket, but Erin's footsteps were so quiet that he didn't realise she was in the room until she was standing right in front of him.

She had changed and brushed her hair, so that it gleamed like a dark waterfall around her shoulders, and a soft woollen dress was hugging her slender hips. He noticed that she frowned slightly when she saw the bottle standing on the table next to the peach blossom bonsai tree.

'Champagne?' she said lightly. 'Why, are we celebrating something?'

'I don't know.' He lifted the bottle from the ice bucket and cold droplets slid onto his fingers. 'At least, not yet.'

'Is this some sort of guessing game?'

'Do you want to try guessing?'

'Okay.' She screwed up her face. 'We're celebrating a successful trip?'

'That's one thing we could drink to, I agree. It has been a very successful trip.' He peeled away the foil and let it flutter to the table. 'Which is why I think we should get married.'

Erin stared at him.

'Did you say *married*—just out of the blue like that?'

'Why not?' There was a hissing little pop as he eased the cork from the bottle. 'What do you say?'

What did she say? Erin swallowed. She didn't have a clue how to respond. She felt perplexed—and bewildered. This had come out of nowhere with no warning whatsoever. And now he was pouring champagne, which was fizzing up the sides of a flute so delicate she was terrified her shaking hand might snap off its fragile stem. She shook her head as he held the flute out towards her.

'Not right now, thanks. This has come as a bit of a shock,' she said, aware of the glaring understatement in her words. She tried to rid her voice of any hope or expectation. 'I mean, *why*? Why do you want to marry me, Dimitri?'

'You don't know?'

'If I knew, I wouldn't have to ask.'

He smiled. 'Because of Leo, of course.'

Of course.

Erin nodded. The logical part of her brain had known that all along but that didn't protect her from the sudden stupid lurch of disappointment which chilled her skin. And she didn't want to be *disappointed*. She wanted to be cool and calm and impartial. Just like him. She wanted to treat a proposal of marriage with the same kind of careless interest as it had been offered. 'And how would that work?' she said.

'Isn't it obvious?'

'Not to me, no. I'm not in the habit of getting random proposals of marriage from men who only a short time ago were barely able to look at me without being furious. You'll have to talk me through it.'

He turned the swell of music down by a fraction and

one of the logs in the fireplace spat out a shoal of bright sparks. 'You must realise that I've grown very fond of Leo.'

She nodded. 'That's good.'

'And I consider you an excellent mother. I told you that.'

'Again, that's very good. But neither of these facts are reasons enough for us to get married, Dimitri.'

'No, they aren't. But there are other considerations, too. Financially you cannot deny that you struggle, while, fortunately, I do not. And my wealth could help make both your lives considerably more comfortable.'

She tried to smile. 'You realise you don't have to put a gold band on my finger in order to pay maintenance?'

The second movement of the concerto came to a finish and the fire spat again—a hissing and angry sound this time.

'Damn you, Erin Turner.' Dimitri's words fell softly and fervently into the short silence which followed. 'Do you really want me to spell this out for you?'

She met his eyes. 'I'm afraid you're going to have to.'

'It's more than just about the money. I want to be *there* for him,' he said, his voice growing deep, and passionate. 'To be there for the ordinary things—not just the high days and holidays. I want grumpy mornings as well as Christmas morning. I want to be hands-on—not absent for most of the time. To give him what I never had.'

Erin stared at him as a bubble of hope began to rise inside her—even though she was doing everything in her power not to get ahead of herself. In case it was futile. In case it hurt her in a way she'd vowed she would never let herself get hurt. 'And you would marry me in order to achieve that?'

'Yes,' he said emphatically. 'I would. Because I've come to realise that you are the perfect woman for me.'

Erin blinked because now hope was refusing to listen

to her reservations. It was hurtling through her body like a runaway train and flattening everything in its track. 'I am?'

His icy eyes glittered. 'Indeed you are. I like the way that you don't try to manipulate me or covet my money, or possessions.' He paused. 'And, of course, you drive me wild in bed. Wilder than I ever thought possible, *zvezda moya*.'

'And that's enough?'

'No, it is not. But you have another attribute which is rare. So rare that I have never found it before. The silver bullet, if you like—which is that you don't love me. You don't believe in love. Well, neither do I.' He smiled. 'Now, isn't that just a match made in heaven?'

Her knees went weak and Erin only just managed to stop herself from crumpling as she listened to his cruel parody of a marriage proposal. Everything a man was traditionally supposed to say at a time like this, he had twisted round. He had made dark what was supposed to be light. He had projected a future which would make their proposed union into nothing but a *mockery*. A pastiche of a marriage, which would be little better than the one which had ruined his own life.

'And you think that's the kind of example I want to set my son?' she questioned, her voice trembling with a hurt she could no longer hide. 'That I want him growing up with two people who are proud of never experiencing an emotion which has driven the human race since the beginning of time?'

'I didn't say I was proud of it.'

'I don't care what you said,' she hissed, aware that her sense of logic was haemorrhaging by the second.

'And I don't understand either your outrage or your objections,' he snapped. 'You were happy enough to marry Chico for financial security, weren't you? When we both know he wasn't offering you half the benefits you could get from me.'

'You're disgusting,' she snapped as she heard the unmistakable sexual allusion which had roughened his voice. Did he really think *that* could sway her? That his skill between the sheets would make her forget all her principles? She shook her head. 'I don't need a heartless man to bankroll the life I want for Leo and me. I can achieve what I need all by myself, Dimitri, and what's more—I'm going to. There's nothing to stop us moving out of London and going to live in a cheaper part of England. There's a whole lot of beautiful countryside just waiting out there.'

'But think how much easier it would be with me behind you.'

'But that's where you're completely wrong.' She shook her head as she stared at him, aware of the crackling fire and the heavy beat of her heart. 'Because I've suddenly discovered a fundamental flaw in my own argument.'

'I don't understand,' he said coldly.

Maybe because she was only just beginning to understand herself. She sucked in a deep breath, realising that she was laying everything on the line here. But why run from the truth any more? Surely it was better to feel *something* rather than nothing. To live rather than to exist. Because Dimitri had been right about one thing and that was that you couldn't protect yourself against being hurt. That being hurt was part of life itself.

'I thought I didn't believe in love,' she said slowly. 'But the irony is that somewhere along the way I've fallen in love with you, Dimitri. I didn't want to. I still don't want to—because you're the last man in the world any sane woman would choose to be in love with. You're cold and you're heartless and you don't give out your trust very easily. But don't they say that the heart takes no prisoners? I started loving you a long time ago, and, no matter how hard I've tried to get you out of my system, it seems that none of my methods have worked.' She gave a wry smile. 'Oh, don't worry—I'm not asking you to reciprocate, because I realise you can't. But obviously I can't marry you under these circumstances. It wouldn't be fair—not to you, nor to me and especially not to Leo.'

'Why not?'

'Because unrequited love doesn't work,' she said impatiently. 'It's a recipe for disaster—everyone knows that! And love doesn't really last. All the books say it changes once all that new sex wears off.'

'But hasn't your parents' love affair lasted?'

She glared at him, wondering why he was trying to argue for something he didn't believe in. Was it just because he always liked to win? She stared at the two glasses of champagne, which had now stopped fizzing. 'They are the exception which proves the rule,' she said quietly. 'And they're ordinary people—not oligarchs. My father doesn't have women throwing themselves at him every minute of the day, like you do. You're only objecting because I'm not doing what you want me to do. But the reality is that you'll grow bored with me and start looking round for someone younger and prettier—and I couldn't bear that. I'm just being realistic and facing facts, because falling in love doesn't mean I've had part of my brain removed. I'm doing you a favour, Dimitri. I'm not going to limit your time with Leo—in fact, I'll do everything in my power to make sure you see as much of him as you want. But I'm not going to marry you. Do you understand?'

CHAPTER TWELVE

DAMN HER.

Just *damn* her.

Dimitri glowered. He would not... He would *not* be emotionally blackmailed.

He studied the antique bowl containing the grouping of bonsai trees which adorned the polished desk of his London office—an exquisite planting of seven Foemina Junipers, which had been created by a Japanese master. It had taken a lot for Dimitri to persuade the man to sell it, because he had needed convincing that the trees would be properly cared for and kept in the right conditions. It had occurred to Dimitri at the time that the plants' welfare had been of far greater concern to the master than the astronomical price tag which accompanied it.

Usually, just staring at the priceless piece of horticulture brought him some kind of peace, but not today. He studied the bowl. The idea that something as enormous as a tree could be clipped and contained into a size small enough to keep on a man's desk had always appealed to his dark sense of humour. But he realised that he also enjoyed the element of control essential for successful bonsai care. Conditions needed to be monitored daily, with nothing left to chance. Any sign of rampant growth needed to be ruthlessly cut away. It was man controlling nature. And it was a representation of how he liked to live his life.

Until now.

Now he was discovering that not everything could be controlled. With a heavy sigh he sat back in his chair and thought about Erin. She had meant it when she'd turned down his proposal of marriage. He couldn't quite believe it at first, but she had. There had been no wavering or sign she might be softening—not during the flight back from Moscow or the journey at the other end, when he'd dropped her and Leo off at the café.

She had made him feel...

What?

He swallowed. She had made him feel powerless. For the first time in a long time, he had come up against someone who would not be moulded to his formidable will, no matter how many enticements he offered her.

He had tried telling himself she was right. Much better that he had as much contact with his son without risking the messy emotional fallout of sharing his life with another person. He'd returned from Russia determined to seek his pleasure elsewhere and had flicked through the stack of invitations which were waiting for him.

But all he could think about was a pair of green eyes and a woman who only smiled when she wanted to.

He thought about the things she'd said and his eyes focused on the Foemina Junipers again. Had she been trying to tell him that the conditions essential for maintaining a successful marriage needed to be right, just as with the bonsai? Just as you couldn't grow a tiny tree in barren soil, neither could a relationship flourish properly without love and care and commitment? Was that what she had meant?

Damn her.

He waited two days for her to change her mind and come running and he waited in vain. His days seemed drawn-out and tedious and the nights were even worse. He hadn't slept this badly since the time he'd cut out vodka. Saturday morning dawned and, after a largely sleepless night, he drove himself round to the café, where he sat outside the citrus-decked exterior in his big car—half expecting Erin to come storming out and demand to know what he was doing there. Or perhaps send Leo out to talk to him, because wouldn't that have been an easy way to break the stand-off which had sprung up between them?

But nobody came. He could see her sister behind the counter—her eyes big behind her owl-like spectacles—but she didn't wave at him to come in.

He got out of the car and locked it, his heart pounding as he pushed open the café door. It was warm and crowded with customers, with mothers and fathers and little children as well as a couple wearing party clothes who didn't appear to have been to bed. Several people looked up as the jangling bell announced his arrival, and stayed looking.

Walking straight over to the counter, he smiled at the woman who stood there, drying coffee cups.

'It's Tara, isn't it?' he said. 'I'm Dimitri.'

'I know who you are,' she said flatly. 'And Leo's at Saturday morning football, I'm afraid.'

'It isn't Leo I've come to see. It's Erin.'

There was a slight pause as she looked around before

lowering her voice, as if she didn't want to put her livelihood at risk by engaging in some kind of showdown
with the tall man who had just walked into her café.

'Erin doesn't want to see you.'

'Well, I'm not leaving here until she does. So perhaps
you'd like to pour me a cup of coffee and I'll wait over
there while you tell her that? Black, no sugar, please.'

Tara's mouth opened and closed, before she disappeared into the back behind some sort of curtain and
Dimitri walked over to a table near the window and
sat down. A woman who was sitting on her own at a
nearby table smiled at him, but he didn't smile back.
He didn't feel like smiling—least of all to some bottle
blonde who might as well have had the word 'available'
tattooed across her forehead.

A shadow fell over the table and he looked up to
see Erin standing there. Over her jeans and sweater,
she was wearing an apron which emphasised her tiny
waist—but she didn't look great. In fact, she looked terrible. Her face was pale and her green eyes were dark
and shadowed.

'Perhaps you'd like to drag your attention away from
that woman for a moment,' she said tightly, 'and tell me
what you're doing here?'

'You haven't brought my coffee.'

'You're not getting any coffee.' Pulling out the chair
opposite him, she sat down and leaned across the table
and began speaking in a low voice. 'Look, you're welcome to come and see Leo any time you want—I already told you that—but you really have to give me
some warning before you do. I can't just have you turning up here out of the blue like this.'

'Why not?'

'You know why not. Because it's too…disturbing. We have to try to learn to be…' She hesitated. 'I don't know. If not exactly *friends*, then certainly two parents who can interact amicably with each other.'

He nodded, his eyes not leaving her face. 'But I thought we *were* friends, Erin. More than friends. Don't you know that I'm closer to you than I've ever been to anyone else?'

'I don't want to hear this—'

'And let me tell you something else,' he interrupted. 'Something I've never told you before. Something which happened when you came round to my apartment, to tell me about the baby.'

'You mean when I found you hungover, with the naked woman and the porn films?'

'And you looked down your nose at me,' he said slowly. 'Just like you're trying to do now, only this time you aren't making such a good job of it. But back then you didn't like what you saw and you told me so in no uncertain terms. You told me a lot of home truths that day, Erin. You blasted me and my lifestyle and left me feeling dazed. Because nobody had ever spoken to me like that before. And then you handed in your notice and walked away.'

'I don't understand what this has to do with any-thing,' she said. 'We already know this.'

'But you don't know what I did next,' he said. 'At first I tried to convince myself I was glad you'd gone and that you had no right to judge me. But I couldn't stop thinking about the things you'd said. And the more I thought about them, the more I realised they were true. You left me feeling bad about myself and I had to ask myself what I was intending to do about it. So

I went away and cleaned up my act. I quit the booze and the gambling and the women.' He saw her face and shrugged. 'Well, maybe not all the women, but I started to be more discriminating about it. And I got off that merry-go-round of self-destruction you'd highlighted so accurately.' He leaned across the table towards her. 'You were the catalyst which made me examine my life and turn it around. So I owe you, Erin. I owe you big-time.'

'Thanks very much. And if you want my congratulations, then you have them—but I still don't see why you're bringing all this up now.'

'Don't you? Though why should you when I've only just realised myself? When it's taken me all this time to admit what's been staring me in the face for so long. That you've had a profound and lasting influence on me.' He waited for a minute and then drew a deep breath. 'That I love you—and I don't want to spend my life without you in it.'

She didn't answer, not at first—just nodded her head. 'Dimitri,' she said at last, sounding as if she was trying desperately to keep her voice from breaking. 'Listen to me. I'm not going to change my mind about marrying you—so please don't say things you don't mean.'

'But I *do* mean it. Every word I speak straight from here.' And he placed his hand over his heart.

'Will you stop it?' she hissed. 'Everybody's looking at us.'

'I don't care.' He took her left hand between his palms and thought how cold her fingers felt. How stiff her body language was as she sat there facing him. 'Just tell me that it's not too late,' he said. 'Tell me that you still love me—as you did that night in Russia. Tell me that you'll marry me and spend the rest of your life with me.'

Erin was aware that pretty much everyone in the café knew what was happening. Even if they couldn't hear—and Dimitri was making no attempt whatsoever to lower his voice—then it was now glaringly obvious, because he was digging into the pocket of his suit jacket and pulling out a small box.

He flipped open the lid and she could see the dazzle as the light caught the glittering band of diamonds in the centre of which was one enormous and flawless stone, and from behind the counter she heard Tara gasp.

'I have had this ring fashioned from the very finest diamonds in my mine,' he said. 'But if it's too big or too flashy, we can get you something else. We could buy you something antique and special in Moscow or Paris, if that's what you'd prefer. I'd just like you to wear it in the meantime, because I want to see it on your finger. Because ironically, despite having run all my life from matrimony, I have now become its greatest advocate. That is...' he stared at her '...if you'll agree to marry me?'

Erin saw the flicker of uncertainty in his eyes—so brief that she might have imagined it—and somehow it made her love him even more. Dimitri uncertain? Whoever would have thought it? It was something as impossible to imagine as him making such a public and romantic proposal in an East End café. She had tried to stop loving him, but somehow it just wouldn't work and now she had accepted that it was never going to. He was complicated, there was no doubt about that. He was brilliant at some things but not so good at others. Feelings and emotion, mainly...those were the things he liked to hide away—at least until now. But now she understood why. And didn't he need her love just as badly as she wanted to give it? 'Oh, Dimitri,' she whispered. 'Of course I'll marry you. I—'

But her words were drowned out by his laugh of pleasure as he rose to his feet and walked round to her side of the table, where he lifted her to her feet. He stared into her face for what seemed like a long time before he started to kiss her, and all the customers—except for the blonde—burst into a spontaneous round of clapping and cheering.

In the commotion, the ring fell to the ground and remained missing until Leo and his friends came back from football later that morning, crawling around on their hands and knees until it was located underneath the skirting board. They were rewarded with ice cream and cola and the promise of a trip to watch Chelsea play, and Erin overheard Leo saying to his best friend, 'That's my *daddy*.'

She blinked a little at that, because she didn't actually remember telling him that. And that was when it all became real and tears of happiness began to slide down her cheeks.

EPILOGUE

LEO GOT HIS snowman after all—along with sleigh bells and fairy lights and the realisation that having a Russian father and an English mother meant he could actually celebrate *two* Christmases, instead of one. The first was spent in England, with Dimitri flying Erin's parents in from Australia as a surprise and Tara closing down the café for a whole fortnight. Dimitri booked an entire floor of the Granchester Hotel for the festivities, which famously had the biggest tree in London—if you didn't count the one in Trafalgar Square.

And somewhere amid all the excitement, they got married. They exchanged their vows and, for those heartfelt moments, felt like the only two people in the world. Outside, the ground glittered with frost and Erin wore a hooded white cashmere cloak over her long, silk dress. With Leo at her side as proud ring bearer, she carried camomile daisies—the national flower of Russia—mixed with white freesia, which were her mother's favourites. Chico was invited but had flown back to Brazil to tell his parents he was gay and no longer intended to live a lie. Saladin was also invited but his favourite and most valuable horse was injured and he was at his wits' end.

Their second Christmas of the year was spent in Russia, where the holiday was traditionally celebrated on January the seventh and nothing was eaten all day, until the first star had been seen in the sky, when a dish called *kutia* was taken from a shared bowl, to signify unity. And if once upon a time Leo would have turned his nose up at the thought of walnut-and-fruit-studded porridge, he dug into the dish with enthusiasm as the three of them ate their meal together. Erin remembered staring at her son in amazement, and thinking how much he'd changed.

How much they'd all changed.

Leo had blossomed beneath the warm glow of his father's love—a love which Dimitri had confessed he wasn't sure he'd be able to show, just as he wasn't sure if he was capable of being a good father. Erin guessed that wasn't surprising, because if you'd never been properly fathered when you were a little boy, then how would you know how it worked? But Dimitri had worked it out. Of course he had. Her cold, proud Russian had melted— morphing into a man with so much love to give that it made her heart sing just to think about it.

She'd changed, too. The dark fears and insecurities which had nudged the corners of her soul were now a thing of the past. She recognised that it was more than Dimitri's love which had helped her to accomplish that. It was finding her own inner strength and conviction. She'd been strong enough to tell him that she wouldn't settle for second best. To show him that she could and would live independently, even if that was the harder option. Sometimes you needed to be prepared to walk away from the thing you most wanted, in order to get it to come to you.

She lay back against the sofa while the fire crackled

and waited while Dimitri read Leo a bedtime story. He would be down in a minute and tomorrow they were taking him and Anatoly sleighing. And after that they would probably build yet *another* snowman.

She sighed.

'Such a very big sigh,' Dimitri observed softly as he walked into the room and the light from the crackling fire turned his hair red-gold.

'A happy sigh.'

'Oh?'

She looked up at him as he joined her on the sofa, his arm sliding around her back, and automatically she snuggled up to him. 'I was just thinking how lucky I am. Lucky to have met you and had your baby. Lucky to be with you now.'

He looked down at her very intently as he brushed the hair away from her face. 'And all the in-between years? The wasted years?'

She shook her head. 'No, not that. I've been thinking about that and they definitely weren't wasted. They were learning years. Growing years—and growing is always painful. Unless of course you happen to be a bonsai tree, in which case you don't even get the chance!'

He smiled. 'Any ideas what you'd like to do tonight?'

'Surprise me.'

His smile deepened as he cupped her face in his hands and moved his own close enough for her to feel the warmth of his breath.

'I'm going to pour you a glass of champagne and tell you how much I love you, before thrashing you at P'yanitsa.'

'A busy schedule,' she observed.

'Very busy,' he agreed as his lips brushed over hers. 'And after that…'

'After that…what?' she questioned breathlessly as his fingertips brushed over her breast.

'On second thoughts,' he said roughly, 'maybe the P'yanitsa can wait…'

* * * * *

Luis's reputation needs restoring after a scandalous business feud. Chloe will pay for her part in it—by marrying him! Their attraction is explosive, but Luis requires more than blackmail to make Chloe his bride...

Read on for a sneak preview of
Michelle Smart's next story
MARRIAGE MADE IN BLACKMAIL,
part of the **RINGS OF VENGEANCE** trilogy.

"You want me to move?"

"Yes."

A gleam pulsed in his eyes. "Make me."

Instead of closing her hand into a fist and aiming it at his nose as he deserved, Chloe placed it flat on his cheek.

An unwitting sigh escaped from her lips as she drank in the ruggedly handsome features she had dreamed about for so long. The texture of his skin was so different from her own, smooth but with the bristles of his stubble breaking through...had he not shaved? She had never seen his face anything other than clean-shaven.

He was close enough for her to catch the faint trace of coffee and the more potent scent of his cologne.

Luis was the cause of all this chaos rampaging through her. She hated him so much, but the feelings she'd carried for him for all these years were still there, refusing to die, making her doubt herself and what she'd believed to be the truth.

Her lips tingled, yearning to feel his mouth on hers again, all her senses springing to life and waving surrender flags at her.

Just kiss him...

Closing her eyes tightly, Chloe gathered all her wits about her, wriggled out from under him and sat up.

Her lungs didn't want to work properly, and she had to force air into them.

She shifted to the side, needing physical distance, suddenly terrified of what would happen if she were to brush against him or touch him in any form again.

Fighting to clear her head of the fog clouding it, she blinked rapidly and said, "Do I have your word that your feud with Benjamin ends with our marriage?"

Things had gone far enough. It was time to put an end to it.

"*Sì.* Marry me and it ends."

Don't miss
MARRIAGE MADE IN BLACKMAIL,
available August 2018,
and the first part of Michelle Smart's
RINGS OF VENGEANCE *trilogy*
BILLIONAIRE'S BRIDE FOR REVENGE,
available now wherever Harlequin Presents® books
and ebooks are sold.

www.Harlequin.com

Want to give in to temptation with
steamy tales of irresistible desire?

Check out **Harlequin® Presents®**,
Harlequin® Desire and
Harlequin® Kimani™ Romance books!

New books available every month!

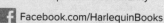

CONNECT WITH US AT:

Harlequin.com/Community

Facebook.com/HarlequinBooks

Twitter.com/HarlequinBooks

Instagram.com/HarlequinBooks

Pinterest.com/HarlequinBooks

ReaderService.com

**ROMANCE WHEN
YOU NEED IT**

PGENRE2017

Need an adrenaline rush from nail-biting tales
(and irresistible males)?

Check out **Harlequin® Intrigue®**
and **Harlequin® Romantic Suspense** books!

New books available every month!

CONNECT WITH US AT:

Harlequin.com/Community

 Facebook.com/HarlequinBooks

 Twitter.com/HarlequinBooks

 Instagram.com/HarlequinBooks

 Pinterest.com/HarlequinBooks

ReaderService.com

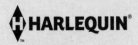

**ROMANCE WHEN
YOU NEED IT**

SGENRE2017

Earn points from all your Harlequin book purchases from wherever you shop.

Turn your points into *FREE BOOKS* of your choice OR
EXCLUSIVE GIFTS from your favorite authors or series.

Join for FREE today at
www.HarlequinMyRewards.com.

Harlequin My Rewards is a free program (no fees) without any commitments or obligations.

MYR17